Reviewers love *New York Times* bestselling author SUSAN ANDERSEN!

Just for Kicks

"Deft characters, smart dialogue, laugh-out-loud moments and sizzling sexual tension (you might want to read Chapter 15 twice) make this hard to put down.... Lovers of romance, passion and laughs should go all in for this one."

—*Publishers Weekly*

"Andersen's follow-up to *Skintight* retains the charm and wit of the previous story, and the sexy sparring between Wolf and Carly leads to some memorable between-the-sheets action. Hot, hot, hot!"

—*Romantic Times BOOKreviews*

Hot & Bothered

"A classic plot line receives a fresh, fun treatment...well-developed secondary characters add depth to this zesty novel, placing it a level beyond most of its competition."

—*Publishers Weekly*

"*Hot & Bothered* has it all: suspense, steam and smart banter. Rocket is a remarkable hero, tough, hard-edged but still kind and tender. We should all be as lucky as Tori!"

—*Romantic Times BOOKreviews*

Skintight

"Andersen again injects magic into a story that would be clichéd in another's hands, delivering warm, vulnerable characters in a touching yet suspenseful read."

—*Publishers Weekly*, starred review

"Written with Andersen's signature sass and sizzle, this book will appeal to fans of Sandra Hill and Rachel Gibson."

—*Booklist*

Dear Reader,

Once upon a time, in a book called *Hot & Bothered,* a couple of teenage kids lived on the streets of Denver. Seventeen-year-old Jared Hamilton was the heroine's runaway brother and a central character in the story. P. J. Morgan was the thirteen-year-old who'd been kicked to the curb by her mother, and when I began the book she was supposed to be only a minor character. But, omigawd. That little girl grabbed me by the throat and simply refused to turn loose until I expanded her part.

I received an amazing amount of e-mail from people wanting to know what was going to happen to P.J. and Jared when they grew up. I was already dying to write their book, but as a reader myself I find it difficult to swallow characters aging fifteen years in a solitary real-time one. But age 'em fifteen years in three? Now, that strikes me as supremely reasonable. Because every weekday when I've got the time, I bang through the swinging door to my kitchen at 2:00 p.m. sharp and turn on the tube to watch *Guiding Light* while I have lunch. And when babies are born in Soap Opera Land they pretty much go upstairs and don't come down again for—you guessed it—three years. At which time they've morphed into teenagers with story lines of their own. So aging Jared and P.J. given that criteria worked for me.

These characters are so special to me. I hope they'll make you laugh, make you cry, make you wet your—well...hmm...maybe not that last thing.

But I do hope they'll grab a piece of your heart, the way they did mine.

Happy reading,

Susan

Susan Andersen

Coming Undone

ISBN-13: 978-0-373-77213-1
ISBN-10: 0-373-77213-0

COMING UNDONE

This edition published by arrangement with Harlequin Books S.A.

www.HQNBooks.com

Printed in U.S.A.

This is dedicated to the women of the industry:

To
Meg Ruley, Dianne Moggy and Margo Lipschultz
for helping me be the best that I can be

To
Margie Mullen and Marianne Szamraj for making
the First Ever Midwest Newsgroup tour so much fun

To
Sue Grimshaw and Kathy Baker
and booksellers everywhere for getting my books
into the hands of readers

And to
The Levy Gang: Pam Nelson, Justine Willis,
Emily Hixon, Kathleen Koelbl, Janet Krey,
Krystal Nelson and (okay, so you're not a woman—
you really need to be mentioned anyhow)
DeVar "Heyyyy, Ladies!" Spight for the
Sizzling Summer Reads Author Tour. I might not
have gotten much sleep, but the laughter and being
treated like a queen more than made up for it.

Thanks to you all

Also by

Susan Andersen

Just for Kicks
Hot & Bothered
Skintight

Coming Undone

PROLOGUE

Headline, *Nashville Tattler*
Country Star of Grammy-Winning Song
"Mama's Girl" Fires Manager Mom!

JARED HAMILTON DIRECTED the cabbie through dark Denver streets to the old Craftsman-style bungalow that housed Semper Fi Investigations. The taxi pulled into the agency's small parking lot and he climbed from the cab, then watched as the departing vehicle's rear lights grew smaller, blinked red and finally disappeared around a corner two blocks away. Flipping up his collar against the late-spring chill, he turned and climbed the covered front porch to let himself into the dark reception area. Down the hallway a single light glowed through the frosted-glass transom over John Miglionni's door. Bypassing his own office, he stuck his head into his brother-in-law's. "Hey. What are you still doing here at this hour?"

John clicked a command on his keyboard and pushed back to look up at him. "I was actually waiting around hoping to see you."

"Why? What's up?" Dropping his overnighter to the floor, Jared flopped down on the chair facing John's desk. "Must be something work-related. You wouldn't be here at eleven forty-five on a Thursday night if anything had happened to Tori and/or the kids."

The other man gave him a faux paternal look. "Haven't I always said you're brighter than the average Joe?"

"Yeah, yeah. So I ask again—what's up?"

John flashed his famous I'm-so-good-someone-really-oughtta-bottle-me smile. "A very lucrative, high-profile assignment came knocking at my door yesterday."

"Way to go, Rocket!" Congratulations just seemed to call for the military handle his brother-in-law had earned years ago in the Marines.

"Yeah, it's a good thing. Except Willie, who was going to handle it, landed in Rose Medical with a busted appendix this afternoon. And I'm eyeball deep in the Sanderford case."

Stretching out his long legs in front of him, Jared folded his hands over his stomach and gave John a cocky smile. "Guess it's lucky for you then that I just wrapped up my case."

"You might not think so once you discover who we've been hired to find."

Unable to imagine such a scenario, he merely raised both eyebrows in inquiry.

"Wild Wind Records retained us to find your old friend Priscilla Jayne."

Jared's heart gave a single heavy slam against the wall of his chest. He knew it was merely the surprise of hearing that name out of the blue—an assumption that was validated when his heartbeat promptly settled down again. "P.J.?" He met Rocket's gaze levelly. "Why would I have a problem with that?"

John gave him an ironic don't-try-to-kid-a-kidder look. "Well, let me see. Maybe because you two shared a couple of the most intense weeks of your lives?"

"Yeah, we did—*fifteen* years ago. Lotsa water under the bridge since then, big brother." He shoved himself a bit straighter in his seat. "So what's the story with country music's hottest new diva? I thought everything was coming up roses for her. How did she come to be missing?"

"Nobody seems to know. But apparently it started Monday when she fired her mother as her manager."

"No shit?" A fierce surge of satisfaction filled Jared. "Good for her. *There's* a comeuppance that was long overdue." He'd detested P.J.'s mom fifteen years ago and he'd bet the family manse the woman hadn't improved appreciably over the years.

"I don't know how good it is for Priscilla's career though, at least in the short term, since her mom's talking trash to every country-music magazine and yellow journalism rag in the country. P.J.'s due to start a big tour in about two weeks and Wild Wind Records is getting very nervous that no one seems to have a clue where she's gotten herself off to. If you accept this case, your mission is going to be twofold. First to locate little Miss Priscilla Jayne. Then to accompany her on her *Steal the Thunder* tour to make sure she doesn't disappear again."

Jared whistled. "The entire tour? Those things can

run pretty long—months and months, some of them." He eyed John warily. "How much time are we talking about?" He wasn't sure how he felt about giving up his privacy for several months of babysitting P. J. Morgan. Their friendship might have been the most important relationship of his existence the summer he was seventeen, but that was a long time ago.

"Five weeks, give or take a stop or two."

Okay, he supposed a little over a month was doable. "Does Wild Wind have any idea how much this could end up costing them?"

"They should. I made a point of spelling it out for them in minute detail. They seemed a lot more concerned about how much it will cost them if their million-dollar baby takes a powder."

"That seems pretty unlikely, don't you think? This sounds like P.J.'s big break. It seems to me she has a vested interest in turning up for something that shows every sign of boosting her career right into the stratosphere."

"Like you said, a lot can change in fifteen years. I've heard more than one report claiming she's butted heads with the big dogs in Nashville pretty regularly the past couple years."

Jared could hardly argue with that. Everything he knew about P. J. Morgan these days he'd gleaned from the occasional television report or newspaper article. And those hinted that she could be difficult and demanding.

So who was he to say differently? Their relationship

had been intense but brief, and was ancient history long before this assignment had come along.

For all he knew, the sweet, feisty little girl he'd once known could very well have grown up to be a stone-cold bitch just like her mama.

CHAPTER ONE

Front cover headline, *Country Now* magazine:
Where in the World is Priscilla Jayne?

"OH, FOR THE LOVE OF PETE!" P. J. Morgan, known on the country music circuit by her first and middle names, tossed aside the magazine and jumped to her feet. "Mysterious disappearance, my butt! Where do they get this crap?" Scary to think *Country Now* was one of the reputable publications. She could only imagine what the tabloids were saying.

Crossing the room to the window, she pulled aside the faded olive drape to look out. Not that there was much to see in this wide-spot-in-the-road rural town. At a time in her life when she could finally afford to stay in posh four-star hotels, it was ironic that she'd instead picked a low-rent motel off a secondary highway on a hot, still Texas plain.

"Well, hey." A humorless laugh escaped her. "You can take the girl out of the trailer park, but there's just no getting that trailer trash out of the girl."

Blowing out a breath, she dropped the curtain and turned away. This wasn't exactly what she'd planned when she'd taken off on Monday. She'd been headed for Los Angeles, a city she had never seen. It had seemed exotic, was a good long way from home and she'd figured not many of its citizens were likely to give a good goddamn where one beginning-to-make-a-name-for-herself country singer had gotten herself off to.

With thoughts of parking herself by a palm tree–shaded pool to drink her fill of fruity concoctions sporting frilly paper umbrellas, she'd driven seventeen hours straight, stopping only to stretch her legs and fill up the tank. When she couldn't keep her eyes open to drive another mile, she'd pulled into the Wind Blew Inn, a clean but ancient motor court in the Texas panhandle. She'd promptly fallen into bed and when she'd awakened thirty-six hours later, she'd stayed put instead of hitting the road once again. Something about this nowhere little town's one-block-long main street reminded her of the never-ending series of hick towns she'd lived in growing up.

And when things go to hell, she always said, stick with the familiar.

Her stomach growled, and she realized she was hungry. What day was it, anyway—Thursday? No, God, it was Friday.

Her appetite had been nonexistent since Monday. And if that wasn't indicative of her state of mind, she didn't know what was. One summer a lifetime ago, she and a boy named Jared had gone hungry together on the streets of Denver. It was an experience that had hardwired her ever after not to miss another meal. Yet, except for about six gallons of coffee and the occasional candy bar grabbed when paying for her gas, she'd barely eaten a bite.

Twisting her hair up off her neck, she reached for her baseball cap and pulled it on, then donned a pair of oversized dark glasses. Slipping a handful of bills into her shorts pocket, she headed for the door.

It was hotter than usual for early June and the swamp cooler laboring in her room's window dripped green-tinged condensation onto the concrete next to the two-step stoop outside her door. Blinking against the glare, she tugged the brim of her navy cap down and set out across the lot.

The Prairie Dog Café was a squat orange building next to Elmerson's Feed and Seed, and P.J. pulled open its screen door to the clatter of heavy crockery, the rumble of male voices discussing crops and Lari White singing about flies on the butter from an old Wurlitzer in the corner. She stepped out of the sun into the smell of frying meat and cigarette smoke. Slipping off her dark glasses, she noticed that the only customers who didn't have John Deere tractor caps planted firmly on their heads had straw Stetsons hooked over the back rails of their chairs.

Conversations faltered for a second, then resumed their accustomed rhythms. P.J. noted she was the only woman in the café this time of day, then shrugged the observation aside and crossed to the counter to claim one of the few vacant red-vinyl swivel seats. If she'd allowed men to intimidate her in her line of work, she would've quit singing about the same time she'd first attempted to go professional. The truth was, she liked the company of men. She worked primarily with them—her backup band consisted of two of the species, and the roadies that set up and broke down shows and transported the equipment from city to city were almost exclusively male.

Moving aside an ashtray, she reached across the counter for a laminated menu stuck in the rear prongs of the stainless steel condiment holder.

A waitress with *Sandy* embroidered above the breast pocket of her pink uniform came over a few minutes later and set a glass of water in front of P.J. "What can I getcha, honey?"

She ordered a ham and swiss on sourdough and knew she should ask for it to go. But the murmur of voices was comforting to a woman accustomed to being surrounded by people and she couldn't quite bring herself to relinquish the sound to return to her too-quiet room.

She realized it wasn't a smart choice, however, when Sandy said something as she clipped her order to the wheel above the pass-through to the kitchen and the short-order cook immediately poked his head through the opening to give P.J. the once-over. She also caught the waitress stealing glances at her as she bustled about the room filling coffee cups and slapping down bills torn from a pad in her apron pocket. Then "Mama's Girl," P.J.'s very first recording, came on the jukebox and with an inward groan she settled a little deeper into her chair.

Sandy brought the bill a moment later. "That's you, isn't it?" she demanded with a tip of her chin toward the Wurlitzer.

P.J. could lie with the best of them and she looked the other woman straight in the eye. "Don't I wish." She smiled wryly. "People are *always* mistaking me for her. Darn shame I can't sing a lick."

"It's you," Sandy insisted. "I saw you on *Austin City Limits* once and I'll never forget your speaking voice."

Damn. Didn't it just figure *that* would give her away? She hated her speaking voice. It was raspy and made her sound as if she were a three-pack-a-day smoker. She'd always figured God had given her a good, strong singing voice to make amends for saddling her with such a ridiculous conversational one.

Still she insisted, "Oh, this isn't the way I usually sound. It's the tag end of a nasty case of laryngitis." But recognizing a blown cover when she saw one, she left a hefty tip and headed for the door. It looked like she might see California after all.

"Pretty cold-blooded to fire your own mama, you ask me," the waitress called after her.

Ouch. Ouchouchouch! Given the mess with her mother earlier this week, Sandy's parting shot was a direct hit.

"Nobody asked you," she muttered under her breath when she was out of earshot. Damn if she intended to make excuses to someone who didn't know the first thing about her relationship with her mother. She stomped back to the Wind Blew Inn.

She had just zipped her suitcase closed and was looking for her flip-flops when there was an authoritative knock on the door.

She stilled, her head raised to stare at the peephole-free door. Dear Lord. Reporters already?

Then she willed herself to relax. *Don't be ridiculous, it's probably just the manager.* Even if Sandy had called someone, which was iffy, the only reporter who could have gotten here this fast would be from a local weekly, and she could be three states away by the time its next edition hit the streets. She crossed to the window and lifted a corner of the curtain, trying to see who was on the other side of the door.

A tall man stood on her tiny stoop, but the angle was wrong to see more than the fact that he had wide shoulders in a navy-blue T-shirt, neatly trimmed brown hair and was wearing a faded pair of jeans. His right forearm, she saw as he raised his fist to knock on the door once again, sported a long, narrow tattoo that undulated subtly with the movement. It was mostly green and almost looked like a praying mantis.

"Ohmigawd."

She lunged for the door, pulling it open. The man jerked back his fist, but she barely even noticed how close it had come to her forehead. Her gaze went first to the tattoo, which was exactly what she'd expected to see, then to the man's face. "Jared?" she whispered. "Jared Hamilton?"

"Hello, P.J."

"Ohmigawd!" she said again. A frisson of pure

pleasure buzzed along her spine and, laughter erupting, she leaped out at him, her arms snaking around his neck in a stranglehold, her legs wrapping around his waist. "Oh. My. God!" Leaning back, she gazed into his face. And grinned. "You sure grew up good."

That was an understatement. He'd been good-looking at seventeen, but now his features were honed in a way that made it nearly impossible to look away. Hard jaw, aristocratic nose, stern mouth with a full lower lip. His hair was still the sun-streaked brown she remembered but he wore it shorter these days. And he'd grown into his long, skinny bones. He was still tall and lean, but his shoulders were wide, his body muscular.

His fingers, which had clasped her butt with a light touch when she'd jumped him, tightened infinitesimally. A slight smile pulled up one corner of his mouth. "You grew up pretty well, yourself."

Well. Not good—*well.* Some of her pleasure dimmed. It was due to Jared that she'd worked as hard as she had in her language arts and English classes in junior high and high school, and her grammar was much better than it had been at thirteen. Not good enough, though, evidently. "Grew up good, grew up well." She shrugged. "Not everyone has the advantage of your prep-school upbringing, rich boy. Some of us are simply never gonna speak like some stick-up-the-butt banker."

"It wasn't a put-down, Peej." His hands slid from her rear to her hips. "It was merely an observation. You look great."

"Oh. Well. Thank you." Unwrapping her legs from around his waist and loosening her choke hold on his neck, she allowed him to set her back on her feet just inside the door. Curling her bare toes into the worn motel carpet, she tipped her head back to look up at him. "Want to come in?"

"Absolutely." He stepped over the threshold.

Her native caution belatedly kicked in as she backed deeper into the room. "What on earth are you doing here? This isn't exactly your type of accommodations."

"I wouldn't have thought it was yours, either, these days."

His eyes were the same gray-green she remembered, but no longer did the fear and worry she'd once seen reflected in them exist. Instead a watchfulness lingered in their mossy depths, a cool reserve that she had a difficult time reconciling with the boy she'd known. And she was beginning to get a bad feeling in her stomach. "What brings you to the Wind Blew Inn, Jared? How did you find me?" She inhaled sharply as sudden suspicion hit her like a bomb out of the blue. "Oh, jeez, tell me you're not a reporter!"

"For Christ sake, Peej." His dark eyebrows slammed together over his nose. "That would be the last occupation I'd choose!"

She'd forgotten for a moment about his own persecution by the press back in the days when he'd been the number-one suspect in his father's murder. "Of course it is. I'm sorry, J," she said, the old nickname slipping out easily beneath the press of old memories of a time when he'd been the one person in the world who made her feel safe. "I forgot all about your dad." But her desire to make peace only went so far and she narrowed her eyes at him. "So why are you here?"

Straightening to his full height, he met her suspicious gaze head-on. "Wild Wind Records hired me to see that you get to all your shows while you're on tour."

"They did what?" She couldn't possibly have heard that correctly.

He merely looked at her, however, and her stomach went hollow. She hadn't felt this stunned since the time one of her mother's boyfriends had backhanded her for sassing him. "My label hired a watchdog?"

"If you care to look at it that way."

Anger started low and slow but escalated faster than smoldering embers sprayed with kerosene. She straightened to her full if less than impressive height. "No one gets to accuse me of being irresponsible. I've been taking care of business as long as I can remember!"

He shrugged. "I'm merely telling you what I was hired to do."

"Well, bully for you." She strode back to the flimsy door, yanked it open and gave her one-time true friend a pointed stare. "It's been a long time, Jared, and it was good to see you again. Don't let the door hit you in the butt on your way out." She hated that her breathing had grown so ragged she was nearly panting, and, inhaling and exhaling a deep breath, she got herself back under control.

"I've been getting myself to gigs since I was eighteen

years old," she continued quietly. "I'm damned if I plan to blow my career now by failing to show up for the biggest concerts of my life." It was probably unfair to hold Jared responsible for the mess she was in, but learning her label felt compelled to hire someone to ensure she showed up for her own tour was a huge slap in the face. Not to mention he was handy and she was disappointed that he'd turned out to be nothing like the boy who'd filled so many of her daydreams over the years.

He didn't move. "Sorry, P.J.," he said, but he didn't sound the least bit conciliatory to her. "But we signed a contract."

"Who's we, Bosco? *I* didn't sign any contract."

"No, but Wild Wind Records and Semper Fi Investigations did."

"Semper Fi?" Small world. Just Tuesday she'd had occasion to mention that very name—and not in conjunction with the U.S. Marines' motto. "The agency of that P.I. who found us in Denver?"

"Yeah. You remember him? He's my brother-in-law now."

"Of course I remember him." John Miglionni had been nice to her, had been, in fact, one of the first adults who'd ever treated her as if she had as much worth as anyone else on God's green earth. But the smile that tickled the corners of her lips at the memory of the tall, dark man slid into a scowl as she stared up into the face of another long and lanky man. "You're a private investigator, too?"

He nodded. "Yeah. We do that and personal security."

"Huh. I thought for sure you'd be the CEO of some whoop-de-do-dah corporation by now."

He snorted.

"Guess not. Well, how nice for you. Now go away."

"Not gonna happen, Peej."

She had to tip her head way back to meet his gaze and frustration sizzled along her nerve endings. He was big and steely and she had zero chance of physically ejecting him from her room.

But if there was one thing she knew, it was how to bluff. So she looked him in the eye and said calmly, "Fine. Then I guess I'll just have to call the police and let *them* remove you."

He shrugged and sat in the room's only chair. Sliding down on his tailbone, he stretched his long legs out what appeared to be halfway across the room and crossed his arms over his chest. "Go ahead."

Crap. Like she could afford to add another indignity to the scandal that was already dogging her footsteps. But she crossed to the telephone and picked up the receiver. When Jared simply slouched deeper into his seat and watched her with cool eyes, she punched out a number she had only this week memorized.

The phone on the other end of the line picked up. "Benjamin McGrath Management Company," said a professionally dulcet female voice.

"This is Priscilla Jayne Morgan."

"One moment please—I'll connect you with Mr. McGrath," the woman said without further ado and the line went silent as P.J. was placed on hold.

Almost as quickly, her call went through to her new manager. "P.J.," Ben McGrath said in his brisk New England-accented voice. "What can I do for you?"

"I have a situation here. There's a man named Jared Hamilton who refuses to leave my room. He says he's here from—"

"Semper Fi Investigations."

Her stomach sank but she prayed that when she glanced at Jared her face didn't show the sudden distress jittering her nerves. He was watching her with a slight frown pulling his eyebrows together.

"Do you mind?" she said coldly. "I'd like a moment of privacy."

He climbed to his feet and walked out the door, closing it quietly behind him.

P.J. turned back to the phone. "You *know?* What the hell is going on, Ben?"

"You haven't seen any of the tabloids lately, I take it."

"No, only *Country Now* magazine. That was bad enough, so I was afraid to see what twist the rags might have given the story."

"Smart girl. Wild Wind is nervous about all the publicity your mother is generating. She's got them convinced you have a history of running away when the going gets rough. She went public with your time in Denver when you were a kid."

"*What?* Why would she do that? I didn't run away back then—she threw me out!" But indignation couldn't hold a candle to the sickness churning in her stomach. Oh God, everyone knew. Her own mother had seen to it that everyone knew she'd lived on the streets at one time.

"I know. But Wild Wind is afraid you're going to renege on your obligations and—"

"I've never reneged on a contract in my life!"

"You're preaching to the choir, Priscilla. But you keep tying my hands by refusing to let me go on record with all the garbage your mother's pulled. So when Wild Wind insisted on hiring a babysitter to assure you get to your concerts, all I could do was suggest who they hire. Let me go public with what really happened with your mom and—"

"No. I told you before, I'm not going to talk about that." It was bad enough the world knew she'd been homeless for a while. The last thing she could bear was for everyone to discover that her mother had never loved her.

Ben's sigh filtered down the line. "If you ever come to your senses I'll put the proper spin on all the shit that's been flying around. Until then I thought if you had to have an escort, you might at least prefer someone who was once good to you."

"Right this minute, Ben, I regret telling you about him at all." She'd only done so because he'd insisted on hearing everything that might be used against her. Revealing that time in her life had led to mentioning the boy who'd kept a scared-to-death thirteen-year-old girl from losing all hope. That, in turn, had given her such a warm, fuzzy rush that she'd then confided how John Miglionni and Jared's sister, Tori, had rescued them.

"The truth is, I didn't expect your old friend to be assigned to the case. A business like mine doesn't generate the need to locate private eyes or security specialists as a rule. But when this came up I remembered you mentioning the Semper Fi agency, and I thought it might at least be a place to start."

Well, I guess that'll teach me to be so damn chatty, she thought bitterly.

"I actually had the owner in mind to handle this—figuring someone you once admired might make the situation more bearable. I didn't know Hamilton worked there until Miglionni called to let me know how the agency planned to handle the assignment," Ben said. "And I'm sorry for the necessity, Priscilla, but Wild Wind insists. This is your big break—"

"I thought that was when I won the Grammy."

"That was your *first* break. This tour is the one that's going to put you on the map. So I'm afraid you're just going to have to suck it up and do what your label wants."

She managed to hang on to her temper long enough to get off the phone, but she was seething by the time she hung up.

She'd worked one job or another since she was fifteen years old. She had been the family breadwinner more often than not, and Wild Wind dared suggest she couldn't be trusted to show up for a series of contracted concerts?

Staring out the window, she scowled at Jared, who lounged against the wall on the shady side of the court, his hands in his pockets and one foot propped against the faded cinderblock. He had an eye on her room and, catching her peering out the window, he straightened and headed across the lot.

Her spine snapped as straight and steely as a length of rebar. Enough was enough. Mama was sufficient trouble all on her own—P.J. didn't need the embarrassment of a watchdog on top of it.

She'd had it with handlers and people telling her what to do. She wasn't stupid—singing was the only thing she could call her own and she had every intention of showing up for her shows.

But the tour didn't start for a couple weeks, and she needed some alone time to lick her wounds and get centered and focused before it began. She sure as hell didn't need her one-time best friend to herd her toward her first gig like a blue heeler with one calf. And while it appeared she had no choice but to put up with him once the tour began, she saw no reason to tolerate his escort until then.

So let him catch up with her in Portland. Because the first opportunity she got, she was shaking Jared Hamilton from her heels like the dust of all those dinky towns she'd left behind.

CHAPTER TWO

Mama claims Priscilla Jayne has a history of running away when the going gets tough. Stay tuned for our interview with Jodeen Morgan following our eye-in-the-sky traffic report.

—Jay Pollen, morning DJ of KXPS,
Kickin' Country Radio

STANDING IN THE Wind Blew Inn parking lot, Jared thought for sure the feeble light from the quarter moon riding the western sky was playing tricks on his eyes. His gut said it wasn't, however, and staring at the four flat tires on his rented Lexus, he swore like a sailor and kicked one of the hubcaps above the flattened rubber.

Then his reaction brought him up short. What the hell was he doing? He didn't lose control—he jumped head-first into the fray and didn't stop swinging until he came out on top. Pissing and moaning and kicking tires wasn't going to get the job done. Pulling his cell phone from a pocket, he punched in the Semper Fi agency's number.

But the minute he heard his brother-in-law's voice, his frustration boiled over. "She ditched me," he snarled. "Do you believe this? It hasn't even been one full day and she frigging ditched me!"

There was an instant of silence, then Rocket let loose a big belly laugh. "I always did like that girl."

"Sure, yuk it up. *I'm* real amused, I can tell you."

"I can hear that." Rocket's voice sobered, but Jared was pretty sure he could still hear amusement lacing its undertones. "What happened?"

"She played me like a goddamn Stradivarius." And how. From the moment she'd opened the door of that dingy little motel room and taken a flying leap to wrap herself around him like a chimp in a monkey-puzzle tree, he'd been hammered by memories.

Of her saving his life fifteen years ago by showing him the ropes when he'd fled Colorado Springs for the streets of Denver—even though she, like everyone else in their Centennial State, had believed he'd killed his father.

Of her pedal-to-the-metal personality—that what-you-see-is-what-you-get emotionality that had been the primary characteristic of the thirteen-year-old he'd known.

Of the crushing guilt he'd once felt for the random flashes of lust that her underfed, flat-chested little body had inspired in him.

She was still slight of build and her breasts were probably little more than a mouthful even now. But her arms and legs were rounder and her collarbones had lost that half-starved scrawniness they'd had. And she had a surprisingly full, round ass. His palms still retained the luxurious feel of its curves resting in his hands.

"You're not an easy guy to play," Rocket said slowly. "So how did P.J. manage it?"

Tucking the phone between his ear and shoulder, Jared rubbed his palms down the outer seams of his Levi's to rid himself of the memory. He no longer needed to feel guilty about whatever attraction P.J. might hold for him, but he wasn't about to act on it, either. He was a professional and he had a job to do.

Yeah, right. Some professional, hotshot. She shook you off without breaking a sweat. He squared his shoulders. Fine then. He didn't mix business and pleasure. "I forgot the cardinal rule," he admitted.

"Let your guard down, did you?"

"Big-time. She was so happy to see me until I told her why I was there." That still blew him away, the way her face had gone incandescent when she'd first opened the door and seen him standing on her stoop. As if she hadn't been the one to cut him out of her life. "Then, when she discovered her record company had hired me to accompany her to her concerts, she was pissed. But she got over it—or so I thought. The minute I relaxed my guard, though, she ditched my ass."

"Big deal, so you made a mistake and treated her like the average missing person," John said easily. "Anyone would have done the same."

"You wouldn't."

"Yeah, I probably would have. I only saw P.J. a few times fifteen years ago and still she stands out in my memory. I've never forgotten that feisty independence. But you know what really sticks in my mind? What a sweet little nougat she was. She might have acted all tough on the outside, but she had that break-your-heart vulnerable center. It's easy to forget how street-savvy and fast on her feet she could be."

"That's a fact. But while I don't disagree about the girl she used to be, Rocket, it wasn't you she made a fool of. So P.J. had better hope she's a damn sight faster than me," Jared said grimly. "Because I've got a job to do and no one—not an old friend and sure as hell no up-and-coming country diva with a reputation for unreliability—is going to get in the way of my doing it."

HE CAUGHT UP WITH HER in Idaho six days later. Since that was five days longer than he'd anticipated it taking him, he wasn't feeling particularly charitable as he watched P.J. test the lock on her hotel-room door, pocket the key card, then turn in his direction. Stepping into the narrow alcove that housed the ice and vending machines, he watched her walk past, allowed a few seconds to go by, then stepped out again. If she'd bothered to glance over her shoulder he'd be in plain view, but her focus was apparently front and center.

He sauntered a quarter of the length of the corridor behind her, watching the flex of that lush, round butt in a sprayed-on pair of blue jeans. She wore a straw Stetson on her head and a rose-spattered transparent little black shirt over a black camisole-type top. Hearing the elevator ding a car's arrival, he picked up his pace and slipped between the doors just as they were closing.

"Hi there," he said as she stared up at him, her golden-brown eyes wide with shock. Letting the doors close, he reached out to punch the Stop button. "So, where we headed? Out to dinner?"

She didn't respond, merely gaped at him, and he shrugged. "I see you picked a nicer hotel this time. Still not as fancy as your newfound status might suggest, but definitely a major step up from the Wind Blew Inn—"

"How did you find me?" Her cheeks were flushed an irate rose, and her eyes—those almond-shaped, slanted cat eyes—looked even more exotic when offset by the blush.

He slammed shut the part of him that admired the image and answered the question. "You're still driving your own truck. Hitting those three ATMs the day you ditched me was a smart move, but you should have lost the pickup at the same time and paid cash for its replacement." His attention wandered from the conversation. With her short, not-exactly-voluptuous body and her long, rich, chestnut-brown hair, she was the antithesis of all the statuesque blond beauties that seemed to dominate country-music videos these days. At the same time, she was very...watchable. Very compelling.

Not that she was sucking *him* in that way. He wasn't a compel-me kind of guy. With a fierce mental shake, he gazed at her down the length of his nose. "Which reminds me, you owe me $67.50 for the service I had to call to reinflate my tires."

The last iota of shock fled her eyes and they snapped fire at him. Yet her voice was cool, composed and un-Peejlike when she said, "Yeah, right. Hold your breath waiting for me to cut you that check, pal."

He shrugged. "I suppose it is a bit unreasonable to expect you to fork over the dough. Forget I even brought it up." He flashed her his biggest smile to show how magnanimous he could be. "I'll just add it to Wild Wind's bill."

She gave him a flat-eyed stare. "Go away, Jared."

"Not gonna happen, Priscilla. And since we covered this ground the last time I saw you, I suggest you learn to deal with it." Reminded of the less-than-merry chase that she'd led him on, however, he felt his jaw grow tight. He unclenched his teeth and sucked in a quiet breath.

She settled her cowgirl hat more firmly over her shiny curls and scowled up at him. "What is this? I don't need to be in Portland for the first concert until the twenty-second." She met his gaze head-on. "So why exactly are you here now? And what were you doing at the Wind Blew Inn last week?"

Shit. She would ask the tough questions—the very ones he'd asked himself, then dodged answering because there wasn't a satisfactory reply. Oh, his rationale for running her to ground today was easy enough—it had taken him damn near an entire week to find her after she'd left him standing in the Texas panhandle with four flat tires and his thumb up his ass. He sure as hell wasn't about to risk losing track of her again in case it took him that long or longer to find her the next time. But as far as making his presence known to her last week went? That was a little harder to justify.

And he'd clearly waited too long to reply, because she gave him a shot to the solar plexus with the heel of her hand. "Well?"

"Hey!" Refusing to let her see that she'd knocked the wind from his chest, he grabbed her wrist and plucked her hand away from his breastbone. "No touching."

Still, the action was so quintessentially the P.J. he'd known that it became clear without further examination what had brought him to the Wind Blew Inn nearly two weeks before he needed to approach her.

Curiosity.

It had been curiosity, pure and simple. Ordinarily he would have monitored her movements until they were nearer the date of her first concert, but his desire to discover if there were still remnants of his old friend had proven stronger than his usual bedrock-solid professionalism.

And no doubt about it, remnants remained.

She blinked. "Since when don't you like touching? You used to be a regular Mister Touchy-Feely."

"Was not."

"Were so. Remember that condo construction site we stayed in the night before your sister found you? You musta put your arm around me half a dozen times."

He took a step closer. "Yeah, because you were afraid of a stupid little thunder-and-lightning storm."

She thrust her delicately pointed chin ceilingward. "As I remember it, pal, it was because *you* wanted comforting."

"You are so full of sh—" Cutting himself off, he took a step back. Jesus. What was he doing arguing with her like he was still seventeen years old? He punched the button to get the elevator car moving again. "That was then," he said stiffly. "This is now."

"Yeah? Well, I liked you better then. I thought you were the smartest, handsomest guy in the world. Now I know you're nothing but a cold-hearted son of a bitch."

"And proud of it," he said, telling himself her assessment didn't pinch.

The elevator reached the first floor and the doors swooshed open. Resting his palm against the small of P.J.'s back, Jared escorted her from the car. "Where were you going? To dinner?" He could only hope, since it was nearly nine p.m. and he was starving.

"I ate at six o'clock like the regular folks do," she said coolly. "Only idiots and preppy rich boys have supper at nine in the evening." She gave him an insulting once-over. "Which, come to think of it, are probably one and the same."

"Fine." He halted her with a hand on her arm. "We can head back upstairs so you can pack, then."

She jerked her arm free. "Screw you, Hamilton. I have eight days until I have to be at my first gig. I might not have any choice when it comes to your escorting me to my concerts, but I sure as hell don't have to let you dictate my actions until then." The look she leveled on him said she was serious as a heart attack. "I *will* call the cops this time if you press me on this—and the devil with the bad press."

Her face adopted a mulish expression he remembered. "And to hell with Wild Wind Records, too. They never should have hired someone to squire me around like some flighty eighth-grader. God knows they shouldn't have simply taken Mama's version of my character as gospel." The obdurate expression solidified. "Maybe I should just cut my losses with them and call it a day."

Swell. The Semper Fi Agency ought to look real good in her label's eyes when he informed them that not only would he not be accompanying their hot new talent as agreed, but that because of him she was dumping them, as well. Nothing like setting the gold standard in the investigational/security world. "Don't you think you should have a little dialogue with Wild Wind before you just walk away?"

"Why?" Stepping close, she got in his face. "Did they have so much as one conversation with me? No, sir. They sicced you on me without bothering to discover that Mama has a great big ax to grind."

Double-damn hell. He recognized that look. Telling the old P.J. what to do had always merely entrenched her in her position, and to hell with whether it was a defensible one or not. So he pasted a bored look on his face and shrugged. "Hey, you want to tank your career, that's fine with me. It probably didn't mean that much to you in the first place, so what the hey. Easy come, easy go, right?"

"No, that's not right!" She drilled him in the chest with a blunt fingertip. "You don't know diddly about how hard I worked to get here."

People in the lobby were turning to look at her, and Jared had to admit she was something to behold when she was all fired up. Somehow, though, he doubted telling her she was hot when she was angry would earn him any points. Wrapping his fist around her finger, he removed it from his pec. "Then use your head. You don't just toss aside something you've worked years to attain because you're hacked off. Just what did your mother do, anyhow?" The question was partly to divert her attention before she imploded, but mostly because he really wanted to know what it had taken for P.J. to finally see her mother for what she was.

A shield slammed shut in her eyes. "None of your damn business." She jerked her finger free. "You're not my friend anymore. You're Wild Wind's lackey."

Stung, he straightened to his full height. "I'm nobody's lackey, baby. I'm my own man."

"So you say. I'll have to take your word for that, but either way you have no authority over me, so get out of my way. I've got places to go, people to see." She pushed around him and headed for the exit to the parking garage.

He fell into step beside her, his long legs easily

matching the brisk stride of her shorter ones. "Where we going?"

She stopped. Glared up at him.

Then sighed.

"You're not going to leave me be, are you?"

"Nope."

"Fine." She started for the garage once again. "Do what you gotta do—I can't keep you out of public places. But don't get any ideas that I'm just going to roll over to make your job easy for you. And don't even think you're riding with me."

"I wouldn't dream of it. I'll follow in my own car."

"If you can keep up."

He could, but only because he'd found a spot in the garage not far from where she'd parked. He'd barely turned over the engine in his rented SUV when she peeled out of the garage like a bullet from a .45, and he had to remain alert just to keep her in sight as she headed out of town. In between driving like Dale Earnhardt Jr. in order to stay on her tail, he spent time on his cell phone finessing arrangements with the hotel they'd just left.

Fifteen minutes later, she pulled into the graveled lot of a huge clapboard tavern with the name Guitars and Hot Cars spelled out in flaming red neon across the roof. P.J. had hopped out of her pickup and was striding toward the honky-tonk's massive double doors before he'd found a spot to park in the acre-wide lot.

The joint was jumping when Jared let himself in a few minutes later. The lights were dim, the music loud and the dance floor packed. There were a lot of women wearing straw Stetsons and skintight jeans. He was beginning to think P.J. had given him the slip out the back when he spotted her sitting at the bar talking ninety miles an hour to a bartender with no neck, tattoos on his massive biceps and a blue bandana tied around his bullet-shaped shaved head. For all his tough appearance, the man had a stunned look in his close-set eyes as he divided his attention between pouring a shot from a bottle of Wild Turkey and staring at her. Jared could identify, knowing from experience that P.J. could talk the balls off a brass monkey.

"The band's about to break. I'll go get Burt," the bartender was saying as Jared walked up. "He's gonna flip that you actually showed up." Placing the shot glass in front of her, he gave the bar a meaty slap and laughed.

"Thanks, Wayne."

"Are you kidding me? He thought you was playin' games with him for sure. He's gonna be so jazzed." Shaking his head, Wayne pulled the towel from his shoulder, wiped a drop of bourbon off the countertop, then called someone over to relieve him. Surprisingly agile for a man his size, he hopped the bar as soon as his replacement arrived and disappeared down the back hallway.

Jared took the vacant stool next to her. "Got a hot date?"

He thought she was going to ignore him, but after a second of silence she hitched the shoulder nearest him. "You bet." She tossed back the shot, shuddered a little, then turned to look him in the eye. "I'm primed. I'm pumped. Raring to go. Me and Burt are gonna do the bed boogie till we burn down the house."

To his surprise, he discovered that the thought ground at something deep in his gut. He could barely wrap his mind around P.J. as a woman, much less a sexual woman who sat in bars tossing back shots and talking about doing a stranger. But that was his problem, so he merely gave her a cool-eyed gaze. "Obviously you've had a change of heart about sex since the last time I saw you."

Swiveling her stool in his direction, she gave his forehead a light rap with her knuckles. "Hello! I was thirteen years old the last time we discussed sex. Of course I've had a change of heart."

"Well...good, then. Fine. That's real healthy."

Her clear amber eyes looked into his as if she could read his soul and her mouth quirked up in a knowing smile. "Isn't it just?"

An older, heavyset man bustled up just then, and, treating Jared as if he were suddenly invisible, P.J. twisted her stool around an additional quarter turn to face the new arrival. Her face lit up in a million-watt smile. "You must be Burt." She thrust her hand out.

The man grasped it and pumped enthusiastically. "Oh, man. It really is you. I thought for sure Wayne was shittin', er, that is, foolin' me."

"No, sir. As I told you on the phone, I'd really like an opportunity to perform with the band, if they don't mind."

"Oh, man," he said again. "They're gonna go ape. Why don'tcha come with me and I'll introduce you."

"That would be great." She turned to Jared. "And here you thought I'd come to have sex with the man."

Burt looked aghast. "What? Why would anyone think such a thing?"

"Darned if I know," she said sorrowfully. "There are some people in the world who are just sick puppies."

The older man shot him a look of disgust and cupped a protective hand around P.J.'s elbow.

Jared watched them walk away. "What a card," he said through tight teeth as they disappeared into the crowd. Ignoring the pretty blonde in the leopard-print cowgirl hat who offered him an inviting smile as she slid onto P.J.'s vacated stool, he reached for the bowl of peanuts on the bar. This had been the longest goddamn day.

And apparently it wasn't over yet.

CHAPTER THREE

Headline, *Country Billboard*:
Priscilla Jayne's Sophomore Album *Watch Me Fly*
Soars Despite Controversy

P.J. FINISHED STRATEGIZING with the band over the order of the playlist and walked up to one of the two mics, adjusting it to her shorter height. "Hell-o, Pocatelló! My name is Priscilla Jayne and Cold Creek has kindly agreed to let me play with them this evening. I hope you don't mind my horning in."

The audience roared its approval and she grinned, flooded with pleasure. God, she loved this. Singing was the only thing she'd ever had that was hers alone and when she performed, all the crap in her life just disappeared for a while. Her glance went to Jared at the bar, but immediately she brought her attention back where it belonged—with her audience.

"You probably already know Cold Creek's lead singer, Ron Taber. He and I have never sung together before—but if you won't hold the occasional screw-up against us, we promise to give you the best show we possibly can. Now, we know you came here to dance, so let's hear those boots out on the floor, because we're starting out tonight with Shania Twain's 'I Ain't No Quitter.'" Leaning into the microphone, she sang, *He drinks...*

The drummer and steel guitarist jumped in with a two-note counterpoint.

He smokes...

As the band repeated the counterpoint, Ron Taber leaned into his mic, made a half turn to look at her, and joined in.

He curses, swears and he tells bad jokes...

The bar patrons poured onto the dance floor and P.J. and the band kept them there by playing everything from "Billy's Got His Beer Goggles On" to "Hicktown" to her own "Let the Party Begin." Not until the dancers nearest the stage looked good and sweaty did P.J. say, "We're gonna slow things down now with a little number called 'Mama's Girl.'"

Some of the dancers snickered, and she acknowledged them with a crooked smile. "I know, I know—it's an ironic choice, given the headlines in the rags these days." Her gaze involuntarily sought out Jared. Then she snapped her attention back where it belonged. "But do me a favor and don't believe everything you read, okay?" She turned to the band. "Hit it, boys."

They launched into the intro and she brought the mic to her lips. Looking beyond the lights to the shadowy tables ringing the dance floor, she sang:

She was eighteen years old and all alone
When a slick-talking man on the Thurston County road

Slowed down his car and said
Let me give you a ride.

It *was* ironic, all things considered, but despite everything she still loved this song. Her friend Nell had written it, and from the very first time P.J. had heard it, its story and haunting melody had resonated with her. It'd also accessed feelings she was ashamed to acknowledge. For how did one admit to all the guilty longings for the kind of mother she'd always wished she'd had? "Mama's Girl" had hit on her most heartfelt, number-one fantasy—a mother who loved her daughter unconditionally and made sacrifices to assure her child's happiness.

It was a pipe dream, of course, but every time she sang the song she could almost make herself believe that it was true—that the saga of a single mother whose every thought began and ended with her daughter's welfare was *her* story. Even now, after Mama had tried to rob her blind and had smeared bits and pieces of her life across the media, the emotional connection to the mother of her song kept sucking her back into the fantasy.

Unfortunately, that had caused her to dig herself into a great big pit with the media when "Mama's Girl" started racking up airtime. But what should she have said when they'd asked if the lyrics were based on her own experiences—that the woman in the song was so far removed from her real mother that it wasn't even funny? That she sang an ode to a nameless, faceless woman she'd give her left arm to have been raised by?

No, not faceless, P.J. admitted. She had never forgotten Jared's sister, Victoria, or the way she'd treated her daughter, Esme. Had never been able to erase the memory of the love stamped all over the woman's face whenever she'd looked at her little girl. Nor had P.J. forgotten Victoria's generosity—not when Tori had given her the most beautiful dollhouse she'd ever seen when P.J. had left Denver to go back to live with Mama.

So every time she sang this song, Victoria's was the face she envisioned.

By the time they finished the set, P.J. was all jacked up with the euphoria of performing. Fans stopped her every two steps as soon as she left the stage, but she smiled and laughed and happily talked with them. She was in a fine mood by the time she reached the bar.

"Great show," Wayne said.

"Thanks, it was fun. Can I have a large, *large* club soda, please?"

"You bet. You want something stronger to go along with it? Another shot of Wild Turkey, maybe? It's on the house."

"No, thanks. One shot lubes up my pipes. Anything more throws off my timing. But I appreciate the offer."

He brought her a tall club soda and she drank it down in one long swallow. Laughing, Wayne took the glass from her hand, refilled it with the soda gun, squeezed a wedge of lime into it and handed it back to her. A second later the waitresses converged on the bar and he left to attend to the break's rush orders.

"Looks like you've got this crowd wrapped around

your little finger," Jared's voice suddenly said directly into her right ear.

Sensation shivered from the point of entry all the way down her side and she swiveled to face him. He was wedged between her stool and the one next to it, looking hot in his worn jeans and white tank top with a white shirt hanging open over it. He smiled down at her. She noticed, however, that the smile didn't quite reach his eyes. That seemed to occur a lot—and she realized anew that although she'd known the boy almost inside out, she didn't know squat about the man he had become. "I enjoy meeting fans," she said coolly.

He slid onto the stool next to hers. "You were really good up there."

Okay, she'd admit it: his praise thrilled her. But attributing it to a momentary blast from the past, she merely inclined her head. "Thanks."

"So what are you doing in a podunk bar when you're slated to begin a tour of big-time venues?"

"Doing what I love best—jamming with other musicians." She shrugged. "And if I can exert a little damage control with the fans at the same time, so much the better."

"You'd do a lot more damage control if you gave an interview to one of the magazines or CMT."

"Well, thank you for that advice. If the time ever comes when I wanna see my private life dissected in front of millions, I'll be sure to keep it in mind." She shook her head in disgust. "I thought you'd be the one person to understand the effect all this media attention has on a person's psyche. But I guess you've changed even more than I'd already noticed." Hopping off the stool, she stalked across the bar to the back exit.

"P.J.!"

She didn't even slow down.

Dammit, he'd brought her wonderful mood crashing to earth and she resented the hell out of him for it. This had been the happiest she'd felt in almost two weeks.

Losing the performance high, however, was nothing compared to the way he'd crushed her second-favorite fantasy. For years she'd carried the dream of him around in her heart. For a brief while he'd been her hero, and she'd missed him like crazy when her mother had first let her come home after Rocket rescued her and Jared from the streets. But she'd seen the mansion Jared lived in, and the seeds of Mama's insistence that a rich boy like him had no time for a girl like her had found fertile ground. So when she and Mama moved mere days after reuniting, she'd let her relationship with Jared lapse.

She'd dreamed of him, though. God, had she dreamed of him! And long before she'd ever believed she might have an actual shot at realizing her fantasy of becoming a country singer, she'd made up scenarios in her head of one day running into him. She, of course, would be the hottest singing sensation since the coalminer's daughter. He would be so struck by her beauty and talent that he'd beg her to marry him on the spot. And they'd live happily ever after in a nice house with a really big yard full of dogs and cats and stuff.

"Juvenile bullshit," she muttered now, pushing through the back door into the brisk evening air.

She shivered. It had been about seventy degrees earlier today but the town was nestled in the western foothills of the Rockies and the temperature felt as if it had dropped thirty degrees. Rubbing her arms as the sweat she'd worked up onstage encountered the chilly air, she eyed the cartons of empties stacked next to the Dumpster. She separated out one and sat on it. Planting her elbow on her knee, she rested her chin in her palm.

After a moment it occurred to her that although she was tired of being jerked around, just sitting on her butt stewing about it didn't seem to be getting her anywhere. So maybe it was time to get up and actually do something.

She marched back into the bar, located Wayne and walked up to him. "See that guy over there?" She indicated Jared with a lift of her little finger.

"Yeah. Seen him talking to you a minute ago. Then I seen you taking off, lookin' mad enough to chew nails. He bothering you?"

"Yes. Can something be done about it?"

"You betcha." He pulled out a sawn-off oar from beneath the bar and raised it in the air over his head.

"Whoa, whoa, *whoa!* I don't want him beaten up."

He grinned at her. "I'm not gonna hit him. This is just to signal Bubba."

"Who's Bub— Whoa."

A man the size of a refrigerator appeared next to her, and Wayne jutted his chin toward Jared, who was sitting down the bar a ways, killing off a bowl of peanuts. "Man in the white shirt is bothering the lady here," he said softly.

"I'm sorry about that, ma'am," Bubba said in a quiet, surprisingly high-pitched voice as he politely inclined his head to P.J. "I'll see to it he doesn't do that again."

"Without violence, right?"

"Yes, ma'am." He started to turn away, then turned back and gave the front of his white straw cowboy hat a courteous tug. "Enjoyed your singing."

"Thank you." She turned bemused eyes to Wayne as Bubba ambled away. "Big boy."

"Oh, yeah."

They both watched as Bubba walked up to Jared, leaned down and said something in his ear. Jared turned his head to stare at P.J., his face impassive but eyes hot, before nodding and climbing to his feet. He dropped a couple of bills on the bar then strode across the room and out the front door.

Take that, she thought, watching until the door closed behind him. *How do* you *like being the one with no power over what's happening to you?* She turned back to Wayne. "You have any bottled water?"

"Sure."

"Let me have one of those, wouldja? I need something to sip onstage." She wasn't stupid—she knew she hadn't gotten rid of Jared permanently. But for the moment at least he wasn't sitting there raining on her parade. She was used to being in charge of her life, but too many things had been happening lately without her input. It had to stop.

And to that end, she felt as if she'd taken her first steps. Maybe only baby steps, but it felt good all the same to be proactive again. Her heart regained some of the lightness she'd been feeling before Jared had ruined her mood.

By the time she and Cold Creek closed down their final set at close to two in the morning she was flying high. She talked to the band while they broke down the drums and packed the stringed instruments in their cases. But when they invited her to join them for an after-hours drink, she declined. The shot she'd tossed back before the first set had long worn off, but she didn't think it was a good idea to have another drink just before she climbed behind the wheel. Plus she wanted to get out of town before the press got wind of tonight's gig and hunted her down—but she could use a few hours' sleep first. So she thanked them, thanked Burt and Wayne and Bubba, and headed out to the nearly empty lot.

Jared's SUV was still parked across the lot, but she shrugged and headed for her truck. If her luck held, maybe she'd make it back to the hotel and gain her room without having to talk to him. Laughing, she dashed to her pickup. So far, so good. No headlights flashed on the Lexus and its engine didn't fire up. She unlocked the driver's side and opened the door.

"Took you long enough."

"Holy crap!" Her breath exploded from her lungs and her heart slammed up against the wall of her chest. She slapped a hand to her breast to contain it. Seeing Jared lounging on his tailbone on the passenger side of the bench seat, a black felt cowboy hat pulled low over his eyes and his long legs crossed at the ankle and propped up on the dashboard by the steering wheel, made her good cheer go up in smoke. "What are you *doing* here? How did you get in? And where did you get that hat?"

"Waiting for you. Picked the lock. And I found the hat behind the seat. I look pretty hot in it, don't I?"

He did, dammit. "The color's appropriate, anyhow."

"Bad guy, black hat?"

"Why, yes, now that you mention it." She gave him her best wide-eyed innocent look, as if that wasn't exactly what she'd implied.

"At least I know enough to look inside a vehicle before I climb in."

She rolled her eyes. "So do you often help yourself to other men's stuff?"

His eyes were a now-you-see-it-now-you-don't gleam beneath the brim. "Can't say that I do. But I had lots of time to kill, and when I found this—" he touched a lazy finger to the hat's brim "—I realized I need a nice Stetson if I'm going to be on a country-music tour. Want to fit in, don'tcha know."

"Well, get your own. That one's Hank's. And it's not a Stetson, city boy. It's a Resistol." She smacked his calf. "Get your feet off my dash." When he complied, she climbed in and closed the door. The overhead light blinked off.

"Who's Hank? Your boyfriend?"

"My fiddle player."

Jared didn't know why he gave a damn one way or

the other, but he was glad to hear it belonged to a member of her band. He looked at her as she fired up her truck. She had pretty skin; it looked creamy even washed by the faint green-and-gold glow thrown off by the dash. He cleared his throat. "You okay to drive?"

"Sure. I had one drink when we first got here, but I sweated it all out by the time we finished the first set." Putting the pickup in gear, she released the brake.

And drove the hundred yards to the other side of the lot, where she stopped next to his Lexus. "Don't let the door hit you in the butt."

"You seem to say that to me a lot," he said, fishing his keys from his pocket and climbing out. He leaned in to speak to her through the crack in the window. "Lock your damn doors, okay? I'll see you back at the hotel."

She made a rude noise, and the minute he stepped back, she peeled away, leaving the smell of scorched rubber and exhaust in her wake.

He just grinned, because he'd had plenty of time to study his map while he'd waited for her. Driving hell for leather on the alternate route he'd memorized, he made it to the hotel ahead of her. He collected his room key, detoured through the coffee shop to grab a handful of spoons and forks off the table nearest the door and was in time to smile at P.J.'s disgruntlement when he stepped onto the elevator with her. "Déjà vu."

"Ha-ha." She eyed the leather satchel in his hand and the canvas backpack slung by one strap from his shoulder. But it was his fistful of cutlery that she addressed. "You're stealing hotel silverware? What, you lose your trust fund or something?"

"Nah. I gave it away."

She pushed away from the wall she'd been leaning against. "You gave away all your money?"

"Not all of it. Just the lion's share."

She stared at him openmouthed. "But that's…that is so—"

"Philanthropic? Altruistic? Unbelievably generous?"

"*Nuts.* That's just plain nuts. A person has to work too damn hard for his money to just give it all away."

He shrugged. "I didn't earn the money that I donated to charity. It came, as you so astutely pointed out, from a trust fund set up by my father and from the bearer bonds that got him killed. Or maybe you didn't hear about the latter." A tinge of bitterness he couldn't prevent entered his tone. "After all, you'd taken a powder by then, hadn't you?"

She tipped her head so he could no longer see her eyes in the shadow of her hat brim. "I did so hear," she muttered.

The car arrived at their floor and he waved her out ahead of him. She stepped into the alcove with alacrity but then hesitated and turned back to him. "I'm sorry," she said grudgingly.

"Are you? What for?"

"For making those rich-boy cracks."

He laughed. "Honey, I'm still rich. I'm just not obscenely wealthy like I was before." He followed her off the elevator.

She backed up a step. "What are you doing?"

"Would you believe walking you to your door?"

"This isn't a date! I don't need to be walked to my door."

"In that case, I'm walking me to mine."

She blew out an aggravated breath. "Fine. Whatever. I'm too tired to figure out your riddles. I'm going to bed." She turned on her heel and stalked off.

Once again he found himself walking behind her, eyeing the irritated twitch of her butt. After her performance with the band, he figured she had reason to be tired.

She'd knocked his socks off tonight. He'd heard her music before, of course, so he'd already known she had a powerhouse voice. But listening to a CD and watching her perform live was like comparing silver to platinum. A record didn't showcase the incredible contrast between her raspy speaking voice and that full-throated way she had of belting out a melody.

And she *moved* onstage. From the instant she'd sashayed up to the microphone, she'd been in motion. Either her hips had been swinging, or her arms had been in the air or she'd been bopping in place while holding the mic out for the audience to sing the chorus of a song. All that energy in motion had been like a time warp back to the days when she used to dance backward in front of him so she could talk his ear off while they walked the sidewalks of Denver. Except tonight there'd been a confusing overlay of vivid woman superimposed atop the memory of the child she'd been then.

An overlay he was dead determined to ignore.

She stopped at the door to room 617 and inserted her card. When the light turned green she pushed down the handle. She was halfway into the little hallway inside the door before she appeared to notice him opening the door to room 619.

She shot back out into the corridor and faced him, hands on her hips. "You're *next door?*"

"Handy, isn't it? We have connecting rooms."

She made a sound like pressure escaping a steam valve and stormed into hers. "I'll be sure to lock my side," he heard her say as she slammed the door shut.

"Nah, really?" he murmured as he closed his own door behind him. Opening the closet, he dumped his satchel on the luggage rack, then sloughed the backpack off his shoulder as he continued into the room. Dropping it and his fistful of flatware onto the bed, he sat down and stared at the wall as a wave of exhaustion swept over him. It had been a long day.

And it wasn't over yet. Pulling the backpack closer, he unzipped it and rummaged through the main compartment until he located a spool of fishing line. Then he moved up the mattress until his back pressed against the headboard, laid out the utensils he'd taken from the coffee shop and started tying them, one next to the other, on the line. He fastened one end of the filament to the nightstand lamp's finial, then fed out the line down the short hallway, looped it around the doorknob to the open bathroom door and ran it between the threshold and the bottom of the door to the hallway.

Quietly making his way to P.J.'s room, he looped the line around her door handle, tied an angler's knot and cut the remainder of the spool free.

Returning to his room, he stripped down, brushed his teeth and went to bed.

The sound of his bathroom door slamming and a half dozen forks and spoons clanking together as they danced on the line next to the bed woke him half an hour later. Rolling from bed, he tugged on his jeans and headed for the door.

As he pulled it open he heard a muffled thud and P.J.'s voice exclaiming, "What the—?"

Strolling out into the corridor, he saw her bending over to peer at the line stretched across her doorway. Her suitcase lay on its back half in, half out of her room.

"Going somewhere, P.J.?"

She raised furious eyes. "What the hell is this?"

"A rudimentary but effective alarm system. Checking out?"

"I'd considered it. I want to leave town before the press gets wind that I'm here." She looked at his naked chest, then raised resentful eyes to meet his gaze. "But I guess it can wait till morning." Whispering a curse, she dragged her bag back into her room and slammed the door.

Score one for his side. With a satisfied smile, Jared reset his line and returned to his room, as well.

Now maybe they could both get a few hours' sleep.

CHAPTER FOUR

And on the music front, a little birdie just told me that singer Priscilla Jayne hired power agent Ben McGrath to replace the mother she fired.
—"Dishing With Charley" columnist Charlene Baines, *Nashville News Today*

WHEN THE ALARM WENT OFF at eight the next morning P.J. had no idea where she was for a few disoriented moments. Then the smell of cigarette smoke on her skin and in her hair registered—that all-too-familiar reek of bars and honky-tonks. The stench brought last night's events rushing back and she crawled out of bed and stumbled over to the complimentary coffeemaker to assemble a pot. The minute it started burbling she stuck her cup in the coffeepot space. When it was full she exchanged it for the glass container and knocked the drink back in one long swallow.

Finally feeling awake enough to quit stumbling over her own feet, she headed for the bathroom to take a quick shower. Then she dried off, pulled on a short cotton two-flounce lime green skirt and a white tank top and threw her toiletries into her suitcase. Bundling last night's smoke-saturated outfit into a plastic bag, she tucked it alongside her cosmetic pouch and zipped the suitcase closed.

After piling her belongings next to the door, she called down to the front desk. "This is Priscilla Morgan in room 617," she said in a tremulous voice when they picked up. "Would you send up the manager, please? Right away? And I need my bill prepared for checkout."

There was a knock on her door within five minutes. P.J. opened it the barest crack and peered out.

"Miss Morgan? I'm Jed Turner, the manager. You requested to speak to me?" She saw him stare down at the fishing line tied to her door knob, watched as his gaze tracked it along the hallway. "What is this?"

"That's what I wanted to talk to you about," she whispered. "The man next door is stalking me."

"He's *what?*"

"Shh. Please." She cast a nervous eye in the direction of room 619. "He's been following me for days, and last night he somehow discovered which room I was in and managed to get accommodations in the one next door." She let out a shuddery sigh. "He tied that line to my door. It leads to his room where it's tied to something that forms a rudimentary alarm system. I know because he told me so last night when I tried to leave." She looked up at the manager. "I'm scared, Mr. Turner. I think he's…disturbed, and I can't get out of my room without him knowing."

"Well, we'll just see about that," the manager said grimly. "Stay put. I'll be right back."

Oh, crap. She'd hoped to be out of here before he confronted Jared.

But Turner didn't go next door. He walked down the hallway in the opposite direction and, as promised, was back in less than five minutes. Producing a pocket knife, he sliced the line from the doorknob. "Will you come out here for a second and hold this?"

P.J. stepped out into the corridor and took the severed filament from his grasp.

"Keep applying tension to it," the manager instructed in a low voice.

"Where did you get this stuff?" she asked as he tapped a fine nail into the doorframe.

"From our maintenance foreman."

She gave him her best awed smile. "You are so clever!"

He stood a little taller, but merely said, "If you'll step over here to this side of me and continue holding the line taut I'll fasten it to the brad."

She watched him tie the line around the nail.

"There!" he whispered in satisfaction.

She dashed into her room and grabbed her stuff. "Thank you so much!" she said as she rolled it out. "I'll just stop at the desk and check out. Thank you!"

"Um, wait a minute, Miss Morgan. I called the sheriff's office when I went to Maintenance. You're going to need to stick around to talk to them."

Uh-oh. But P.J. hadn't spent time as a kid scamming tourists out of their spare change for nothing. She knew how to think on her feet. Giving him an earnest nod, she said, "Sure. Let me just check out and put my things in my car, then I'll come back up." She flashed him big, imploring eyes. "Please. Won't you stay here to make sure he doesn't get away? I want to put as many miles between me and this pervert as I possibly can, and I'm scared to death he'll somehow find out that the sheriff is coming. God!" Allowing a little hysteria to enter her voice, she grasped his arm. "What if he gets away? What if he lies in wait somewhere to follow me *again?*"

Turner gave her a comforting pat. "No, no, that's not going to happen. I'll stay right here to be sure he doesn't go anywhere."

"You are so wonderful. Do you want me to come back up here?" She glanced nervously down the hallway. "Or...maybe I could meet with the sheriff downstairs?"

"My office would probably be the best place. Have the desk clerk direct you there and ask them to page me as soon as the sheriff arrives."

"Oh, my gosh, thank you, *thank you!* You've truly been my hero."

It took her only minutes to check out. She was on the road heading out of town moments after that, conveniently having failed to pass on the request to page the manager.

Envisioning Jared's face when he found himself all tangled up in red tape, she laughed as she hit the city limits and punched the pedal to the metal. Score one for the girl in the white hat.

IT TOOK JARED ALL DAY to track P.J. down. Sitting in the foliage-filled atrium of a downtown Red Lion hotel in

Spokane, Washington, he ate a club sandwich while keeping an eye on both the entrance to the bank of elevators and the stairs that came down from the two interior balconies overlooking the lobby.

Much as he hated to admit it, she'd caught him off guard. He didn't know precisely how she'd conned the manager of the hotel in Pocatello, but her performance must have really been something, because the guy had been all over him the minute he'd opened the door to a peremptory knock. The damn sheriff had even been called in and he'd had to do some fancy dancing to avoid having his ass hauled down to the county clink. Luckily he had a copy of the contract that the agency had signed with Wild Wind Records.

It hadn't hurt, either, that P.J. had vanished. By the time Turner hauled him down to his office, only to discover the sheriff had been there for some time but P.J. hadn't made an appearance at all and no one had been instructed to contact him, it was obvious he'd begun to suspect he'd been played. An involuntary grin tugged at Jared's lips now.

No shit, Sherlock.

Not that he had much to chortle about, himself. He'd underestimated her. From everything he'd seen so far, he would have sworn P.J. would do just about anything to avoid turning the light of media attention on herself. She sure as hell kept dodging having to deal with all the bullshit her mother was spreading. And unless Jodeen Morgan had changed dramatically since their Denver days, he had to believe one session of straight talk from P.J. and her old lady's guns would be spiked. The fact that P.J. wasn't doing a damn thing about it had led him to believe she wouldn't make a fuss over his homemade alarm system, either.

Looked like he'd been wrong on that front.

Before he'd fallen asleep last night it had occurred to him that hooking up with her this early was probably a mistake and that maybe he ought to back off and just keep his eye on her from a distance until her tour started. Well, screw that. Her trying to get him arrested for *stalking,* for crissake, had made this personal.

He came to attention when P.J. suddenly came into sight, skipping blithely down the staircase just as he was killing off his sandwich. It was an hour to sunset and he hadn't known if she'd go out at all. If so, though, he would have expected her to be dressed for hitting the club circuit like she'd been last night. Instead, she wore a sports bra, an abbreviated pair of shorts and running shoes. A CamelBak hydration system was strapped to her back.

She was a runner? That wasn't something he ever would have guessed. He watched her cross the atrium.

It didn't take a detective to figure out she was going for a run—which meant that sooner or later she'd be right back where she'd started: here. No sense in leaving this beautifully air-conditioned hotel to get all hot and sweaty following her around.

Then he sighed. Because this morning's stunt was still fresh in his mind, and what if this were a ruse? She could easily have spotted him from the upstairs landing, in which case he wouldn't put it past her to have called the bell captain to load her luggage into her truck. And wouldn't he look like an ass if he sat here for the next hour and a half waiting for her to return, when for all he knew she was jogging her way to Timbuktu.

Standing up, he glanced down at his Teva sandals. Shit. He was asking Rocket for a raise. He wasn't being paid nearly enough for this crap. He watched her exit through the front entrance, then followed.

Like a breath-stealing, run-amok forest fire, a wall of heat hit him the moment he stepped outside, and he damn near trod on P.J.'s heels when he unexpectedly came up behind her where she stood stretching. With the image of blue hip-hugger boy shorts stretched taut over that amazing butt seared into his retinas, he backpedaled out of sight until she set off at an easy clip down the path that fronted the hotel. Once she disappeared around the corner, he started out behind her.

He followed her past the pool at the back of the hotel and by the umbrella tables until she reached a little bridge that crossed the river to the hundred-acre island that formed Riverfront Park. She picked up her pace and they ran at a decent clip past the forestry shelter and the pavilion with its carnival rides and IMAX theater, through greenery and meadows, down to the place where the gondolas took off overhead and past a bunch of sculptures.

Heating up, he stripped off his T-shirt as he ran. Even then, he had to stop at the hand-carved wooden carousel to catch his breath. Pressing one hand to the stitch in his side, he braced the other against a bench back and bent over, blowing hard. He looked beyond the kids leaning out to try for the brass ring to where P.J. was running by a structure that he heard a parent call the Garbage Goat. Thinking he would kill for a bottle of water, he blew out a breath and started after her again, ignoring the hot spot that his sandal was rubbing on the ball of his right foot.

They jogged past a giant interactive sculpture shaped like a Radio Flyer red wagon and farther along passed a floating stage. They turned left over another little bridge, then P.J. turned left again and they pounded past a Vietnam veterans' memorial with a soaring clock tower in the background. That brought them back near the forestry shelter and he watched a trickle of sweat roll between her shoulder blades as she ran in place while giving another connected island they hadn't covered a considering gaze. Another drop coasted down the shallow groove of her spine and disappeared into the low-cut bandless waist of her little blue shorts.

Christ, had the temperature just spiked another twenty degrees? He could see the headline now: *Semper Fi Detective Strokes Out on Measly One-Mile Run.* Lucky for him, he knew he could count on his sister to spend time at his bedside wiping the drool from his chin. John, on the other hand, would probably just show up to laugh at him.

To his eternal relief, P.J. turned back toward the first bridge.

Figuring he could safely assume she was headed back to the hotel, he slacked off his pace. Then his professional self demanded, *And you're going to discover her room number* how *from back here?*

"Crap." Blowing out a breath, he picked up his speed again.

She'd disappeared by the time he got in sight of the pool again and, swearing to himself, he put on a further burst of speed.

"Enjoy your run?"

He skidded to a halt, his head whipping around.

P.J. sat at one of the umbrella tables on the rail-enclosed deck, her feet up on the chair next to her. He walked back. "You knew I was behind you the entire time?"

"Hard to miss the sound of those sandals slapping on the path." She nodded at his feet. "You run pretty good for a man in Tevas."

He swung over the railing onto the deck and took a chair across from her. "Gimme your water."

"Get your own drink."

He leaned toward her. "I sold my favorite baseball card for you. Give me the goddamn water!"

"That was fifteen years ago, and you sold it for both of us, not just me." But she shoved the CamelBak she'd removed across the table.

He swooped the backpacklike hydration system up, stuck the mouthpiece between his lips and nearly sucked the well dry. When he came up for air, he found her gazing at his naked chest.

"You might want to put your shirt on," she said dryly. "I think this is one of those no shirt, no shoes, no service places."

"Then they must not get a helluva lot of business. It's next to a damn pool."

"That's a point." A valid one, P.J. saw when she looked around and saw a few of the diners still in bathing attire. She was nevertheless relieved to see him raise his right hip and fish his navy T-shirt from his back pocket, where he'd stuffed the shirt's tail. All that bare skin stretched over all that well-defined muscle and bone made her a little nervous. So she gave him a wiseacre smirk. "Who would have guessed that you'd turn out to be so buff?"

He pulled the shirt on over his head then flexed an impressively muscular bicep at her. "You a fool for muscles?"

"Oh, yeah." She laid it on thick, batting her eyes and doing the pitty-pat thing with her hand on her heart. "They just make me weak all over."

"Uh-huh." As she'd hoped, he thought she was yanking his chain, even though the sight of his shoulders and chest and ridged abdomen did make her feel a little giddy.

Lord Almighty, girl. Get a grip.

Clearly she had to get out more. She'd determined as a kid not to get sucked into the penchant that seemed to run rampant in so many of the small-town women she'd known—that longing for a man, any man, to stand between them and the lonelies. She'd always patted herself on the back for striking a healthy balance. So okay, she'd admit that recently she'd been concentrating on her career so much that her love life was pretty much nonexistent. Still, she certainly hadn't turned her back on men altogether.

Maybe she was going a little overboard on the vocation side of the equation these days, though, if the sight of one well-muscled chest gave her palpitations like those of a fourteen-year-old exposed to her first crush. That was a little on the awkward side.

All the same, the girlish giddies had her feeling pretty cheerful.

"So, when did you start running?" Jared asked, interrupting her thoughts.

"When I was sixteen. One of the schools I attended had a track team and Mama and I actually stayed in town long enough for me to join it." Only to be told to pack up again two days after their first meet.

"You do it to maintain that great ass?"

"No. I do it for my singing."

He gave her a blank look and she explained, "The lungs are a bellows, Hamilton. Running improves my wind, which improves my ability to sustain a note." She studied him from beneath her lashes. "So you think I have a great ass?"

To her surprise, dull color climbed his neck to flush his jaw and cheeks. "Hey, I'm a red-blooded man. I've noticed your butt in a, you know, general sort of way."

"Boys will be boys," she agreed dryly. And just like that, she found herself no longer pissed at him. The not quite disguised discomfort in a man she would have sworn didn't have a self-conscious bone in his body reminded her of the boy she'd once adored.

Besides, what had started out feeling like one big slap in the face—Jared's determination to keep tabs on her and his vow to deliver her to her concerts—was actually turning into something of a godsend. This game of cat-and-mouse they played kept her from trying to rewrite her history with Mama over and over again.

Who woulda thunk it? Truth was, though, she couldn't remember the last occasion spent offstage when she'd had this good a time. He was kind of stimulating company and it amused her to keep him on his toes.

Maybe that was why, when he asked out of the blue what her mother had done to make P.J. fire her, she didn't blow him off the way she had that day in the Texas panhandle.

"She cooked the books."

He stared at her. "She *embezzled* from you?"

Raw pain swamped her and she really wished she had blown him off. But she shrugged as if it were no big deal and dipped her chin in assent.

"That *bitch.*"

She'd always hated it when he'd bad-mouthed Jodeen. It was one thing for her to do so but something else entirely for anyone else to take a shot, and her jaw automatically shot up. But she resisted getting in his face about it. Because he was right. Much as she hated to admit it, he was one hundred percent correct.

Mama was a bitch. She likely always had been, but P.J. had refused to let herself see it.

Still, she hoped like hell her sorrow over acknowledging it now didn't show. Climbing to her feet, she gathered her CamelBak. "Well, gee," she said as if she didn't have a care in the world. "This's been swell. But our little whatchamacallit—our truce thingie—"

"Détente?"

"Yeah, that. Is over. Don't go thinking this changes anything. And you really don't want to start expecting I'll make things painless for you between now and the start of my tour. Because I won't. I'm still unhappy about having a guard dog. I'm not about to roll over and make your job easier." And if she had to stifle a silly little pang of regret, that would be her secret.

He yawned. "I'll keep that in mind."

His boredom shot her moment of remorse to hell, and she almost smiled in gratitude. "Just as long as you know." She started back toward the hotel entrance. "I don't want to hear no whining that you weren't warned."

CHAPTER FIVE

Headline, *Modern Twang Weekly*:
Priscilla Jayne Sighted Playing Small-Town Bars
Across the West

WHEN THE MAN OPENED his mailbox to discover a manila envelope from the clipping service he'd recently subscribed to, he came the closest to smiling that he had in a long time. "Praise the Lord," he murmured and marched back up the path to his house with a brisker stride than usual. Pleasure suffused him at the prospect of reading about Priscilla Jayne. He admired everything he knew of her.

Well, that wasn't quite accurate. He didn't approve of her song about drinking and partying that was getting so much airplay these days. But at the same time… "'Honor thy father and thy mother,'" he said with conviction, "that thy days may be long upon the land that the Lord thy God giveth thee." Exodus 20:12 was one of the Bible's most pertinent passages and Priscilla Jayne grasped its importance. That made her a woman in a million in this immoral age they lived in.

Certainly his own daughter had never shown him the respect he deserved.

He brought himself up short with an impatient shake of his head. *No.* He wouldn't think about that.

Not now. Not today.

The moment he entered his modest frame house, the man went straight to the dining room, where he drew the drapes against prying eyes and the hot, Midwestern sun. Except then it was too dim and the overhead light didn't help much. He'd been waiting for these articles with far too much anticipation to miss a single word.

He fetched the gooseneck lamp from the living room, arranged it where it would do the most good and plugged it in.

Nodding in satisfaction, he made a quick trip to the kitchen to pour himself a glass of iced tea but was too impatient to drink it at the kitchen table as was his custom. He brought it back to the dining room and, after placing the glass just so on a paper napkin he'd positioned in the exact center of the heart-of-pine trestle table, he slit open the envelope. Shaking its contents onto the pristine surface, he meticulously aligned the papers, took a sip of his tea and restored the glass to the precise spot from which he'd retrieved it. Heart quickening in anticipation, he reached for the first article.

After reading it, however, his heart pounded with another emotion. Priscilla Jayne had fired her mother as her manager?

That wasn't following the fifth commandment. That wasn't being a proper daughter at all.

Still, it was one piece of writing, and that from one of the more sensationalistic publications. Perhaps they had skewed the story in order to sell more copies of their rag. Those kind of journals were sued all the time for doing exactly that. He reached for the next article in the pile.

Several minutes later, he'd gone through the entire stack of material. He sat back with his fist clenched next to the newly straightened pile. What had happened to all those pretty sentiments Priscilla Jayne had expressed on that CMT interview he'd watched several months back? She'd seemed so different from the usual young woman of today—more moral, more *pure*. Certainly as different from his daughter, Mary, as a woman could get. He had developed an instant and total admiration for her.

But she wasn't honoring her mother now in any manner that he could see. Fingernails biting into his palms, he glared at the faded wallpaper on the far wall without actually seeing it.

That was just plain wrong.

"THANK YOU AND GOOD NIGHT, Klamath Falls! You've been a great audience!" Stepping back from the mic, P.J. blotted perspiration from her forehead with the back of her wrist and reached for her water bottle. The throng crowding the dance floor and the tables surrounding it roared their approval, and she grinned. But it was late, she'd been doing this for seven nights straight, and when the lights slowly dimmed onstage, exhaustion rolled over her. She walked over to thank the band she'd jammed with tonight, then climbed down from the stage.

Tomorrow she'd catch up with her band in Portland. Between traveling and the sound check she had scheduled at the arena to prepare for the tour's first concert that evening, it was bound to be a long and busy day. But that was tomorrow. Tonight she just wanted her bed at the Crater Lake Lodge.

The thought of her room perked her up, and she cast a triumphant smile in Jared's direction. Not that he likely saw it, sitting as he was at the back of the room with his legs stretched out beneath the table in front of him, his arms crossed over his chest and his new charcoal-gray Resistol pulled low over his eyes. It didn't matter, though. He might be unaware of her satisfaction, but she still hugged the coup of reserving the last room at the inn to her breast. According to the desk clerk, the beautiful old wood-and-fieldstone lodge was booked months in advance. P.J. had only scored a room herself due to fortunate timing and a last-minute cancellation.

She strode across the bar and pushed out the door, shrugging into a sweater as she crossed the lot to her truck. She'd finally learned to come prepared for the Pacific Northwest's cool-to-downright-chilly evening temperatures. Picking up her pace, she hit the remote entry button on her keychain and heard the soft thunk of locks disengaging.

"The world as we know it came to a screeching halt

tonight," Jared said from behind her. "You didn't have me tossed out of the tavern. I hardly knew how to act when I didn't have to cool my jets in the parking lot for two or three hours."

It said something about their week-long battle of one-upmanship that she wasn't even startled to hear his voice come out of the dark. Feeling exultant to have come out on top tonight—other times having gone back and forth between them pretty equally—she bestowed her most beatific smile on him.

"Considering you'll be spending the rest of the night shivering in your car, I figured I should probably let you gather all the comfort you could from the bar."

"At the very least." He gazed down at her. "Pretty damn pleased with yourself, aren't you?"

"I am." She executed a little victory dance as she pulled the door open, then climbed up into the cab of the truck. Slamming the door shut, she turned on the ignition and punched the window button. When the glass had glided down she reached out to chuck him gently under his chin. Stubble pricked her fingertip and she snatched back her hand. Cleared her throat.

Then gave him a cocky smile. "See ya around, sucker."

Since she planned to go straight to bed for what remained of the night and there was no point in sneaking out of the lodge in the morning when Jared knew exactly where she was headed, she meant she'd see him tomorrow.

But she hadn't eaten in hours and when hunger sent her out to raid the vending machine in the ice room shortly after settling into her room, it never occurred to her to look down when she opened the door. The next thing she knew, her shin smacked up against a hard barrier and she heard a grunt as her forward momentum sent her lurching over the object blocking her door. Sprawling onto her hands and one knee on the carpeted corridor, she cranked her head around to see what had happened.

Her bare feet were hooked over Jared's midsection. Pulling them free, she swiveled on her knees to face him, pushed back to sit on her heels and gave him a straight-armed shot to the shoulder. "What the hell do you think you're doing? I could have broken my neck."

Rubbing at the spot she'd just smacked, he fixed sleepy eyes on her and yawned. "Well, I *was* sleeping before you tried to break my ribs." His cheek resting on the arm curled above his head, he reached out his free hand to cup her bare thigh just above her kneecap.

"In the *hallway,* like a bum in a doorway." She jerked her leg from his light grasp. "What are you, nuts?"

"Quite possibly. But if you read the sign driving up the road, you know the elevation here is seventy-one hundred feet. Only someone completely nuts would sleep outside where it's fortysomething freaking degrees when there's a nice warm hallway right here. Not to mention room to stretch out." Pushing up on his forearm, his heavy-lidded gaze tracked a path from her legs to her faded red boxers to her tank top to her scrubbed face, making her aware of how awful she must look. "And who's going to see me at two-thirty in the morning?" he asked without heat. "I set my watch to be out of here before most people stir."

"Most people. But it'd only take one early riser to catch you."

"Big deal. I'll tell 'em my wife kicked me out. Trust me, honey, if it's a guy, that'll do the trick. The man hasn't been born who doesn't understand the lack of logic in the female mind."

She shot him a look that should have dropped him in his tracks, but unfortunately looks really couldn't kill. "I oughtta kick you again just for drill."

Reaching behind her, he wrapped his hand around the foot she'd nailed him with and kneaded his fingers along her arch. His forearm was warm against her leg, his touch firm as it dug into just the right muscles, and her fatigue swirled away like water down a drain. But when his thumb brushed the curve of her butt where it rested on her heels, she shifted away.

He shrugged and brought his hand back to scratch his stomach. "You only get one free shot, short stuff, and you've already used yours." Then he gave her a wheedling smile. "You've got a nice big room. Why don't you let me sleep on your couch instead?"

"I don't have a couch."

"Your floor, then."

"Dream on, Hamilton."

"C'mon, what's the worst that could happen?" Then his green eyes suddenly went heavy with something other than exhaustion. "You afraid I might make a move on you?"

"What?" Disquieted, edgy, she surged up on her knees. "Of course not!" That truly hadn't occurred to her, but once the image was planted in her mind, it stuck there like a burr to a saddle blanket.

He moved onto his knees, as well, and he towered over her, the sudden expanse of his hard chest in a soft gray T-shirt her only view. "I think you are," he said in a low voice, and she jerked her gaze up to lock on his. "I think you're afraid I might try to kiss you." He looked her over from her lips to her breasts to her bare legs. "Maybe put my hands on you."

"That's crazy! I never—" And she hadn't, not once since she was a kid who'd learned better than to hang on to unattainable dreams—and even then her fantasies had never traveled any further than an innocent press of lips. But her own gaze glanced off his mouth now, dropped to his hands.

She jumped to her feet. "You're certifiable! Get out of my way. I'm not listening to this crap." Pushing past him as he, too, stood up, she fumbled with the key card, unable to get back into her room fast enough.

She thought she felt his fingers brush one of her curls, and when the light finally turned green, she pushed the door wide in her haste to get away from him. But Jared's hand was right there, splayed against the painted panel to prevent her from closing the door firmly in his face when she whirled back to do precisely that.

"Where's the fire, Peej?" he said softly. "I merely asked if you were worried about my intentions. I didn't say you needed to be. I'm a professional. I don't slap the make to my clients."

"I'm not your client," she snapped, then could have kicked herself. But, this had been a *game?* Humiliated for thinking he had been putting the moves on her—and worse, that she'd responded to them—she thrust her chin up and took a giant step forward to prove to him—to herself—that no cut-rate Romeo could intimidate *her.* "Still, that's good to hear. I was beginning to think you'd lost every standard you once had."

"Not a chance, baby," he murmured, smiling faintly.

For the briefest instant, her traitorous gaze drifted toward his lips, but she quickly jerked it away. "Good night," she said flatly.

This time when she stepped back and leaned her weight against the panel, he let her shut the door between them. Face hot, blood burning hotter, she stalked into the bedroom and threw herself facedown on the bed.

It was a long, long time before she finally fell asleep.

P.J.'s RIGHT, JARED thought for about the hundredth time eight hours later. *You* are *certifiable.* Approaching the cutoff where Highway 160 met up with I-5 outside of Medford, he scowled at the tailgate of her truck as she roared up the road in front of him. Then his thoughts bounced back to the same damn situation he'd been stewing over since two-thirty this morning. The one that had thrown him and P.J. and their history and his reason for being in her company into one big jumble.

It was messy enough already. What the devil had he been thinking to bring sex into the equation?

He'd love to claim it was all part and parcel of their ongoing attempts this past week to outdo each other. But even though he hadn't hesitated to give Peej the impression that it had been nothing more than a golden opportunity to one-up her, he couldn't sell that story to himself. Because rattling her and making her aware of him hadn't been a result of any genius design on his part. He'd simply touched her, looked at her in those worn little red boxer shorts and snug tank top, and his brain had short-circuited and his mouth had started spewing out the thoughts that had been crowding *his* mind, not hers.

Then he'd had the stones to tell her he was a professional. God, that was rich. He'd be lucky if she didn't slap a sexual harassment charge against him.

His brows snapped together. What *had* he been thinking? His professionalism had long been one of, if not *the* most important aspects of his life. So why the hell was he endangering everything he'd worked so hard to accomplish to play who's-on-top-now with P.J.?

Because while it might feel like fun and games, it was threatening his self-respect. And unnecessarily so—he'd known a week ago he didn't need to personally accompany her until the tour officially began. But it had been surprisingly enjoyable to match wits with her, and his life had been so fucking serious for such a long time. And, okay, so maybe he felt more alive than he had in ages, but that was a piss-poor excuse. He only had two things he could count on in his life—his family and his work. That wasn't so frigging much that he could afford to blow off one of them.

Thinking of the other fifty percent reminded him of an event he'd missed at home. Happy to divert thoughts that kept circling like vultures waiting for the corpse, he picked up his cell phone from the seat next to him and punched his sister's number.

The phone on the other end of the line rang three times before it was picked up. "Hello," Victoria said and her voice, warm and familiar, was a balm to his raw nerves.

"Hey, Tori."

"Jared! How are you doing? Have you seen P.J. yet?"

"I'm fine. And yeah, I've seen her." *Several times, in a number of situations.*

She laughed. "Dumb question. Of course you have. John told me you were traveling with her—I just forgot for a minute."

"Ah, caught you at work, did I?"

"Yes. I'm trying out a new design, so my thoughts are a little scattered. It's a Greek temple. Very different, but fun. Although I'm having a tough time imagining what kind of dolls will feel at home in it."

"Maybe Goddess Barbie or Toga Ken. Or maybe it's actually for an adult. Your dollhouses are so amazing I'm guessing they aren't always ordered for kids."

"You sweet-talker, you." Then her voice turned brisk. "But enough about me. Tell me all about P.J."

"She's still fast on her feet and a smart mouth. Other than that, not much to tell."

"Not much to—Jared Hamilton! Don't tell me you haven't rekindled your friendship!"

Shit. This was exactly the conversation he'd hoped to avoid. "I'm here on a job, Victoria."

"And your point is? That little girl was the closest friend you ever had. You can't seriously be holding yourself as emotionally distant from her as you do from everyone but me and Rocket and the kids."

"Christ. What is it with you guys? Like I told John, we were close, but that was a lifetime ago. *She* tossed the friendship away, not me!" But feeling cracks developing in his normally smooth facade, he pulled himself up short. Drawing in a calming breath, he ordered himself to picture the Rocky Mountains. He was a glacier peak, impregnable and remote. He did not lose control.

Calmer, he felt a bite of satisfaction at how composed and patient he sounded when he said, "Look, is Esme around? That's the reason I called."

"Aw, sweetie," she said in a voice so understanding that for a moment it endangered his hard-won composure. "Hang on a second. I'll see if I can find her."

The telephone went on hold, and Jared pictured his sister in her attic studio tracking Esme down via the intercom system wired into every room of her and Rocket's big, rambling Denver home.

Then the line opened up again and his niece's voice said, "Hullo, Uncle Jared!"

"Hey, pipsqueak. Or should I say college graduate pipsqueak? Congratulations, kid. I'm sorry I missed the ceremony, but a gift is in the mail."

"Lovely. But as it happens, you didn't miss a thing." Traces of her first six years in England colored her voice. "I didn't graduate."

"What?" He took his eyes off the road for an instant to give the phone a blank look. "What happened?"

"Turns out my high school French classes don't count toward my foreign language obligation because I failed the competency test I took for college entry. Only no one bothered to tell me that until just now, which I think is complete and utter bollocks. Regardless, I'm stuck taking a French class summer quarter."

"Sorry to hear it, Es." He waited a beat, then said, "Send me back my prez."

"You wanker!" She laughed. "Just try to get it back. You always give great gifts."

"So you're taking one class this summer. That sounds cushy enough. What are you doing the rest of the time, lounging by a pool?"

"I wish. I'm working part time at Daddy's."

"He's letting you muck around at Semper Fi?" He injected the proper horror into his voice. "A girl who couldn't even graduate college? What are the chances of there being a business to come back to when I'm finished with this job?"

"Pretty decent, considering Gert doesn't let me do a damn thing without supervision. Shouldn't she be retired by now? She must be eighty years old."

"Seventy-four. And retire to do what? Crochet doilies?"

"You sound just like her." Amusement laced her voice. "And I have to admit, the woman's a machine. I'm running my arse off just trying to keep up with her."

"She keeps us all slapped into shape," he agreed. "Well, listen, kid. I'm running into traffic and it looks like there's some road construction ahead, so I'd better hang up and pay attention. Keep your nose to the grindstone and I'll see you when we get to Denver."

"Mum got us tickets to Priscilla Jayne's concert. She said I met her once, but I don't remember. I've listened to her new CD, though, and it's actually good."

He grinned. "I'll be sure to pass on your effusive praise."

"That didn't come out right. I guess I just thought all country music was twangy, but hers isn't. I really like her voice and her songs tell great stories. I'm looking forward to hearing her in concert."

"She puts on a helluva show," he said, thinking of her energy knocking them dead in honky-tonks across three states. "I'll see if I can't get you backstage passes."

"Sweet."

When they disconnected a minute later, Jared emptied his mind of everything but the need to concentrate on the sudden backup on a stretch of freeway that moments ago had been nearly empty.

Once traffic opened up again, however, his mind went straight back to the subject it had been worrying since the wee hours of the morning. He was like some damn hamster on a wheel, he thought with disgust, running his ass off to get nowhere. He had to knock it off.

One thing was certain, though. He was glad the tour was finally starting.

Because it was bound to be a whole lot easier getting back on professional footing with a mess of people around to dilute the effect of one-on-one time spent with P.J.

CHAPTER SIX

Hyperlinked headline, NightTrainToNashville.net:
Priscilla Jayne Kicks Off *Steal the Thunder* Tour

"WELL, LOOK WHO'S HERE," said a familiar voice as P.J. strode onto the stage in the Portland venue later that afternoon. "Hey, little girl. Early as usual, I see."

She grinned at Hank Hartley, who stood a short distance away tuning his banjo, his fiddle carefully nestled in its open case at his feet. He gazed at her with warm hazel eyes from beneath the brim of his ever-present leather bush hat, a small return grin playing around his lips. "Sound check's not for another twenty minutes, babe," he informed her.

"What can I say, H.H.? Promptness is a hard habit to break." She raised her eyebrows at him. "But I don't have to tell *you* that. You got here even earlier than me."

Laughing, he crossed the short distance still separating them and hauled her into his wiry arms. Strong as a bear at forty, he gave her a big hug that left her feet dangling off the floor and the neck of his banjo digging into her spine. She drew in his familiar scent of tobacco, aged leather headgear and wrist straps, and Drakkar

Noir cologne. The top of her head bumped the underside of his hat and, reaching up to hold it in place with one hand, he set her gently back on her feet.

"I'm sorry about your mom and all the shit with the press," he said gently.

"Aw, thanks, Hank." She touched the little sandy-brown soul patch beneath his bottom lip, the single silky surface in a hundred-miles-of-bad-highway craggy face. "It's been a…challenging few weeks."

"I bet." Gently he hooked one of her curls behind her ear. But several strands snagged on fingertips callused from years of playing stringed instruments and pulled free again. With a whispered curse, he smoothed it back to join the rest. Then, looking beyond her, his eyes narrowed. "Who's this?"

She knew who she'd see before she turned. But she glanced over her shoulder anyway. Jared stood several feet away, hands in his pockets and his posture relaxed, observing them.

Sighing, she turned back to Hank. "My watchdog," she admitted and briefly explained Wild Wind's burning desire to insure their investment.

"The *hell* you say!" Easygoing eyes gone hard, he stepped around her and, pausing only long enough to lay down his banjo, strode toward Jared. "Listen, pal—"

Alarmed, she sprinted after him. While Jared might be a full head taller and didn't appear particularly worried, she'd once seen Hank flatten a man a good deal beefier than Mister Oh-so-nonchalant Hamilton would be even if he supersized his meals for the next ten years.

Idiot that he was, Jared looked completely unruffled as he faced the irate musician—his only concession to the approaching threat to pull his hands free of his pockets. "You're taking issue with the wrong man," he said evenly as Hank rocked to a halt in front of him. "Take it up with Wild Wind. I'm just doing the job they hired me to do."

"Good for you." Hank gave Jared a flat stare. "But she's right where she's supposed to be, isn't she? So you can take a hike."

For a second Jared's posture lost its easy slouch and a dangerous expression flared in his eyes. Then he shrugged and walked away, disappearing into the shadows of the left wing.

P.J. watched him go, telling herself she didn't feel disappointed. Hell, no—that would be just plain ridiculous. She *saluted* Hank for routing him—she should have thought of that whole I'm-here-so-now-you-can-go-away deal herself. As for the big hollow space in her stomach, she just wished she'd grabbed something to eat was all. The sound check could take quite a while depending on how good the acoustics were and how well the new backup band meshed with her way of playing.

Joining Hank, she slipped her arm through his. "My hero," she said, batting her lashes at him.

He snorted.

"Have you seen Eddie or Nell yet?"

"Last I saw Eddie, he was romancing the front-office girl. Haven't spotted Nell."

"I'm here," a soft voice said and they both turned. A plump, medium-height woman materialized from the shadows of the right wing, where her medium-brown braid and medium-dark clothing had rendered her invisible.

"Nell!" P.J. dashed across the stage to give her only real female friend a fierce hug. "I'm so glad to see you." Stepping back, she held Nell at arm's length. "Now, are you sure you want to do this again this year? I mean, why be tour manager when you can make more money and work less hours as a songwriter?"

"What, and give up all this glamorous travel?" Nell looked around the stage, bare of everything except Hank's instruments and pieces of the bandstand that the roadies were setting up for the extra musicians Wild Wind had hired for the tour, then out at the empty theater.

Following her gaze, P.J. saw with a jolt that Jared hadn't left at all. He sat in the front row, one ankle propped on his opposite knee. The only other person out there was the sound man in his booth at the back of the main floor. Having introduced herself to him earlier, she dragged her attention from the last guy she'd expected to see front and center and returned it to her friend. "Is the bus here yet?"

"Yes. I just spoke to the driver and he's pumped. Apparently he's a huge country-music fan and is looking forward to driving you. Thinks you're darn near as good as Patsy Cline."

"Get out. Nobody's as good as Patsy." Then she laughed. "But whataya say we go check out our new ride as soon as we finish the sound check? We're going to have to make a decision about buying our own bus after this tour, I suppose. I'll have to run it by Ma—" Renewed pain was a razor in her throat and she cleared the clogged tissues gingerly. "Um, Ben, I mean."

Nell squeezed her hand. "I'm real sorry, Peej." She hesitated, then straightened her shoulders. "But I have to say something that I've been biting back for years."

"What's that?"

"Your mama's a bitch."

P.J. choked, stared at her friend for a frozen moment…then laughed like a coyote. Hank howled, too, and she saw that he was closer than she'd realized. They exchanged delighted glances.

It wasn't the sentiment so much as the sentiment coming from Nell's mouth. Because she was soft-spoken, eschewed makeup and wore clothes that made her blend into the woodwork, people often assumed she was a mouse. She wasn't; she had a wicked sense of humor and usually didn't hesitate to state her opinions.

At the same time she was genuinely nice and a good friend, and P.J. didn't doubt for a moment that Nell loved her. "So, how long have you been keeping that to yourself?"

"Pretty much forever," Nell admitted. "I know how much you wanted to have a made-for-TV family relationship with her."

"Yeah, pretty desperate, huh? On one level I've always known the person she is. Damn, she kicked me out of the house when I was thirteen years old. And I have a feeling it took some pretty strong threats on the part of a woman named Gert to get her to take me back again."

"Is that why you made her your manager? Thinking that if you gave her carte blanche over your career she'd love you the way you deserve? Because, I gotta tell you, I never understood that."

"No—that would have been halfway understandable at least." A roadie wheeled past part of the risers that would elevate the backup band at the rear of the stage, and P.J. got out of his path then moved to the front of center stage where she wouldn't have to keep dodging the crew.

Nell and Hank came right along with her, and she gave them a look. "You're not going to let this go, are you?"

"Nope." Hank reached into his shirt pocket where his smokes resided, then apparently remembered where he was and let his hand drop.

"Not a chance," Nell agreed.

P.J. sighed her defeat. "Okay, then. The real irony here? I never set out to make her my manager at all. She began showing up at some of my shows back in my bar-singing days when I first started to draw crowds. And one night Ron Brubaker stopped by to check me out."

"Mercer Records Brubaker? That was your first label, right?"

"Yeah."

"So Jodeen was there the night Brubaker came in," Nell prompted. "What'd she do?"

"Sashayed straight to him and started talking me up. After the show Ron came over, introduced himself and told me how proud of me my mama was. The next thing I know I'm being offered a contract to play in a much larger venue while—are you ready for it?—I cut my first record."

"It was your first big break," Hank said.

"With Ron Brubaker, who's famous for not tolerating problem clients. What was I gonna do? You know how hard it is to break into this business and I was bending over backward trying to look as professional as possible. Mama had charmed his pants off. So I let the fact that she was written into the contract as my manager slide. And then, of course, I was stuck with her." She looked at her friends. "And I know what you're thinking. After I split from Mercer over those widely publicized 'creative differences,' I could have dumped her. But—I admit it, okay?—I liked having her like me for the first time in my life. And right up until she started helping herself to my money, she actually did a pretty decent job of representing me."

Then she raised her chin. She knew she'd been needy and had shown poor judgment, but the last thing she wanted was their pity. "Long story short, I was an idiot. So I guess I'm getting what I deserve."

"Bullshit," Hank growled.

"Complete and utter BS," Nell agreed. Reaching out, she gave P.J.'s arm a comforting rub. But her expression was serious—and perhaps a little bit hurt—as she said, "Why have I never heard about this before today?"

Because she hated, hated, *hated* anyone realizing what a chump she could be when it came to her mother. Hell, she'd just as soon not admit to it now, but Nell was right. They'd been friends longer than P.J. had ever had the opportunity to be with anyone else. And friends deserved the truth.

"It happened before we met," she said carefully. "And in truth, Nell? I'm not exactly proud of how easily I've let Mama manipulate me over the years."

"Ah, hon, that's not *your* shame. That rests entirely on your mother's should—"

"Hey, tiny thang!" a cheerful male voice interrupted. "How's my best girl?"

"Hey, Eddie," P.J. replied without turning around. She'd know the voice of her guitarist anywhere—not to mention the dreamy admiration she could see forming on Nell's face and the exasperation on Hank's. Then she was swooped up into strong arms and whirled in a fast, tight circle. Slinging an arm around Eddie's neck, she hung on until he slowed down, then gave his handsome face a friendly pat. Eddie Brashear was charming, talented and not to be trusted farther than you could throw him when it came to the fairer sex. P.J. had helped clean up more of his messes than she cared to remember. *Someone* had to pick up the pieces when his woman of the moment learned that fidelity wasn't part of his vocabulary, and God knew it was never Eddie.

But he was the perfect diversion from having to chronicle more of her dysfunctional relationship with Jodeen and she was happy he was there.

"You're late," Hank snapped as Eddie set P.J. back on her feet.

"Chill out, old man. Some of us have better things to do than show up half an hour early for sound check. Besides, the roadies are just now finishing setting up." Turning to Nell, he chucked her under the chin. "How are you, sweet thing? Glowing as ever, I see."

She blushed, Hank snarled and P.J., deciding it was pretty much business as usual, said, "Whataya say we get this show on the road?" She walked over to the musicians who were tuning up their instruments in the bandstand and introduced herself.

"We're going to be working hand in glove for a lot of shows for the next several weeks," she told them once she had their names semistraight in her mind. "So let's get started finding out how we sound together." The stage lights came on with a series of loud clanks and she shielded her eyes from the glare as she turned to look out into the theater. "Billy, you ready out there?"

"You betcha."

"Then let's give this a whirl." She looked over her shoulder at Eddie, who'd plugged in his electric guitar and was fitting its strap over his head, and at Hank, who had picked up his fiddle, and said, "We'll start with 'Let the Party Begin.'"

For the next hour and a half they ran through song after

song, making adjustments and finalizing the order of the playlist. When they finished the final number P.J. danced around to face the backup band. "God, I love this business! You guys rocked! Beer's on me in my dressing room after the show." She glanced over at Nell, who nodded and wrote on her clipboard. Then, after waiting for the cheer that had greeted her announcement to die down, she said, "Let's bring 'em to their feet out there tonight."

Collecting Nell on her way offstage, she decided to forgo checking out the new bus in favor of heading straight to her dressing room for some downtime before she had to get ready for the show. When she caught another glimpse of Jared sitting by himself in the front row, however, her steps slowed.

He looked so…alone. When she stopped to think about it, in fact, he *always* seemed to be alone.

Well, duh. She picked up her pace again, striding offstage toward the corridor that led to her dressing room. What did she expect—for him to behave like the Grand Poo-bah of Party Central? He was here to do a job that he clearly took seriously.

Still…

Not once in any of the bars the two of them had hit this past week had she seen Jared chat up a woman or dance with one or even exchange small talk with a bartender. He'd simply sat off by himself. Even jammed shoulder-to-shoulder on a stool at the bar he'd projected an unapproachable manner that was every bit as effective as a neon No Trespassing sign.

Sounds like a personal problem to me, girlfriend.

Damn tootin'. She began walking so quickly that Nell had to ask her to slow down.

She complied, but her friend's request barely even registered. It just didn't sit right to exclude Jared from the after-show party when she'd invited everyone else. She didn't like the job he was hired to do, or him for taking it. But if anyone knew what it felt like to always be left out of events everyone else in the world seemed to be invited to, it was her.

Crap.

Stopping, she reached for Nell's arm to bring her to a halt, as well, and leaned to murmur in her ear. Then, feeling like the world's biggest chump, she stalked down the corridor to her dressing room.

"MR. HAMILTON?"

Jared looked at the woman making her way down the center aisle that he was walking up. "Yes," he acknowledged, stopping when they met at Row 14. He peered through the dim lighting at the unadorned brunette in front of him. "Nell, isn't it?"

"Yes, sir." She blinked up at him. "How did you know?"

"The acoustics in here are outstanding."

"Yes, isn't this a fabulous theater?" Then alarm widened her eyes as two and two belatedly added up to a sum that told her he'd overheard P.J.'s private conversation with her and the fiddle player. "Ohmigawd."

She looked so stricken that he reached out to give

the hands she'd begun wringing a pat. They were ice cold beneath his fingers. "I don't make it a practice to gossip about my clients," he assured her gently. "And I never talk to the press. Consider me your priest. P.J.'s business is her own."

Fingers stilling, she gave him a dry look. "Yes, I'm sure *priest* is the first word that pops into women's minds when they look at you."

Surprised by her sass when he would have thought she wouldn't say boo if she'd been born a ghost, he missed the beginning of her next question.

"—call her P.J. when she's more widely known as Priscilla?"

"Huh? Oh. P.J. and I knew each other for about five minutes a long time ago."

"*Did* you? Funny, she didn't mention that."

"As I said, it was a long time ago—lot of water under the bridge since those days."

"Interesting, though." Then she seemed to collect herself. "But that's neither here nor there. You're probably wondering why I stopped you."

He merely regarded her with polite attentiveness.

"Yes, well." She shifted her weight. "I wanted to invite you to the after-show party. It's in P.J.'s dressing room, which is down the hall that leads from backstage."

He stared at her in surprise. "I'm invited to the party? I would've thought I'd be the last person she'd want there."

"And you might be." Eyebrows performing a lightning up and down equivalent of a facial shrug, she looked him in the eye. "But P.J. spent her entire childhood being left out of things because she was rarely in one town long enough to get to know her schoolmates. So she sees to it that the same doesn't happen to others. She's the most inclusive person I know. And speaking of the party—" she glanced at her watch "—I have some refreshments to order. So we'll see you later, right?"

"I don't know. It doesn't sound like my kind of thing."

"Well, you'd know that better than me. But if you decide to attend, it's in the room with the tinfoil star on the door." Thrusting out her hand, she gave him a firm shake when he extended his own. "See you later, Mr. Hamilton."

"Jared," he corrected.

"You really should try to make it tonight, Jared. It's a great way to get to know the people you're going to be traveling with for the next month."

To his surprise he found himself wanting to grill her about some of those people—particularly the two band members who'd been so fast to manhandle P.J. this afternoon. He couldn't help but wonder if the hints of animosity he'd witnessed between them were due to a rivalry over her.

But he shrugged it aside as unimportant, wished Nell a good day and watched as she walked back up the aisle. Then he turned his attention back to the conversation he'd inadvertently eavesdropped on.

Contrary to what he'd let Nell believe, he hadn't overheard more than a snippet here and there of the conversation between her, P.J. and the fiddle player until they'd moved to the center of the stage, almost directly in front of him. Then the talk had suddenly turned crystal clear, even if it had been conducted in low tones that he doubted carried to the sound man's booth in the back of the theater.

Apparently he wasn't the only one who'd wondered why P.J. had made Jodeen Morgan her manager. He wasn't quite certain, however, how to reconcile her explanation with the girl he used to know. The old P.J. would never have allowed that manager clause to be included in her contract.

Or, shit, maybe she would have. He was the product of a seriously screwed up father/son relationship himself, so if anyone ought to know what it was to constantly hope for a parent's affection—even though the fact you'd never received it should've knocked the need right out of you—he was the one. And what the hell did he know about what it took to break into the music business anyway? The chances of getting a record deal at all had to be mighty slim, never mind having reached the heights P.J. was beginning to enjoy.

So who was he to second-guess her decisions? They'd led her to hiring an undeserving mother. Big deal. He'd once made a decision that had left him standing accused of murdering his father.

During which time P.J. had stood by him even though she, like everyone else, had believed he'd committed the crime.

He'd reserve judgment until he had some actual facts. And he'd go to her frigging after-show party, as well.

If only to find out what the story was with those two bickering band members of hers.

CHAPTER SEVEN

"Rumor Has It" column,
Country Connection magazine:
What Up-and-Coming Star Refuses to Talk About
Her Current Problems?

SHORTLY AFTER MIDNIGHT P.J. and Nell barreled through the stage door into the brisk early-morning air.

"What a great night," P.J. declared, pulling her sweater on as they clattered down the steps into the alley. Still juiced from the rousing success of her tour's first concert and its rowdy after-party in her crammed-to-capacity dressing room, she bopped down the narrow passageway. "We sold out! For tonight and tomorrow night *both,* the production manager told me. I know this is the smallest venue we're playing this tour, but still. How cool is that?"

"Very cool." Nell smiled at her.

"And it's such a great theater. Man, the acoustics!" She made a face. "Although I gotta admit I'd rather not think about the sort of sounds it projected to the furthermost seats back in its dirty-movie days."

"Say what?"

"That's something else the manager passed along. Apparently the theater was a porn house throughout the seventies and eighties." She grinned at her friend. "Have I hit the big time, or what?"

Reaching the sidewalk, she spun to skip backward down the block in front of Nell, still talking ninety miles an hour right up until the moment her back smacked up against a cool metal surface.

Nell made a grand sweeping gesture. "Your tour bus, madam."

Spreading her arms wide, fingers pressed against the smooth metal at her back, she laughed. "You might have warned me."

"What, and miss seeing how far you'd travel without once checking to see where you were going?" Nell hitched a smooth-skinned shoulder. "I don't think so. Girl's gotta grab her jollies where she can."

"And here I thought I could count on you to be my guide." She pushed away, then whirled to check out her new home away from home. "Whoa. Is this thing monstrous big or what? And so shiny. I *love* shiny." Admiring the tonal design that seemed to stretch forever along the bus's silver exterior, she was so focused on checking out the immense vehicle that the sudden pneumatic wheeze of its door opening startled a squeak out of her.

She guffawed. "Okay, that's embarrassing. I thought only cartoon girls seeing mice said 'eek.'" Flapping her hand dismissively as she climbed aboard, she shot a smile at Hank, who had a hip perched against the driver's seat, before continuing over her shoulder,

"Still, life is good. Ain't nothin' gonna ruin my mood tonight."

"Uh, I'm sorry as can be, Peej," Hank said, "but I wouldn't be so sure about that." When she turned back to look at him in surprise, he jerked his chin toward the small lounge that began behind the partitioned driver's seat.

Turning her head to follow the direction he indicated, her gaze ran smack up against Jared, slouched down on one of the burgundy leather couch-benches. Shock ripped through her and she discovered Hank was right. Her good mood blew away like smoke in a stiff breeze. She fixed her best evil eye on the trespasser.

Not that he was looking. Long legs stretched across the aisle, his new charcoal Resistol tipped low over his eyes, he might have been sleeping for all the attention he paid. She marched over and used her toe to tap his ankle a little more forcefully than was probably necessary. "What are you doing here?"

Thumbing up the brim of his hat, Jared raised his head to look at her. Something jittered along his nerve endings when their gazes clashed and, jerking his away, he surveyed her from the rolled brim of her straw cowboy hat to the short halter-neck black dress she'd worn for her concert, paired now with a little black cashmere sweater. He studied her long, primary-colored graduated-bead necklace with its large oval pendant and the chunky red, blue and yellow bangles on her wrists, before skimming downward. He'd noticed before that she wore a lot of skirts these days and, eyes lingering for a second on her bare legs and narrow feet in their barely there red sandals, he could see why.

Slowly, he returned his gaze to her face. "Trying to figure out which bunk is mine," he said.

"Which bunk—?" It was clear that for a moment she'd either forgotten the question she'd asked or—more likely—found his reply incomprehensible. "Why would you think any bunk on this bus would be assigned to you?"

"Because Wild Wind Records told me I'd be staying with the band on the bus during the tour."

"Chickenshits didn't even bother to pass the news on to us," Eddie said as he entered the lounge from the bunk aisle on the other side of the galley.

Jared knew the comment probably wasn't aimed at him. He had already gone a couple rounds with Hank before the women arrived and was feeling a little defensive, but he got the impression Eddie had a tough time dredging up any kind of lasting interest in anything that didn't sport tits. Still, he climbed to his feet, stuffed his hands in his pockets and said, "I agree they could stand to improve their communication skills."

That was nothing short of the truth. But it was late, everybody was tired and this wasn't the time to get into it. "That's nothing to do with me, though. It's something you really should take up with them."

"Which you can be sure we'll do," Nell said, slinging a protective arm around P.J.'s shoulders and moving her back a step, making him realize for the first time how close they'd been standing. The other woman met his gaze squarely. "Seeing's how we only have your word for it that you're even supposed to be here."

Nothing like being Mr. Popular. He hitched a shoulder. "Hey, do what you have to do," he said as if he didn't give a damn. "But it would be pretty stupid of me to invent something so easily verified, don't you think?"

With a final glower, Hank turned his attention to P.J. "You want me to toss his ass off the bus until we find out what's what?"

Jared reined in the temper threatening to slip its leash, but he couldn't prevent his eyes from narrowing at the musician or taking an aggressive step closer. "You're welcome to try, champ."

Hank promptly went chest-to-chest with him and something inside Jared howled to know just what the hell P.J.'s relationship was with this clown. He'd watched through the crush of musicians and roadies at the post-concert party in that broom closet they'd called a dressing room, but he could have sworn the fiddle player had spent more time watching Nell than Peej. So why did the guy keep acting like a jealous lover?

"Knock it off, both of you," P.J. ordered, muscling between them. The heat of her shoulder and hip burned through his clothing for a second before she got a hand on his and Hank's chests and shoved them back a step. Then she stepped back herself, dividing a glare between them.

"It's bad enough that my label's treating me like an

irresponsible eighteen-year-old," she snapped. "I don't need you two acting like a couple of junkyard dogs on top of it." Then she blew out a weary-sounding breath and looked at her band member. "But he's right, Hank. I suppose we should make sure Wild Wind authorized him to share the bus with us, but it would be beyond dumb to lie about something so easy to check—and the Jared I knew was never stupid. Besides, face it, it's their bus."

For just a second her voice held a forlorn note. Then faster than the speed of light she gave an oh well, who-the-hell-gives-a-rip shrug and turned her attention to him. "Pick whatever bunk's available after Hank and Eddie choose theirs." Turning away, she added, "Which reminds me—I'd better go grab one for myself."

"Uh-uh, girlfriend," Nell said from the front of the bus. "You get the stateroom."

P.J. jerked around to stare at her friend, then walked forward to join the other woman. "The what?"

"Stateroom, honey. As in an honest-to-gawd bedroom at the end of the bus. It's got two double beds and an actual door. With a *lock*." Nell grinned. "Can you say privacy? No tumbling out of a claustrophobic little enclosed bunk for you, Morgan."

"Or you, either, Husner. Two doubles sounds like a bed apiece to me." She whooped, hooked Nell around the neck and planted a smooch on her cheek. "We're outnumbered at the best of times in this biz. I say us girls gotta stick together. Oh, man, a room. I am so off to bed." She started boogying her way down the aisle with the same exuberance she'd shown when she'd first entered the bus but came to a dead stop when she reached the spot where Jared stood blocking the aisle.

He couldn't have said why he didn't get out of her way, but he stood his ground.

"Excuse me," she said politely enough, but the look in her eyes as they met his suggested she'd be pleased as punch to apply her fist to his nose. Not that she gave voice to the desire by so much as a word or inflection. "It's been a long day," she said neutrally, "and I've got a radio satellite tour scheduled to start at five a.m. So if it's all the same to you, I'd really like to catch at least a few hours' sleep."

Feeling like a bully who'd burst her balloon not once but twice tonight, he stepped aside and watched her continue down the aisle toward the rear of the bus. "What's a satellite tour?" he inquired of her back.

The stateroom door closing between them was his only reply and he turned to look at the remaining occupants.

Eddie merely said, "I'm off," and left the bus.

Hank rummaged through the compact fridge beneath the galley's counter.

"Hand me that bottle of Jack Daniels, will you, Hank?" Nell said. "I could stand a shot."

And Jared got it—he was lower than a cockroach and they couldn't be bothered to step on him, never mind talk to him. He reclaimed his spot on the bench seat.

After pouring a shot of whiskey into a stubby glass and tossing it back, however, Nell apparently decided to take pity on him, for she abruptly turned, leaned her hip against the galley counter and gave him a level look—a vast improvement over her earlier you're-the-shit-on-the-bottom-of-P.J.'s-shoe glare.

"A satellite tour is a series of radio interviews conducted over the phone via satellite," she said. "They're usually set up for the morning commute programs, which means getting up before dawn if you're on the west coast. At least Peej doesn't have any east coast ones scheduled."

"Yeah," Hank agreed. "It'd be a shame to add anything else to her burden. Between Wild Wind's insulting behavior and you playing watchdog, she's got pretty much all she can bear."

"Then maybe I should just go to bed and get out of everyone's hair."

"Well, you could do that," Hank agreed. "It'd be a damn shame, though, if you got all settled and we had to roust you out when *we're* ready to go to bed. Since you might pick one of the bunks we want."

Like there was any *might* about it. Slumping down on his tailbone, he tipped the brim of his hat back down over his eyes, stretched out his legs and crossed his arms over his chest, willing himself to outwait P.J.'s band members without complaint—even if God alone knew when Eddie would return. *But, shit.*

Just...shit.

THE MAN WAS DRIVING to his job as a security guard in Iowa City when he heard Priscilla Jayne's name mentioned on the radio. Keeping one eye on the truck tailgating him down Highway 38 as he slowed for the approach to I-80, he reached over and turned up the volume.

"—so stay tuned," the DJ said. "This is Dan the Man McVann and the morning crew. We'll be right back to talk a little smack with Priscilla Jayne after these brief messages from our sponsor."

The man didn't find them all that brief and he fidgeted in his seat as he waited for the interminable commercials to cease. He'd written three letters to Priscilla Jayne this spring but hadn't received so much as a single reply in return. They'd been wonderfully flattering notes, too—well, at least the first two. The one he'd written last Saturday had rightly taken her to task over her lack of respect for her mother.

"And we're back!" The DJ's voice broke into the man's growing agitation. "This morning's guest is Priscilla Jayne, whose new CD *Watch Me Fly* we've been watching fly off the shelves at an amazing rate since hitting the stores last week. Welcome!"

"Thank you, Dan," said the raspy voice the man remembered from the show he'd seen her on. "I'm happy to be here."

"As I just mentioned to our listeners, your new CD is burning up the charts."

"Yes, isn't it great?" Her laughter rolled out of the speakers. "It seems to be doing very well, and I'm so grateful to my fans for their support."

The man, who had found himself smiling at the rich

sound of her laugh, scowled. "Then you might try responding when they go to the trouble of writing you."

"Your critically acclaimed debut album *Outside Looking In* spent a record ten weeks atop the Country Albums Chart and has been certified double platinum for sales in excess of two million," Dan the Man said. "Do you find it daunting knowing how much your sophomore album has to live up to?"

"It scares the bejeebers out of me if I let myself think about it too long or too hard," she agreed. "But I try to just take everything day by day. I'm very proud of *Watch Me Fly* and hope my audience will find the album as singable as I do. I love the entire project, but if listeners take away nothing else I have faith that they'll at least enjoy a song or two. I believe we've got some really great singles on this CD."

"I guess so!" the DJ heartily concurred. "'Let the Party Begin' debuted at number three on Billboard's Country Album Chart and 'Crying Myself to Sleep' at number seven."

"It's been an excellent week," she said in that easy, friendly voice. "Unfortunately, I spent most of it driving cross-country to get to Portland, where I played my first concert on the new tour last night. So I haven't had much time to savor it."

"Speaking of your cross-country drive, I wonder if you could put to rest a rumor that's going around," the DJ said.

The man went on alert but instead of asking about Priscilla Jayne's mother the way he should have,

McVann said, "Some of the journals are claiming you were spotted playing all kinds of bars across the West last week. True or false?"

The DJ's "morning crew" chimed in with their guesses, but the man ignored them as he awaited Priscilla Jayne's response.

"That's actually true," she said. "I got my start playing honky-tonks and clubs. Plus, growing up I lived in—man, I can't even tell you how many wide-spot-in-the-road towns. I had a week to kill on my way to Portland, so I stopped along the way at some taverns in a few small towns and jammed with the local bands."

"That must have thrilled them."

"It thrilled *me* to play with so many gifted musicians. The truth is a good part of this business comes down to blind luck. There's so much talent out there, even if much of it never goes any further than playing gigs at local taverns."

Dan the Man didn't appear to have much interest in non–platinum-selling performers. "So are you driving yourself from concert to concert?"

"No, I'm traveling on the bus Wild Wind hired for us. Concerts are scheduled almost daily, so for the most part we'll finish one performance, get on the bus and sleep while Marvin, our driver, delivers us to the next destination."

"What did you do with your car, then—leave it in Portland?"

"No. It's being driven back to Aspen."

"That's where you live these days?"

"Yes. I'm a brand-new home owner—or at least it still feels brand-new. I bought a house last year."

"You mentioned earlier that you moved around a lot."

"I did and I hated it." Then she laughed. "And I know choosing a career that puts me on the road for a good part of the year when I've spent most of my life craving a home I didn't have to up and leave at the drop of a hat must sound like a—whatchamacallit—a paradox. But having a place I can call my own makes all the difference."

"Because it'll always be there for you to go back to when the touring is over?"

"Exactly!" Her raspy voice was full of warm approbation that he understood her feelings so well.

There was an infinitesimal pause, then the DJ said, "So if a stable home life is so important to you, why did you fire your mother?"

The man in the car let up on the gas pedal as he sat straighter in his seat. "Excellent question."

Dead air filled the airwaves for several long seconds. Then Priscilla Jayne said in a voice not exactly cold but definitely no longer warm, "Excuse me while I pull the knife out of my heart." She gave a theatrical grunt. "There—and only the minimum of blood, too, as long as I keep my finger in the hole."

Laughter came from the morning crew, but the man didn't understand what they found so amusing. He didn't find the singer's flippancy one bit appropriate.

"I gotta hand it to you, Dan the Man," she said. "You slid that blade in slicker than the devil."

"Yet still you didn't answer my question."

"Noticed that, did you? Well, let me see if I can put this in a way you'll understand. My personal life is exactly that. Personal. I don't mind putting it all out there in my songs. I do mind flopping my private business onto the table for wholesale consumption by a bunch of people who don't know the first thing about it." Her voice warmed. "Marina, you still there?"

"You bet," replied one of the sidekicks.

"Can I ask you a personal question?"

"Sure, I guess."

"What's your relationship with your mother?"

"Why, it's fi—that is, it's…nothing I care to talk about on the radio."

"I hear that, sister. And I rest my case."

"Yet *your* mother has gone on record to state you broke her heart," the DJ insisted.

"Well, what can I tell you, Dan?" she said lightly. "There's just no pleasing some people."

The interview wound up a minute later but long after the radio crew signed off, long after the man clocked in at work and commenced his rounds, he continued to seethe.

Because this was wrong. This was just plain wrong. Priscilla Jayne lacked all reverence for her mother and she shouldn't be allowed to get away with such flagrant disrespect.

Well maybe, just maybe, she wouldn't. Because he had several weeks of vacation time coming.

And he just might use them to teach her a lesson in honoring her parent.

CHAPTER EIGHT

Headline, *Country Billboard*:
Priscilla Jayne Singles "Let the Party Begin" and "Crying Myself to Sleep" Lighting Up the Charts

"HEY, IT'S ME," Jared said the moment his brother-in-law answered the phone. P.J.'s concert filtered faintly through the thick walls of the San Francisco arena behind him. "I need the name and number of the suit who hired us for this assignment. I've been leaving messages at Wild Wind for the past three days, but either he's dodging me, which doesn't make sense, or I'm not asking to speak to the right guy."

"We have a problem?"

"Aside from wasting our time playing watchdog for a clueless client, you mean?"

"O-kay." John's voice was slow and easy. "You wanna expound on that a bit? But make it quick, wouldja? Sympathetic as I am to the plight of the poor working stiff, I don't count myself among your number for the next fourteen days."

Jared felt the tension that had been building over the course of the past week begin to unwind at John's mellow voice and offbeat sense of humor. "You heading up to the cabin?"

"Yep. In about twenty minutes. Just me and Tori."

"No kids?"

"Well, okay, me and Tori and Grayson and two of his very large, always hungry and extremely loud friends."

Jared grinned at the thought of his nephew and his friends wreaking havoc with John's downtime. "Es staying in town?"

"Yep. Running her and Gray's and your future children's inheritance into the ground while I wet a fishing line or two. Which, in the interests of getting this vacation on the road, brings us back to your request. Why do you feel we're wasting our time accompanying P.J. on her tour?"

"It's make-work, Rocket. There's not a damn thing for me to do here—an illustration of P.J.'s face oughtta be next to *consummate professional* in the dictionary."

"I'm not sure *consummate professional* is actually in the dictionary," John murmured. "Not linked together, anyhow."

He ignored the interruption. "It's clear to anyone with eyes in their head that this tour is important to her. She doesn't need anyone to get her to her concerts, she sure as hell makes her sound checks without assistance and with the exception of the first show in Portland, where we had the only two-night engagement so far, she's been on the tour bus within a half-hour of each show's closing."

"So what do you think compelled them to hire us?"

"I honest to God don't know." Leaning against the arena's concrete exterior wall, Jared settled his shoulders more squarely to absorb the residual heat still stored from the day's high-eighties temperatures, enjoying the warmth that seeped through his T-shirt to the slowly relaxing muscles below. "Wild Wind has a bundle tied up in this tour and there's a lot of negative press out there making it sound as if P.J.'s unreliable. But it's common knowledge it's been stirred up by her mother, so why the hell would they take Jodeen's version of the situation as gospel?"

"Because people tend to believe where there's smoke there's fire and P.J. hasn't exactly been fighting to tell her side of the story?"

"Okay, human nature being what it is, I get that. But they don't once ask their new million-dollar baby what's going on? From everything I've seen so far they're doing a bang-up job on the logistics of this tour. Yet their approach with P.J. is friggin' passive/aggressive. They just slapped a watchdog on her without bothering to discuss the problem. Why hasn't anyone picked up a goddamn phone to deal directly with her?"

"Is that what you'd recommend?"

"Hell, yes. They could probably learn the real story and have a team of spin doctors slanting the sympathy factor back where it belongs in a heartbeat if they'd just take five lousy minutes out of their schedule to talk to her. I'd also warn them that this is no way to build loyalty in their performers. They're putting a lot of money into building P.J.'s career. But if they treat her like a rebellious teenager at the same time, why would she want to stay with them once the tour is done?"

"Yeah, I can see where she might find it insulting to go about her business in a professional manner only to have them sic the dogs on her anyway. So!" His voice turned brisk. "You clearly know what you're doing and you've got a game plan. You don't need my input, except to tell you the guy you want to contact is Charles Croffut. Call Gert in the morning to get the number to his direct line."

Jared grinned, for he could all but hear the sound of his brother-in-law rubbing his hands together in anticipation of his vacation. "Thanks, John. Kiss Tori for me and cast a line or two in my name. In fact, if I free myself up within the next couple days I just might join you."

"Good. You can be in charge of entertaining Gray and his friends."

He heard himself laugh for the first time in days. "I was thinking more along the line of getting in some fly fishing, but I'm always open to negotiation."

"Tell P.J. we're looking forward to seeing her concert when we get back to town. Or hell, just plant a kiss on her from me—whichever strikes your fancy. Me, I'm going fishing and getting in some serious snuggle time with my woman."

Jared was still smiling when they hung up an instant later. Warmth and acceptance were the gifts from Tori and John that kept on giving. They'd taken him in when he was seventeen and parented him with the same even-handedness they'd used to raise Esme and, later, Grayson. Their support and love had turned around the remainder of his childhood. It was through their example that he'd learned how to become a responsible adult.

Before them, acceptance hadn't been a quality he'd experienced much in his life. He'd grown up with increasingly younger stepmothers uninterested in getting to know him and a father impossible to satisfy. Negativity had been his screw-you response. Not exactly a mature one, he knew, but at the time he'd figured what the hell. If he couldn't make his dad pay attention to him for the things he'd done right, he'd simply earn the old man's notice by smoking, drinking and getting himself pierced, tattooed and expelled from the series of boarding schools his father sent him to.

Not that anything he'd done had made a damn bit of difference, he admitted now, and even after all these years he couldn't prevent a grimace. His father simply hadn't cared about anyone but Ford Evans Hamilton. Not his son or his daughter. Not his granddaughter or any of his wives. And in the end his megalomania had gotten him killed.

For a brief, awful time during his seventeenth summer, Jared had thought he'd murdered him, because in a knee-jerk reaction to being told he should have been aborted, he'd lashed out and shoved his father, knocking him to the floor where Ford had struck his head on the corner of a marble hearth. Unable to find a pulse, panicked, Jared had run as far and as fast from his father's Colorado Springs mansion as he could get.

And, ironically, had been found by P. J. Morgan, the only other person ever to offer him wholehearted acceptance.

Being a homeless teen on the streets of Denver—of any city—was a precarious and terrifying existence. He and P.J. had lived hand to mouth, day to day, and he'd felt perpetually dirty, hungry and so scared it was a constant ache in his stomach, a churning in his bowels. Yet for the first time in his life he'd had a friend who'd allowed him simply to be…him. Survival might have been stripped down to its rawest, meanest form, but he hadn't felt the need to put on a front with P.J.—a state of affairs so novel and freeing he'd actually felt real moments of happiness in the midst of all the horror. Before that summer he'd found it necessary to keep his mask firmly in place to guard against people discovering who the real Jared Hamilton was. It just led to being shipped off or left behind, and he'd had enough of that shit.

To this day he had a tendency to keep his guard up around everyone except family. Where once it had been from necessity, however, now it was mostly out of habit.

And entirely beside the point, he thought, giving himself a mental shake. The salient point here was that while in the end P.J., too, had left him behind, she'd still saved his life. If she hadn't attached herself to him the way she had, he wasn't sure he would have survived. It wasn't simply because she'd been on the streets longer than he and knew more about the resources available to them. She'd given him her wholehearted, unconditional admiration, had *believed* in him, and that had meant the world to him. It had kept him going.

So he'd repay her once and for all by getting Wild Wind off her back. Then she could get on with her career and he could get back to his life.

And if that struck him as just the tiniest bit boring, so be it.

P.J. PICKED UP HER PACE, sprinting the last hundred yards of her late-morning run. Then, slowing to a walk, she rounded the corner of the somewhere-in-California arena she was scheduled to perform in that night and found Jared slouched comfortably in a lawn chair on the tarmac outside the tour bus.

"Hey," he said as she began her cool-down walk from the front of the bus to its rear and back again.

"Hey, yourself." Covertly eyeing him as he lounged in the webbed chair sipping something tall and refreshing-looking, she yanked a hand towel from the waistband of her shorts and paced past him dabbing at her forehead, temples and throat. She didn't know how he managed it, but no matter what he wore he always looked as if he'd just stepped off the cover of some upscale men's magazine. He'd been like that during their time on the streets, she remembered. Even homeless he'd looked like a prep-school boy half the time—especially the days they'd been able to cadge a shower at Sock's Place, the church drop-in center catering to kids in jeopardy.

She, on the other hand, always seemed to be sweaty or disheveled. She shot him a sour look. "My run just didn't seem the same this morning," she sniped. "What with you not breathing down my neck and all."

He merely raised a dark eyebrow, then reached down and picked up another tall glass that had been on the ground next to his chair. He held it out to her. "Lemonade?"

She accepted it with a suspicious look. "What are you up to, Hamilton?"

The grin he flashed her was all white teeth. "Trusting as ever, I see."

"I know you, remember?"

"Yeah, you do. So you have to know I'd never deliberately hurt you. I have some news, in fact, that's just the opposite."

For some reason a silky little ribbon of disquiet unfurled in her stomach, and she changed the subject. "Where the hell are we?"

"What?"

"What town are we in?" she asked impatiently. "I know it's southern California, because there's palm trees all over the place. But we've played so many cities this week and I slept like the dead during the drive last night, and I've lost track. I can't recall offhand where we're supposed to be playing tonight—but it doesn't feel the way I imagined L.A. would."

"We're in Bakersfield."

"Ah. Inland, then. No wonder it's so hot." She blotted up more sweat, chugged down half the drink he'd given her in one long swallow, then lowered the glass. Touching the back of her wrist to her lips, she gazed at him and inhaled. Then quietly she exhaled. "So what's the good news?"

"I'm leaving."

No.

She swallowed the protest unsaid, but her heart began to bang in her chest and she couldn't quite catch her breath. "You're…? Why? Is it because Hank's been giving you a bad time?"

"What? No, of course not. It's because you're right. You've behaved like a professional and your label is treating you like a kid who needs to be sent to her room."

"So you're—what?—handing me off to the devil I don't know?"

"Huh?"

"You know that expression 'Better the devil you know'? Well, that would be you. I don't necessarily see replacing you with an unfamiliar devil as a huge improvement."

"Aw, I'm touched." He flowed up out of his chair and crossed the short distance separating them to stand in front of her. "Except there's not going to be a new devil. I talked to them, Peej. And I made them understand how insulting it is to just accept your mother's propaganda as fact without so much as checking with you for the real story."

Great. Her heart pounded harder yet. "I'm not talking to them or anyone else about my mother."

"I figured that might be your stand, so I told them she embezzled money from you."

"You did *what?*" The sudden ice lining her gut battled for supremacy over the flames of fury licking through her veins and, pushing up onto her toes, she went nose-to-nose with him. "You had no *right!* My private life is just that and now Wild Wind's gonna splash it all over the goddamn media."

"No, they're going to keep the news to themselves," he interrupted quietly. Catching a damp strand of hair dangling over her left eye with a gentle fingertip, he looped it behind her ear. "They agree with you that it's your business." The same finger stroked a nerve-rich patch of skin below her earlobe. "And they're real impressed with the publicity you garnered for yourself with those honky-tonk drop-ins. Also, since your sales are apparently soaring, they've decided there's no such thing as bad publicity. So they'll leave it alone unless you say otherwise. They don't want to lose you."

"Why would they assume they would?"

"I, uh, might have mentioned that could be a result of treating you like you don't know what you're doing."

She thumped him on the chest. "Damn you, J, I don't know whether I oughtta thank you or knee you in the nuts."

"I vote for the former." But he took a step back and his expression erased faster than a fire-hosed blackboard.

She could have screamed. She'd honestly thought that if nothing else came of Jared's unexpected drop into her life, she'd at least finally get some closure on a few of her more ancient dreams. "Why do you do that?" she demanded.

"Do what?"

"That." She waved at his face. "That bland expression. That big mental step back you take. What happened to you? You used to be so open."

A harsh laugh exploded out of him. "I was never open."

"Yes, you were. With me, you were."

He gave her an *are-you-for-real?* look. "You think? Well, look where that got me."

"What's that supposed to mean?"

He merely gave her the blank-eyed stare again and she shook her head in frustration. "Tell me!"

"What is it that you want to hear, Peej?" he asked and stepped closer again. But he stopped out of reach. "That you were the best friend I ever had? Fine. You were. For about five minutes." His eyes were dark and shuttered as he looked down at her. "Then you gave me a phony phone number and disappeared from my life."

She jerked in shock. "That number was real! Mama just packed us up and moved a couple days later."

"Uh-huh. And you never got another phone?"

"I—"

"No, wait, I believe you did. But somehow you never called to give me that number, did you?"

"I—"

"I got it anyhow, you know. Rocket tracked you down to Wyoming."

"You had the Wyoming number?" She blinked up at him. "You never called me." She wondered how different her life might have been if he had.

"I was going to. Until I found out you'd given the number to Gert. Not to me—Gert." He met her eyes with a cool, bored gaze. "Then I wised up. Never let it be said this boy can't take a hint."

"I wanted to call you!" she cried. "You don't know how much I wanted to. But you were so educated, so…rich."

"What?" He shook his head. Then his eyes went from cool and disinterested to flat-out furious and between one heartbeat and the next he was towering over her, radiating so much rage and heat she was surprised she didn't go up in flames. "What difference did the size of my trust fund make? You and I shared something no one else could truly understand, but you waltzed off because I was *rich?* You *knew* that didn't matter."

"Yes, it did!" She could still remember exactly the way she'd felt when she'd learned he had a cook like someone in the movies, when she'd seen the Colorado Springs mansion he'd called home and heard him correct her grammar. She hadn't needed Mama's whispers that a rich boy like him would have no use for a girl like her to make her feel unworthy. "You lived in a palace. I lived in a trailer! You had your sister and John and your niece and your baseball buddies. You were exonerated of your father's murder. You didn't need me. Your life was perfect. Mine was—"

"Perfect?" he roared. "Fucking *perfect?*"

Her driver poked his head out the bus door. "You okay, Miz Morgan?"

"Yes, thank you, Marvin," she said, barely sparing him a glance. Her attention locked on the hint of pain peeking out of Jared's eyes. Her heart beating an erratic tattoo, she began to suspect she had been wrong all those years ago. "I'm fine."

"Okay, then," he said with palpable reluctance and directed a hard glare at Jared. "Yell if you need help." He withdrew back into the bus.

Jared wrapped his hand around her upper arm and marched her away from the vehicle. When they'd reached a point he apparently found sufficiently removed, he dropped his light grip on her as if she were covered in toxic waste and casually slid his hands in his pockets. The pain she'd glimpsed was neatly tucked away once more and he gazed at her with that recently familiar lack of emotion.

"Yes," he agreed coolly, "I had my family and that was great. But my baseball friends were left behind when we moved up to Denver. And would you like to know what most people remembered about my father's murder, Priscilla Jayne?"

Nothing good, she was guessing, if the remote look in his eyes was anything to go by. Still she nodded.

"It wasn't that I was exonerated or that someone else was ultimately convicted. It was that I was accused of it. People don't remember the retractions, honey. They remember the headlines and the talking heads rehashing the manhunt for suspected murderer Jared Hamilton night after night."

"I'm sorry." Reaching out hesitant fingertips, she stroked them along his forearm. His skin under her hand was warm and firm.

He slid his arm out from beneath her touch. "Not a problem," he said carelessly. "It was a long time ago. So, listen, it's been real, but I've got some packing to do."

He started to turn away, but she grabbed his arm. "Jared, please," she said, hanging on when he merely stood and gazed at her gripping fingers as if they belonged to a stranger. "I don't want to part like this."

"Then we won't," he said with that careful politeness. "My flight leaves tomorrow night from L.A., so I'm going to ride down there with you. We'll chat. Catch up."

Yeah, sure they would. It didn't take a genius to see that was never going to happen and her temper started to percolate.

Maybe it was his well-mannered distance that put her back up. Maybe it was—she didn't know—something else entirely. His refusal to show a genuine emotion for longer than two seconds running, perhaps. Whatever it was, if this was goodbye, they were damn well going to say it her way.

"We'll have to do that," she agreed with a polite smile of her own. "But before you go, I have something to say."

"What?"

"Get your head down here," she snapped. "I'm not going to scream this out for any Tom, Dick or Harry who might be hanging around to hear. I'm on enough tabloid covers as it is."

He dipped his head obligingly and, reaching up, she slid both hands into the soft, cool strands of his hair. Then, yanking his head closer yet, she rose onto her toes and locked mouths with him.

She wasn't sure what she'd intended—or, okay, if she'd planned anything at all. But if she had, she was pretty sure it would've been something along the lines of a brief, hot kiss that she directed. Instead she lost control of the situation the minute their lips touched. Between one moment and the next, it seemed, it was all teeth and tongues and runaway heat. She found herself plastered to the hard warmth of Jared's long body while his hands splayed over her butt, keeping her close.

And, oh God, it felt good.

Too good. She could barely think. Ripping her mouth free, she stepped back.

"Take that with you when you go," she said, and if her voice sounded even raspier than usual, well, it couldn't be helped. Head held high, she whirled on her heel and strode back to the bus.

It took every ounce of willpower she possessed to not look back.

CHAPTER NINE

Headline, *Nashville Tattler*:
Mama Promises More Revelations about Priscilla Jayne's Shocking Secret Life

"DID YOU SEE THIS SHIT?" Furious, Hank stormed onto the stage and thrust the tabloid at Nell. "Shocking secret life, my ass. Something's gotta be done about P.J.'s old lady."

Taking the paper, Nell skimmed the article. "Jodeen doesn't seem to actually reveal any shocking secrets," she murmured when she finished. "Funny how that's often the way with these rags, isn't it?"

He snorted. "Like there's anything to reveal. Something's got to be done," he repeated.

"Like what? You going to take out a contract on her?"

He pretended to consider it. "Not a bad idea." Her startled look dredged forth a faint smile. "No, I'm not planning anything violent. But why the hell doesn't P.J. do something?"

Nell gave him a level look. "What's your mom like?"

"Mine?" His smile grew. "She's great."

"Thought you were wonderful, told you you could accomplish anything you applied yourself to?"

"Yep, that's my mama."

"P.J.'s mama pretty much ignored her or told her what a burden she was up until the day Peej showed signs of becoming a money machine Jodeen could cash in on."

He scowled. "My point exactly."

"Oh, you don't think you would've spent a good part of your life hoping your mother would somehow turn into the kind you were lucky enough to be raised by?"

"Hell, n—" But he cut himself off and thought about it. "I don't know. Maybe."

"I have a friend who's an E.R. nurse. She sees abused kids way too much, kids with broken bones whose X-rays show too many previous breaks to be accidental. And the one true constant, she once told me, is that they all deny their parents had anything to do with their injuries. It's a built-in defense mechanism, because the truth is just too ugly to admit."

"Shit."

"Yeah." Then she shook her head. "We can't do anything about Priscilla's bad luck in the parent pool and I doubt she'd appreciate knowing we were discussing it. So you want to help me with a song I've been working on instead? I've practiced it over and over again on piano, but I'd love to hear how it sounds on fiddle."

"You bet." Man, he liked this woman. She was smart

and funny and talented—and he'd bet the bank she'd be one warm, round armful if he could ever get her there.

But she had a yen for Eddie. Idiot Eddie, for crissake, who would never in a million years appreciate a woman like her the way she deserved to be appreciated. And that was supposing the fool could manage to look past the superficial in the first place, which, considering how far removed Nell was from the twenty-something airheads in sprayed-on Lycra that Eddie generally went for, wasn't likely.

He had to admit, though, that his band mate, for all that he couldn't keep his pants zipped for more than four or five hours at a pop, didn't pretend to be anything other than what he was. He was honest and up front about his shortcomings.

Maybe I oughtta take a lesson, Hank thought. Because he knew damn well if Eddie were ever interested in Nell, he wouldn't dither around about it. He'd let her know right away.

Not wanting to think about it any longer, Hank reached for his fiddle.

"Wait." Nell put a soft hand over his as he tucked the instrument under his chin and raised his bow. "Let's change the note here to C flat."

He leaned into her to see what she was pointing at on the sheet. "This one?"

"No, the one next to it there, see?"

A fresh, elusive fragrance tickled his nose. But instead of complimenting her on it or telling her what pretty skin she had or how much he enjoyed spending time like this with her, he merely nodded and began to play the new song.

And berated himself for being such a goddamn chicken-liver.

JARED BLEW OUT A BREATH, squared his shoulders and climbed onto the arena stage through the almost ladder-like stairs at the back of the boards. He was so tense he felt as though one false move and he'd fracture into so many tiny pieces he'd look like a damn mosaic. And wasn't that insane? How could one little kiss unleash fifteen years of suppressed emotion?

It shouldn't be able to.

Yet, oh, man, it had. Unleashed it big-time. The back of his tongue still retained P.J.'s taste, his palms itched and his fingers kept wanting to curl into the shape of that luxuriant curve of her butt.

But he trusted intellect, not strong emotions. Fifteen years ago he'd lost his temper and as a result he'd thought for a brief, awful time that he'd killed his own father. In the wake of it, once his life had finally stabilized in Tori and John's care, he'd made himself a vow that he would never again let his feelings take control. Because just look where that had gotten him. He'd quit acting in the heat of the moment, had given up committing any rash acts at all. The stronger his emotions were, in fact, the more likely he was to rein himself in. If there was a small part of him that was exhausted by always having to guard against a spontaneous reaction, it was a small price to pay. Because the truth was he just couldn't trust what might happen if he ever let go.

Which made his reaction earlier with P.J. all the more shocking. He'd formed that resolution years ago, and considering how well it had always worked for him he'd just naturally assumed it was an established fact by now.

Not so, apparently. Because his ironclad control had sure as hell slipped with her.

And slipped big.

It was bad enough he'd allowed her to anger him with that crap about his "perfect" life. In the short time they'd been reunited, she'd managed to rile him faster than anyone he'd ever known. But he always got himself back in hand fairly quickly. And he'd done so today as well.

Only to lose it completely when she'd kissed him.

Holy shit. A kiss was a kiss was a kiss—or that's what he'd always believed, anyhow. Kisses were nice and they led to activities that were even nicer. But face it, they were pretty much interchangeable.

Not hers. A harsh breath exploded from his lungs. Hers had damn near blown the top of his head off.

He was going to pretend it hadn't, though. He was going to corral her before sound check and have that catch-up talk he'd told her they'd have. He was going to chat and smile and keep it light and friendly. He'd keep his hands in his pockets and his gaze off her mouth. And afterward he'd ride that midnight bus down to L.A. with her.

Then he was getting the hell back to Denver, where life had boundaries he understood.

P.J. wasn't onstage when he rounded the huge speaker blocking his view of most of it, but he hadn't expected her to be. He'd come extra early by design.

Hank and Nell had come even earlier. They sat on stools on the left side of the stage, Hank playing a stanza or two of a song on his fiddle before Nell interrupted, made a notation on some sheets of paper she held, then waved at him to continue.

Well, shit. Nell was a sweetheart, but Hank sure didn't top the list of people he was dying to see.

But those were the breaks. As that old philosopher Mick Jagger said, you can't always get what you want. Releasing his frustration on a hearty exhalation, he assumed a pleasant expression and shoved his hands into his pockets as he sauntered across the stage.

Hank spotted him first and the slight smile curving his lips disappeared. "Aw, hell." Lowering his fiddle, he gave Jared his usual what-the-hell-are-you-doing-in-my-territory fixed stare. Then he turned to Nell. "Hand me that paper, will you, darlin'?"

She passed him a tabloid-sized newspaper and the musician immediately thrust it at Jared. "Here. Why don't you make yourself useful for a change and do something about this?"

"Hank," Nell remonstrated without heat.

Jared looked down at what was indeed a tabloid and swore when he saw the headline. Then he shut out the others to read the entire article.

When he finished, he didn't kick it across the stage or reach for the closest book of matches to torch it the way he wanted. Instead he handed it with extra care back to Nell. "God, I despise that woman," he murmured to himself, his gaze still locked on the *Nashville Tattler* and its screaming headline even as Nell twisted to put the paper away. "She was malicious fifteen years ago and she hasn't changed a bit."

"You know P.J.'s mother?" Nell asked.

He looked up, surprised that he'd actually said it out loud. Then he gave a mental shrug. What the hell—he'd given up caring who knew about his earlier days a long time ago. "We've never met, but I know she's a liar and a lousy mother. That story in the rags a while back about P.J. running away from home when she was thirteen? Pure bullshit. Her mother kicked her out."

"And you would know this how?" Hank demanded skeptically.

"By living on the streets with me," P.J.'s voice came from behind him.

Aw, crap. He turned to face her. He'd give a lot not to have had her overhear this particular conversation. But that cat had slipped its cage.

"Yeah, right," Hank guffawed. "Mister Hundred-Dollar T-shirt, here? Pull the other one."

Tired of the other man's attitude, Jared gave him a flat-eyed stare. "What, you think bad parenting can't cross the socioeconomic line? Think again, pal. I had a dad who made Peej's mom look like Mother Teresa."

"Sez you." P.J. snorted. "My mother was barely getting warmed up when your dad took that letter opener through the heart."

Oh, gawd. She couldn't believe she was *joking* about this! Yet there was something liberating about being able to do so after all the years of pretending that if only she wished hard enough everything would turn out okay. The truth was her mother was never going to be the parent she'd spent a lifetime dreaming of. And while she wasn't close to being ready to share that with the rest of the world, she could at least admit it to the people here. She was among friends.

Well, two of them were, anyway.

Jared looked down at her with a coolly raised eyebrow. "And that doesn't tell you something right there—that he was murdered and according to Rocket and Tori they had more suspects than they knew what to do with, but I was the top pick anyhow? If Dad had survived your mother would have had to hang her head in shame. The woman was a piker compared to my old man. Hell, she wasn't even in the same league—she was strictly the minors."

She saw the stunned looks on Nell's and Hank's faces and couldn't prevent a wry smile. Because she and Jared might not be friends in the normal sense of the word, but their time in Denver had forged a bond that would never break no matter how thin they stretched it. If she never saw him again after tomorrow the experience they'd shared as kids would still be a link that connected them forever. They'd survived things together that most people couldn't even imagine.

Jared turned those imperturbable eyes on Hank. "So do me a favor, buddy, and quit making assumptions. You don't know the first damn thing about me."

Hank stiffened and P.J. took a casual step forward that put her between them.

Jared merely put his long hands on her shoulders and leaned over her head. "But because I live to brighten your day, I will tell you that I'm out of here after we get to L.A."

"And not a moment too soon," Hank muttered. But the look he gave Jared was more thoughtful than his usual you-asshole glare.

She, on the other hand, just felt sort of edgy. Dissatisfied. "Where's Eddie?" she demanded and winced at her petulant tone.

"I'm here, babe."

He stood in the wings with a young blonde beneath the drape of his arm. This one looked barely legal and P.J. was fresh out of patience. "If you'd be so kind?"

"You betcha." Giving the blonde a final squeeze, he set her loose and strolled onto the stage.

She turned to Hank. "And our backup band?"

"They're down in the passageway, most of them," he said. "I'll tell 'em it's time." He disappeared behind the speakers and yelled down the steps. Men's voices replied from the cavernous corridor below, then footsteps sounded on the stairs.

"Good," she said, even though nothing felt all that good to her at the moment. "I don't know about the rest of you, but I've got things to do. So whataya say we get this under way? Is the soundman here?"

An affirmation came from the darkened orchestra pit and P.J. nodded. "All right, then. Let's go."

Watching Jared saunter toward the wing where the

blonde stood, it took her a moment to realize Hank was talking to her. She turned to him. "Huh?"

"We playing this in the usual order? I'm trying to figure out banjo or fiddle for the first song."

"Oh." She had to think a second, then shrugged when it still didn't pop to mind. "Yeah, usual order." Whatever that was.

"Banjo, then."

She gave her head an impatient shake as he turned away to exchange instruments. What the hell was the matter with her? If the constant traveling was catching up with her already that didn't bode well. They'd barely gotten started.

Nell shuffled what looked like a song score to the back of her clipboard and walked to center stage to check off the musicians who were beginning to trickle onto the bandstand. When everyone was assembled, she turned to P.J. and nodded. "We're good to go."

"Okay, let's get right to it," she said. She just couldn't get in the mood for this today and wanted it over and done with as quickly as possible.

The musicians were launching into the first number when a short metallic screech rent the air overhead. Musical notes trailed off as everyone stopped to listen, but the noise had ceased. They raised their instruments again, but before they could launch back into the beginning of the song the sound came again—a short, high-pitched shriek that ended almost as quickly as it had begun.

Everyone looked up. "What the hell?" someone muttered.

Then there was a longer attenuated screech, and the next thing P.J. knew, Jared was racing toward them. "Clear the stage!" he yelled, and when everyone still stood frozen in shock, he leaped into the air.

And took Nell to the floor in a flying tackle just before a huge metal light on a cable that had been severed on one side came swooping with the velocity of a home-run ball straight through the spot where she'd stood a second ago.

"Stay down," P.J. heard him order as her friend began to struggle beneath him. He hunched over her, clearly prepared to take the brunt of the light if it swung back their way.

And sure enough, they were still in its trajectory when it reached the cable's apex and started its return swing. From what she could judge from where she stood, P.J. thought it was probably high enough off the ground to pass right over them.

But she wouldn't want to bet the bank on it. And finally she moved. "Can somebody get that?" she yelled and raced toward them.

Hank passed her and threw himself in the light's path, catching it before it reached the pair on the floor. P.J. heard Hank's breath explode from his lungs as the fixture hit him in the diaphragm, but he bent and wrapped his arms around it, hugging it to himself. "Jesus," he whispered and let go of the metal casing to grab hold of the cable that still attached it to the overhead beams. Angry red marks marred his inner forearms.

"Ohmigawd, it's hot, isn't it?"

He shrugged, and she gave herself a head slap.

"Stupid question. Of course it is."

He passed the broken fixture to Eddie, who'd come to help, and squatted down next to Jared and Nell. "Y'all okay?"

"I'm fine." Jared lifted himself off Nell but knelt beside her, gently touching the back of her head and her shoulders. "How about you? Are you all right? Did I bruise you?"

"Um." She rolled over gingerly then pushed herself up into a sitting position. She blinked from him to Hank. "What the hell happened?"

The portly stage manager arrived, out of breath and apologetic. P.J. stepped between him and Hank when her musician looked ready to charge like an enraged bull. She gave the manager her best no-nonsense look. "You want to tell me what happened here?"

"I'm sorry, Miss Morgan. We won't really know until we take the light back to our electrician and have him look at it."

"That's not good enough," Hank snarled. "Nell could have been seriously hurt."

"But I wasn't," she said and with Jared's assistance climbed to her feet. She crossed over to Hank and patted his arm. "I'm fine. A little the worse for wear and shook up, but fine. Don't blame him. Accidents happen."

But nerves that stemmed from more than having to wait for the stage crew to finish checking the remaining lights before they were allowed to get back to it were in evidence throughout the sound check. And their music during the actual concert later that evening was edgier than usual. When the last note was sung, P.J. knew that she for one hadn't given her best performance. Fortunately the audience hadn't seemed to notice.

Uncertain she could blame it strictly on the accident, she was subdued and feeling down as she washed off her stage makeup in the dressing room after the show. When she stepped out into the vast corridor a short while later, she was happy to see that Nell had waited for her. They fell into step and the sound of their shoes striking the linoleum-over-cement floors bounced off the concrete-block walls. Harsh overhead fluorescent tubing negated the late hour.

"I'll be happy to see the last of this town," Nell said.

"Yeah, me, too." But part of her wasn't quite ready to move on, no matter how much she'd been looking forward to seeing L.A.

Hank was smoking a cigarette on the tarmac outside the bus when they arrived and Jared stood a few feet away, his shoulders and one foot propped against the vehicle's silver exterior.

"What are you guys doing out here?" P.J. asked as she and Nell walked up, surprised to see them together.

"Marvin's not here," Jared replied and pushed away from the bus. He gave it a slap. "He left this buggy locked up tight, which is actually a good thing, if inconvenient."

"Where could he have gone? He's usually around when we need him."

Jared shrugged and Hank rolled the paper tube of his cigarette between his fingers until the coal dropped to the ground. Stepping on it, he disposed of the dead butt in a nearby trash can, then walked over to join them. "Interesting concert tonight," he said.

"Yeah," she agreed glumly. "Not our best."

"Having a missile on a string come hurtling outta the blue tends to put a crimp in a band's style."

Marvin came bustling up. "I'm sorry, Miz Morgan," he said, his sparse gingery red hair standing up in electrified tufts. "A kid told me I had a call from home in the front office, but it musta been a practical joke because the office was locked when I got there and my wife didn't have a clue what I was talking about when I called her back." He grimaced apologetically. "I shoulda known she'da just called me on my cell."

Jared stiffened and put a hand out to stop Marvin from unlocking the bus. He indicated the flashlight in the driver's utility belt. "Can I borrow that?"

Marvin hesitated, but then handed it over. "Sure, I guess."

Jared played the light down the doors then got down on the ground and shined it up beneath the bus's carriage.

P.J.'s stomach sank. Oh God. That didn't look good.

"What the hell are you doing?" Hank demanded. "Looking for a goddamn bomb or something?"

"We had a fixture break today that shouldn't have," Jared replied calmly. "It was no doubt an accident, but—"

"You're right," Hank interrupted, glancing at Nell. "There's no such thing as overkill when it comes to safety. You need any help?"

As the driver exclaimed in alarm, obviously hearing

of today's event for the first time, Jared said, "Yeah, go to about the midpoint and see if anything looks out of place when I shine the light that way."

Nell explained to Marvin about the incident with the light and her and Jared's part in it as the men went over the bus. Then it was her turn to exclaim when P.J. contributed the part where Hank had caught the light and gotten burned for his efforts.

Minutes later the men climbed to their feet. "It's fine," Jared said and handed the driver back his flashlight. "Go ahead and unlock it."

Marvin did so but paused in the midst of putting his foot on the first step after the doors opened. "What's this?"

Jared muscled him aside and reached down to pick up a crumpled manila envelope that had clearly been crammed under the door. Holding it by the corners he climbed into the bus and walked to the little galley table. "Hit the lights, will you, Marvin?"

P.J. was right beside Jared when he turned back from getting a steak knife from the drawer, but he intercepted her hand when she reached out for the envelope.

"It's addressed to me," she protested, looking down at the block printing that spelled out *PRISCILLA JAYNE.*

"I know. But try to touch it as little as possible in case we have to turn it over to the cops."

"Who the hell are you?" Hank demanded, and only then did P.J. realize that both he and Nell had crowded behind her. "You're awful damn cautious for a record company's stooge."

"I'm not a Wild Wind employee. I'm a partner in Semper Fi Investigations, the agency that Wild Wind hired for this job." He slid the blade tip under the sealed flap.

"Semper Fi, huh? You were a Marine?"

He nodded, clearly intent on his mission to open the envelope with as little contact as possible, and P.J. jerked her gaze away from his hands to stare at him in surprise.

"You were?"

"Yeah. Not a lifer like Rocket, but I put in my four years." He sliced the blade along the envelope's fold. Glancing over his shoulder at Hank, he said, "Semper Fi specializes in investigations and security." Then he turned his attention back to the job at hand and extracted his blade from the now-slit mailer. "Let's see what we've got."

Carefully he tipped out the contents, which turned out to be a single sheet of glossy magazine paper.

Tilting her head to one side, she realized it was a half-page photo that had been taken of her for an article in *Country Connection* magazine several months ago. For a second she merely stared down at it without understanding.

"Aw, shit!" Hank growled, and it was then that horror began to seep through her incomprehension.

For where her photographed eyes had been were blank holes. And printed across her chest in more of those block letters were the words *IF THINE EYE OFFEND THEE, PLUCK IT OUT.*

CHAPTER TEN

Hyperlink, www.CelebrityCafe.com/Country
Priscilla Jayne Single "Crying Myself to Sleep"
Goes Digital Gold!

LOUNGING AT THE TABLE in the galley, Jared watched P.J. exit her sleeping quarters at the back of the bus the following morning and stumble down the hallway to the coffeepot in the galley. "So," he informed the back of her head. "It turns out I'm not leaving after all." Even as he braced for an argument, he couldn't prevent the faint smile that tugged up the corners of his lips. She had one helluva case of bedhead.

They'd spent what remained of last night at a Bakersfield police station and hadn't hit the road to L.A. until well after three a.m. He'd set his alarm for four hours later in order to talk to Croffut at Wild Wind Records in Nashville. Following that conversation he'd sat in the galley drinking coffee and making notes until P.J. finally emerged from her room.

She turned to give him an owlish blink, her face still blurry with sleep. "Wha?"

A bifold rustled open down the hall and Hank rolled

out of his sleeper, wearing a pair of unzipped jeans and nothing else—not even the bush hat that Jared had never seen him without. "He said he's back on the job."

"Which I'm sure thrills the hell out of you." He hung on to his cool because that's what he did. But, dammit to hell. If Peej had objections he'd counter them. It would be a lot easier, however, if he wasn't being double-teamed.

"I don't know if thrilled is the word I'd use," Hank said mildly. "But to my surprise I actually think it's a good idea."

Jared stared. "You…what?"

"I know, who'da thunk it, huh?" Zipping up his jeans, Hank, too, ambled over to the coffeepot. Giving his bare stomach an absent-minded scratch, he poured himself a cup. He swallowed a sip, finger-combed his hair, which Jared noted was receding slightly, into a rough sort of order and gave Jared a level look over the cup's rim. "You looked like you knew what you were doing last night and that's more than any of the rest of us can say. For instance, sick as that note to P.J. was, I probably would have blown off taking it to the cops since our schedule gave us no choice but to turn right around and leave town the minute they were through with us."

"But we needed to have the incident on record in case she—you—" he turned to include P.J. in the conversation since this concerned her most of all "—receive anything else like it. Not to mention that cops have the juice to check for fingerprints."

"So you said," Hank agreed. "And you were right.

You were also right to make sure we handled that piece-of-shit correspondence as little as possible to give the cops a better chance of getting usable prints from it—another detail that never would've occurred to me. And you exhibited a cool head under pressure at sound check. Your actions saved Nell one helluva knock off her feet. So I think you're probably our best bet for keeping P.J. safe."

"I agree."

Jared's head whipped around at P.J.'s raspy voice. "You do?"

"Yeah. Having someone who knew what to do last night was the only thing that kept me from freaking. And like Hank, I was blown away by the way you rescued Nell."

"Me, too," Nell said, entering the galley. Unlike the other two, she was dressed and her hair was neatly braided. She seemed to falter for a second when her gaze touched on Hank, but either that was his imagination or she had an immediate recovery. Stopping in front of Jared, she looked up at him with solemn blue eyes. "Things happened so fast and furiously yesterday I didn't even thank you for getting me out of the light's way." Rising onto her toes, she kissed his cheek, then settled back on her heels. "Thank you. I shudder to think of the damage it could have done if you hadn't intervened."

It wasn't often he was caught flatfooted, but he was staggered by their responses. He'd prepared himself to fight them all if necessary and instead they made him feel…welcome. "Yes, well." He rolled his shoulders uncomfortably, then squared them with an impatient snap. For God's sake, he was a professional. "I'm glad you're okay, but it was nothing. I was just doing my job." He turned to P.J. and said briskly, "I'll need to know your schedule from now on. What's on your agenda today?"

"I have a radio interview at one. Then sound check at four."

He made a notation in his notebook then glanced up at her. "Is this another of those satellite interviews that you conduct over the phone?"

"No." She shoved a hank of her bed-messy hair behind her ear. "From now on they're all live."

"In that case, plan on me accompanying you."

"All right."

"Don't plan on going *anywhere* by yourself from this point forward. That means either me, Hank, Nell or someone else you trust is to be with you when you're around the arena areas. And I'm with you when you go out in public."

She grimaced, but nodded gamely. "Gotcha."

Seeing her put a brave face on, he relented. "That letter might have been a one-shot deal and it might not even have anything to do with the incident with the light. But we don't bet your safety on it. Until we know otherwise we treat everything as connected and we stay vigilant. Where's Eddie?"

"Still in bed," Hank said. "Want me to roust him?"

"No. He's hardly ever around, so his part in this

isn't as crucial as yours and Nell's. But fill him in when he gets up, will you? Because when he is here he has to be every bit as watchful as the rest of you."

P.J. looked up at him. "Should I be afraid, J?"

His stomach tightening at hearing the diminutive she'd given his name years ago, he reached without thinking to touch a gentle fingertip to the point of her chin. "No, just aware. Just stay aware, Peej."

P.J. didn't think that would be a problem. She hadn't been kidding about being freaked last night and she had every intention of keeping her eyes peeled from now on. Nothing was going to get past her.

But later that afternoon as she discussed her career on the air with a Los Angeles DJ called Lonesome Jack, the thought of Jared not leaving the tour after all kept scratching at the back of her mind—and her emotions vacillated wildly.

On the one hand, her inner little girl, who'd once given him a leading role in her most heartfelt dreams, still lingered in some of the more shadowy corners of her psyche. And Jared's take-charge attitude last night had played right into those fantasies. He'd known exactly what should be done and had organized her, Nell and Hank with a competent lack of fuss into doing it. It had been enormously comforting.

"We've talked about the success of 'Crying Myself to Sleep' and 'Let the Party Begin,'" Lonesome Jack interrupted her thoughts. "Did you write those songs yourself?"

"Just 'Crying Myself to Sleep.'" On the other hand,

she wasn't a little girl anymore. And if she'd had any idea Jared would be hanging around instead of leaving, she never would have kissed him the way she had. How was she supposed to deal with him with *that* forever in the back of her mind?

Then she shoved the ping-ponging viewpoints aside and concentrated on her interview. "That one came from moving around a lot as a kid and feeling like an outsider every time I landed in a new town."

"How much of your own music do you write?"

"I probably pen about a third of my songs."

"What's your favorite?"

She laughed. "I don't know this from firsthand experience, mind you, but I gotta imagine picking just one song from all the ones I dragged kicking and screaming from my soul must be a little like having to name your favorite child." Then she gave Lonesome Jack a grin. "Still, that said, I have a sneaking fondness for 'Designated Driver.'"

"The one about drinking and not driving."

She gave him a wry smile. "Bless you—you've obviously listened to the entire CD. But yes. I doubt I lived in a town growing up that had a population of more than two thousand souls. And a common denominator with hick towns everywhere is teenage drinking."

"You think that's due to a lack of other available entertainment?"

"Probably. Boondock towns rarely have a movie theater, let alone the type of underage, liquor-free clubs where kids can go to party. You can always find a beer blast somewhere, though. And in at least six of the towns I lived in, students died or were seriously injured in alcohol-related accidents. That makes this subject close to my heart. So if even one kid takes my song to heart and picks a designated driver before he or she goes out to party in the woods or at the lake I'll be one happy woman."

"Wouldn't it be more responsible to tell kids not to drink in the first place?"

"Absolutely. I don't know how realistic it is, though. In an ideal world preaching would make an impact, but I can't honestly say I've ever seen the just-say-no principle work. The desire to fit in is a lot more immediate and compelling than some country singer's opinion. God knows peer pressure is alive and well. Probably even more so in small-town America than in its bigger-city counterparts, where I'm sure it's bad enough."

"You might have a point," Lonesome Jack said. "Listeners, what do you think? Let's open the lines now and take a few calls." He pointed to his engineer, who toggled open a line, and said, "Hi, you're on the air. Who am I speaking to?"

"My name is Benjamin McGrath," said a familiar voice.

P.J. straightened in her chair. "Ben?" She glanced at the disc jockey in confusion.

He winked at her. "Please welcome Priscilla Jayne's manager, cowgirls and cowpokes," he said to his listeners in a hearty DJ voice.

"I'm calling to congratulate her on the success of her

single 'Crying Myself to Sleep,'" Ben said. "It's the second record on her *Watch Me Fly* album to go digital gold. I have in my hand a copy of a certificate commemorating the sale of more than one hundred thousand downloads. I overnighted the original and it will be presented at tomorrow night's concert. Congratulations, Priscilla."

A laugh bubbled out of her. "Ohmigawd. Seriously?"

"Absolutely," Lonesome Jack said, then leaned into the microphone. "So listen up, all you fans out there. If you don't have your ticket to Priscilla Jayne's concert yet and you'd like to see the official presentation, you'll want to run, not walk, to your nearest Ticketmaster. Uh-oh, wait a second. Marley's signaling me." He leaned over to hear as his coworker spoke in his ear, then returned to the mic.

"Erase what I just said," he drawled. "It appears both concerts have sold out. But don't despair, my little buckaroos, because we here at KPIX are still the proud owners of a block of tickets. And for the next ten lucky listeners to be the ninth caller when they hear this—" he played the opening bars of "Crying Myself to Sleep" "—you'll not only be our guest to hear Priscilla Jayne's concert, but you'll be issued a backstage pass so you can personally offer her your congratulations after the show."

Jazzed up yet vaguely uneasy, P.J. had to concentrate in order to answer the number of legitimate phone-in calls that followed. She was still in a daze and bouncing from one emotion to another as she wrapped up the interview with the DJ and thanked him not only for having her on today's show and the airtime his station devoted to her music, but for the part he'd played as well in staging the news of her single going digital gold. Leaving the soundbooth, she floated down the hallway to the reception area where she promptly bounced off Jared's chest when she walked right into him without seeing him. She distantly heard Lonesome Jack's program playing softly through speakers mounted on the wall.

"Hey." Wrapping his hands around her shoulders, he steadied her, then held her at arm's length to grin down at her. "Congratulations! How cool was that? You didn't know anything about it, I take it?"

"No." Then, because his open expression reminded her of the boy she'd known back when they were each other's only support system, she admitted, "For years I dreamed of the kind of success I'm beginning to enjoy. But now that it's coming my way—" She broke off, because she'd just gotten excellent news and truly didn't know why she wasn't simply bouncing with joy.

"You're seeing there's more than one side to it," he suggested. "There's the good part—the being paid like a queen, having your work loved by many and seeing your records go gold. But there's a downside, too. Your private life is fodder for sleazy journalists to spread across their rags for every Tom, Dick and Harry to consume with their morning Wheaties, and you've got a potential stalker who apparently feels perfectly justified in sending you sick, incomprehensible messages."

"*Yes!*" Relief surged through her that he understood, and, stepping forward, she leaned her forehead against his chest in sheer gratitude. He smelled of soap and man and laundered cotton, and her itchy restlessness settled as she breathed him in. She rocked her head back and forth against the solid warmth of his chest. "I know nobody likes a whiner, J. But that photo really shook me up."

"Hell, yes, it shook you. You wouldn't be human if it hadn't." Cruising his hands up over the curve of her shoulders, he slid them in to lightly encircle her neck, his thumbs resting on her collarbones and his fingertips working the vertical slope of her nape like a maestro coaxing a symphony out of a sax. "But I'm good at my job and I'm telling you this flat out—I will keep you safe. Trust me."

She raised her head to gaze up at him. Usually when a man said, "Trust me," it was the last thing she was inclined to do. But Jared meant trust him as a professional, and in that arena she did.

It made her uneasy to realize that she'd apparently been harboring a secret wish to trust him on a more personal level, as well. But she merely met his eyes and nodded. Then she drew a deep breath and eased it out before taking a casual step back. When his hands slipped away to drop to his side she shivered against the sudden lack of warmth in the air-conditioned lobby.

"I'll do that," she said, then cast a meaningful glance

at the receptionist, who was clearly pretending she wasn't straining her ears for all she was worth in an attempt to overhear their conversation. "Right now, though, I think we better ask little Miss Nosy over there to call us a cab."

NELL LAY QUIETLY in her bed in the stateroom she shared with P.J. and stared through the stygian gloom as if she could actually see the ceiling that hid behind the darkness overhead. When the linens on the other bed rustled quietly, she turned her head in that direction. "You awake?"

"Yeah."

"Good interview today. I meant to tell you earlier that I'd tuned in to listen. I was impressed Lonesome Jack didn't once bring up the business with your mother." She smiled in the darkness. "But then he had an entirely different surprise in mind, didn't he?"

They'd celebrated when P.J. had returned from the radio station, but then it'd been time for sound check, after which she'd had a hundred details to see to. And when those had been done P.J.'d had to get her stage makeup done and get dressed for the concert. The next thing Nell knew it had been showtime. This was the first opportunity she'd had to discuss anything in private with her friend.

She heard a return smile in P.J.'s voice when she said, "Wasn't that something? I called Ben back as soon as we quit partying and of course he'd staged the whole thing. But he also said the positive press is starting to outweigh the negative—and that the bad stuff probably fueled sales, anyway." She blew out a noisy sigh. "What a business."

"Yeah, it's lunatic." Nell hesitated, then said casually, "This is changing the subject, but have you ever seen Hank without a shirt on before today?"

"Sure, once or twice. It's a rare thing, though." P.J. laughed. "Too bad, too. The boy's got a six-pack on him, doesn't he?"

"I'll say." It had blown her away. She didn't know why, exactly—he generally wore his shirts neatly tucked in and it wasn't as if she'd ever seen them stretched over a beer belly or anything. It was just…

She'd never once considered him in a sexual way. "He's no Eddie," she said, thinking out loud. "But—" Seeing him half-naked and disheveled as she had this morning had made her look at him in a brand-new way.

"He might not flaunt it like Eddie does, but his build leaves Mr. I've-got-the-attention-span-of-a-gnat's in the shade." P.J.'s bedding rustled once again and her voice sounded closer, as if she'd rolled to face her. "He's more man than Eddie will ever be, if you ask me."

"Oh, I know. I like him a lot. He's easy to talk to and he's professional and really talented. But Eddie is so gorgeous." She shook her head. "And my God, that makes me sound shallow."

"Ya think?"

"I know, I know. But the thing is, I've had a crush on that man for what seems like forever."

"Yeah." P.J.'s voice was soft in the darkness.

"And I realize he's never going to look at me the way he does his parade of sweet young things. Still..." She drew in a deep breath, then eased it out again. "I want to fix myself up a bit. Trouble is, I was born without the girly gene, which means I don't have the first idea where to start. You always look pulled together, though, with all your dresses and skirts and funky jewelry."

"A woman named Gert, who took me in after my homeless spell, bought me the first dress I ever owned that wasn't a hand-me-down," P.J. said. "I'd pretty much lived in jeans and T-shirts up until then, and that little sundress made me feel so feminine that I started buying more whenever I could get the moons to align."

"And how does one accomplish that?"

P.J. laughed. "Well, in my case it was when I'd scratched together a few bucks and Wal-Mart had a sale. Those skirts and dresses made me feel good about myself during a period when that wasn't often the case."

Nell turned on her side to face her friend who, now that Nell's eyes had adjusted, was a dim outline in the other bed. Tucking her bent arm beneath her head, she said, "Would you go shopping with me, Peej? Help me find a few pieces that are flattering and get a haircut and some makeup and stuff? Just a little makeup," she quickly qualified. "I know myself well enough to realize I'll never use anything too complicated."

"Are you kidding me?" P.J. pushed up in the next bed. "That would be a wonderful break. And this is L.A., baby. There's gotta be all kinds of great shopping in this town."

An edge of panic niggled her stomach. "I'm not talking about Rodeo Drive or anything."

"No foolin'. I may have graduated from Wal-Mart, but I still can't bring myself to pay three hundred dollars for a little T-shirt or six hundred dollars for a pair of shoes. Maybe next year."

"That's the attitude we like to hear." She grinned in the lessening dark. "Now that you're a big hotshot Digital Gold performer and all."

P.J. made a rude noise. Then she suddenly went very still. "Oh, man," she whispered. "This is too good."

"What is?"

"Well, it just occurred to me. You heard Jared this morning. He insists on attaching himself to me as my own personal bodyguard." She flopped onto her back, kicking her legs in the air and laughing like a loon. Even after she had finally settled down, her teeth were a light beacon in the dim room. "How you think he's gonna like spending the day shopping and hitting the salons with the girls?"

CHAPTER ELEVEN

Jodeen Morgan signs with literary agent Sue Mitchell. Can we expect a book deal in the future?
—"Dishing With Charley" columnist Charlene Baines, *Nashville News Today*

IT WAS GOING TO BE A long day.

Jared sprawled on the trendy pink love seat that dominated the waiting area of the Mane Event salon. Stretching across the small couch at an angle, he extended one foot out onto the floor, his opposite knee drawn up and deliberately positioned spread-eagle across the seat to discourage any of the black-kimono-wearing clientele surrounding him from getting the wrong idea. Sharing his space was not an option.

Rock music pounded out of the overhead speakers, which P.J. insisted was a good thing. She claimed that anyone who tuned in heavy metal as their normal listening preference was unlikely to be familiar with the country music world—let alone its gossip. And that, she asserted, made her anonymous—which in turn gave her a heaven-sent opportunity to be just like any other woman in the place.

God knew the salon was packed to the rafters with the species. There were tall women, short women, skinny women, fat women and every size and shape in between. There were women who had hip down pat, women who looked as if they spent every spare minute taking lessons from country club pros and matronly women—although there were a damn sight fewer of those.

The joint was awash in estrogen, and female voices wove over and under the thumping music as they chatted about stuff both more mundane and way more intimate than any snippet of conversation he'd ever overheard Esme or his sister have with their friends. It was like being in a foreign country—one where the air was ripe with the scents of shampoo, hairspray and a witch's brew of chemicals.

He was tempted to hook a finger beneath the collar of his shirt and tug it away from his throat. He resisted because one, with its two top buttons unfastened, his collar wasn't the least bit constrictive and two, the gesture would be too revealing. But man, did he feel out of his element.

Two women, one seated to his right and the other three chairs down, talked on their cell phones. Everyone else either flipped with varying degrees of interest through magazines dedicated to hairstyles, movie stars or fashion-and-beauty tip stuff or visited with each other. In many cases they did both.

He was coming in for his share of curious looks, as well, probably because he was the only appreciably straight guy in Girlyville. For the most part it was nothing more than a quick peek over the top of a magazine or a new client faltering briefly when she turned from the reception desk and saw him sitting there. One of the cell phone talkers, however, and a brunette facing him on an Eames-style chair down against the other wall, subjected him to slow, bold, up-and-down inspections. The phone chatterer was checking out his package and the brunette, catching him glance her way, opened her lips, gave them a lascivious circle with her tongue and pantomimed a kiss.

Now, Jared wasn't a shy guy and ordinarily he'd welcome a little female attention. But not only was he badly outnumbered by the gentler sex, he was on the job. Plus the tenor of some of the attention focused on him was a helluva lot more predatory than that of an admiring woman catching his eye in a bar. For the first time he fully appreciated how women walking the gauntlet of whistling construction workers must feel. Sexual aggression wasn't appealing in either gender.

Coolly he returned Phone Chick and Miss Kissyface's comprehensive appraisals, letting his own gaze conduct a leisurely assessment from head to toe before pointedly turning his attention elsewhere. And if he started to suffer a persistent little get-me-out-of-here itch, well, he'd just keep that to himself.

He hoped.

No. His face went stony. There was no "hope" about it—he would. *You're a trained professional,* he reminded himself grimly. *There hasn't been a sissified beauty palace built that has the chops to take that away from you.*

But it was sure as hell a different world in here.

He looked past the reception desk into the heart of the pink and black salon. The rituals practiced back there were a mystery to him. He could see Nell seated at a station down near the end of the room. A girl with black and fuchsia hair had whacked the tour manager's braid off at the nape, secured its cut end with a pink ribbon and set it like a trophy on the counter in front of her. Miss Two-tone had then snipped up a storm until he'd swear more hair lay on the floor around Nell's chair than was still attached to her head. He didn't know squat about this stuff, of course, so he had to assume she'd look great when the stylist was finished. Right now, however, what hair was left bristled with layers of aluminum foil. He saw at least two other patrons sporting a similar look, making the lot of them appear for all the world like alien invaders from a fifties-era B movie.

A stylist had already trimmed P.J.'s hair and tamed her usual tumble of curls into a sleek, straight waterfall that cascaded over her shoulders. Currently seated on an elevated chair over in the alcove, the long skirt of her red dress rucked up between her thighs, she sipped something from a delicate china cup and carried on a rapid-fire conversation with the technician painting her toes. He couldn't make out what she was saying, but if her frequent laughter was any indication she was having the time of her life. A slight smile curved his lips. It was good to see her enjoying herself. It had been a tense couple of days.

She shuffled his way a short while later. Glancing down, he took note of disposable green and yellow Hawaiian-print flip-flops on her feet and rainbow-colored separators that spread her red-tipped toes. With a bemused shake of his head, he shifted to make room for her on the love seat.

"Shades, J?" she demanded, dropping down next to him, only to immediately hitch up one bun. "Ow. What's this thing made of, bricks?"

"I was thinking poured concrete, myself."

Her lips quirked up, but almost in the same instant she went all stern on him. "Don't change the subject. What's with the Ray-Bans? Could you *be* any more conspicuous? Everyone probably thinks you're FBI."

He slid the sunglasses in question down his nose and peered over their black rims at her. "Hey, it's blinding in here." And that was true as far as it went; sunshine did pour through the window onto the left side of his face.

It just wasn't the real reason he'd donned them.

She apparently knew it, too. "Uh-huh." She gave him a swift elbow to the ribs. "More like you're hiding out from all the babes wanting to jump your bones."

"Yeah, right," he scoffed. Nodding his head toward two particularly aggressive blondes who'd replaced Phone Chick and Kissyface, he said, "I was thinking of asking those two to join me in a little ménage à trois." God knows they'd been staring holes through him for the past several minutes and hadn't bothered to keep their voices down when they'd exchanged the increasingly raunchy methods they'd like to use to wear him out.

Then he broke like a cheap china plate. "Jesus, Peej," he said in a low voice. "Is there a sign over my head that says Fresh Meat, Come and Get It or something? You should *hear* some of the trash they've been talking. If a guy said half the shit they've suggested he'd be sued for sexual harassment."

She laughed. But leaning into him, she also butted her head against his chest like a kitten seeking attention. "Poor baby."

With no conscious decision on his part he found himself threading his fingers into her shiny chestnut hair to hold her in place.

Peering around him at the two women under discussion, she finger-walked her way down his row of shirt buttons until she reached his stomach, which she proceeded to pet. "Back off, ladies," she told them in a low but firm voice. "He's mine."

The blonde with the more impressive implants made a rude sound. "There's nothing to you," she said, subjecting P.J. to an insolent up-and-down appraisal. "Maybe the big guy's ready for something a little more exciting."

"There *is* nothing more exciting than what she gives me," Jared said flatly. Then awareness burned through him at the feel of P.J.'s delicately curved breast pressed against his side and he turned his head to look down at her. "Is there, baby?" he demanded softly. And he lowered his head to kiss her.

He'd been telling himself ever since she'd laid that wet one on him the other day that it hadn't truly fried every circuit in his brain. But he'd been fooling himself.

Because her lips were soft—God, so soft and sweet—and the interior of her mouth was sweeter still, tasting like green tea and hot, willing woman.

It was that last thing, her willingness, that nearly pushed him over the edge and made him want to lay her back on this uncomfortable little love seat and punch that compliance into overdrive until both of them were revving full throttle.

Instead he geared himself down. Deliberately he kept his kiss brief and restrained. And when he came up for air he told himself that the entire performance had merely been for show.

But he knew better. And he could have kicked his own butt around the block. So much for his big claim of professionalism anytime, anyplace.

"Well, that did the trick," P.J. murmured cheerfully. "It appears the Porn Twins have finally taken the hint."

He looked over to see that the blondes had indeed moved their attention elsewhere. Then he turned wary eyes back on P.J.

And little by little the tension in his shoulders eased. Thank God she at least seemed to believe he'd kissed her with the sole purpose of getting the blondes off his back.

The Twins had been called back for their appointments by the time Nell came out. Whistling when he got a look at her, Jared rose to his feet. "Wow. You look...fabulous."

She did. Her dark hair had been cut short to feather around her temples, forehead and nape, and it stuck up on the crown in soft, modish spikes. She had beautiful skin and the highlights around her face not only accentuated it but made her eyes look bluer.

"*Muy* fabulous," P.J. agreed. "You look so hip."

Nell laughed. "Oh my God, I do, don't I?" In an age-old feminine gesture, she touched her fingers to her hair. "I thought I was going to wet my pants when Rachel chopped off my braid, but I really like it." She gave her head a shake. "It feels so light."

"Did you remember it, by the way?" he asked her, noticing that her hands were empty.

"Hmm?"

"Your braid. I saw your beautician—Rachel, is it?—set it on the counter in front of you. Did you forget to grab it?"

"Oh. No." She smiled up at him. "They're keeping it for the Locks for Love program."

He must have looked as blank as he felt, because P.J. said, "Nell donated it to a charity that makes wigs for cancer victims."

"Whoa." Leaning down, he kissed the tour manager on the cheek. "You are one classy lady."

Their next stop was a department store makeup counter and while it was hardly the activity he would have chosen to while away an hour he discovered he didn't really mind the time spent there. Nell's quiet delight in her haircut and the changes wrought by some lipstick, blush and mascara were endearing, and he liked the way P.J. was equally delighted for her friend. In fact, the entire day, from what he could tell, seemed to have been designed with Nell in mind.

Not that P.J. didn't throw herself wholeheartedly into a shopping spree of her own. She, too, bought lipstick, two cosmetic brushes and some eye stuff. Given their hand-to-mouth existence back in the day, he had to admit he got a kick out of seeing her with money to burn and clearly enjoying the hell out of spending it.

He was still in a pretty mellow mood when the women moved their shopping bender up to the second floor. Nell stopped in the misses section but after a quick low-voiced consultation, P.J. kept going.

He followed her to the junior department where he stood out of the way with his hands in his pockets and watched as she shuffled hangers on the round stands boasting markdown signs of fifty to seventy-five percent off. "Country music must not pay as well as I thought if you're reduced to shopping the clearance rack," he said wryly.

P.J. barely spared him a glance. "You try finding summer stuff in the summer," she said and selected a skirt that started out denim but then exploded at the hipline into three short flounces of frothy, lightweight material with bits of lace and lines of ribbon appliquéd all over them. "Their fall lines are already out."

"Yeah, I've never understood that not being able to buy the clothes you need in the season you need it."

"Me, either." She gathered an amazing number of separates off the sale racks, shoved them into his arms, then led him to the lingerie department where she selected slinky little camisoles and tank tops in a rainbow of colors. Carrying those herself, she led him back to the misses section in search of Nell.

"Looks like you found a few things," she said to her friend when they met up, indicating the armload Nell clutched to her breast.

"There's an advantage to being a size fourteen."

"Aside from being a nice, warm armful, you mean?" Jared asked and the elated smile she flashed him tugged up the corner of his own mouth.

"Yes, aside from that, you honey-tongued devil." Cheeks flushed, Nell turned back to P.J. "He makes me feel desirable and totes your stuff. This shopping with a man riff ain't half bad." Then her brows furrowed slightly as she indicated the jumble of clothing in her arms. "What do you think of my selections?" she demanded. "Am I headed in the right direction?"

P.J. inspected Nell's choices one by one. "This one looks too baggy," she decided of a dark, shapeless dress, and Nell put it back on the rack. "Ooh. I like this jacket and these three tops. And I see you hit the lingerie department, too."

"Damn few tank tops to be found otherwise," Nell agreed.

"Tell me about it." P.J. vetoed one other selection and applauded the rest.

"I'll give these a try then." Nell reclaimed the hangers containing the clothes that had survived the cut and nodded at the fragile tops in P.J.'s hands. "What about you? You ready to try some stuff on?"

"Yep." P.J. headed down the aisle, crooking her finger at Jared over her shoulder. "Come, boy."

Nell's head whipped around as if to assess his reaction to her friend's insolence. He merely tugged a lock of hair falling over his forehead and murmured, "Yes, ma'am."

"Oh my," Nell said. "This just keeps getting better and better."

A moment later P.J. indicated a nice overstuffed chair situated outside the women's dressing room. "Have a seat," she invited. "You might as well get comfortable, because this is gonna take a while."

He kind of enjoyed himself at first. P.J. insisted they could use a man's perspective and he liked seeing the flush on Nell's cheeks and her pleased expression every time she came out to model an outfit that he approved.

P.J. modeled her picks, as well. And for a while he got a charge out of watching her parade out of the dressing room to twirl in front of him, then turn this way and that to assess every angle in the triple mirror situated not far from his chair.

After twenty minutes of being constantly asked to endorse her choices, however, he'd had enough. He'd been trying to ignore his attraction to her ever since he'd signed on for this job, but his determination to hold himself aloof only worked as long as he manned the ramparts, maintained the defenses. And somewhere between the salon and this comfy chair outside the women's dressing rooms, he'd let his guard down.

Big mistake. Because now P.J. had begun modeling

those damn little underwear tops and spandex pants. And he was starting to sweat.

"Do these make my butt look too big?" she asked, twisting to look at her reflection in the mirror. The fingers of her right hand splayed atop the anatomy in question, which pulled her elbow back and thrust her breasts forward.

"You're kidding, right?" His gaze was all over the full curve challenging the stretch in the little black capris that she eyed so critically. "You've got a great ass." His fingers flexed, tempted almost beyond bearing to reach out and palm a handful.

"That's what I'm always telling her," Nell called from inside one of the dressing rooms. "J-Lo's got nothing on our girl."

"You think?" She turned around and looked at him uncertainly. "Then it's this top. I look like a boy, don't I? Damn, I've been waiting my entire life to grow a decent rack, but some things never change."

"Jesus, P.J." But tearing his gaze away from the sweet little cupcakes pressing slight but insistent curves in the cherry-red satin chemise, he looked into her eyes and saw genuine anxiety.

It was crazy. She was a rising star in an impossibly tough industry. She brought fans to their feet every night and this very evening she was to be awarded a prestigious plaque. She was loaded with talent, she was pretty…yet the insecure little girl he'd once known still lurked inside of her.

He rose to his feet, took her by the shoulders and

turned her back to face the mirror. The top of her head barely reached the hollow of his throat and she looked dainty and feminine against his more muscular frame. Reaching around, he smoothed her top from just beneath her breasts to the exquisite garment's hem. "Trust me," he said in a low voice as the material pulled tight against her tits, "these are sweeter than sugar. There's not a man on earth is ever gonna mistake you for a boy." The satin under his hands was slippery smooth, the flesh beneath that warm and alive. He watched his hands in the mirror as if they belonged to someone else as they cupped the slight bottom swells, watched his thumbs as they swept like windshield wiper blades from her outside curves to her nipples. He observed those nipples shoot from soft quiescence to hard little bullets beneath the luxurious red fabric. "Not any man with blood in his veins," he reiterated, pressing the stiff crests between the sides of his index finger and the pads of his thumbs.

Her head lolled against his chest and her eyes grew sleepy-lazy as they stared in the mirror at the hands on her breasts. He watched her watching.

Then his brain belatedly kicked in. *What the hell are you doing?*

He jerked his big paws to her upper arms and stepped back, holding her steady when she staggered at the removal of the support that had been propping her up.

He cleared his throat. "So, we just about done here? It's getting late." He raised his voice. "How about you,

Nell? You almost ready to go?" A couple of women had come and gone while they'd been back in this corner, but had he even checked to see if anyone was around before he'd manhandled her? Hell, no.

Stupid! Stupid, stupid, stupid! God, he was a moron.

He did his best to make up for it, however, acting cool and businesslike as he encouraged the women to speed up the remainder of their try-ons, pay for their purchases and climb in the cab he'd called to take them back to the arena. But he had his doubts that his sudden professionalism fooled anyone. He couldn't really say about Peej, he supposed, since she was avoiding eye contact with him as assiduously as he was avoiding it with her. But Nell, whom he'd learned over the course of the day might be quiet but was far from meek and sure as hell didn't lack for intelligence, had a speculative gleam in her eyes whenever she looked at either of them.

Traffic was a nightmare and no one said a word to alleviate the tension inside the taxi as it crawled down the freeway. When they finally pulled up to the tour bus P.J. turned to him and coolly addressed a point beyond his left shoulder. "I'd like you to help take this stuff inside, then come with me to my dressing room."

He did as she asked but walking by her side toward the arena a short while later, he didn't hold out much hope for a pleasant conversation once they reached their destination. They were both silent at the moment, but he had no doubt that P.J. would have plenty to say once they hit her dressing room. And he was pretty sure what he was going to hear.

Hit the road, Jack—or whatever the country equivalent was.

Her posture was stiff as she stopped before the door to her room. Opening it, she waved him in like a grande dame. Gut roiling, he complied with her gesture and she closed the door behind them. Certain that this was the end, he abruptly realized that he wasn't even remotely ready to call this assignment—or whatever was happening between them—quits.

He was even less prepared for her to leap on him, wrap her legs around his waist and rock her mouth over his.

CHAPTER TWELVE

Hyperlink, www.JuicyCountry.com
How Faith Hill, Priscilla Jayne and Shania Twain
Stay Slender. And How You Can, Too!

P.J. PLUNGED HER HANDS into Jared's hair, held him fast and kissed him as if her life depended on it. And maybe it did, because she'd never felt quite this way—all hot blood, pounding pulses and nerve endings that arced and snapped like a downed power line. Ever since that ended-way-too-soon smooch in the salon she'd been primed. Beyond primed, really. And that business in front of the mirror had merely been gasoline on the fire.

In public. Dear God, she'd been ready and willing to get naked and do the hump-de-hump with Jared Hamilton, the star of her girlhood dreams, in the middle of an upscale department store. His sexual experience was clearly lightyears beyond her own.

But, man, oh, man, was she ever prepared to play catch-up!

He ripped his mouth free. "Wait…no…wait," he panted. "We can't do this." But his hands gripping her bottom flexed and kneaded and pulled her in, undulating her against a hard-as-hickory baton that pushed beneath her rucked-up skirt and settled between her legs to tell a different story.

A story that had her body singing the give-it-to-me song. She licked her lips and nodded earnestly. "Uh-huh. We can."

"God, yes, maybe." He drew in a deep breath. Blew it out. Then his heavy-lidded eyes, which burned with green fire between dense, tangled lashes, cooled the tiniest bit. "But we do it my way."

Her own eyes narrowed. "Your way doesn't include things like whips or chains, does it?"

"Nope."

"Anything painful?"

A rusty-sounding laugh escaped him. "No pain, baby—only pleasure."

"Well, alrighty then. But I want more kisses."

"Oh, I'll give you kisses."

Why did that sound almost like a threat?

She didn't have time to pursue the question because Jared, true to his word, lowered his head and kissed her again. He kissed her with such adroitness, with such skill, that she was barely even cognizant of being carried across the room. All she knew or cared about was that his mouth was hot and his lips exerted an exciting suction and his tongue set a languid, carnal rhythm that drove her to the edge of sanity.

That caused her breath to hitch and her lips to cling helplessly.

That made her arms drop limply to her sides even as

her heels dug into his muscular rear to hold him in place.

The dressing room's acoustical-tile ceiling took a sudden twirling spin when he lowered her onto the day bed in the corner. He came down on top of her and, linking their fingers, pressed the backs of her hands into the thin coverlet on either side of her shoulders. Pushing up onto his forearms, he flung his hair out of his face. Several strands promptly fell forward again and his dark eyebrows snapped together, patently displeased with the insurrection.

P.J. wanted to laugh out loud. Given the slant of his lower lip, the streaky disheveled hair refusing to conform to his command and those broad shoulders in their richly textured heavy-cream-colored cotton, she thought he looked like a sulky fallen angel. She half expected monstrous feathery wings to unfold and rustle with disgruntlement.

Lifting their connected hands, he hunched a shoulder and bent his head to swipe the fallen locks out of his way with his raised forearm. They fell right back out of alignment. His mouth still retaining its sullen cast, he shrugged and resettled their twined hands back onto the spread, staring down at her.

"Frigging hair," he growled. Then his gaze sharpened on her and it was as if every bit of his concentration suddenly refocused. "God, you're sweet."

She grinned up at him. "Aren't I a peach?" she agreed, wiggling pleasurably beneath him. "And you're—oh God, Jared, you're so hot."

His mouth finally crooking up, he settled a little deeper atop her. "Yeah?"

"Oh, yeah." It gave her palpitations just thinking about it. "All that's missing is Josh Turner crooning from the stereo." At his baffled look, she sang in the lowest register she could manage:

"Baby, lock the door and turn the lights down low.
Put some music on that's soft and slow."

In her conversational voice she admitted, "'Course, it's not quite the same when I sing it. He's got that wonderful deep voice going for him. And okay, it's a couple of years old. But ever since the first time I heard it playing on the radio I've thought of it as the ultimate makeout song."

"Well then, baby, lock the door and turn the lights down low."

Laughing, she disentangled her fingers from his grasp to cup the back of his head and pull him back down for another kiss. One touch of his lips, however, and her laughter faded as jangled nerve endings that had temporarily settled down jitter-danced back to life. He'd lowered his head to comply with her unspoken demand for his mouth, but a space of several inches still separated their upper torsos. Finding the distance unacceptable, she moaned and lifted to press her breasts against his chest.

As if someone had kicked the slats out from under him, he collapsed on her, thrusting the hands he'd been using to prop himself up into her hair. His sudden weight drove the breath from her lungs, but she didn't care. Breathing was overrated. His mouth was savage, passionate, and, loving it, P.J. dove headfirst into the madness.

For several long minutes she burned out of control. Her skin felt hot and tight, her pulse pounded in her throat, her wrists, her nipples and deep between her legs, and her only thought was that she wanted to tear Jared's clothes off and rub her body all over his. She'd been turned on a few times in her life. Never, however, had she experienced anything close to this level of unrestrained need. She felt as if she'd literally die if she didn't get naked with the man soon.

Jared seemed every bit as crazed. His fierce kiss pushed her head into the mattress, his hands gripped rather than seduced and he breathed like a bull maddened by a matador's cape.

Then he suddenly raised his head and pushed up on his palms. Breath sawing in and out of his lungs, he hung his head and stared down at her. After a moment he cleared his throat. "We've gotta slow down or in about four minutes there'll be nothing left but a pile of ashes."

Not slowing down seemed like a better plan to her. She'd never been the recipient of a burning-out-of-control-until-there's-nothing-left-but-the-ashes kind of passion. It sounded exciting. "And this would be bad because...?"

"Because our first time ought to last more than a couple of minutes."

She was marshalling an argument for a longer, slower second time when he lowered his head and kissed the side of her neck. "Because I wanna watch you come undone," he murmured into her ear, his voice a harsh growl that raised a fine wash of goose bumps down her entire left side. Moving a little lower, he used his lips, his tongue, to even more devastating effect. "But I can't do that if I'm racing to the finish line, can I?" he demanded. "And I'm dying to watch you come, P.J.—at least once, maybe two or three times—before I really cut loose."

Okay, it was official, she was about to have an orgasm from his words alone. She would have sworn that wasn't possible but his firm, I'm-in-charge mouth that was lightly sucking, licking, biting its way down her throat was almost redundant.

Well, maybe not.

She clenched her thigh muscles to keep from squirming and cleared her throat even as she tipped her head back to give him more room to maneuver. "Hearing a lot of words here, Hamilton. Where's the action that goes with it?"

Oh, thank you, thank you, Jesus, for not letting my voice crack. It was bad enough she had the chest of a fourteen-year-old boy without sounding like one as well just when she most needed to sound like a woman.

"You want action, honey? I can give you that." Jared's hands left a wash of heat the length of her throat and across the expanse of her chest, which was bared by the wide peasant neckline of her red dress. He stroked its gathered edge. "Did I tell you how much I like this dress?" he murmured. Long fingers lazily brushed back and forth, back and forth, from the crest of her nearly bared shoulders to the spot where his fingertips met at the bow between the slight rise of her breasts. Then they glided back up her to shoulders and his eyelids drooped and his head lowered, allowing his lips to follow the trail his hands had forged.

Pushing up on her elbows, P.J. watched his fingertips pinch the drawstrings that held the bodice together between her breasts.

"I've wanted to do this all day," he said. And, his gaze on the slender cords of fabric in his hands, he pulled the ends, slowly untying the bow as if he were about to unveil a great work of art instead of a barely there set of boobs.

The neckline widened in a V down to the smocking that hugged her midsection from beneath her breasts to her hips, where the skirt, which under ordinary circumstances would have fallen to calf length in three tiered flounces, was bunched above her knees. Only her nipples preserved her modesty—and that by the barest of margins. Distended with arousal, they hooked the bodice in place. She watched Jared gaze at them as if weighing the merits of scooping the soft red fabric to the far side of the thrusting points. Apparently deciding to leave her covered, he rolled off her onto his side.

Propping himself up on one elbow, he reached out to smooth his free hand up her thigh. Slowly he bent his head over the cotton that covered her left nipple.

Almost before she had time to register his mouth's amazing warmth and dampness, he looked up, met her gaze, and sucked. Hard.

It was like being hotwired to lightning and, breath exploding from her lungs, she arched into his mouth. Unharnessed power shot straight through her from the nipple he worked with such craft and skill to the tight, wet, aching spot deep between her legs.

Elbows melting out from under her, she found herself flat on her back once again, thighs sprawling wide until her right knee nudged up against his hard stomach. It occurred to her then that she was just lying here accepting everything he did as if it were her due. Thinking to offer a little reciprocal attention, she tried rolling to face him.

"No." His hands, gentle but firm, held her in place and his lips upped the suction on the damp fabric rapidly turning transparent over her nipple.

Omigawd, Omigawd. It took everything she had to pull herself back from the edge long enough to pant, "But you're doing all the work."

He mumbled something she didn't catch. "What?"

Raising his head, he shot her a wry smile. "Sorry. Talking with my mouth full. I said I'll get mine in due time. But if all those prep schools I got bounced out of taught me nothing else, they at least drummed one rule into my head. Ladies first."

He bent his head over her again, but this time he tugged on the little cap sleeves until they slid off her shoulders. "Well, look at this," he said, gazing down at her breasts, which had escaped their tenuous imprisonment, and at her arms pinioned to her side by the narrow sleeves he'd pulled midway down. "A two-fer. Your breasts all bare and pink, and a little light bondage allowing me do whatever I want with them." His gaze flashed up, pinned her in place. "With you."

Blushing, she tried to free her arms. The neckline with its loosened drawstring gave her some leeway, but still she could only widen the distance between her arms and her torso an inch or two before the material held firm. She began plucking at the midriff smocking in an attempt to tug the bodice to a point where she had a prayer of shedding it.

Rising onto his knees, Jared threw a leg over her hips to straddle her, effectively pinning the dress in place. "You claustrophobic, baby?"

"No."

Easing down to make room for himself between her legs, he lapped her shallow cleavage, gazing up at her as he did so. "Then why not just go with the flow?"

"You said you weren't into chains."

"And you don't see me using any, do you? I just want to make you feel good. And you've got such sensitive little tits I think we ought to see if I can make you come just by playing with them."

"What?" A laugh escaped her, but to her embarrassment it cracked right down the middle. "Of course you can't!"

"Bet I can. They're so responsive."

P.J. snorted. "They're so little they barely exist," she

said flatly, giving the tiny offerings under discussion a disgusted look. Being flat on her back sure didn't improve their stature.

"The hell they don't. They're nearly a handful and that's all I need. They're gorgeous, so quit putting them down." He licked his way up the slight slope toward the center of her left breast. "And these aren't little at all, are they?" He blew on her nipples before pinching them between his thumbs and forefingers.

She bit her tongue to keep from mewling like a cat in heat. But God, that felt good! And he was right. She rather liked her nipples—they were the most prominent part of her boobs. Pale pink protuberances that thrust skyward from puffy areolae, they were quite long when cold or excited—and God knew they were excited right now. Not to mention really, really receptive to the way he kept alternating the force of his clasp on them from the lightest pressure to an almost but not quite painful compression.

He seemed to know it, too. "I think all your nerve endings in these babies are right on the surface." Giving the morsels in his fingers a tug, he lightly bit first one tip then the other.

A single quick, hard contraction deep between her legs made her cry out.

"Jesus." Jared clenched his teeth to keep his head from blowing off his shoulders. "You really did get off. Not a real big one, maybe, but an orgasm's an orgasm." Oh, man, he was hanging by a thread here. Moving up her lithe body, he planted a fierce kiss on her lips. "Again," he demanded the instant he came up for air. He was determined to concentrate on her pleasure. He had to in order to keep from burying himself in her receptive body with one savage stroke and driving toward his own satisfaction like a freight train jumping the tracks. It wasn't only that he prided himself on being a thoughtful lover. He never relinquished control. Never.

Well, okay, eventually he did. But not until the last possible moment.

And he wasn't about to let little Priscilla Jayne Morgan be the exception to his rule.

He was hard-pressed to keep that affirmation in the front of his mind where it belonged, however, as he slid his hand up under her dress and finally brushed his fingertips against the lacy panties stretching the thinnest of barriers between him and a little slice of heaven. They came away damp with her arousal and it didn't matter what he did to keep hold of the situation—he could feel his grip slipping another degree.

"Again," he repeated in desperation and insinuated his fingertips beneath the scalloped hip band. The next thing he knew they were sliding between buttery feminine folds.

"Oh!" Her hips arched up off the bed.

He sucked for a breath he hoped would actually penetrate beyond the superior lobes of his lungs. Closing his eyes, he concentrated on the feel of her hot flesh beneath his fingers. He feathered the slippery little nugget of her clitoris, then stroked his fingers downward. When he reached her opening, he gently circled the ring of muscle guarding her entrance until her thighs began to clamp down on his hand and restlessly spread apart, close around him and sprawl open. Then he eased his forefinger inside.

"God," he breathed, and it was a benediction rather than a curse. Bowing his head, he rested his forehead against hers. "You feel so good," he whispered. "So hot and wet. So tight." *Very* tight, now that he'd mentioned it. The way that molten sheath clamped around the single digit he'd slipped in her you'd think nothing larger could possibly fit. He raised his head to stare down at her. "How long has it been for you?"

"Huh?" Her eyes slowly focused. "I don't know, a year? Maybe two."

And he'd float an educated guess here that she hadn't exactly been working the bars on a nightly basis before that. Or that her version of working them had meant singing onstage with a nice, wide protective gulf between her and a club full of interested men. "Sweet," he murmured and kissed her.

She kissed him back with the boundless enthusiasm that made her Peej and his tongue soon developed a synchronized rhythm with the finger he pumped in and out of her. When she began making little squeaky noises and thrusting her hips up off the bed, he flattened his palm against her plump, wet cleft and ground the heel of his hand over her clit.

She went off like a rocket.

Then she went limp, her beautiful rump hitting the

spread, her legs sprawling akimbo and her arms flopping heavily to her sides. With a final lingering pass up the creamy furrow of her sex, he slid his hand up to stroke her stomach. "You still breathing?"

A faint sigh was his only response.

"O—kay." Propping his head in his hand, he looked down at her. Her cheeks were flushed, her pretty bottom lip had gone slack and her eyes were closed. Her breasts were bare but her skirt still covered her to midthigh. White lace panties pooled around her right ankle, and he vaguely remembered her thrusting them down to give his hand more room to maneuver.

It occurred to him he hadn't gotten to view what he'd been touching. He was just starting to contemplate inching up her skirt and seeing what sort of damage he could do with his tongue when she crawled up out of her indolent sprawl. Climbing onto her knees, she gave his unsupported shoulder a shove and knocked him onto his back. She swung a leg over his hips and settled astride him, for an instant simply sitting squarely on his dick.

He stared spellbound up at her bare breasts, pleasure firing every atom of his being. Showcased by the red cotton hug-her-ribs smocking and the now drooping top she'd slid her arms from, they were all subtle curves and projectile nipples. Tearing his gaze away, he looked past them into Peej's determined amber eyes.

"You've got too many clothes on," she said and pointed to his shirt. "Take it off."

He unbuttoned his shirt down to where the skirt of

her dress billowed over his lap. She looked down the length of her nose at him and daintily grasped two fistfuls of fabric to raise it out of his way. He unfastened the last button and pulled the tails from his waistband. Crunching up, he shrugged it off his shoulders, wrestled it down his arms and shook it free. He lowered himself back on the bed.

Her hands immediately smoothed over his bare pecs and, electrified by her touch, he looked up. P.J. was watching her fingers slide over him.

"You've got a gorgeous chest," she said dreamily without lifting her gaze from her hands, which she used to outline his collarbone before trailing along the bony ridges of his shoulders. "Great shoulders."

Then she scooted down his body to trace her fingers along each muscle of his stomach. "*Really* great abs." Lying flat between his spread legs, she bent her head and kissed his stomach while her hands unbuckled his belt and dealt with the button on his waistband.

He jerked, his hands reaching for the silky fall of her hair. "P.J."

"It's okay," she whispered and lowered the zipper on his jeans.

No, it wasn't. He had to get control here or things were going to go to hell. Fast. "I'm kind of on edge, baby." And her breath on his fly threatened to shove him right into the abyss.

"Excellent." Her hand disappeared into his pants and his hips shot off the mattress when he felt her fingers clamp around his cock.

"Holy shit! Holy fucking sh—" Air hissed through his clenched teeth. He had to take charge here quick.

But God, it felt so good and he wanted so bad to see her hand on him.

A wish that was granted when she took advantage of his raised hips to yank his Levi's down around his thighs. His dick sprang free to point at the ceiling and she promptly wrapped it once again in her competent little fist.

Looking down, he saw its head push through her grip as she began a stroke that ended at the very root of his shaft. Oh, God, oh, God. He had to get a handle on this before he embarrassed himself. He was a glacier peak, he told himself, impregnable and remote.

Yeah, right.

He was fucking Mount Vesuvius. Ready to blow.

"I'm not going to last," he admitted as his hips instigated a rhythm that pushed him in and out of the snug tunnel her palm and fingers formed. He fumbled for his wallet in his sagging back pocket and, wrestling it free, fished out his lone rubber. She thrust out a peremptory palm and he slapped the condom in it.

The minute she had him suited up and her dress removed and sent sailing over the side of the bed, he grasped her nearest thigh and urged her to straddle him. He held her full, firm ass in both hands while she slowly impaled herself.

The feel of her wet, muscular heat slowly parting to accommodate his length and the sight of him disappearing inside her had him sucking for breath. She lowered herself in careful increments and he had to grit his teeth against the urge to slam her down with one powerful jerk of his hands and thrust of his hips. "Aw, Jesus, Peej. You're killing me." The control he took such pride in was hanging by a thread, and to distract himself he released her butt and raised his hands to toy with her nipples.

A wordless exclamation exploded out of her and she dropped the last couple of inches, seating him fully inside her. "Oh!" She blinked startled eyes at him.

"*Yes,*" he said fervently and ground up into her.

"Oh," she said again, only this time it was with a duel syllable, ohmigawd-this-feels-so-*good* rising inflection. Bracing her hands behind her, utilizing the power of her strong runner's thighs, she rose up his length then sank back down. Rose up and sank back down.

And oh, God, he was too close. Close to losing his mind. Close to coming like a fire hose. *Have to see to Peej's needs first,* his last remaining brain cells insisted even as he thrust up into each descending slam of her hips. *Gotta get her over.* Still determinedly manipulating her right breast, he brought his right hand down to delve between the wet folds that rose from where she engulfed him. He ran his thumb up and down the slippery cleft before zeroing in on her clitoris. *That* he plucked in concert to the firm tugs on her nipple and the rhythmic slaps of their bodies meeting and retreating.

"Jared?" Passion-blurred eyes stared down at him

and he felt the beginning ripples of her orgasm gathering force. "Oh, God, *Jared?*"

Thankyouthankyouthankyou. "That's it, baby," he panted. "Come for me." He gentled his touch between her legs, firmly gripped the pink spike of her nipple. "Please, Peej, I need you to come, because I don't think I can hold out any long—"

His breath exploded from his lungs as she contracted around him, a beautiful furnace-hot wet-velvet clenching fist that emptied his mind and shattered his control. The last thing he saw was P.J. clutching her breasts and throwing back her head, a hoarse moan purling from her throat. Then his eyes blurred and he was a fucking machine driving for his own satisfaction. He pounded, pounded, pounded up into her. Then, shoving deep and holding there, he roared out her name and came.

And came. In jet after jet of scalding sensation. Until, exhausted, he collapsed back onto the mattress.

Slowly his vision cleared and he stared up at her perched astride his hips like some wet-dream equestrian mastering the English saddle.

Then she melted atop him like a Dalí watch, resting her head on his chest as she made subtle adjustments to find the optimum position. "That was amazing," she said in her raspy voice. "You really know your way around this sex stuff, don't you?"

He wrapped one arm around her waist and curved his free hand around the warm swell of her left buttock to hold her close, wanting to stay inside her as long as possible. "It helps to have the right partner," he replied, pressing a kiss on the top of her head. A contentment he'd never known radiated from his heart clear out to his fingers and his toes and he turned his cheek to rest against her shiny brown hair. "How'd you get to be so damn sweet?"

"Hmm?" she murmured. Then he felt her lips tilt up against his pectoral. "I told you, I'm a peach."

"I'm serious. You were dragged from pillar to post, didn't have a single advantage and never got a day's nurturing out of your old lady in your life. But not only are you a rising star in an impossible industry, you *are* a peach. You're funny and warm and kind. Your band loves you and I've heard more than one roadie say you're the nicest performer they've ever worked for. So how did you get to be such a sweetheart?"

She'd been wiggling around, but now she stilled. "Umm," she said nonchalantly. But an instant later, a warm drop slid across his pec and down the curve of his ribs to the sheet.

His heart slammed in his chest and his head jerked up, chin dipping to look down at her. "Are you crying?"

"Hell, no," she said gruffly, but another drop slid down his ribs.

"Ah, baby, don't do that. I'm sorry. Was it what I said about your mom? I didn't mean to upset you."

"No!" She rubbed her wet eyes against the swell of his chest then lifted her head to look up at him. "No, you didn't. That was one of the nicest things anyone's ever said to me."

Aw, hell. She *was* sweet—giving and open and talented and an all-round better person than he.

And he had a feeling he was so screwed.

He didn't doubt for a moment that tomorrow he'd regret letting his guard down. Yes, sir, tomorrow he was going to have a stern talk with himself about professional ethics. Once again he would gather his defenses. Rebuild his walls.

But for today he merely tightened his arms around her.

CHAPTER THIRTEEN

Headline, *World Weekly Inquisitor*:
Mum Says Egyptian Mummy is
Priscilla Jayne's Father

NELL WAS JAZZED AS SHE headed down the tunnel to the arena, her clipboard in hand. No one had been around this afternoon to appreciate her Cinderellalike transformation but that was about to change. Primed to show off her new do and duds, she was through sitting in the tour bus all by her lonesome. She had work to do, people to see. Hell, she was mere moments away from a captive audience and she intended to capitalize on it.

Sometimes a woman simply had to strut her stuff.

It had been a long time since she'd felt like strutting anything, but she felt attractive tonight. Smart. Stylish. Almost…sexy.

Showing her badge to the guard, she tested her wiles by making eye contact and shooting him a flirtatious smile. She got an appreciative grin in return. *Oh, yeah.* Striding through the arena's backstage area, she beamed. *Ladies and gentlemen, allow me to present Nell Husner. Tour manager. Songwriter extraordinaire.*

Last of the red-hot mamas.

Hey, who cared if the guard was eighty-five if he was a day?

Gigs that ran at the same venue for longer than one night were rare on this tour, but this was day two of one of them. That meant she didn't have to reinvent the wheel, which made her workload lighter than usual. She made her usual rounds and checked to see that everything was running with the same efficiency she'd set in place yesterday. But this evening felt as if it were more about having her ego stroked than doing her job. Because everywhere she went people complimented her on her makeover.

She could hardly wait to hear what Eddie would have to say about it.

He hadn't yet arrived when she strode onto the stage, but that was hardly news. Hank was there, however, and she crossed the stage toward him.

He had his butt perched against a wooden stool, his left leg stretched out and his foot in its scuffed boot planted firmly on the floor to brace himself. His right knee was raised to support his banjo, his boot heel hooked over one of the stool's higher rungs. Head bent over the instrument, he adjusted the second fret, his hat brim concealing all but his lower lip with its little underlying soul patch and the strong angle of his chin. Then almost as if he felt her scrutiny he looked up.

For an instant he merely gave her a blank look, as if she were a stranger who'd wandered onto the stage by mistake. Then slowly he straightened and rose from the stool. Without looking behind him, he reached back to set his banjo on the seat he'd just vacated.

"Holy shit," he breathed. "Nell? Is that you?" He watched her approach with intent eyes then walked a circle around her. Stopping when he came full loop to face her once again, he looked her over from head to toe, then reversed the journey back to her face. "*Wow.*" Then he shook his head, dull color climbing his throat. "Sorry. I'm not exactly Mr. Articulate. I must have been standing in the wrong line the day they handed out the silver tongues."

"Could have fooled me," she said as warmth radiated from her heart to her farthermost extremities. "*Wow* is exactly the way I'm feeling today. That makes you sound pretty darn eloquent to me."

He pursed his lips in a silent whistle. "You look fantastic. Well, you always look great. But now you're even…more so. I didn't realize you were so—" his hands sketched a vague outline of her curves "—uh, so…"

"Plump?" Some of her pleasure dimmed and for the first time she felt uncertain about her decision to give up her comfortable baggy clothing. "Fat?"

"No, are you kidding me? Lush. Man, God, so lush. Did you hang on to your old clothes? Because I think we oughtta cover you back up. You're giving me a heart attack here."

She grinned at him. "I decided I'm shooting for the red-hot-mama look." A zaftig red-hot mama perhaps, but still.

He nodded earnestly. “You hit your target.”

“And you say you’re not articulate,” she scoffed, giving his stomach a poke. The rock-hard surface made her recall the look of him with his shirt off and, heat stealing up her face, she immediately retracted her fingers.

One of the extra musicians came over and asked her to settle a dispute about the seating arrangement in the horn section. When she got back from forging a compromise that pleased both parties, P.J. and Jared had arrived. They looked different than they had a short while ago, more content somehow, less edgy. But Nell barely had time to register the impression before Eddie strolled onto the stage and blew it clean out of her mind. Her heartbeat picked up its pace.

He greeted P.J. first as he always did and complimented her sleekly straight hair.

“I’m enjoying it while it lasts,” P.J. said. “Which is pretty much until I have to wash it. I sure don’t have the patience to wield a blow-dryer for the time it takes to get it this smooth myself.”

Eddie turned to Nell. “And you, sweet thing. You’re looking particularly radiant tonight. You lose some weight or something?”

Heart stilling, she simply stared at him for an instant.

“Christ, Brashear,” Hank muttered. “Could you *be* a bigger idiot?”

Omigawd, was her first clear thought. *He doesn’t know the first damn thing about me.* She’d spent nearly two years mooning over Eddie Brashear, with his dirty-blond hair and his bedroom eyes, and he had obviously never paid her the slightest attention in return. Which really shouldn't catch her by surprise. She was a far cry from his usual barely legal blond bimbo.

"You are an idiot," P.J. agreed and Jared stepped up to Nell, sliding an arm around her shoulders and walking her away.

"What?" Eddie demanded in a baffled voice. "What's everyone so bent out of shape about?"

"Well, don't I feel like a fool," she murmured as Jared escorted her to the wings.

He squeezed her shoulders. "Don't. Hank called it right. The guy's a complete moron."

Stopping in the shadow of the left wing, she stepped back to look at him. "Well, you know, thinking back, it occurs to me that this isn't exactly a new phenomenon. I've simply ignored the fact that every compliment he's ever given me has been a variation of the same theme. So who's the real moron here, Jared? *You're glowing* and *you're radiant* are clearly the currency he expends on the plump, pushing-forty crowd. I'm the one who read into it what I wanted it to mean. Every damn time."

He shrugged. "You can't choose who you fall in love with."

A sharp laugh that was dangerously near hysteria escaped her and she clapped her fingers to her mouth. She quickly got herself under control but her lips retained their crooked slant when she dropped her hand and looked up at him. "Well, here's the thing.

Being in love would at least be a decent excuse. What I felt for Eddie suddenly feels more like some crush a none-too-deep thirteen-year-old might have developed for the cute new boy in school." She looked Jared in his pretty green eyes. "Which—and here's how much depth I've gained at thirty-eight—is now stone-cold dead."

"That's actually a good thing," he said without sentiment. "I'd hate to think of you carrying a torch for the guy. Because have you ever *looked* at the girls he hangs out with? They may be cute and they're certainly built. But if even half of them have graduated from jailbait, I'd be very surprised. And talking about deep, don't you have to wonder if that's because he knows that one conversation between him and a real woman would send her screaming into the night?"

"Come to think of it, I don't believe I ever have had an actual conversation with Eddie." She smiled crookedly. "I was too busy lusting from afar." Feeling much better, she reached out and gave his hand a squeeze. "Thanks, Jared. You're a nice man. I, on the other hand, am not so nice. And I do believe I'm going to spend the night writing a new song. One about a man that a good-hearted woman thought was a diamond, but who turned out to be nothing but a pretty piece of paste." A melody started tickling the back of her mind and she smiled. "I'll have to give it some thought, because I especially want this song to be one of P.J.'s top sellers."

"Whoa." His eyebrows rose. "Let me guess—so Eddie can play it night after night on the next tour and hear it getting airtime on the radio and never have a clue it's about him?"

She smiled at him approvingly. "You're much quicker than he is."

"And you are one diabolical woman. What will you name it?"

"I don't know. Carly Simon already took 'You're So Vain.'" She shrugged. "But I'll come up with something. 'Eddie's a Blind Jerk Jackass' is probably a little obvious. I think I'll shoot for something more along the lines of a little inside joke that only a few of my closest friends will understand."

Jared studied her for a moment then shook his head. "Remind me never to piss you off."

THE MAN SLAMMED THE telephone receiver back in its cradle and stalked a short path from one end of his motel room to the other. This was wrong, just plain wrong! He should have won a ticket and a backstage pass to tonight's Priscilla Jayne concert by now. Instead, even though he'd diligently called every time he'd heard the opening notes to "Crying Myself to Sleep," he had yet to manage getting through to the radio station. It was frustrating, irritating, and the busy signal that assaulted his ear with every attempt was beginning to make him very, very angry.

"Forgive me, Father." Sinking to his knees beside the bed he prayed for patience and the Lord's guidance. He apologized for his lack of faith when he knew perfectly well that his quest was just and his Creator would provide the means to contact Priscilla Jayne in His own way and on His own schedule.

Early evening waned without the man ever reaching KPIX, but by then he had mastered acceptance. Because giving himself over to a higher power had opened a space in his mind that allowed an alternate idea to occur to him. He let himself out of his motel room and headed toward Hollywood Boulevard a half-block over.

He hadn't been pleased about having to stay this close to California's Sodom and Gomorrah and had kept his distance from the famous street. Given a choice, he'd prefer not to rub shoulders with so many sinners. He wasn't made of money, however, and at least his motel was clean, within reasonable proximity to the place he needed to be and relatively inexpensive.

It was ironic, then, that this boulevard of broken dreams and perversions might now turn out to be exactly what he was looking for.

Except...Hollywood Boulevard wasn't at all what he'd anticipated. Where were the string of tattoo parlors, the scandalous lingerie stores, the hookers and the dealers? He tramped street after street but saw nothing but a clean new shopping complex, an equally new metro station and restored hotels and shop fronts. He should have been pleased that such a corrupt town was cleaning up its decadent neighborhoods. And he was.

But for just this evening a decadent neighborhood had been the kind of place where he could reasonably expect to find what he needed.

He sure couldn't find it in this new and improved district, and he was ready to call it a night and head back to the motel when he saw the devil's handmaiden leaning against a light standard. He stopped short on the sidewalk. Glancing up at a street sign, he realized he'd walked all the way to the seedy beginning of downtown L.A. He stared at the woman on the opposite side of the boulevard.

Clearly she would know where he could find what he was looking for.

Still he hesitated, because even understanding that she was a sign sent to him from above, he didn't want to approach her. With her huge shock of brassy hair, her makeup that looked as if it had been slapped on with a spackling knife, her inch-long squared-off fingernails painted a Jezebel red and at least six tattoos, she reminded him of his daughter, Mary. And that was a personal failure he didn't care to revisit tonight.

Time was growing short, however, and he didn't have many options left. All he could do at this juncture was command himself to keep his gaze above the woman's neck. But her great, bulbous breasts in their low-cut, skintight, zebra-print top and her skirt so scandalously short it barely covered the essentials were lures designed to tempt the virtuous from their path. The long, muscular snake draped around her neck had more volume to it than her entire wardrobe combined.

By rights she ought to hang her head in shame. Instead, when she saw the disapproval he could not completely disguise, she mocked him with her salacious behavior. She laughed a husky siren's laugh, proposed indecent act after indecent act and shook her whore's teats in his face. He longed to take her in hand the way he once had Mary, to do what he had been unable to do for his own daughter and set her feet firmly on the road to redemption.

But he forced himself to swallow the inclination and be civil. He needed information and he'd learned the hard way that a soft voice was more effective than thundering threats of hell and damnation.

But if ever a female cried out for punishment it was this unrepentant harlot before him.

She refused to give him the information he sought until he paid her thirty dollars. When he then discovered that he would have to drive down to Yorba Linda for his purchase he longed to unleash the power of his righteousness upon her, to castigate and renounce her for the hell-bound sinner she was. He choked down that impulse, as well. Instead he thanked her for her time and hiked back to his motel. There he collected his uniform, tidied it with a lint brush and carried it out to his car where he carefully laid it on the pristine backseat. After consulting his map, he drove back to Hollywood Boulevard, where he turned left and headed for Highway 101.

There was an accident not far from where 60 East merged with 57 South and the snarled traffic barely inched along for the next forty-five minutes. The longer he was stuck in it the more he stewed about the store closing before he could get there. Why hadn't he called for the shop's hours before he'd set out to drive these heathen freeways?

But he received yet another reminder that the Lord was his Shepherd when he arrived with twenty minutes to spare before the store closed for the night. *Oh, ye of little faith,* he chastised himself as he marched through the door.

The clerk was dressed head to foot in black, had green and black hair, a tattooed asp on her neck and multiple piercings. She was also a nonstop talker who followed him around the store extolling the virtues and drawbacks of her merchandise. The man would have preferred a little privacy to mull over his choices, but he gave in with good grace when it became clear he wasn't going to be granted that wish. He made his selection and talked pleasantly to the clerk as she boxed up his item. Ten minutes later he was on the freeway back to Los Angeles.

He was pushing the far boundaries of the timeframe he'd set for himself when he finally neared the arena where Priscilla Jayne was holding her concert. All the same he pulled into a service station and changed into his uniform. The restroom's disgusting condition made his skin crawl and he washed his hands three times before letting himself out. Even then he couldn't relax until he'd also gone over them with one of the antiseptic wipes he kept in his glove box.

He drove around the peripheries of the arena until he located the tour bus he'd identified as belonging to Priscilla Jayne. It was in the lot near the backstage tunnel, and, parking his car in the shadows of an alley half a block away, he sank low in his seat to observe the bus for signs of occupancy.

All was quiet. A faint glow filtered through a couple of the black tinted windows, but he couldn't see any activity going on behind them. Which made it impossible to tell who was on the bus. That was unacceptable. He was on a mission and he needed to know that Priscilla Jayne and her entourage were elsewhere while the bus driver was on board. Was that so much to ask?

Considering that without the driver, his mission fell apart.

Well, perhaps the driver was on the bus. It was even probable. There was only one way to find out, however. Climbing from the car, the man straightened his uniform, settled his hat low over his forehead and reached back into the vehicle for the package. He set off with a purposeful stride for the bus.

He was about fifty yards away when the sound of approaching laughter floated up the ramp from the arena entrance down below. He melted into a shadow until he could see who emerged. To his surprise and momentary pleasure, Priscilla Jayne herself walked into view, hugging a large plaque to her chest. She whirled at the top of the ramp, and he watched her skirt lift up to twirl around her legs. She laughed and slapped it down, dancing backward in front of a cigarette-smoking man who was likely a drug user by the dissipated look of him; a woman with short, messy brown hair and full-figured curves that ought to be decently covered by clothing much less form-fitting than what she had on and a tall man with a loose-limbed walk but a vigilant air about him.

Like the moon pulls the tides, the man's gaze was drawn back to Priscilla Jayne. She was so animated, even prettier and more joyous in person, that it was difficult to look away.

Then he gritted his teeth in disgust. The attraction of the flesh was the *last* thing he should be thinking about. That was the devil, whispering temptation in his ear.

"Get thee behind me, Satan," he muttered. So close. He had been so *close!* Anger at being denied his goal was a slow fire inside of him that threatened to burst into full flame.

He firmly stamped it out. Turning away from the noisy group, he headed back to his car. It was disappointing, yes.

But there was always tomorrow.

CHAPTER FOURTEEN

"Rumor Has It" column,
Country Connection magazine:
What On-Tour Singer Currently Feuding With Her Mama Has a Mystery Hunk Climbing Aboard Her Bus Every Night?

FIVE CITIES, FIVE CONCERTS, five drive-all-night bus rides. And now, with the morning sun lighting their way, they were rolling through town number six.

P.J. watched Denver unfold outside the window and memories of living on its streets, first by herself, then with Jared, began piling up faster than she knew how to handle. She stole a quickie peek at the banquette where J sat engrossed in a book, sipping a cup of coffee.

He didn't spare her so much as a glance in return.

Of course not. Acid cramped her stomach. Never mind that Denver was where they'd met, the city where they'd gone through so much together, where they'd relied on each other to stay sane. She'd taught him every bit of street savvy she'd learned there. He'd comforted her, talked to her, been her friend. Hell, even though he was a person of interest wanted for questioning in his father's murder, he'd risked exposure to face down a pervert for her—all because she'd called Mama begging to come home and had been told she'd made her bed and could just lie in it. When she'd flipped out as a result and was about to throw herself over the edge, Jared had pulled her back.

But no, never mind all that.

Because ever since L.A. he'd gone back to being Mr. Professional Bodyguard or Security Guy or whatever the hell he was supposed to be. And she was ready to scream.

Or cry.

Or—hey, here was an idea—shoot him.

The last option was gaining favor by the minute. For really, it beat the heck out of crying. And screaming was so bad for the voice.

Not to mention that she was just plain ticked. Because try as she might, she couldn't get their incredible encounter out of her mind.

She had never known sex could *be* like that. It had blown her away, and she'd thought of little else for the past six days. Not merely about the orgasms, either, which had been a revelation all their own. But about the comfort of being in his arms afterward, the feel of his voice rumbling beneath her ear and speaking over her head at the same time as he'd said those nice, nice things about her. She had felt close to him in a way she'd never felt with anyone else. She'd felt safe.

Jared apparently hadn't found it particularly special. Otherwise he wouldn't be so freaking determined to act as if it had never happened.

Her life had been turned upside down and inside out, while his—

Well, his clearly hadn't. Not if he could go from what they had shared back to treating her like good ol' Peej.

She'd probably stunk at it. She was twenty-eight years old and hardly a virgin, but neither did she have a lot of know-how on her side. She'd been nineteen the first time she'd done the deed, years behind most of the girls she'd known. Nineteen when Johnny Ripley had sweet-talked her out of her panties in the bed of his pickup truck down at the end of the dirt road next to old man Hemming's orchard. The experience had been messy and uncomfortable and had cured her of her crush on Johnny but good.

It had improved with the next guy, but not by leaps and bounds. Same thing with the guy after that—it had been better, but not by much. The truth was, she'd mostly been too busy trying to get her foot in the music-industry door to bother with it much.

Then Jared had come roaring back into her life and introduced her to Sex with a capital *Ssss.*

And at the risk of repeating herself, she'd probably stunk like a skunk at it.

Well, she didn't care. So what if he was some hotshot stud between the sheets and she did the wild thing with all the expertise of the thirteen-year-old he'd known back when? She had other skills. Hell, dollars to doughnuts the only place Jared could carry a tune was in the shower.

But that wasn't a place she cared to picture him in, since she knew only too well how good he looked in it. They'd made love there, too.

Besides, maybe he was sorry they had done it *because* of his memories of the girl she'd once been. Or it was possible that he didn't like women who made the first move. Of course, if she'd waited for him to make it, they probably never would have had sex at all, and she refused to be sorry that they had. Or maybe—

"Arrgh!" She thunked her head against the window.

"You okay?" Nell asked vaguely, looking up from the score she'd been laboring over night and day since L.A.

"Yeah, sure." *Ducky.* She dredged up a smile for her friend, but inside she was screaming, *Get me out of here!* It was only eight a.m. and already she was sick of being cooped up on this bus with everyone.

It had never occurred to her when they'd first set out on this tour that such close contact with her band might develop into a problem. And, really, it hadn't—at least not into a big one. But she had to get away for a while. Maybe check into a nice hotel, sign herself up for a few spa treatments. They were a good eight hours away from the sound check for tonight's show, and what was the point of being a big-whoop singing sensation if she couldn't get away every now and then to enjoy the benefits? Everyone was a little edgy from so much togetherness; they were beginning to rub on each other's nerves.

About the only one who hadn't gotten on hers the past several days was Nell. That was a two-edged sword though, because not only did her friend have her hands full with managerial duties, she'd been spending every moment not devoted to her paying job hunched over her music sheets, composing. Songwriting drew her deep inside herself. P.J. knew how time-consuming it could be, and she respected the process too well to interrupt the flow.

At the same time, she was tired of tiptoeing around. She hadn't turned the television on or the stereo up for days now for fear of disturbing Nell's concentration. Running would have been an outlet, but even that had been denied her more often than not. Jared insisted she only run when he could accompany her but then he'd had one excuse after another not to do so. And her stress levels had kept building and building.

Until she felt ready to explode.

Well, she'd reached her saturation point. Between being back in Denver and being stuck in close quarters with Jared, wondering every damn time she opened a door if he'd be on the other side of it—knowing that even if he was he'd only ignore the fact they'd had sheet-scorching sex—she needed to clear her head. Needed to gain some perspective.

They were playing three cities on this leg of the tour. Tonight's show was near here. Denver was centrally located between the other two cities, and following the Colorado College gig in Colorado Springs tomorrow night they even had an honest-to-God day off before playing Fort Collins. So her mind was made up. She was getting herself a big private room and commuting to the next three concerts.

Jared, of course, would feel that it was his job to accompany her, which would defeat the purpose of the exercise. So why tell him? It wasn't like there'd been any further contact from the weirdo in Bakersfield. That disturbingly doctored magazine spread thankfully had been a one-shot deal.

While Marvin pulled into the Red Rock Amphitheater's lot west of town, talked to an attendant, then jockeyed the bus into a space reserved for performers, P.J. came up with a possible way to get out from under Jared's indifferent yet watchful eyes. Going back to the stateroom, she packed a small overnight bag and made two phone calls.

When she came out again she collected her backstage pass from Nell. For one crazy moment she considered simply making a break for the door, but knew she wouldn't get far. So she asked for Jared's pass, as well, then walked over to him where he still sat at the table. "Come with me."

Placing his finger in his book to mark his place, he looked up at her. "Where?"

"I want to check out my dressing room." Seeing his gaze grow wary didn't exactly knock her on her butt with surprise, considering what had happened the last time they'd been in one together. But it stabbed her to the quick.

No. She sucked in a breath, straightened her spine. His suspicion didn't hurt; it pissed her off. Just what did he think she was going to do, demand he *service* her? "Look," she snapped, "I can go by myself, if you'd rather not. You're the one who keeps harping about taking someone with me every damn place I go."

"Did I say no? Christ. Give me a minute to change gears." He climbed to his feet and followed her off the bus, his book still in hand.

They didn't speak, and a tension that neither acknowledged grew with every step that brought them closer to the assigned room. When they reached a door with her name on it, he took a step back and looked at her with shuttered eyes. "I'll wait out here."

"Whatever. I'm not rushing for you, though, so you might wanna get comfortable." She nodded at his book. "You may just get to finish that." Opening the door, she paused to glance at him over her shoulder. "You want to—" A huge yawn caught her unawares and she went with the flow, dropping her bag to stretch her arms in opposite directions as she inhaled a lungful of air, then expelled it in a long, squeaky, attenuated breath. "Sorry," she said once it passed. "You want to come in and grab a chair?"

Taking another brisk step back, he tipped his chin toward the corridor they'd just traversed. "I saw one down by those props. I'll go grab that."

"Suit yourself." She essayed an indifferent shrug even though her first inclination was to break into a happy dance.

She walked into the room but immediately stepped back out into the hall when he strode away. Slipping off her sandals, she watched until he was halfway down the long hallway, then grabbed her bag, eased the dressing room door closed behind her and raced down the corridor in the opposite direction. Reaching the exit, she glanced back and saw him leaning over a stack of old scenery. His shirt strained across his shoulders, his jeans pulled tight over his muscular butt, and for a moment she stood frozen, staring at him. Then she caught herself and pushed through the door before he could see her. She put her shoes back on and jogged around to the front of the venue.

A taxi arrived scant moments after she'd reached the arena's main entrance and she slid inside. "Hotel Teatro in Denver, please."

The morning rush-hour traffic doubled what should have been a twenty-minute ride back to Denver, but eventually the cab pulled up to the long sidewalk awning that protected patrons of the boutique hotel from the elements as they crossed the sidewalk to the ornate front entrance. A doorman came forward to open her door.

"Good morning, miss."

"Good morning." She relinquished her overnight bag to the bellman who came out for it, then followed him into the hotel. Pausing inside, she managed to take in the sweeping staircase, the rich use of marble throughout the lobby and the intricate ceiling without gawking. It was a near thing though, for first-rate hotels were still pretty new to her. Trying her best to project an image of a woman who frequented places like this all the time, she turned through the archway to her left to check in at the front desk.

In short order she'd been escorted to her suite and

shown the amenities. She tipped the bellman, closed the door behind him and leaned back against the smooth wood with a sigh of relief. Then she pushed away and went into the bedroom to unpack. After calling room service she flopped down to watch a morning show while she waited for her breakfast to arrive. Propping her feet on the coffee table, she gazed around contentedly. This was heaven.

Not long after she'd finished eating, however, she began to grow antsy. For all that she'd been dying for some privacy, she was accustomed to being surrounded by people. And without someone to share it with she didn't quite know what to do with the entire day that stretched in front of her.

She supposed she could watch more television. But a little viewing went a long way and at the moment she wasn't interested in anything on the schedule. She could go shopping or work on the song that had been scratching at the back of her mind for a while now. Except shopping was more fun with a friend and the song still had some percolating to do before she could even begin to delve into it.

Then, just like that, it came to her what she wanted to do.

She wanted to see Gert MacDellar. Years ago John Miglionni had located Jared for J's sister and in tracking him down had gotten P.J. as a bonus. When they sent Jared home to Colorado Springs, John's office manager, Gert, had taken P.J. in until Mama could be convinced to take her back. She had discovered later that Gert had also seen to it that her mother *got* convinced, and on Gert's schedule, not Jodeen's. For months Mama had bad-mouthed the older woman something awful as a blunt and bossy old broad. But P.J. had adored Gert for those very reasons. She had known exactly where she stood with her and Gert had treated her the way P.J. always imagined real families treated each other.

They'd kept in sporadic touch over the years but P.J. hadn't actually seen Gert in person since the day the crotchety old woman had carefully packed the new dresses she'd bought P.J. into a sturdy suitcase and driven her down to Mama's trailer in Pueblo.

Energized, P.J. called the concierge desk for a taxi.

If she also felt a brief jitter of unease, she shoved it aside. Maybe it was reckless to waltz into Jared's business, but—what the hell—he was safely stashed out at the amphitheater. Besides, it had been a tough week. She was due to catch a break.

If she had second thoughts when her ride pulled into the small parking lot that fronted Semper Fi Investigations' converted Arts-and-Crafts-style house, it had nothing to do with J. Maybe Gert wouldn't want to see her. Yes, she had responded to P.J.'s occasional letters, but maybe that was just old-lady good manners. Gert probably wouldn't even recognize her, and then P.J. would have to introduce herself and everyone would feel awkward and—

"You will get out now?" the cabbie asked in his musical accent.

"Yeah." Taking a deep, controlled breath, she opened the door and stepped out. The taxi immediately reversed in a tight, fast turn, rocked to a halt, then shot out of the lot. It was already at the corner light by the time she climbed the stairs to the covered front porch. A discreet chime sounded when she opened the door.

Going from bright sunshine to dimmer indoor lighting blinded her and for a minute she simply stood on the threshold. Then an irascible voice said, "Close the door. We're not paying to air-condition the great outdoors."

P.J. laughed, her nerves settling. That was the Gert she'd known, and she could see her now, seated behind her enormous oak desk, sporting the same blue-tinted up-do and cat's-eye glasses she'd had the last time P.J. had seen her. "You said the same thing to me fifteen years ago."

"Then you don't learn very fast, do—" Cutting herself off, the elderly woman with the ramrod posture rose to her feet, her hand going to her bony chest. "P.J.?" She rounded the desk and strode over, stopping right in front of her. "Well, my God. It *is* you."

"Hello, Gert. It's been a long time but you haven't changed a bit."

"And you're all grown-up. But that voice is the same. I should have known it from the first word out of your mouth." She reached out a hand as if to touch P.J.'s face, but then let it drop to her side. And that glimpse of uncertainty made P.J. lose her own.

Closing the distance between them, she gave Gert a hug.

The old lady squeezed her fiercely in return, then held her at arm's length to conduct a comprehensive appraisal. "You might not have grown any taller, missy, but you grew up real pretty. You finally have a little meat on your bones."

She grinned. "That started in your kitchen with the brownies you made. You still have that Felix the Cat clock on your wall?" She'd loved Gert's house. It had been a seven-room ode to the forties and fifties.

"Yep. Everything's essentially the same. Thank you for the tickets to your concert, by the way."

Pleasure lit her up from the inside out. "You're coming, then?"

"Well, of course I'm coming. I wouldn't miss seeing you in action."

"Mac, have you seen the Pedersen file?" A tall sun-streaked brunette with a faint British accent strode into the room. "The blasted thing has disappeared." Seeing P.J., she halted midstep. "I'm sorry. I didn't realize anyone else was here." Then her dark eyes went wide. "Omigawd. You're Priscilla Jayne!"

It always surprised her—and thrilled her a little—to be recognized. She stepped forward, her hand extended. "Yes. How do you do?"

"This is Jared's niece, Esme," Gert said, then to the young woman added astringently, "Try not to drool."

"You won't remember this," P.J. said to the brunette, "but I met you once, a long time ago."

"I'm afraid I don't, but Mum's told me about it."

"How is your mother? I have a song called 'Mama's Girl' that makes me think of her every time I sing it."

"*My* mum? Not your own?"

"No. Well." *Good going, Morgan. You couldn't keep your mouth shut?* Then she squared her shoulders and met Esme's gaze head-on. "I was a thirteen-year-old who'd been thrown out of my house when I met your mother and saw how much she loved you. It made a lasting impression on me."

Esme reached out and touched her arm. "I'm sorry. That was frightfully rude of me. Mum would be really honored to know you feel that way." Her gaze dropped to P.J.'s denim and froth skirt. "What a smashing piece."

"Isn't it great?" Running her hands down the garment she'd bought on the Los Angeles shopping trip, she smiled. "I was telling my friend Nell just last week that Gert started me on my love affair with skirts and dresses."

"You knew Mac before today then?"

"Yes. I lived with her for a short period. She bought me my very first non-hand-me-down dress."

Esme turned to the old woman. "You never told me that Priscilla Jayne lived with you."

"Yes, there's a surprise, dear. That I don't tell a twenty-one-year-old girl everything about my life."

P.J. grinned and gave Gert's hip a little bump. She knew the old lady's gruffness rubbed some people the wrong way, but she loved it. Because she knew it for what it was: a very thin layer over a solid-gold core.

"Is that what brings you here? A visit with Gert?"

"Yes."

"Did you know my dad, too?" Without awaiting an answer, she whirled off down the hall. "Daddy! You'll never guess who's here!"

"You might not surmise it from her constant chatter," Gert said wryly, "but she's a very bright young woman."

P.J. hadn't really considered the fact that she might see John, and her heart took a funny skip. She'd had such mixed feelings about him as a kid. Mostly she'd admired him and felt grateful to him for getting her and J off the streets. But a big chunk of her had been pea-green jealous of the way Jared had hero-worshipped the man who would become his brother-in-law.

But when he sauntered out of his office, fifteen years older but still lean and tall and easy in his skin, she smiled, her momentary unease dissolving. His black hair was dusted gray at the temples and was no longer worn in a long ponytail. But he hadn't lost an iota of the cool she remembered and still carried the same air of confidence and competency that even her thirteen-year-old self had known defined him.

"Well, look who's here," he said with a warm smile. "Little Priscilla Jayne Morgan, all grown-up."

"Hello, Rocket."

"Omigawd," Esme said. "Nobody calls him Rocket anymore."

"Except your mother and Jared," John said dryly, hooking an elbow around his daughter's neck and scrubbing his knuckles over her scalp. "And Coop and Ronnie and Zach and Lily and all their assorted kids."

She grinned. "Yeah, except for them."

Sliding his arm down to circle her shoulders, he hugged her to his side and directed his attention back to P.J. "So where's Jared?"

Her heart gave another of those funny skips but she gestured vaguely. "Out at the amphitheater. It's so big that the security walk-through should take up half the morning." Which wasn't exactly a lie—a walk-through *would* take half the day…if such a thing existed. She flashed him an insouciant smile. "Besides, there's nowhere safer than with you, don'tcha think?"

"I suppose that's a point. Congratulations on your success, by the way. Tori and I have been loving the hell out of watching your career rise." His cell phone rang in his pocket and he pulled it out to check the screen. "Excuse me for a minute. This is a call I have to take." He loped back down the hall and disappeared into his office.

Esme came back to P.J. and for a moment simply stood gazing down at her. "You're so tiny."

"Compared to you and your father and Jared, I am," she agreed. "I feel like a munchkin."

"I didn't mean that rudely. It's just that your voice is so big I assumed you would be, too." Esme gave her a crooked smile. "Which merely proves that axiom about what *assume* makes of you and me, I suppose. Speaking of Jared—"

"Did your mother get the tickets I sent?"

Esme's face lit up. "Yes! How lovely of you. Mum had already bought some, but not in such a premium area! My best friend Rebecca is so jealous. We gave our old tickets to her and her parents."

Conversation around Esme never lagged, and P.J. found it easy to allow the young woman to take it where she would. She squeezed in chats with Gert in between Esme's topics and found herself having a perfectly lovely time. When the front door opened behind her she was seated in a chair pulled up to Gert's desk, her feet propped up on a pulled-out file drawer while she sipped iced tea from a tall, frosty glass. As she laughed a big belly laugh at an acerbic comment Gert had just made, it occurred to her that this was the most relaxed she'd felt all week.

A condition that promptly imploded when Jared's irate voice growled, "Security walk-through, my ass! What the hell do you think you're doing?"

CHAPTER FIFTEEN

Headline, *Country Billboard*:
Priscilla Jayne Concerts Playing to Sellout Crowds

"HEY, UNCLE JARED!" Esme rushed over, her face alight with her habitual enthusiasm.

"Hey, pipsqueak." He leaned down to give her a fleeting peck on the lips, but barely broke stride in his unwavering advance on P.J.

He stopped in front of her, his hands firmly in his pockets to keep from doing her bodily injury. When he'd realized she was no longer in her dressing room—that she hadn't *been* in the room the entire time he'd been sitting guard outside of it—his gut had turned into a mass of screaming nerve endings. She'd willfully put herself in danger on his watch.

That he wasn't happy about it was an understatement. "Say goodbye, P.J."

She looked up from her conversation with Mac, meeting his gaze dismissively. "When I'm ready."

He knew that stubborn look, but he was royally pissed and that trumped mulishness hands down. He wasn't about to take no for an answer. "Say. Goodbye," he commanded through gritted teeth, hauling her to her feet.

"Jared," Esme said uncertainly and Mac's eyes narrowed. But his willingness to carry little Miss Escape Artist out the front door—thrown over his shoulder like a sack of spuds if necessary—must have shown. P.J. turned to Mac.

"Thank you for treating me to the most fun I've had all week," she said warmly, rising onto her toes to plant a kiss on the older woman's cheek. "You come see me tonight after the show." She turned to his niece. "You, too, Esme. It was so good to see you again. Tell your mama I'm looking forward to seeing her tonight, as well." Projecting her voice to reach down the hallway, she said, "You can come, too, Rocket. If you absolutely must."

John's laughter floated out of his office.

Jared said his own goodbyes, then marched P.J. out the agency door, across the porch and down the steps to the Jeep he'd retrieved on his only detour between the amphitheater and here.

Tense silence filled the Jeep as he drove them out of the parking lot. The more he thought about the worry she'd caused him, the more his neck muscles tightened. If he hadn't finally called John to admit he'd lost her, he'd probably still be tearing the venue apart looking for her.

To his surprise, P.J. broke the silence between them. He'd have sworn she'd rather choke than cave first. "Take me to the Teatro."

Okay, so it was a command rather than an attempt to escape his displeasure. Clenching his teeth against the urge to snarl, he said in a neutral tone, "You're going back to the amphitheater with me."

"No, Jared, I'm not. I'm already checked into the hotel. Take me there."

"You are not staying at a goddamn hotel," he barked. "I won't have it." Hearing himself, everything inside him stilled.

Then the nerve endings that had begun to settle down recommenced their hot, mortified dance of agitation. Jesus. He sounded exactly like his father at his autocratic worst. He might have been channeling the old man from the grave, so closely had his tone come to the one that had hounded his adolescence.

Sucking up all his ire, he stuffed it away. Then he took a deep breath and blew it out. But it didn't matter what he did, because he recognized this for what it was: one wrong comment, one sideways glance away from blowing sky high. He drew more air into his lungs. *I am a glacier peak, impregnable and remote.*

"We've been through this before," P.J. snapped. "Same song, same dance. Read my lips, Hamilton. You don't get to dictate where I can or cannot stay. I need a break from living with a busload of people and I'm taking one. Drive me to the Teatro. For the next few days you can consider it my home base."

What he considered was just flat out disregarding her wishes. But maybe she could read his mind, because she said flatly, "I'm tired and cranky and you do not want to blow me off. Because I'm warning you, J, I'll pick up the phone and call Wild Wind so fast it'll make your head swirl. And who do you think they'll choose if I demand that either you go or I will?"

He drove her to the Teatro.

He was so angry, though, he could barely see straight. Unleashed emotion was unlike him, and he drew in several deep, silent breaths, trying to get a handle on it. Refusing to let his temper show, he turned his car over to a valet and walked P.J. to the hotel entrance, his clasp on her elbow courteously loose.

"This really isn't necessary, you know," she said, extricating her arm as they entered the lobby. "You can leave me here."

"I need to know where your room is so I can see about getting one nearby. You may have forgotten the threatening note you received last week, but I haven't."

"Of course I haven't forgotten it. But neither have I heard another word from the whack job who sent it."

"And let's hope that continues. But we don't bet your safety on the assumption. You don't have to spend time with me while you're here." He gave her his best ask-me-if-I-give-a-damn look, the one he'd perfected on his father. Then he let his eyes go hard. "But I will do my job."

When she argued no further he accompanied her to the elevator, then down the hallway of her floor. He stood back while she slid the key card into the door slot of her room. But when he followed her inside, she sighed.

Not just your average everyday sigh, either. A *woman sigh.* One of those long-suffering exhalations that only females of the species were truly good at. It was wordless, just a breath of air, really.

Yet it still managed to say, *What have I ever done to deserve being saddled with this horse's ass?*

Temper ratcheting another degree higher, he eyed her butt, noting how firm and round it was, how satisfying it would be to apply the flat of his palm to it. Forcefully.

Jesus, Ace. Shoving his hands deep in his pockets for the second time that day, he followed her into the suite's sumptuous sitting room without noticing the first thing about the decor. What was he thinking? Losing control was *not* in his makeup. And he sure as hell didn't manhandle women! *I am a glacier peak.*

Impregnable.

Remote.

"No, you know what?" he said aloud. "To hell with that."

P.J. swung around to stare at him. "What are you babbling about?"

"I don't babble. And you owe me an apology. I searched every fucking inch of that amphitheater looking for you." He crossed the room to tower over her. "And, baby, you at least told John one truth. The place is immense." He'd never felt such immediate fear as he had upon discovering she was missing. Furious to know he'd suffered that hot gut and cold sweat over what had basically been P.J. messing with his head, he crowded her against the wall. If she had a working brain cell in her head she'd be afraid.

She'd be very afraid.

"Well, boo hoo." Leading with her chin, she scowled up at him. "For the past five days you haven't had two lousy minutes to spare me—so ask me if I give a rip that you had a few bad moments trying to track me down. I've had a lousy *week* and I'll be damned if I'll let you make me feel guilty about my visit with Gert. It's the first decent time I've had since—" Cutting herself off, she slapped hands to his chest and shoved. "Get out of my way. In fact, get out of my room."

He didn't budge. But neither did he put his hands on her. He wanted to, though. Man, did he want to! He'd spent way too much time the past several days reliving their time in that Los Angeles dressing room.

He wasn't stupid; he knew he never should have touched her. Getting her naked, getting *inside* her, had been unethical squared.

But, damn. Merely thinking about it almost blew the top of his head off. Which just went to show that it didn't pay to jump the gun patting yourself on the back. He'd been so cocksure he could hold her at arm's length after holding her skin-to-skin close as she'd gone up in flames. And he'd done it, too, by God. Except…

All he had wanted to do, itched to do, was dying to do, beneath all that self-congratulatory restraint, was take her back to bed.

Glacier, Hamilton. Remember the fucking glacier.

But that was hard to do when the thing was evaporating like mist in the jungle, turning his brain into one big steam bath. His anger was gone, his cool shot to hell. All he had left was a raging red-hot case of lust.

"Is that what you really want?" he asked her hoarsely. "You want me to leave?"

She obviously read his mood, for her eyes changed, went dark and aware. But she angled her chin up at him. "Yes, I—"

"Because I want what we had in that room in L.A." Only he'd have more control this time. He'd make her come again and again and again while staying a little bit removed. While staying in command.

"Oh, *now* you're interested in having sex again?" Her eyes narrowed. "What, you suddenly decide I wasn't so lousy at it after all?"

"What?" He stared down at her in shock. "Who the hell said anything about you being lousy at it?"

"You've been avoiding me ever since we did the deed, haven't you?"

"Because I'm supposed to be keeping you safe, not fucking you!"

"Which—let me guess—became a consideration only after you discovered how lousy I was in the sack."

"No, which became a consideration when I quit thinking with my little head long enough to realize how unprofessional I'd been. But you… Damn, Peej, where do you get these ideas? You are so far from lousy I can't believe the thought even crossed your mind."

"I am?" The heartbreaking hope in her golden brown eyes gave him a flashback to the thirteen-year-old he'd once known. Then she gave him another shove. "Yeah, right. You're just saying that now because you're horny."

"I'm saying it because it's true." He held her gaze,

thinking surely she couldn't look into his eyes and doubt that. In the spirit of full disclosure, however, he did admit, "I confess to being horny, too, but that's hardly new territory. It seems to be a constant state around you."

She blew a short, pithy raspberry.

"What, you think I'm kidding?" Bending his head, he pressed his mouth to the side of her neck. Her skin was smooth and fragrant and he flicked it with his tongue.

Shivers raced down P.J.'s thighs, a condition that only grew worse when he moved his lips to her ear.

"You remember the night we spent in that new construction site?" he asked. "The night of the storm?"

"Of course I do." She remembered every moment of every day they'd spent together. The night he was talking about had been dark, wet and chilly, with wild displays of lightning and thunder that had scared her silly.

"We'd been cuddling to try and stay warm and you got mad when I moved away. You thought it was because I was getting ready to leave you. But you wanna know the real reason I quit holding you, P.J.?" He didn't wait for her to say yes or no. "I moved because the feel of you against me was starting to give me a hard-on."

Her head reared back, smacking the wall. "Did *not!*" Fingers automatically homing in on the spot she'd just hit, she gingerly massaged the hurt away. But her attention was fixed on Jared.

"Did so. You were only thirteen and I felt like a

perv, but I had a boner a cat couldn't scratch." Brushing her hair aside, he resumed kissing her neck.

Heat shot down her spine and she jerked skittishly. "What are you *doing?*" She batted at his shoulders. "Two seconds ago you were giving me your big screwing-you-is-unprofessional spiel. What happened to that?"

"It went up in smoke." He took the step closer that brought their bodies together and bent his knees until their eyes met. "And you know what? I don't care. Hell, I pretty much patterned myself after Rocket and he slept with my sister when he was working for her. It didn't seem to hurt his professional image any."

"Yeah, well, weren't they pretending to be engaged? You plan on sacrificing yourself on the altar of matrimony for the sake of a little nookie?"

"No." He stepped back smartly. "Uh-uh, no, ma'am. Listen, Peej, you were everything to me as a kid and you're more special than any other woman I know. But I'm not the marrying kind. Trust me on this—I don't have the chops to make a woman happy for more than a week or two running."

Somehow she doubted that. He was handsome, he was rich and he was rock steady. Looks and money might disappear over time, but the steadiness, his sexy competence…*that* would be with him forever. It would always make a woman feel safe.

Still, all the places made warm by having his body pressed against hers felt downright chilly with the distance he'd put between them. And who the hell asked him to marry her anyhow? "Do I *look* like I'm dying to have you drop to your knees and propose?"

His eyebrows met above the thrust of his nose. "No." He sounded almost surly, as if she'd offended him or something. But that was ridiculous—he could only be insulted if he wanted her to marry him, and he'd just made a huge production out of telling her otherwise. So how needy did it make her that she was reading nuances into a matter where none existed?

She scowled. "Then get over yourself. Maybe you should just lay out what it is you do want."

His expression underwent yet another transformation and he stepped forward again. Looking down at her with sexual heat in his gaze, he bowed his head to bring his lips to her ear. "Well, for starters—" the gravelly purr insinuating itself down the whorls made the short hairs on her neck stand on end "—I want to lick you all over."

Luckily the wall at her back was holding her up because her knees turned to Jell-O. Locking them, she gave him her coolest appraisal. "Maybe I don't want to be licked by someone who, by his own admission, can't produce the goods for more than a week or two."

That amused him, apparently, for she felt his lips curve against her ear. "Oh, I can produce, baby. The question is how long good sex will outweigh my defects in your eyes." He swiveled his hips against hers and his erection was a hard, heavy ridge pressing the folds of her skirt between her legs.

She lowered her lids to prevent him from seeing her

eyes cross. "Well, I'll tell you what." Proud of how composed she sounded, she tugged his T-shirt from the waistband of his jeans. After a second spent admiring the hard, flat planes she'd exposed, she looked up to meet his gaze. "Why don't you shoot for a brand-new personal best here? I'm happy to do the wild thing with you, but only if you try to keep those defects to a minimum until the end of the tour. The last thing we need is a big breakup in the middle of it. I don't think I can take the drama of having to work with someone I've just dumped."

"Yes, ma'am." He unfastened the long row of tiny pearlescent buttons down the front of her aqua top. "I'll do my best to keep you pleased." Wrapping his hands around her hips, he straightened to his full height, lifting her against the wall.

Then he kissed her, full-tilt boogie.

Adrift in an immediate maelstrom of sensation, she anchored herself by wrapping her arms around his neck and her legs around his waist.

He slid his hands beneath her skirt and grasped her bottom, his splayed fingers so hot through the fragile satin of her panties that she wouldn't be surprised if they melted beneath his touch. Snugging her to the steely length of his penis, he rocked against her with carnal intent. He was the barest fraction off-target and, crossing her ankles behind his back, she lifted the millimeter it took to make that hard ridge hit just the right spot. "Oh!" she whispered against his marauding mouth, her fingers biting into his shoulders. "Oh, *please.*"

And please her he did—until she hurtled off the edge of the universe.

"God." He continued grinding against her, prolonging her orgasm. "That *sound.* You squeaked just like that when you yawned outside the dressing room earlier." She went limp against him and he stepped back, gathering her in his arms before she could slide bonelessly to the floor. He carried her over to the bed, laid her upon the coverlet and came down on top of her, bracing himself on his forearms. "I'd been trying like hell to stay away from you," he said in a rough voice. "Then you made that I'm-coming sound and it damn near erased all my hard-won resolve. I wanted to nail you right there against the door in the amphitheater corridor."

"Ah." Her heart gave a mad thump, but she nodded sagely. "That explains your hotfooting it down the hall for a chair when there were probably a couple in the dressing room. Which I appreciated, by the way, since it allowed me to make my escape."

"Don't remind me. We're going to talk about that...but not right this minute." He slid down her body, divesting her of clothing as he went. "I've still got that licking fantasy to fulfill."

She was limper than a plate of overcooked fettuccini by the time he finished with her more than an hour later. "You've gotta quit doing that," she murmured into the chest she lay half draped over.

"Doing what?" He stroked her from the top of her head to the base of her spine.

"Giving me too many orgasms."

His hand stilled. Raising his head and tucking his chin, he stared down at her, his eyebrows elevated. "Is that even possible?"

"You wouldn't think so, would ya? Yet it is if you only get one and I get, like, a bazillion."

"So coming a lot is a bad thing?"

She blew out a breath and found the energy to lift her head long enough to stack her hands on his warm chest. She propped her chin on them. "'Course not. But if it's such a good thing, then why are you only having one to my many?"

"Hello!" He circled a hand over her bottom. "Women—multiple orgasms." He made the same gesture over his sex, which currently lay dormant upon his thigh. "Men—recovery time."

"Fine. But I'm an equal-opportunity lover. And I'm sure you could manage to get it up twice. You took an hour with me before you even dropped your pants. And maybe you could cut my orgasms down to, oh, say, four. That way you'd be ahead one hundred percent, and I—well, maybe I might be able to summon the energy to move in something under an hour. Right now I've got spaghetti bones."

He laid his head back on the pillow and resumed stroking her. "Well, okay. But I gotta warn you, once I cut back I might not be willing to pick up a heavier load again. So don't come whining to me if you want more and I say no."

"I'll try my best to keep a stiff upper lip," she said dryly.

"See that you do."

Eventually they had to get up and get dressed, but P.J. retained her ultra-mellow mood during the drive back to the amphitheater and all through sound check. Walking over to the bus to grab a couple items to take back to the hotel with her, she gave Jared a lazy smile. "Man. I feel amazing. Usually I only feel this relaxed after a shot or two of Wild Turkey."

"I'm glad to be of assistance." He hooked an arm around her shoulders and looked down at her. "Not to rain on your parade, but we have to talk about you ditching me this morning."

"Must we? I told you, I needed a break and you were just adding to my stress level."

"I'm sorry about that. But I'm being paid to see to it that you don't go off by yourself. Trust me, you don't want to be on your own if the whack job, as you called him, makes a return appearance."

"Oh, please." She stopped at the door to the bus and looked up at him. "Do you honestly believe he was anything but a one-shot deal?"

"I hope to hell he was exactly that. I really do. But as I told you before, I'm not betting your safety on it."

Because she understood what he was saying on an intellectual level—even while the thought of constant surveillance felt stifling on an emotional one—she let it go. "Hi, Marvin," she greeted the driver as the door swished open and she boarded the bus.

"Hiya, Miz Morgan. I put your package on your bed."

"Thanks," she said absently, thinking ahead to what she needed to grab. She strode straight toward her stateroom.

"What package?" Jared asked.

"The one the security guy said Miz Morgan told him to give me to put in her room."

"Is that true?" he called after her. "Were you expecting something from last week's shopping trip, maybe?"

"Hmm?" She greeted Hank as she passed him lounging in an open-curtained sleeping berth reading a James Lee Cooper book, then entered her room. "Oh, look!" she said, dropping her purse on the built-in counter and crossing to the beautifully wrapped package on her bed.

It was fairly large, about the size of three stacked boot boxes. She reached for the iridescent ribbon.

"Don't touch that!"

She gaped over her shoulder at Jared as he burst into the room. "What?"

"Did you or did you not ask a security guard to deliver this to your room?"

"No. Of course not."

He squatted down to inspect the package. "Well, that's what the man who delivered it told Marvin." He pressed his ear to the side of the package. "And you don't open unexplained gifts without a few precautions."

"No, I suppose not. Is it *ticking?*"

"No." He looked up at her. "Go stand outside the door."

"What? No."

Jared rose to his feet, grasped her by the shoulders and backed her out the door. "Stay there."

"I'm not going to leave you to deal with that on your own."

"Stay there!" he barked. "Dealing with it is my job."

Hank rolled out of the berth behind her. "What's going on?"

"Unexplained package," Jared said succinctly. "See that she stays out of the room."

"You got it."

"Hank," she protested, but he merely wrapped a sinewy arm around her shoulders and hugged her to his side. She watched with her heart in her mouth as Jared went back to the package.

He examined it up, down and sideways, then reached for the tips of the ribbon.

She held her breath as he untied it, but nothing happened. Nothing happened when he carefully unwrapped it, either. But she saw his back stiffen when he lifted its lid free with a ballpoint pen.

"What?" she demanded, pulling against Hank's hold. "What is it?"

"Shit," Jared said.

She broke free and crossed the room, but stopped dead when she saw what the package contained. Her lips drew back from her teeth in revulsion.

For uncoiling out of the box, tongue flicking and head weaving, was a big orange and gold snake.

CHAPTER SIXTEEN

Hyperlink, www.JuicyCountry.com
Priscilla Jayne Named Among Country's
Top 10 Cuties

"OMIGAWD, OMIGAWD, OMIGAWD." P.J. couldn't backpedal from the bed fast enough. But neither could she seem to rip her gaze from the narrow, reptilian head rising above the lip of the box. She watched hypnotized as the snake slithered over the container's side. When it touched the comforter and began to wind across the bed, Jared tossed aside the box lid and grabbed it.

"Are you crazy?" Her backward momentum stopped dead. "Don't *touch* it! It might be poisonous."

"No." He grasped the snake behind its narrow head and just above its tapered tail and, holding it up, stretched the reptile out to what appeared to be a full six feet. "It's a corn snake. I knew a jarhead in North Carolina once who had one for a pet. They're nonpoisonous."

"He had a snake for a *pet?*" She shivered. "I bet he didn't have a lot of girlfriends."

"No shit," Hank agreed.

Jared looked up from studying the snake. "You don't think he's kind of pretty? Look at this coloring."

And from a distance the reptile did have a beauty of sorts. Its skin was gold with vibrant red-orange markings outlined in brown. Had it been behind glass in a zoo, she might even have admired it.

But it wasn't, and she didn't.

"Hank," Jared said. "Check inside the box to see if there's a message. Then get the lid, will you? Try not to touch either too much, though, if you can avoid it. The cops will probably want to dust it for prints."

Hank brushed by her and leaned to peer in the box. "There is something here." He pulled out a sheet of paper by its upper-right corner and traded it for the box lid on the bed. "Ready when you are."

They worked like a team of long standing as Jared returned the snake to the box and Hank slipped on the lid to secure it. Then J bent to read the paper. She and Hank crowded in on either side to see what it said.

I WILL SEND THE TEETH OF BEASTS UPON THEM, WITH THE POISON OF SERPENTS OF THE DUST.
YOU HAVE FAILED TO HONOR THY MOTHER AS THE BIBLE INSTRUCTS.

"It's the same person, isn't it," she said. The tone was consistent with the last message. She glanced uneasily at the box. "Are you sure that snake's not poisonous?"

"Yes. But I'll get on the horn with the cops." Using

his palms on the corners of the box, Jared lifted it off the bed and set it out in the hall. He was already pulling his cell phone from his pocket as he stepped back into the room.

"What 'them'?" she asked suddenly. When both men gave her a blank look, she said, "It says 'I will send the teeth of beasts upon them.' What them? He sent the snake to me."

"It's a biblical reference," Hank said. "From 'Moses' Song' in Deuteronomy. The 'them' refers to the Israelites." When both she and Jared stared at him, he shrugged, flashing them a wry smile. "I'm a southern boy. That's pretty much synonymous with being raised in the church."

Jared turned his attention to the 911 dispatcher that had obviously just picked up and P.J. moved closer to Hank.

"So what this guy is saying, then, is that he's not happy about Mama's version of our relationship? Like *he* knows anything about it." But she waved the brief flash of bitterness aside. "Good thing I had you to interpret, Hank, because I'm not sure I'd have gotten it without you. Seems to me he'd have a better chance putting his message across if he used something that everybody's familiar with whether they're churchgoers or not. You know, like the Lord's Prayer or that Lord is my Shepherd psalm. I know neither makes the point he's trying to get across, but still, there must be something more well known." Her eyes lit up. "I know, maybe that 'a thankless child is sharper than a serpent's tooth' thing. I would've gotten that one."

"Except it's not from the Bible," Hank said.

"Oh." She grimaced. "I guess that shows how important Mama thought religion was to my upbringing. It *sounds* like something that might be in the Bible."

"Yeah, it does. It's Shakespeare, though, and this guy is clearly a zealot, so I doubt that in his mind a playwright's words would fit the bill. Religion's his thing."

"Sending snakes to people he doesn't know anything about doesn't seem very Christian to me."

"I'm talking about the way he apparently views himself, Peej. You're right, though, it isn't the way I was taught. My God is benevolent. And even to the hell and brimstoners, Romans clearly says, 'Vengeance is mine; I will repay, saith the Lord. Therefore if thine enemy hunger, feed him; if he thirst, give him drink. For in doing so thou shalt heap coals upon his head'." He reached out and squeezed her hand. "Which is probably more information than you want or need. This kind of shit just burns me up, though. The guy who sent that snake might consider himself some onward Christian soldier, but that's bull. He's nothing but a stalker."

"Oh God." Ice formed in her stomach as she gaped at Hank. "I hadn't thought about it like that, but that's exactly what this is, isn't it? Stalking. Like with John Lennon."

Sliding his cell phone back into his pocket, Jared rejoined them. "I know it's easier said than done not to worry," he said. "But try at least not to let it make you crazy."

"I know." She grimaced with self-deprecation. "I'm hardly in Lennon's class."

"That's not what I'm saying. I just meant that I'm going to take care of this before it has the chance to escalate to that sort of violence."

"What happened to calling in the cops?"

"Oh, I called them. Unfortunately there's no telling when they'll get here, since no one was hurt or is in immediate danger. That's a good thing, but it makes us a low priority so it could be a while. I think we should put the box in one of the free berths to keep from contaminating it any more than we already have. I can't imagine them not dusting for prints when they get here. If we're lucky our guy will be in the system and that will be the end of it."

"I wouldn't count on it if P.J. is the first person he's stalked," Hank said.

"I know. And I don't plan on standing around waiting for information they may or may not feel like sharing with us even if he is." Jared stowed the box in a berth. Pulling the accordion curtain closed, he called, "Marvin!"

"Yes, sir?" Marvin appeared in the hallway entrance.

"Tell me everything you can remember about the man who delivered the package for Miss Morgan."

The driver blinked, frowned in obvious thought, then said, "He was probably somewhere in his mid-fifties and fit for his age. He was medium tall—say five-ten or -eleven—and he had on a black security uniform."

"I'll check on the color of Red Rock's, but I doubt it will be that easy. How about his hair? What color was it?"

Sweat trickled down Marvin's temple. "Um, I didn't notice. He had on the kind of hat you'd see on cops at a police funeral. You know, like when they're in their dress uniforms?"

"You're very observant," Jared said, but he had to work to keep his voice easy. Because while he spoke the truth, he wanted more. He wanted total recall. He drew and exhaled a calming breath. "Just close your eyes for a minute. Maybe it'll come to you."

Marvin did as he was told, but after a minute his eyes popped open again and he shook his head. "What was in the box, Mr. Hamilton?" he asked anxiously. "Am I in trouble? Because I'm sorry, but it didn't even occur to me to question him when he said Miz Morgan had asked him to deliver her package to the bus. He knew my name, so I just assumed—"

Jared straightened. "He knew your name?"

"Yes, sir."

He turned to P.J. "Where have you said Marvin's name publicly?"

"I—I—I." Biting off the stutter, she stared up at him. Shook her head. "Nowhere."

"Think, Peej. Your driver's name isn't the sort of thing that would be common knowledge, so it's unlikely the man just pulled it out of thin air. I've heard you talk to your audiences at concerts. Have you mentioned Marvin at one of them maybe, or to a backstage worker somewhere? A roadie or makeup woman or—"

"No, I swear."

"During a radio interview?"

"No." Then she paused. "Wait. Yes."

Yes! Now they were getting somewhere. The probability of finding the guy went up significantly with a concrete place to start. "When?"

"It was..." Brow furrowing, she trailed off into silence. "Damn, I can't remember!"

"It's okay," he said softly. "Don't try to force it. Do what I suggested to Marvin. Just close your eyes and let your mind drift."

"Brown!" Marvin exclaimed out of the blue. When everyone looked at him, he said, "The man's hair was sort of sandy-brown and cut short. It might have been graying a bit at the temples."

Jared grinned and slapped the driver on the back. "Good work. When the cops show up, let's see if we can get them to hook you up with a sketch artist."

"Yes, excellent work, Marvin," P.J. said, reaching to pat the driver's hand. "And I'm sorry I put you in this position. Because I do remember now—I mentioned your name on the first satellite radio interview I did. The DJ and I had been talking about the tavern gigs I'd done on my way to Portland. And when he asked if I planned to continue driving myself to the other cities on the tour I said no and mentioned your name."

"It's not a problem, Miz Morgan. I feel bad I let him bamboozle me."

"I suggest we all do better from now on," Jared cut in. "Marvin, we'll make you a list of the people we want to get through to us. You don't accept anything from anyone who's not on it. And, P.J., do not give out any more personal information. Not your friends' names, not the type or color of vehicle you drive and certainly not where you live when you're not on the road."

"Oh, crap. My transgressions just keep piling up."

He turned a slow stare on her. "Meaning?"

Looking guilty, she nevertheless shot her pointy little chin up at him. "That interview where I mentioned Marvin? I also told the DJ I'd bought my first real home in Aspen."

"Dammit, P.J.!" Then he shook off his frustration. Glommed on to his professionalism. "No, it's all right. I would have liked to've known about it a little sooner, but it's all right. The bad news here is also the good news—this guy is clearly trailing you, not hanging around Aspen looking to burn down your house. All the same, I'll call Gert and have her arrange to have a guard put on it."

"Okay, boss."

His first inclination was to snarl that he wasn't screwing around here. But giving her a quick, close inspection, he saw that she knew that. Signs of strain showed beneath her flippancy, and he tamped down a temper he had no business experiencing in the first place. "I should have asked for tapes of the interviews. If I had we would have talked about this sooner and some of the measures I intend to take now would already be in place. I apologize. I should have anticipated something like this." What was it about her, anyway, that got under his skin so easily?

Her head snapping up, she shot him a look of disgust. "Oh, get over yourself, Hamilton. Who the hell could've foreseen a whack job like this popping up?"

"I should have. This tour has you in the public eye and there's been a ton of publicity about you lately. That's exactly the kind of situation that brings out the crazies." But that horse had left the barn, so he shrugged. "What radio station was that interview on? That would give us a more exact place to start."

"I don't remember off the top of my head. Somewhere in the Midwest—in Iowa, I think. Nell would have a copy of the schedule."

The police still hadn't arrived when it was time for P.J. to go to the amphitheater to have her hair and makeup done. But Rocket showed up. After looking to Jared for permission, Marvin let John onto the bus.

His brother-in-law looked as easy as ever as he climbed aboard. Stopping in front of P.J., he gave her a gentle smile. "How are you doing?"

"I'm freaked," she said. "And angry. But basically okay. What are you doing here?"

"Jared called me."

He nodded an acknowledgment when she glanced over at him. "I need to stay here to wait for the police to show up and I don't want you going anywhere alone."

"I put in a call to Detective Ellis," John said, naming a detective they'd both worked with in the past. "Of course, the problem here is jurisdiction, and this belongs to Morrison rather than Denver. Still, she said she'd reach out and see if she couldn't get someone out here ASAP. Meanwhile—" Turning to P.J., he offered his arm. "Whataya say, sweetheart? Can I escort you to the amphitheater?"

P.J. FRETTED ABOUT THE quality of her upcoming performance as she sat through makeup and hair. She was tense and upset and as much as she didn't want it to affect the concert, she didn't see how it could help but do precisely that.

But she'd forgotten to take into account the number-one factor of her existence. Music was, and always had been, her drug of choice. And when she strode out onto the stage and saw the navy sky framed by two soaring three-hundred-foot red sandstone monoliths that were floodlit from below, when she opened her mouth to belt out her first number and the shifting sea of humanity that spread up the slope before her roared to its feet in response, it was the remedy she needed for what ailed her.

Just as it had always been. Euphoria flooded her veins, washing out all the sick anger that had lodged in her stomach ever since she'd seen that snake, read that note. By the time they wrapped up the first song, she knew it was going to be a concert for the record books. "Hello, Red Rocks!"

The audience screamed greetings back.

"Is this the greatest natural amphitheater in the world, or what?"

The roar of nine thousand throats agreed that it was.

When the concert came to a thunderous conclusion an hour and a half later, she was perspiring freely. Clammy clothing and frizzing hair aside, however, she felt marvelous. Accepting a hand towel from Nell when she finally exited the stage, she grinned at her friend and danced in place. "Wow. Was that the best one ever, or what?"

"You rocked," Nell agreed. "I was ready to commiserate with you over that snake business, but you obviously found a way to get past it."

"I was really worried that my performance would reflect how much it shook me up, but I dunno—I got out there and the music just took me away. This has got to be the most beautiful venue I've ever played, and the acoustics are stunning."

"They're incredible," Hank agreed, joining them. "Dynamite concert."

"We were jammin'!" Eddie enthused, strolling up.

"God, weren't we?" She bumped her fist companionably against her band members' arms, then danced in place again, finding it difficult to stand still under the residual adrenaline still surging through her bloodstream. "I was just telling Nell that I thought it was our best one yet."

Jared came over. "Great concert."

She grinned. "That seems to be the general consensus." She looked around for the tall man who had stood watch over her before the show. "Where's John?"

"The cops finished with me just about the time the show began, so I sent him back to catch the rest of it with Tori, Esme and Mac. Let's get you out of here," he said, his gaze in constant motion as he monitored the postconcert activity gearing up in the backstage area. "This is a little too public for my liking." Sliding his hand beneath her elbow, he started to lead her away—and not in the direction of the dressing room.

"Wait, wait!" She pulled against his light grasp, but he didn't let go. "Where are we going? Your family is supposed to meet us back here."

"I told them to meet us at the hotel instead." He turned to Nell, Hank and Eddie. "You're welcome to come, as well."

"Did you get rid of the snake?" P.J. demanded, tapping her foot impatiently until he turned his attention back to her.

"Yes. The cops took it."

"Okay, good." She turned to Nell. "I checked into a room at the T—"

Jared clapped his hand over her mouth. "Keep your voice down."

She nodded and he removed his hand. "I took a room at the Teatro for the next three nights," she said very quietly, finding herself checking out everyone around her, as well. "If you don't want to stay on the bus tonight I'll get you rooms there, too."

"Not this kid," Eddie said. "I've got me a place to stay. In fact, I'd better go find my date. Fan-freakin-tastic show, Peej. Sorry 'bout the snake. There's sure as shit some sick sumbitches out there." Picking up his instrument case, he strolled away.

P.J. turned to Nell. "How about you? Would you like a room in an honest-to-God hotel for a change?"

"Oh. Well." Nell turned to Hank. "Are you staying on the bus?"

"Yes."

"Then thanks for the offer, Peej, but I'll be fine here," she said. "I'd be nervous on my own, but as long as Hank's going to be there I won't have a problem." She gave him an uncertain look. "That is, unless you have other plans?"

"Nope. Why don't we pop us up some popcorn and give that song you've been working on a whirl?"

Nell shot him a brilliant smile. "That sounds like an excellent plan."

A few short moments later P.J. found herself tucked into Jared's Jeep, headed back to Denver. She yawned as the last of her adrenaline drained away. Suddenly she was exhausted.

He glanced over at her. "You coming down off that Rocky Mountain high?"

"Yeah. Pretty obvious, huh? Between the snake and Red Rocks, I was all jacked up. It was one great concert, though. I'd play that venue again in a heart-beat." She shoved herself upright. "What did the cops say, J? Am I going to have to talk to them?"

"No. They dusted for prints and had Marvin work with a sketch artist. Between the first threat, the radio interview, which Nell says was in Iowa City, and today's gift, there are three states involved. So the Morrison police are going to send everything to the FBI."

"God, what a mess. Do you have a copy of the sketch? Maybe I'll recognize the man."

"I'll show it to you later. For now, though, why don't you concentrate on hanging on to that good feeling the show gave you. I know my sister is looking forward to seeing you again."

That brought up a worry of another kind. "What should I do about refreshments? We oughtta offer your family something, but I don't know if we should stop at a deli or order up room service or what." She gave him a tired smile. "You can take the girl out of the honky-tonk but you just can't take that honky-tonk outta the girl."

He looked over at her. "Do you feel like shopping?"

"Not really."

"Then we'll raid the minibar or order up a pot of coffee and some cake or something."

Jared's family and Gert were in the lobby when they arrived and P.J. got a sudden second wind. Laughing, she crossed to greet them.

Esme swooped over to meet her halfway. "Omigawd," she said. "That was the most awesome concert I've ever attended!"

"I felt like it was the best I'd ever given," she agreed. "Isn't that amphitheater something?"

She reached Gert, Victoria and John, but as she started to greet them Jared interrupted. "Let's take this upstairs."

So she snuck peeks at Tori as they walked over to the bank of elevators. "You haven't changed at all," she said as a car arrived and they all stepped in.

The tall brunette laughed and leaned to give her a

smacking kiss on the lips. "That's a bold-faced lie, you sweet thing," she said, patting a hip that might be more padded than it had been fifteen years ago. "But a delightful one, so thank you. You have. You're all grown-up. And so talented."

P.J. actually felt a blush flowing upward from her chest. Shyness had never been her particular curse and she possessed a healthy ego when it came to her talent. Yet an unaccustomed bashfulness overtook her now. "You liked the concert then?" This woman had formed the gold standard of parenting for more than half of her life. Suddenly being face-to-face with her felt like communing with a goddess.

"I *loved* your concert. I stand in awe of your talent."

A huge smile split her face. "I stand in awe of yours, too. I still have the dollhouse you gave me."

"You do?" Victoria looked delighted to hear it.

"Yes. It's one of my most prized possessions. I keep it in my bedroom in my house in Aspen." Stopping in front of the suite, she handed Jared the key card and reached to give Gert a hug. "I'm sorry. I didn't mean to ignore you."

"I don't need entertaining, missy. You had some catching up to do and I was happy to listen. Here." The older woman thrust a foil-covered plate at her. "I brought you some brownies."

"Omigawd." She laughed with delight. "This is perfect. I'll order us up some coffee to go with it."

"Would you mind making mine tea?" Esme asked as they trooped into the suite.

"I'd prefer that, too," Tori agreed. "I'll be zooming 'til dawn if I drink coffee at this hour."

"I'll order a pot of each. And check the minifridge if there's anything else you'd rather have. I know there's a few little bottles of wine in there and there might be beer."

The impromptu party turned out to be so successful it didn't break up until after two o'clock in the morning. After bidding a final farewell to Gert and the Miglionnis, she closed the door behind them, looked at Jared and sighed. "Your family is so great. Do you have any idea how lucky you are to have them?"

He studied her soberly, then reached out to gently grasp her elbow and escort her back into the suite. "Yeah," he said softly. "Yeah, I think I do."

She gazed at him a moment, then said reluctantly, "I suppose I ought to look at that artist's sketch now."

Jared extracted it from a folder on the desk and handed it to her.

Holding her breath, she looked down at it. Then she blew it out in a single harsh exhalation. "I've never seen him before." Rubbing her temples between her thumbs and fingers, she stared up at him. "God, Jared. What am I going to do?"

"Tonight?" he asked gently, smoothing a strand of her hair back into place. "Not a damn thing. Come on." He reached for the buttons on her little gauze top, his gaze filled not with the sexual heat she expected but rather a fierce tenderness that squeezed her heart. "Let's go to bed. Things will look better in the morning."

CHAPTER SEVENTEEN

Headline, *Country Billboard*:
Third Single From Priscilla Jayne's *Watch Me Fly* Album Hits Top Twenty. "Designated Driver" Flying High!

"NO, NO, NO, NO. THAT'S wrong." Nell nudged Hank's shoulder with her own to halt his rendition of her song. "That should be middle C, not an octave below."

Her aroma, a pleasant mixture of soap, shampoo and a hint of perfume, drifted through his senses, and he took a deeper breath to enjoy it more fully. When he turned his head to look at her, he discovered that their faces were suddenly very close.

He cleared his throat. Recalled what they were discussing and sat a little straighter. "I'm telling you, it doesn't sound right in middle C. It's not a dramatic enough change. Listen—and this time don't interrupt until I'm done. Keep Peej's voice in mind." Tucking his fiddle back under his chin, he played her arrangement with the change he'd put in. "Now listen to it your way." He played it as written on the sheet music in his lap.

"*No,* I'm sorry, but you're just plain wr—" She fell silent midprotest, her gaze turning inward as if she were listening to the music again in her head. Then her gaze sharpened on him. "Damn. You're right, it does sound better an octave down. It's unpredictable and more interesting. And with P.J.'s range, that dropping down from second F will probably be the section that ends up sticking in everyone's head."

Snatching the score up off his lap, she reached for her mechanical pencil and erased the half note, replacing it with its lower-octave equivalent. Then, tossing the pencil aside, she curled a soft-skinned hand around the back of his neck, jerked him close and planted a smacking kiss on his lips. She pulled back, turning him loose and giving him a big grin. "You're a genius. Pass me that popcorn."

His brain stalled out like a prop plane with a faulty fuel gauge. Almost instantly, it came roaring back, but as if his life had flashed before his eyes during that lost second, everything suddenly looked brighter, tasted sweeter. He wanted to grab her and pull her back for a deeper kiss. But he froze in his seat, fearing he recognized a friendly peck when he felt one and knowing it would kill him if he had to watch her expression turn from admiration to horror. He held the neck of his fiddle in a death grip and unclenched his fingers one by one until he could set the instrument aside and reach for the bowl of popcorn. He passed it to Nell.

"Thanks."

"Sure." He racked his brain for something to say

that didn't have the words "kiss me" and "please, please, please" in it. His gaze landing on the score, he shot her a little sideways smile. "These lyrics crack me up every time I read them. I guess we can safely say you're over Eddie, huh?" *Jesus, man. That's it?* He could have kicked his own butt around the block. *Your big move is to remind her of Faithless Eddie? No wonder women don't beat a path to your door.*

Thrusting his hand into the popcorn bowl, he grabbed a fistful of the buttered kernels and stuffed them into his mouth before he could embarrass himself with additional inanities. Lord have mercy, he was one smooth operator. Why his mama hadn't named him Lady Killer instead of Hank remained the mystery of the century.

Luckily Nell didn't seem to notice his pitiful small-talk skills. "I am so over him," she agreed. "I'm embarrassed my crush lasted as long as it did. What am I, twelve?" Shaking her head, she cast a rueful glance down the length of her mature, comfortably plump body. "I'd have a hard sell trying to convince anyone of that."

"I wouldn't beat myself up about it if I were you. Eddie has that effect on women. He's got some crazy-ass charisma that I've never understood." He shrugged. "But then I'm not a woman."

"No, you're definitely not that," she agreed. "And yes, Eddie does come off as charismatic. But it's a superficial charm that only goes so far. Once it wears thin he has zero substance to take its place." She shot him a look from beneath her lashes and reached for another handful of popcorn. "Unlike you, who doesn't come across as magnetic at first glance but has substance to burn." Her gaze locked on his, she opened her fist to allow several kernels to trickle into her mouth.

Was she *flirting* with him? He gave the idea a second's thought, then had to stop himself from uttering a skeptical snort. Yeah, right. *You wish, pal.*

He did wish, even though his logical self knew she was just giving him one of those strokes that friends give friends. Their bare feet were propped on a stool she'd dragged out of the stateroom, and he gave the ball of hers a nudge with his big toe. "So let me get this straight—you don't think I'm just bristling with magnetism? Well, hell. I'm completely demoralized."

She blew a short, pithy raspberry.

"What, you think I'm kidding? Listen." He cupped his fingers behind his ear. "Hear that whizzing sound? That's my ego flying around the room backward like a loose balloon. Pretty soon there's not gonna be anything left but its little eyes bugging out. This is it. My life as I know it is over."

She laughed as if he were the wittiest man on earth. Once she wound down, she slumped against his side, holding her stomach. Tilting her head back, she studied him for a moment, then smiled. "You've got butter on your lips, hotshot."

"Huh?" He found himself staring into her blue eyes. The lamplight picked out tiny flecks of gold around the pupil.

"Butter," she repeated and rolled up onto her hip. "Right here." Leaning into him, she lapped delicately at his bottom lip. She pulled back, looked into his eyes, then rose up onto her knees and swung one leg over to straddle his lap. "And right here." Lowering her head, she sipped his top lip between her own.

He grasped her hips, perhaps just a little too forcefully, and moved her back. Raising her head, she looked down at him.

"Don't mess with me if you don't mean it," he said, his voice a hoarse rasp. "Because I've had a jones for you for a helluva long time now."

"Yeah?" She gave him a brilliant smile. "You think I'm a red-hot mama?"

"Yes."

"Good. 'Cuz I've been thinking about what you'd look like naked ever since the day you walked into the galley without your shirt."

His heart kicked like a mule against the wall of his chest, and his hands holding her hips lost their fierce grip. "You have?"

"Mmm-hmm." She squirmed to straddle his lap once more and bent her head to nuzzle his lips. Pulling back just enough to gaze into his eyes, she whispered, "You've gotta know you're built, Hartley."

Happiness was a supernova in his chest. "I've been wanting to get my hands on you for what seems like forever." He did just that, smoothing his palms down the swell of her hips until his fingers finally anchored themselves in the full curves of her butt. Only a couple of thin layers of material separated his hands from her lush, warm flesh.

For the first time she looked uncertain. "I'm not exactly Miss America material, Hank."

"Could've fooled me, sweetheart."

"Oh." She blinked. "Good answer." Her lips curved into a pleased smile. "God, I like you. I think I like you more than any man I've ever known." Rising to her feet, she held a hand out to him. "What do you say we take this to my room?"

"Thank you, Jesus," he said fervently. "Well, that and, how did I get this lucky?"

ALTHOUGH THE MAN SAT surveillance outside the bus all night long, Priscilla Jayne never returned. It wasn't until dawn began sending pale fingers of sunlight across the grounds surrounding the amphitheater that he trudged back to the road where he'd left his rental car. This entire night, which had started out as if the light of Heaven itself shone upon it, had somehow gone straight to the devil.

He'd delivered his admonition to Priscilla Jayne without a hitch. Marvin the driver hadn't suspected a thing, as he had known he wouldn't. It was amazing how far the slightest personal knowledge could take an intelligent man.

He would have given a great deal to be a fly on the wall when Priscilla Jayne unwrapped his gift to her. Accepting the impossibility of his wish, however, he'd found a scalper and paid him a small fortune for a ticket to her show. Deeming it money well spent for the opportunity to see at least a residue of her reaction—no matter how diluted—he had looked forward to the moment he could observe the well-deserved look of fear and uncertainty on her face. He'd thought to catch a glimpse of the remorse she should be feeling, as well.

Yet had he seen any of that?

No.

She'd pranced out onto that stage and behaved as if it were the best night of her life.

He didn't understand it. Had she somehow not gotten his message? He couldn't fathom a scenario in which that was a possibility. He'd stood right there and watched her enter the bus. And although he'd had to leave to hunt up his concert ticket before she had come out again, the driver was certain to have told her she had a package. As any man could testify, one mention was all it would take, for women were greedy, grasping creatures by nature. There wasn't a single one of them who had the strength of character to resist the materialistic lure of a present.

No, she had to have opened it. It was inconceivable that she could have left it untouched.

But if that were so, why in the name of all that was holy hadn't she reacted properly? And just where was she?

Well, wherever it was, she was bound to be back fairly soon. She had a concert in Colorado Springs tonight and in the course of tracking her movements he'd come to realize she must attend to other matters before her shows. It was the only thing that made sense, because the bus always deposited her at the next destination with several hours to spare before that night's performance. So, good. He would take an hour to clean this park filth from his body, then he'd come back to resume his vigil. He needed to see her up close and personal before he could allow himself to rest.

He located a truck stop that was within reasonable distance from the amphitheater and drove there to avail himself of the showers. He was certain that grime clung to him with superglue adhesion, but because he feared he might miss something if he lingered too long, he didn't dare scour his body as many times as he ordinarily would to rid himself of it. He had to settle for scrubbing as hard as he could with his rough loofah instead.

It was the best he could do in the time he'd allowed himself, but it didn't feel like nearly enough. At least when he reached for his towel, however, his skin glowed a satisfying cleansed-soul red.

There was so much filth in the world. And while he knew dirt was part and parcel of nature and that it, too, had been designed by his Maker, he couldn't believe it was intended to touch his person.

Otherwise God wouldn't have given him this strong abhorrence toward it.

He arrived back at Red Rocks with ten minutes to spare in the hour he'd allowed himself. He might as well have spent the extra time in the shower that he'd cut short, because for all his rushing not a thing had changed. The singer's bus was still parked right where it had been when he'd left, and it still looked dark and deserted. He settled down to wait.

And he waited.

And waited.

And *waited.*

During the next several hours, the driver came and went a couple of times. The craggy-faced man with the dark hat and darker aspect who he'd seen in L.A. the night he had first tried to deliver the snake left once and returned. He knew from last night's performance that the man played banjo and fiddle in Priscilla Jayne's band. Both times that he'd seen him outside the bus today, the musician's arm had been draped around the shoulders of the woman with the messy hair and overblown body whom he also remembered from Los Angeles.

He didn't see the man with the watchful eyes.

And he did not see Priscilla Jayne. Not once.

When the band's blond guitar player arrived a short while later and the bus took off minus its star occupant, the man stalked back to his car.

This was unacceptable! It flew in the face of all that was right and moral. Priscilla Jayne was an impertinent daughter and no doubt a promiscuous one, as well, if she was sleeping somewhere other than on her bus. Not to mention that he had put a great deal of consideration into the type of lesson he could impart to warn her to mend her iniquitous ways. Yet had she shown the slightest respect for his efforts?

She had not. Women like her were faithless sinners and that was the truth.

Well, God never let sinners win.

At the same time, God helped those who helped themselves. And the man knew how to help himself. He was going to personally see to it that Priscilla Jayne did not get away with her flagrant disrespect. This was a fight for right and he had a zero-tolerance policy for those who persisted in straying.

His daughter, Mary, had been such a person. He had let her slip through his fingers and he'd been paying the price ever since. He was hanged if he'd tolerate another doing the same.

Not when he knew from hard experience that it led to nothing but trouble.

OH, BOY. SHE WAS IN trouble.

Big.

Big.

Trouble.

Settling into Jared's Jeep for the drive down to Colorado Springs, P.J. covertly studied him. How could she have been so dumb?

How could she have gone and fallen in love with him?

Okay, if she were to be completely factual—which in all honesty she would just as soon avoid—she would have to admit that she had probably been working her way toward this very moment ever since, oh, say…the instant she had opened her motel-room door in that hot

Texas panhandle town and clapped eyes on him again for the first time in fifteen years. It wasn't until last night, however, that he'd hammered that final nail into her coffin.

Because that was when Mr. Jared I'm-going-to-give-you-a-dozen-screaming-orgasms-before-I-allow-myself-my-measly-one Hamilton had forsworn the joys of putting her through her sexual paces to simply hold her in his arms until she'd fallen asleep.

She sighed as she thought of the way she'd tried to stay awake in order to prolong the sheer pleasure of being the recipient of that heart-melting tenderness.

"*What?*" he suddenly demanded.

She jumped, slapping a hand to her galloping heart as she blinked him back into focus. "Holy crap, you about gave me a heart attack!" Not to mention the imminent eyestrain she'd inflicted on herself in her fierce need to watch him from the corner of her eye while simultaneously looking inward at her dilemma. Pulling her knee up onto the seat, she swiveled to face him more squarely. "What d'you mean, *what?*"

"I mean what the hell was that sigh for? And how come you're staring at me."

"Was I staring?" Hey, when caught flatfooted, lie like a politician, that was her motto. "I was just thinking how different things are in Denver since the last time we were together here." That was actually the truth. She had thought about that more than once—just perhaps not right at this exact moment. "It's kind of surreal."

"I can see how it would be." He glanced over at her.

"Especially staying in an uptown hotel just off the Sixteenth Street Mall. How many of our days do you calculate we spent hanging out there?"

"Most of them. I certainly never imagined then that I'd someday stay in a place like the Teatro." A sudden chill passed over her body and she rubbed her bare arms. "And I sure never imagined having the career I have, let alone the stalker to go with it. I guess I really have hit the big time."

He reached over the console to give her knee a rub. Warmth sank into more places than where his hand touched. "I will keep you safe," he stated categorically. "And if the day ever comes when I don't feel I can do that on my own, I'll hire a frigging platoon of bodyguards."

Aw, man. And she was supposed to avoid loving this man *how?*

"I've been thinking about the situation quite a bit," he continued. "And it seems to me that this probably didn't come out of the blue."

She blinked at him. "What do you mean?"

"Do you read all your own fan mail?"

"Not anymore. I used to, but then it got to be too much. I receive more mail than I ever dreamed one person could get."

"So who reads it if you don't? And what happens to it afterward?"

"I've got a fan club that handles it. Why, do you think this guy might've written me?"

Jared nodded. "I think the chances are pretty good

that he has. This sort of thing usually escalates, so it's likely that it started with him sending you fan letters. I need the name of someone I can contact at your fan club to see about getting the letters."

"That would probably be Colleen Borts. She heads the club, at least, and she's superefficient. If anyone could answer your questions, it would be her. I don't know her number off the top of my head, but Nell has it on file."

She sat silent for a moment as he accelerated into the passing lane. But once he'd found a hole in the traffic, moved back into the right lane and resumed his normal speed, she blurted, "Jared, I have to warn you that there are literally thousands of letters." Just the idea of culling one from so many was daunting.

Not so to Jared apparently, for he merely shrugged. "All the more reason to believe a certain percentage of them come from the fringe element. Let's just hope the efficient Ms. Borts has culled those out and put them somewhere safe. Because that could give us the break we're looking for to stop this before it gets really ugly."

She'd swear her heart stopped beating. Then it kicked in, drumming out a faster rhythm than before. Suddenly a man who had been a minor irritant was a much bigger threat to her safety. Or at least that seemed to be the gist of what Jared was saying.

"Ugly." She repeated the word, staring at him. "Is that your take on this? That it's going to get a lot worse before it gets better?"

"I don't know what to think at this point, Peej." His

gaze, when he took it briefly from the road to meet hers, was serious. "I don't know enough yet to predict what the man is capable of. What I do know is that I intend to find out. In the meantime, though, I'm not going to sugarcoat it. I'd rather you be a little spooked, a little on edge, than forget to be aware of what's going on around you. So stay vigilant. But know this." He reached over once again to squeeze her knee. "Anybody looking to hurt you will have to go through me first. You can take that to the bank."

CHAPTER EIGHTEEN

Publishers Monthly's online Publisher's Brunch:
Jodeen Morgan sells *Ungrateful Child,* a tell-all Priscilla Jayne biography, to Janice Harper at Benton, in a five-figure deal by Sue Miller of
Miller Literary Management

GOOD GOD. COULD HE HAVE *sounded* any more melodramatic? Jared itched all over every time he thought of his big declaration.

Not that he hadn't meant it. Anyone wanting a piece of P.J. would have to go through him first. But he had a feeling he might have sounded perhaps a bit too fervent, maybe even to the point where he'd put ideas in her head that weren't destined to ever pan out.

Hell, what was he doing getting this cozy with her in the first place? This was P.J. he was talking about. P.J., who had meant more to him than damn near anyone in the world. The same P.J. who had disappeared from his life without a backward glance. He wasn't allowing himself to get that emotionally invested in her ever again. It hurt too much when she walked away, which she was sure to do once he eliminated this stalker business.

He glanced over at her. And promptly had to repeat his mantra when he saw how pale her face had become as she read from the stack of letters in front of her.

Don't go there, Slick. Gritting his teeth, he went back to his own stack of correspondence. He wasn't getting sucked in by that vulnerable aura of hers again. He'd been there, done that already. And look where it had gotten him, with P.J. gone and him picking up the pieces of his life with a big ol' gaping hole where her support and friendship should have been. Well, never again. He'd learned he could rely on his family and himself and no one else. It was time he started keeping that in mind.

He needed to pull back and put some distance between them, emotionally if not physically, since the latter wasn't achievable on the professional front. He had never claimed to be the cleverest man alive, but usually he only had to get his teeth kicked down his throat once before he learned his lesson. So they were going to have a talk the minute they were alone. He was going to lay down some guidelines so she couldn't claim he'd led her on or made her any promises, implicit or otherwise.

"Here's another I-want-to-marry-you-and-give-you-my-babies entry."

He looked at Hank, wincing when he saw P.J. shudder from the corner of his eye. "Damn. How many does that make?"

The fan club manager had come through for him. Colleen Borts had overnighted a box of the fan letters that she'd felt were disturbing and another that she'd found marginal. He would've preferred recruiting only Hank to help him go through the correspondence, but this was P.J.'s life and he could hardly keep her out of it when she insisted on being included. Besides, it was damn difficult to be the wall standing between her and danger if he was in one room while she was in another.

So here they all were, sitting around the table in the new suite he'd registered for her under his name at a new hotel, reading a disturbingly large number of crank letters.

"Twenty-seven," Nell said, answering the question he'd put to Hank.

"And how many are in the pile from the group I think oughtta be in jail?"

"Eleven."

"I guess there's some consolation in that, huh?" P.J.'s crooked smile didn't quite reach her eyes. "That there are fewer flat-out psychos than guys who just want to keep me barefoot and pregnant between tours?"

Nell scooted her chair closer to P.J.'s, wrapping an arm around her shoulders and giving her a hug. "I'm sorry, girlfriend. This really stinks. Are you sure you want to pore through all this crap? Hank and I could take over for a while if you'd like to go take a walk with Jared or something."

"No, I'm okay." Straightening, she reached for another handful of letters from the box in the middle of the table. "It's creepy and I can't honestly say it's not freaking me out. But it's actually better knowing what the letters say than to be left out of the loop and let my mind provide the content." Her smile was wry and barely there, but a little less forced this time. "I've got a very good imagination."

There was a knock at the door and everyone froze. Jared looked at P.J. "Are you expecting someone?"

"No."

"Then stay here. I'll get it."

When he reached the door he looked through the peephole, and surprise elevated his eyebrows. "Eddie?" he murmured aloud. He glanced over his shoulder at the group inside the suite. Focusing in on P.J. he said, "What's he doing here?"

"I don't know," P.J. said. "I gave him the name of the new hotel and the room number just like I did Hank and Nell, but I didn't actually expect to see him."

With a shrug, he opened the door to the guitar player.

"Hey," Eddie greeted him, sauntering into the hallway that led to the suite. "Whazzup?" Stopping in the archway, he looked at P.J., Hank and Nell around the table. "Hell, I didn't know it was a party. I guess my invite musta got lost in the mail." Coming closer, he peered down at the piles of correspondence on the table and his brow creased. "Whatcha all doin'?"

"Going through P.J.'s fan mail," Nell said.

Shaking his head, he gave them a pitying look. "It's Sunday, people. I mean, I love you to pieces, Peej, but reading your kudos is the best you could think to do on our one day off?"

"What are you doing here?" Hank demanded impatiently. "Why aren't you out with the catch of the day?"

Eddie grimaced and sank down in a chair at the table. "Turns out she was barely nineteen."

Everyone burst into laughter and Hank said what Jared at least was thinking. "You can't honestly have been surprised by that."

"Hey, I make it a point to check their ID," Eddie said with utter seriousness. He sank lower on his tailbone. "Only it turns out this girl's was fake." He shuddered. "Man, I don't ever wanna find myself up on statutory rape charges."

"That only happens if they're under eighteen," Jared assured him.

"Even so, man. I ain't interested in babies. They gotta be at least twenty-one." Picking up the letter closest him, he idly perused it. Then he snapped upright, dropping it on the table as if it had grown teeth. "What the—? That's one sick monkey!"

Jared picked it up and skimmed it. "Yep," he agreed, folding it back into its envelope. "It's another for the oughtta be in jail group."

"There's *more* like this? What the hell's going on?"

With the caveat that Eddie keep it under his hat, he filled the blond musician in. To his surprise, Eddie grabbed a handful of letters from the box and dug right in to help.

They fell back into the easy rhythm that the guitar player's unexpected arrival had momentarily disrupted. They were quiet for the most part, long stretches of uncomplicated silence broken by the occasional conversation or sporadic joke to ease the tension that far too many of these letters produced.

"This is kind of nice, being around adults," Eddie said out of the blue. "Young women have great bodies, but how often can you discuss their hair or their nails or what should be done about their bitch of a roommate who keeps helping herself to their shampoo and mascara?"

"Yeah, there's something to be said for maturity," Nell agreed without a trace of irony.

Jared noticed that Eddie kept glancing at her. He'd shoot Nell a look across the table, his eyebrows furrowed as if trying to figure out the answer to some deep, dark mystery. Then he'd go back to his stack of letters, only to give her another surreptitious look.

Hank noticed it, too. Jared smothered a smile when the other man hitched his chair closer to hers and draped his arm casually across its back.

Eddie shrugged and looked away. But a short while later he started sneaking peeks again.

P.J. had been growing progressively more quiet and pale by the minute, and Nell abruptly pushed back from the table and crossed to the corner of the room where the box of marginal letters sat. Picking it up, she carried it back and dumped it on the table in front of her friend. "Here. I think you oughtta go through this box."

"Oh, no, really, I'm fine—" She cut off the obvious lie and gave Nell a wan smile. "Thanks. Some of this stuff is starting to creep me out."

"No crapola," Eddie said. "Like I said, tiny thang, there's some real sick monkeys out there and celebrity obviously brings them out of the woodwork."

Jared gave Nell a warm smile of approval when she looked his way. He should have thought of giving P.J. the less disturbing correspondence himself.

They had waded through another hour's worth of reading when P.J. suddenly jerked erect. "Oh my God."

Everyone stopped what they were doing and looked at her. "What?" he demanded.

"I think this is him." She rattled the small bundle of papers in her hand. "Listen to this:

> "Dear Miss Jayne,
>
> "'Honor thy father and thy mother: that thy days may be long upon the land which The Lord thy God giveth thee.'
>
> "It is so nice to hear music from a young woman who understands the message writ in Exodus 20:12. Clearly you have your values straight. I trust that you will keep up the good work.
>
> "Yours in Christ,
>
> "Your biggest admirer,
>
> "Luther Menks"

She looked up at them. "The return address is from Tipton, Iowa."

"Bingo," Jared murmured and held a peremptory hand out for the papers.

She passed them over.

Nell's brow pleated. "I get the reference to the honor-thy-mother note that came with the snake," she said. "As well as the fact that the area ties in with the interview you did the day you mentioned Marvin. But it's not exactly a threatening note. Why would Colleen include it in the correspondence she considered marginal?"

"Because of the ones Menks sent subsequently," he answered.

P.J. nodded. "She attached notes to a lot of these explaining why she included them. This was the first one he sent and they put it in a pending file where they hold correspondence for a month before answering. When one arrived that she considered marginal, she looked to see if there had been any previous letters sent by the same man."

"What does the second one say?" Hank asked.

"The second is actually along similar lines," Jared said, looking up from reading the last two letters that Menks had sent. "He admires her, she's one in a million to honor the fifth commandment in this age of parental disrespect, yadda, yadda, yadda. It's the third one that attacks her for not responding to his first two letters and for what he considers her lack of respect toward her mother." He looked at P.J. and saw that most of the color she'd regained reading the less disturbing letters had vanished from her cheeks, leaving her complexion pallid once more. "I know this is disturbing," he told her. "But it's actually good news."

"You think so?" she asked coolly. "Because I found

that quote about all the men of the city stoning me to death kinda bad news."

"What?" Nell stared at them in horror.

"Deuteronomy?" Hank asked, and when Jared nodded he turned to Nell. "The violation of the fifth commandment was a capital offense in the old testament," he told her. "The Bible references it in several different books. It wasn't a one-way street, though—Ephesians tells parents to conduct themselves so as to be worthy of honor. Our guy is obviously selective and only chooses the passages that reinforce his beliefs."

"Which makes him a fanatic, which sounds dangerous," Nell said and turned back to Jared. "And you see this as good news, how?"

"Because we know who we're dealing with now," he said evenly. "I have a name, which makes finding more information possible. And information is power." He turned to P.J. once again. Waited until she looked him in the eye. "The power to stop this psycho dead in his tracks."

P.J. CLOSED THE DOOR behind Nell and the guys and slumped back against it. She felt as if she'd just stepped off one of those whirling carnival rides; her head was reeling and her stomach felt wonky. Today was supposed to have been an opportunity to recoup from the crazy tour schedule, but instead she'd spent it reading sick letters from so-called fans. The stoning reference had just been the cherry on her sundae. What else could possibly go wrong?

Her cell phone rang from the other room.

She jerked in shock, then reined herself in. *Get a grip,* she commanded herself sternly. *Not everything is bad news.*

"You want me to get that?" Jared asked from the suite.

"No." Pushing away from the door, she strode into the sitting room and crossed over to the desk where she was recharging her phone. Looking at the number on the screen she saw it was her manager and picked it up, pushing the talk button. "Hey, Ben. What's up?"

"Priscilla, we've got a situation with your mother that has to be addressed immediately."

A sigh escaped her. "I was afraid it was too much to hope you'd be calling to tell me the album went platinum." Hadn't she known it would be more bad news?

"Oh, that's going to happen, as well, and probably sooner rather than later, considering the strength of your sales," he assured her with his usual no-nonsense Yankee briskness. "Unfortunately, it's not what we need to discuss today."

"What did she do this time?"

"She sold an unauthorized biography about you." He hesitated a second then added, "The working title is *Ungrateful Child.*"

For once pain wasn't the first emotion she experienced over hearing about one of her mother's betrayals. Instead pure unadulterated fury pulsed through her veins. "I'll take care of it," she said in a tight voice and hung up without bothering to exchange the usual pleasantries with her manager. Then, breathing heavily, she punched out her mother's number.

A tanned hand snaked around her side to remove the phone from her hand. "Hey!" She whirled to glare at Jared, who had his thumb firmly on the disconnect button. "What do you think you're doing?"

"I don't know what your mother did this time, but you're practically hyperventilating. Take a few deep breaths and get yourself in control before you call her."

She wanted to snap at him to mind his own damn business and give her back the phone. But he was right. Her mother could push her buttons and turn her inside out faster than anyone she knew. This time Mama had gone too far, and P.J. was determined to stop Jodeen's attempts to make a buck at her expense. To do that, however, she needed to have her wits about her. Doing as Jared directed, she took several deep, calming breaths. A minute later she exhaled noisily and shook out her hands. "Okay. Gimme back the phone."

He looked at her closely. "You sure?"

"Yes."

"Do you want to talk about it first?"

"There's nothing to talk about. That was Ben on the phone. Mama sold a tell-all book that you can be damn sure is going to be filled with lies about me. She named it *Ungrateful Child.*" She took another deep breath, because more than anything else, that grated, and she knew the hurt that lingered beneath her fury would gnaw her confidence to bits if she didn't guard against it. "I plan to have a little heart-to-heart with her."

"You could save yourself a lot of heartache by having that same discussion with her agent."

It was a perfectly reasonable, logical out, and for a moment the temptation to latch onto it beckoned like an umbrella-garnished drink on a tropical beach. Then she shook her head. "Don't tempt me." Dealing with it herself was the adult thing to do—but before she had time to pat herself on the back for her mature handling of the matter, she exploded.

"Ungrateful child, J? *Ungrateful child?* I've put up with her shit my entire life, but I'm through taking the high road. She's crossed the line with this one. If I don't put an end to her crap once and for all, she'll just keep coming up with other schemes to get rich quick, and you can be sure they'll all involve trashing me. I'm tired of it."

He handed her the phone.

She hit the redial button, then had to remind herself to keep breathing when the phone began to ring.

The line was picked up at the other end and Jodeen's voice said, "Hello?"

P.J. stood frozen for a microsecond, then said, "Hello, Mama."

"Well, well, well. If it isn't little Miss Bigshot," her mother drawled. "I didn't think you were lowering yourself to talk to me these days. What can I do for you, missy?"

Her tone was the sound of P.J.'s childhood, that

you're-too-insignificant-to-waste-my-time-on tenor that never failed to set P.J.'s nerves to jangling. Amazingly however, instead of putting her stomach in more of an uproar than it already was over the upcoming confrontation, the you're-worthless tone put her tension on a more manageable level. "For starters, you can drop the new book contract before you embarrass yourself."

Jodeen's laugh had a harsh you-wish edge to it, and the sound of a lighter clicking and the quick inhale on a cigarette came through the line. "I'm not the one's gonna be embarrassed," she said.

"Well, I wouldn't hold my breath waiting for it to be me. *Ungrateful Child,* Mama?"

"It seemed fitting."

"Please. You and I both know that when it came to you I never had a damn thing to be grateful for."

The sound of an exhale drifted down the line and P.J. could picture her mother narrowing her heavily mascaraed eyes against the smoke drifting up from her nostrils, then lazily waving it away from her overprocessed, dyed ash-blond hair.

Jodeen emitted a little grunt of disgust. "How do you know the title, anyway?"

"My new manager actually looks out for my interests. I suggest you call your shiny new agent and withdraw the book before you find yourself hip deep in a libel suit."

Her mother made a rude noise and P.J.'s spine stiffened further.

"You think because I've let you bad-mouth me to

the tabloids recently that I won't make our private problems public now? Guess again. Because truth is a wonderful thing, and a whole lot easier to document than the pack of lies you've no doubt written. For instance, I could call Molly Griffith. Remember her, Mama, the owner of the Buffalo Gals Barbeque in Cortez? Or Sue Redbush from the Cracker Barrel in McFadden or Mike Scraggs from the Red Hot and Blue in Cedar City? Heck, maybe I'll call all three, since all of them thought it was a crying shame that a girl my age had to work so hard in their diners while her mama sat on her butt in her broken-down little trailer. I'm sure they'd just love to testify on my behalf."

"You little bitch."

"You don't know the half of what a bitch I can be. Because I also gave the books you cooked to my manager for safekeeping. And wouldn't all those nice folk who think you're so misused be crushed to hear how you embezzled from the daughter who's supported you since she was a kid? Well, crushed for about five minutes, that is. Then they'll probably be madder than a nest of hornets hit by a stick. Funny how allegiances can turn on a dime. And hey, remember Jared Hamilton? He's standing right here. Say hi to my mama, Jared." She extended the phone toward him.

"Hi, Miz Morgan," he said obligingly from several feet away.

"Jared was there the day I called begging you to let me come home and you hung up on me. Wonder what the people who've been reading that my response to problems is to run away would make of that?"

"Well, let me think—would that be the boy who was wanted for murdering his old man?" Jodeen scoffed. But she didn't sound nearly as confident as she had a few minutes ago.

"Yep, that's him. Except the questioning was dropped even before they caught the person who actually committed the crime. He's a highly respected man from a prominent family. Between the two of you, who do *you* think a jury would believe?" She rubbed at the incipient headache brewing in her temples, but kept her voice hard and firm when she said, "Call your agent, Jodeen. Because if I hear one more slanderous word out of your mouth, if I read one more libelous article, not only will you not make another red cent but I'll make it my life's mission to keep you so tied up in court that you'll be old, gray and so deep in debt that you'll have to reach up just to touch ground long before anything's settled."

Her mother cursed long and inventively.

"Goodbye, Mama." She disconnected the call, then let her arm drop to her side, the phone suddenly feeling as though it weighed twenty pounds.

"Way to go, P.J.!" Feeling like cheering, Jared stared at her with a gleeful admiration that was almost savage in its intensity. If he felt a hint of liberation as well that she wasn't nearly as vulnerable as he had feared, well, he'd just keep that to himself. But listening to her deal with Jodeen had been a pure pleasure from start to finish, because he'd never expected her to stand up to her mother like that. "What a tiger."

She burst into tears and threw herself into his arms.

"Heyyyy." Hauling her in, he held her close, tipping his head down to try to see her sad little face as she babbled a lament in which he caught maybe one word in ten.

He heard her loud and clear, however, when she sighed, rubbed a knuckle under her nose and said, "Can we go to bed now, J? I need you to just hold me for a while."

He stilled for a moment. No, no, no, no, no. This wasn't the agenda he'd planned earlier. This was the time he'd intended to talk to her, to make sure that she understood they were just friends...with benefits...and that he was okay with her moving on when his job here was done. Hell, he was more than okay with it—he was a goddamn glacier peak, impregnable and remote, right?

Damn straight. Beyond his family, he had no need for permanent ties.

But instead of saying any of that he blew out a breath, tucked her under his arm and led her to the bedroom, attributing the inexplicable flicker of reprieve he felt to the fact that his sister and Rocket hadn't raised him to be an ass. He was still going to have that talk with her.

But only a complete jerk would kick her when she was down.

CHAPTER NINETEEN

Headline, Entertainment Section, *Denver Post*:
Colorado's Own Priscilla Jayne Leaves Sellout
Crowds Begging For More

"YOU'RE WHISTLING AGAIN." P.J. looked across the room at Nell as they cleared the dressing room of her belongings after the Fort Collins concert. "You've been whistling a lot lately. Is that the tune for your new song?"

"Mmm-hmm." But color rose in her cheeks.

P.J. paused in the midst of removing her tinfoil star from outside the door to stare at her. "Oh my God." She lifted the star off the nail then stepped back into the room and kicked the door shut behind her. "Nell Husner. You hussy. You've been fiddling with my fiddler." She pointed a finger at her friend. "You and Hank have been doing the deed!"

More color flared in Nell's cheeks but she pointed right back at P.J. "And you and Jared haven't?"

P.J. carefully placed the cheesy star Hank had made her to commemorate their first contract into a box atop the other items she used to personalize every dressing room. Then she looked up at her friend. And grinned.

"Oh, God, we have been. Doing it and *doing* it! And I gotta tell you, it's been so…my God, it's just been so…" She shook her head. "Wow. I don't even have the words. This is probably just plain pitiful to admit at my age, but I had no idea it could be like this." And okay, Jared's insistence on holding himself back to the very last minute might render it not quite perfect. But she had high hopes that he'd start loosening up a little and allowing more reciprocation on her part. And sex with him was still so far above anything she'd ever known with anyone else it wasn't even funny.

Nell grinned back. "I've had a couple of pretty good lovers, but Hank—" Her eyes went dreamy. "Well, he's in a class all his own. That man loves me up so well, I feel the need of a cigarette just talking about it."

"And you don't even smoke."

"I know." Her lips curled up in a secret smile. "Which just goes to show you how good he is."

"I've made some progress on our stalker." Jared looked up from the pages he was gathering from the printer he'd plugged into the galley's outlet. Everyone's attention was riveted on him.

He'd worked like a dog on this project for the past couple days, squeezing it in wherever he could snatch a moment between his regular duties. The information he'd culled today felt like the payoff for all his hard work and a slight smile tugged up the corner of his mouth. "Anyone care to see a photo of the guy?"

"Yes!" Everyone except Eddie, who was out,

gathered around the table. He handed the first photo, a black-and-white head shot from a JPEG he'd gotten from the security firm that employed Menks, to P.J. "It's not the best quality," He warned her. "But it's a start." He looked past her to Marvin, who was peering over her shoulder. "It looks a lot like the guy in the sketch you and the police artist made, but you're the only one who's actually seen him face-to-face. What do you think? Is this the man who delivered the box?"

Marvin studied the photo P.J. passed to him then nodded. "Yes, sir. Like you said, it's not the best picture. But I remember the shape of those ears."

"Good. I'll make copies to hand out to Security at every venue we play. And I'll mention the ears. Anytime there's a single feature to home in on instead of having to make mental adjustments for a total look that may have been altered, the chances for success go up. Best-case scenario, we detain Menks for the police to question. Failing that, it should at least keep him from getting into the concerts. And every opportunity we have to shut him down makes P.J. that much safer."

Glancing at the next item in his notes gave him an additional spurt of satisfaction. "We caught another break. Menks has a daughter named Mary who lives in Amarillo. I'm going to have you drop me off there on our way down to Lubbock. I'll rent a car and catch up with the rest of you as soon as I can." He caught P.J.'s eye. "Don't think I'm abandoning you," he said, "because I'm not. I'm going to give John a call and have him hop a flight out here to stand guard."

"Don't bother," she said. "I'm going with you."

He stilled for a moment, then plastered his best *trust me* expression on his kisser. "That's really not necessary."

"The hell it's not. This is my life we're talking about. If the daughter has something to say I'd like to hear it firsthand, not in some dry report after the fact."

Crap. He still hadn't gotten around to having The Talk with her. Every day he woke up intending to, thinking today was the day. But other matters kept getting in his way. He'd been looking forward to the pit stop in Amarillo as a little time on his own to draw a deep breath and catch a respite from feeling torn between what he should be doing and what he actually was doing to define their relationship. Which he admitted was not a hell of a lot.

Well, sometimes you don't get what you want, and he knew she had every right to be present when he talked to Menks's daughter. "Okay. I was vacillating between whether to arrive unannounced or make an appointment. I guess I'll see if I can set up the latter. That way we can be sure to get you back to Lubbock in time for your concert."

TWENTY-SIX HOURS LATER found them on a street in front of an Enterprise dealership in Amarillo, Texas. P.J. watched her tour bus pull away from the curb, then let Jared escort her into the agency where he made arrangements for a car.

They had passed a community with large houses and lush green lawns coming into town. After leaving the rental shack a short while later, they passed another that was less opulent but still very nice. But the neighborhoods lost all pretension to affluence the farther they drove, until they had degenerated to the kind of area with which P.J. was far too familiar. Eventually they turned off a paved street onto a rutted gravel road between two stunted cottonwood trees. When Jared brought the car to a halt in front of three trailers that looked as if they hadn't seen a lick of maintenance since the Carter Administration, P.J. took one look and felt as if she was thirteen…fifteen…eighteen years old again.

Then she took a deep breath and got a grip. This was no longer her life; she'd pulled herself out of the desolation of trailer parks like this and she was never going back. Squaring her shoulders, she climbed out of the car.

A Wal-Mart ad skittered on the hot, arid wind across the packed-dirt lot as she preceded Jared up rickety stairs to the sagging porch of the middle dwelling. She turned to stare at the dusty cottonwoods, the only source of green in this dun-colored landscape, while he rapped his knuckles against the door.

Turning back when it opened, P.J. saw a woman around her own age. The sun pouring through the doorway highlighted teased bottle-red hair, manmade breasts showcased in a tight tank top and a small tattoo of a laughing devil on the woman's right ankle. She looked at Jared, ignoring P.J. altogether. "You Hamilton?"

"Yes, and this is Priscilla Jayne. Thank you for agreeing to see us."

She shrugged and stepped aside, waving them in. "I dunno what you think I can tell you. I ain't seen the old man in more'n ten years."

The interior of the singlewide had the familiar stench of cigarette smoke embedded in imitation wood paneling. But it was decorated with bright gold and beige brocade-upholstered furniture, gilt-edged lamps and tasseled pillows. It might be garish but it still showed a lot more care than any of the trailers P.J. had ever lived in.

Mary caught her looking around and gave her a narrow-eyed stare. "So you're some big-deal singer, huh? I suppose you think this here's a dump."

"No. I grew up in trailers just like this, and I was actually thinking what a nice job you've done with the place."

"Yeah? Oh...well, then. Thanks." For the first time Mary's defensive attitude lessened. "The club pays pretty good. I'm savin' up my tips for a real apartment. Maybe even one of them townhouses."

"What kind of club do you work for?" Jared asked. "Perhaps we'll stop in before we leave town."

"I doubt it's your thing—it's a gentlemen's club." Her eyes narrowed again as if waiting for him to make something of it.

"Then perhaps not," he commented mildly. "Do you like working there?"

She shrugged. "It's okay. I got me my GED a coupla years back, but so far it ain't been all that good at scorin' me a job that pays better'n the one I already got. So are you a country singer?" She turned back to P.J. "'Cause I don't know nothin' about country music. That's what the old man always listened to."

"Yeah, I am," she said and smiled. "I take it you and your dad didn't get along."

Mary made a rude noise, lit up a cigarette and sank into an armchair, waving them to seats on the couch facing her. "You could say that."

"I sure know how that goes," P.J. said. "Only with me it's my mother."

"My mom was great—right up 'til the day the old man drove her away with his preachin' and moralizing and that freaky cleanliness shit of his. In the world accordin' to Luther Menks, she shouldn't oughtta be doin' this and wasn't supposta do that. Well, she finally had enough, I guess, and flew the coop with another man. And from that day on he said she was dead to us and wouldn't let me see her." She sucked hard on her cigarette. "I'll never forgive him for that, or for the fact that she'd been dead two goddamn *years* by the time I finally wised up and hit the road. The sonovabitch knew it, but he didn't bother telling me until the day I was leavin' and demanded her address." She glared at them through the smoke of her exhalation. "And I don't care what anyone says, she didn't go to hell!"

"Of course she didn't," P.J. agreed, feeling slightly

sick. "If anyone deserves a special place in hell, it's a parent who would suggest such a thing to his kid."

"Fuckin' A." She exhaled smoke through her nostrils. "You want a soda or something?"

"Sure. That'd be nice."

Jared shifted quietly at her side when Mary left for the kitchenette, then reached over to stroke her knee. "It's a good thing you came along."

"Yeah, for all she works in a tittie bar and seems to have a good handle on playing men, I don't think your gender is at the top of her hit parade." She couldn't prevent the anxiety that seeped into her voice when she said, "Menks sounds like he's been a loose cannon for a long time, J."

He nodded, but gave her knee another comforting pat as Mary returned with three cans of Coke. Thanking the young woman as he accepted his, he popped the top, took a gulp, then said, "Do you think your father has it in him to be dangerous, Mary?"

She paused with her own can halfway to her lips to stare at him, then slowly lowered it without taking a drink. "I…jeez, I don't know. I never seen him do anything dangerous but he's sure got a screw loose. I watched the other parents at church when I was a kid, and none of them was fanatical like my old man. And like I said, it's been a long time since I seen him. Why? Has he done something?"

"He sent me a magazine article that had my eyes cut out of the photo," P.J. said. "Then he had a corn snake delivered to me care of my tour bus."

"A *snake?*" She stared at P.J., goggle-eyed. "Why?"

"Apparently he feels I'm not honoring my mother."

"Shit." Her heavily made-up eyes hardened. "That sounds like him, all right. That honoring thy parents stuff was his main bitch with me, too. A snake." She shook her head. "Man. That's just plain freaky."

"He also seems to be stalking her," Jared added.

"As in he actually left Iowa?"

"Yes." He gave her an abbreviated rundown of the man who had delivered the snake and showed her the police artist's sketch.

"That's him, all right. Holy crap. It sounds like he's totally gone round the bend."

Jared asked her several more questions, but it was obvious that Mary didn't have a clue what her father was up to these days and was blown away to hear of his recent activities.

When they got up to go, P.J. shook Mary's hand. "I know you said country music's not your thing, not to mention that you're probably working tonight," she said. "But I'm playing down in Lubbock at the Municipal Coliseum and I'd love to have you come as my guest."

"Oh, I don't know." Mary shifted her weight onto one foot, standing hip-shot. "I got tonight off, but it really ain't my cup of tea."

She gave the other woman a crooked smile. "Believe me, if anyone understands that knee-jerk need to stay away from stuff her parent likes, it's me. But tell you what—I'll leave a couple of tickets at the will-call office under your name just in case you change your mind. If you don't wanna use them it's no biggie."

But in the car heading out of town a short while later, P.J. looked over at Jared. "Other than confirming Menks is every bit as loony tunes as we feared, I'm not sure what we gained from that."

"Me, either." He took his eyes off the road for a second to glance over at her. "Only time will tell if something comes of it or not." He shrugged as if it didn't matter one way or the other, but when he pinned her in his sights once again the intensity of his gaze told another story. "I'll tell you what, though. I'd rather take the time to track down each and every lead than let one slip by, only to find out later it was the one thing that we should have been looking into in order to keep you safe."

THE SUN HAD SET BUT a sliver of moon rode the eastern sky as Luther Menks clutched his concert ticket and tried to keep from touching anyone in the crush of people surrounding him—a goal that simply wasn't workable in a crowd that pressed and jostled as it surged forward, funneling down toward the entrances to the Lubbock Municipal Coliseum. He shuddered, hating all this sweat-and-perfume scented, unclean humanity. But taking deep breaths, he held on, for soon he would be seated in a darkened arena where an assigned seat would keep the concertgoers on either side from getting too close as he watched Priscilla Jayne perform.

Surely tonight would be the night she repented her sinful ways. The scalpers' tickets to the last three concerts had been astronomical—far too rich for his budget—so he'd had no way of judging if the impact of the lesson he'd tried to impart had improved her attitude since the Red Rocks concert. By now she'd had plenty of time to reconsider her behavior and adjust it to fit the confines of good Christian morality. Or that was his sincerest hope, at least.

Because only then would he be able to forgive her her trespasses.

He was still twenty feet away from the manned turnstile when he became aware of grumblings in the crowd around him.

"What the fuck's the hold-up, dude?" the youth tromping on his heels demanded of his circle of raucous foul-mouthed friends.

"I've never seen the lines move this slowly," said a woman in a pair of neatly pressed slacks and a prim blouse to a girl wearing a short denim skirt and a cowgirl hat.

"What they doin', looking for someone or something?" demanded a thuggish-looking fellow with a hoop earring and a bandana tied around his bald head.

The latter question made the short hairs on the back of Luther's neck stand up and bristle. Were they looking for someone?

Were they looking for *him?*

That had better not be the case.

Because that would mean Priscilla Jayne hadn't

repented her morally abhorrent ways at all. Just the thought was enough to dredge forth a rage that was startlingly close to the surface. Like a swarm of roused bees it began humming throughout his nervous system.

But he was putting the honey before the hive here. Blowing out a breath, he fisted and flexed the fingers of his free hand in an attempt to release some of his tension. He was definitely getting ahead of himself. There was no real reason to believe that A, the sentries manning the entrances were looking for anyone and B, that even if they were, it was him. The buzz of his wrath began to die.

He watched the security guard as he neared the entrance he'd be using. When he approached a point a few yards from the doorway, he saw the man's gaze drift to the group of complaining young men behind him. Suddenly it snapped back to make full eye contact with him and the other man's eyes widened. The guard immediately turned his attention to others in their line but Menks had been in the business for years and he knew when someone had been made.

And the only possible way he would ever be recognized was if Priscilla Jayne's soul was so far beyond salvation that she couldn't even recognize a helping hand when it was extended to her.

Suppressing his resurrected fury, Luther instinctively sidestepped through the line that was winnowing down from three and four people abreast to one or two the nearer they got to the individual entrances. He whirled to go against the widening flow behind him like a salmon fighting his way upstream.

Looking over his shoulder, he saw the security guard wave someone over to take his place at the turnstile then jump the gate to come after him. Barely registering the protests that followed in his wake, he zigzagged through the crowd, pushing and shoving, crouched as low as he could manage in order to fly beneath the radar as he prayed to his Maker that the guard had lost sight of him in the man's own efforts to get through the throng of concertgoers.

The mob eventually spit him out at the back of the lines. Shuddering, he slapped and brushed at himself, trying to dislodge the germ-infested filth from his hands, his arms, his hair. Then he made himself desist, knowing that he didn't have time for this now. As much as he detested the multitude of close-packed bodies, he was exposed out here in the open, so he wove through the more loosely packed crowds at the back of the gathering, working his way toward the parking lot.

He briefly considered trying another entrance, knowing from experience that some security employees were more diligent than others. But he decided against it.

He had been given a sign, and an intelligent man only ignored one of those at his own peril. Clearly it was time to withdraw to somewhere safer and reevaluate the situation. But cold anger filled him.

Priscilla Jayne didn't know who she was dealing with, and she had better beware. Because he had God on his side.

And she had just bought herself more trouble than she could imagine.

CHAPTER TWENTY

And on the music front, a little birdie tells me there's a sudden spate of heightened security at Priscilla Jayne concerts.
—"Dishing With Charley" columnist Charlene Baines, *Nashville News Today*

RUBBER BURNED. BRAKES SCREAMED. And Jared went from a sound sleep to crashing against the imitation-leather folding curtain of his sleeping berth when the bus tipped to an inexplicable forty-five degree angle. Opening his eyes to the pitch-dark night, he heard a thump out in the hall between the berths, followed by a spate of creative cursing. But before he had time to worry about anyone else's safety the bus slammed down on all four tires and he was thrown back against the cubicle's outside wall. The sound of air brakes from another vehicle shrieked past and P.J. and Nell's raised voices exploded in an anxious babble of high-pitched confusion behind their stateroom door. He unsnapped the flap and shoved it back.

Eddie was sprawled out across the hallway floor, buck naked and cussing a blue streak as he simultaneously rubbed one flank and checked his elbow. Hank was swearing, as well, as he clutched at the half-opened accordion curtain with one hand, his abdominal muscles standing out in stark relief as he hauled his upper body back into his berth.

The stateroom door burst open and the women tumbled out.

“Shit!” Lurching up onto the hip he’d been nursing, Eddie reached into his berth and snatched out a cowboy hat, which he whipped over his lap.

It made Jared realize that he himself was standing there in nothing but his boxers and he grabbed a pair of jeans from his own compartment. Pulling them on, he gave first P.J. then the rest of her crew a swift assessment. “Everyone okay?”

The general consensus was that they were and he nodded. “Good. Let’s find out what the hell happened. Marvin!” It suddenly registered that P.J. wore only a skimpy white tank top and bikini panties and Nell had on an almost see-through baby-doll nightie. “You two might want to grab your robes,” he said. “And, Eddie, trade your hat for a pair of jeans. Marvin!” Looking toward the front of the bus he saw that the driver wasn’t behind the wheel. “Where the hell did he go?”

He strode up the aisle past the galley to the front, where he saw the door standing open. Jumping down to the bottom step, he leaned out into the night. A barely visible but steady drizzle misted his bare shoulders and he shivered. “Marvin?” God, what time was it, anyway? He felt as if he’d slept for hours, yet when he glanced at his watch he saw that not even two had passed since he'd gone to bed.

Masculine voices laced with frustration rose and fell on the other side of a shallow ditch that ran a short distance alongside the road—a trench that Jared abruptly realized their bus now straddled. He leaned out the door. "Marvin, that you?"

"Yeah, I'm here, Mr. Hamilton."

Locating the driver in the black-on-black shadow cast by the bus, he was just in time to see Marvin stumble away from the back end, lean over and be sick. When he straightened a moment later a burly man who had been standing in even deeper shadow stepped out to give him a companionable thump on the back. Jared saw the tail end of a semi across the road and assumed he was its driver.

Taking in the rain-slicked roads, he climbed down to help Marvin back onto the bus, shivering anew at the damp ground beneath the soles of his feet. "You okay?"

"Yes...no...I'm not sure. How about everyone else?"

"Shaken but unharmed. Come on, it's wet out here." He turned to the trucker. "You, too, sir. Come in out of the rain." He offered his hand. "I'm Jared Hamilton."

"Red Conroy." The man shook hands with a firm, hard grip and followed them onto the bus.

P.J. and posse, dressed in jeans and T-shirts, crowded the galley. When he brought the two drivers within the circle of light from a lamp someone had turned on he saw that Marvin was roughly the color of his once-crisp white shirt. "You don't look so hot. Did you hit your head?"

"No, sir."

"You have any other injuries that might need attention?"

"No."

"Then you want to tell me what went down here tonight?"

"Yes, what happened?" P.J. asked, stepping forward to touch gentle fingertips to the driver's shoulders as he leaned forward, gripping his knees with white-knuckled hands, his head hanging. "Are you sure you're all right?"

"Yeah, I'm just rattled," he said shakily and slowly straightened. "I've been a driver for twenty-three years and until today I've never had a ticket, much less an accident."

"Was it the rain?" Jared asked.

"That might have contributed to it. A shower blew up out of nowhere and the highway's slippery." But he cut himself off, shaking his head.

"The roads are slick," the trucker named Red agreed. "But it was that crazy-ass driver in the black pickup who caused this."

Marvin nodded. "Yeah. The rain wouldn't have made a lick of difference if not for that damn reckless yahoo playing games with me."

Jared's instincts started quivering like bird dogs on point. "What yahoo is that?" he asked in a carefully neutral voice.

"You mind if I sit down?"

"Damn, Marvin, of course not. I should have gotten

you settled sooner." He turned to the trucker, who had no doubt gotten his handle from his receding crop of gingery curls. "You, too, Mr. Conroy. Grab a seat."

"Call me Red," the trucker invited as he moved to accept one of the captain's chairs Jared indicated.

Marvin collapsed onto the other one and hugged himself as if he were cold. He looked shell-shocked. "About twenty minutes ago a car came roaring up on my tail," he said. "Until then, except for the occasional trucker like Red here hauling their loads back up north, I'd had the road pretty much to myself."

Hank, who had disappeared for a moment, returned with towels, which he handed to Marvin and Red. He tossed the last one to Jared. Nell handed the drivers each a steaming cup of coffee.

The bus's AC had gone off when the engine was shut down and Marvin had clearly had more things on his mind than to turn on the backup generator. It was growing muggy, but he hugged his towel around his shoulders like a shawl before cradling his mug in both hands. "The guy flashed his lights like he wanted to pass me, so I moved to the edge of the shoulder and he went roaring by. I figured he'd be nothing but a red taillight in the distance before long." He buried his nose in the cup, took a cautious sip.

"But he wasn't?"

"No, sir." Marvin looked up at him. "Right away he slows down to under thirty miles an hour. But when I started to pull into the passing lane, he punched it. I tried to pass him anyway for a coupla minutes, but anytime it looked like I had a shot at getting by he moved in front of me. Short of ramming him, there wasn't much I could do to stop him from blocking my way. So I dropped back. But the leg to Houston is a long one and I couldn't afford to have the hour and forty-five minutes it oughtta take to reach I-20 turn into almost four. So I pulled out into the passing lane again."

"And I'm guessing he punched it once more."

"Yes, sir. But I put the pedal to the metal this time and held it there, thinking maybe I could power past him, since he was driving an older model pickup that looked like it'd seen better days. I also kinda hoped he'd get tired of screwing around and just let me by. So there we were, roarin' down the highway side by side…until I saw Red's semi headed toward us."

"Oh, my god," P.J. breathed and gave his shoulder a squeeze.

"He was still a good ways away," he assured her, reaching up to give her hand a fatherly pat. "You've probably noticed for yourself how far down the road you can see in this area." Then he looked over at Jared. "I had a cushion of several miles before I had to worry about that rig turning into a problem, so I started edging toward the other driver, hoping he'd get a clue about the law of tonnage and get the hell out of my way. But he didn't budge and I've had 'safety first' drummed into my head from the day I got my first car, so I had to concede the road to him and drop back."

The driver's eyes held a vestige of the shock he must have felt at the time. "Except he dropped back, too. He wouldn't let me pass him and he wouldn't let me fall back, and that rig was starting to get a little too close for comfort. Red obviously thought so, too, because his air horn started wailing."

"I thought at first Marvin musta been drinking or something, the way that bus was all over the road. But when I slowed down I could see that asshole in the pickup truck—beg pardon, ladies—wasn't allowing him to get back in his lane."

"I was about to bail into the oil field on Red's side of the road but—" Stumbling to a halt, Marvin brought fisted hands up and ground the heels into his temples.

"But the sonovabitch swerved at him," Red said, picking up the narrative when it became clear Marvin needed a minute. "Swerved right the hell at the side of the bus."

"And I was so surprised that I swerved too hard myself to avoid him."

"Anyone woulda," Red assured him. "Dodging the crap that sumbitch was hurling gives a whole new meaning to defensive driving."

"No, I really did overcorrect. Plus I was sure I'd caught his bumper, which probably gave my wheels that final boost off the ground. But when I got off the bus half expecting to find him flipped on the side of the road there was nothing there. So now I don't know, maybe I just thought I hooked him. And I'm sorry, Miz Morgan, Mr. Hamilton." Coffee sloshed in his cup and he gripped it tighter in a blatant attempt to stop his hands from trembling. "But it happened so fast. For a few seconds there I thought I was gonna roll it for sure."

"You didn't, though, and no one was hurt," Jared assured him evenly. Someone could have been though. They all could have been smeared on the highway and he was pretty sure he knew who was responsible.

It sure as hell wasn't Marvin, who hadn't signed on for any of this shit. "Did you get a license number?"

"Yes, sir. Considering how much time I spent behind that Ford, I had what seemed like hours to memorize it." He rattled off the number, then gave Jared a level look. "It was an Iowa plate."

"I'M SORRY ABOUT THE ROOM." Jared leaned against the hotel room's doorjamb and watched P.J. set out toiletries on the bathroom counter.

"Yeah?" She looked up from arranging a bewildering array of makeup. "Why's that?"

He scratched his thumbnail beneath his lower lip, thinking she looked like she was about fifteen years old with her hair pulled up in that high bouncy ponytail. "Well, it's not exactly a suite at the Teatro, is it? Or even a particularly great standard room." And she deserved better.

"Yeah, pretty damn inefficient of you not to know this was a big conference week in Houston," she said sternly. Then she slugged him in the arm. "C'mon! You got Marvin through his interview with the cops, poured whiskey down his throat to cure his shakes and drove the bus to Abilene yourself while he slept it off. You got the rest of us on a flight to Houston so he can take his time driving here and got us all rooms in this perfectly fine hotel."

"Which rates maybe two stars, and then only if you squint real hard."

"Hey, that's a star and a half more than anywhere I stayed before this Priscilla Jayne thing started taking on a life of its own. But we were talking about you—about how cool under pressure you are. And about how you're my hero. In fact—" Abandoning her unpacking, she crossed over to him and reached for the fastenings on the button-down pinstriped shirt he wore with his jeans. "I think you deserve a little reward for all your hard work."

He'd been steeling himself to put a little more distance between them, not less. In the past twelve and a half hours he'd managed to put up a good front for P.J. and her crew. It sure as hell hadn't stopped him, however, from thinking almost nonstop about what could have happened during that whole bus-being-run-off-the-road debacle.

And the possibilities of what might have been scared the bejesus out of him. The sheriff in the small town where they'd reported the incident promised to run the plates, but Jared didn't need confirmation to know Luther Menks was behind the run-in. There weren't enough coincidences in the world for it to be otherwise.

The mere fact that Menks would pit his ratty old pickup truck against a megaton bus was scarier 'n hell. No one could accurately predict how another driver would react, but the first scenario to occur to a rational man would involve being run off the road himself.

That seemed to be the point though, didn't it? Menks wasn't rational. And now the damn tabloids had published a picture guaranteed to splash fuel on the fire if Menks read that sort of trash. It had actually been an innocent moment—just Jared giving Peej a steadying hand off the bus when her own hands were full. But the photographer had managed to shoot it in such a way that he seemed to be hovering over her like a lover. Then the paper had given it a screaming headline to ensure everyone thought the two of them were fucking like rabbits.

Imagine what they could have done with the truth. The thought made him laugh without humor.

He hoped like hell Menks didn't read the tabloids. The tenor of the notes the guy had sent P.J. suggested he was about as far from the type to do so as a person could get, which just might be the only break they'd catch in this mess. Publications of that nature were probably too secular for Menks's taste.

It was more likely, in fact, that he'd believe he had God on his side—those same notes certainly put it within the realm of possibility. But that merely upped the psycho factor and made the situation hairier yet, because it meant Menks had no brakes in place to slow himself down. And given the danger that kind of fanaticism presented to Peej, the last thing she needed was to be personally involved with her security specialist. Not only did it lack all semblance of professionalism on his part—something that used to actually mean something to him—but it put her at even greater risk than she already was.

Yet even knowing all that he still found himself saying, "Reward, huh?" and picking her up by the hips to carry her out into the bedroom.

Laughing, she wrapped her legs around his waist, hooked her arms around his neck and pulled herself up to take a bite of his bottom lip. Shuddering with arousal, he started making a mental list of all the moves he needed to put on her before he could allow himself to lose himself in her sweet body.

But when he dumped her on the bed and reached for her little yellow cotton top with every intention of stripping her bare, she slapped his hands away. Giving him a stern look, she scooted to sit against the headboard. "You first."

"Huh?"

"You. First. It's a simple concept, Hamilton. Get naked."

Was she crazy? How was he supposed to stay in command if he wasn't wearing a stitch? Because feeling her skin against his before he'd taken care of her at least once was just asking to shoot his control all to hell and gone.

Slowly unfastening the buttons she hadn't already released, he started knee-walking across the mattress. "I'm gonna get to that. But first—"

"Uh-uh." The authoritative crossing-guard palm she thrust at him from the end of her rigidly held arm stopped him in his tracks. "There's no first about it. Strip, Mister."

Damn. "Okay, okay." His mind spinning through

possible ways around the situation, he backed off the bed and made a slow production out of shedding his shirt, then peeling down his pants.

"Yee-haw." Fanning herself, she gave him a crooked smile. "That little bump and grind would probably earn you a ten-dollar tip at Chippendale's. Too bad my purse is clear across the room or I'd tuck one in your waistband myself. Lose the boxers, J."

He pushed them down his hips and kicked free. "What time is sound check? Look, maybe we shouldn't be starting something we don't really have time to fin—" Yeah, right. Glancing down at himself, he shut up. Like she was going to believe he couldn't find the time to squeeze in a little tussle among the sheets when his dick was pointed at her like a compass needle at magnetic north.

"Oh, trust me, we have plenty of time." Pushing away from the headboard, she rolled up onto her knees and made her way to him across the mattress. "All we have to do is cut out ninety percent of my orgasms. I think I can survive on one." She reached for him. "Just this once."

Oh, shit, she'd caught on to that? And did she also know *why* he concentrated so fiercely on her pleasure—had she guessed that he was afraid to get lost in his own? No, wrong word—he wasn't *afraid* of anything. It merely didn't pay.

All thought fled his mind at the feel of her hand wrapping around his sex, and the breath he sucked in was so sharp and sudden he damn near strangled on it.

But mother of God. Her fingers clamped his hard-on, and she squeezed her fist all the way down to its root. Then slid it up. Then down again.

He couldn't look; he was not going to look. That would be the kiss of death for sure. *I am a glacier peak, impreg—*

"Whoa!" Breath exploded from his lungs at the hot, wet vise abruptly constricting the head of his dick and he looked down before he could stop himself.

And damn near lost it on the spot.

P.J. held his cock in a two-fisted grip, choking up on it like a batter getting ready to make a grand slam. But it was her mouth and her eyes that riveted his attention. That sweet, sweet mouth that belted out soaring, electrifying music night after night was wrapped around him, her lips a pretty suctioning seal holding his dick hostage. Her eyes were all dark feathery lashes, clear whites and caramel-brown irises, watching him up the length of his body.

"Jeezzzus!" His hands came down to grip her head and his hips drove forward, pumping himself deeper into the hot, slick depths. He pulled back, then pressed forward again.

And her lips clung and her cheeks hollowed and those beautiful almond-shaped, slanted cat eyes continued to stare up at him.

Panic bloomed. He was minutes, probably seconds if he were to be honest, from losing it entirely and using her like some back-alley hooker.

So what? whispered the devil sitting on his shoulder. *Does she look reluctant to you?*

Man, that is so not the point, his better self argued. *This is Peej, for God's sake. The little girl who thought sex sounded like one great big ick factor.*

Oh, buddy, the devil cackled. *That's no little girl down there sucking your—*

He pulled himself free. Took a hasty, mother-may-I-worthy giant step backward.

For a second her mouth retained its openmouthed oval. Then, closing it, she blinked up at him. Her tongue came out to slick over her lips and it was all he could do not to groan.

"What?" she demanded, looking up at him all sleepy-eyed. "Why did we stop?"

"I, uh." His mind blanked out for a minute. Then he gave himself a mental shake. "I don't want to get off all by myself. It's time for a little togetherness."

"Ooh." She wiggled in place. "I can work with that." Flopping back onto the pillows, she crooked a finger at him. "C'mere, big boy."

He dropped down over her, but immediately pushed up onto his palms and toes on the mattress when he felt her skin, all silky and warm against his own. Still his erection brushed the cleft between her legs and even with her shorts as a protective barrier he knew he had to do something fast or lose what tiny vestige of authority he had left over the situation. Pushing back to kneel between her sprawled legs, he reached down to unzip her Bermudas. She raised her hips to help facilitate their removal. She helped again when he stripped off her little sleeveless blouse and removed her panties.

But when he ignored her invitation to come lie in her arms, and bent instead to bestow a gentle kiss against her inner thigh, she moved restively and said, "Don't."

He raised his head. "Huh?"

"You said you were ready for some togetherness. Well, let's have it." She held up her arms. "Lay on me. I want to feel you inside me."

"I'm gonna get to that," he agreed, a too-familiar alarm itching along his nerve endings. "In one second." As soon as he took the edge off for her. Just one little orgasm—he didn't plan to go overboard here—and then he'd do whatever she asked. His hands sliding up the juncture of her thighs until he could part her slick, dewy folds with his thumbs, he lowered his head again.

The next thing he knew the sole of her foot had slapped against the ball of his shoulder and she'd straightened her leg with a snap. He flew over onto his back. Shaking his hair out of his eyes, he pushed up on his elbow. "What the hell, Peej?"

"*I said,* don't." She scrambled to sit up, grabbing a pillow that she hugged to her chest. "I'm so tired of this shit, J."

"Huh?" he demanded as if he didn't understand. But his heart thundered in his chest.

"I don't need my tank topped off half a dozen times before we get to the down and dirty, you-inside-of-me good stuff. I don't want ten perfect orgasms from Johnny Stud, I want one goddamn real one with the real you—a you who just *once* it would be nice to see as out of control as I am."

His blood roared in his ears, his breath stopped up in his lungs and his heart tried to pound its way out of his chest. He feared if he looked down at his hands he'd see them shaking.

Well, to hell with that. He was damned if he'd let her reduce him to the messed-up teenager he'd worked so hard to leave behind. "Let me get this straight—me wanting to get you off is a *bad* thing?"

"It is when it's all about you being in control!"

His gut churning out enough acid to dissolve a navy tanker, he sat up. "What are you, a shrink now? Where do you get this shit?" He forced a laugh. "Control, my ass. You take a course in Psychobabble 101 or something?"

Flinging aside her pillow, she rolled up onto her knees. Naked, with that petite stature, narrow frame and barely there little breasts, she should have looked like a child.

She didn't.

She might be diminutive but an Amazon warrior couldn't have displayed more power. Conviction radiated off her in waves as she looked him in the eye.

"What do you call it, Jared, when you insist on giving me a set number of orgasms before allowing yourself your one?" She knee-walked a little closer. "You think if you do me, if you make me scream and moan, I won't notice that we're not really together in this?" She moved closer yet. "You think I won't notice that while you're making me come and come and come you're holding yourself back?" She jabbed him in the sternum. "Don't tell *me* you don't have control issues—I've been on the receiving end of them! And you know what I think?"

"No, but I'm just fucking breathless to hear."

"I think you're scared. Of what, I don't know, but—"

"That's bullshit!" he shot back and, whipping out an arm, jerked her to him. "You want me out of control, Peej? Fine. I'll show you out-of-control." And, lowering his head, he slammed his mouth down on hers, laying a kiss on her that was all teeth and tongue and brain-hazed sexuality.

She went up in flames in his arms and within minutes he was flat on his back, deep inside of her with his hands on her tits as she rode him like a rodeo queen, her head flung back and her nails digging into his shoulders. He could feel his testicles drawing up and a climax building at the base of his dick, and he brought a hand down from her breast to delve between her legs for her clitoris. But he had a feeling it was too little, too late, that he was about to get off without her.

As he felt his vision beginning to blur and his hips starting to lift her clear off her knees with the force of his mindless thrusting, however, she suddenly whispered something that was either an imprecation or a prayer. Then the tight sheath gripping his erection compressed around him like a satin-lined fist. Thrusting high one last time, he gritted his teeth and went off like a rocket.

A second later P.J. collapsed upon his chest, boneless as a sleeping child, and he wrapped her in his arms. Damn. He didn't feel half bad. Letting go hadn't been as traumatic as he'd expected. And basking in that lack of tension, he should have simply held her and enjoyed the afterglow.

But the hit his ego had taken with her analysis of his motives fostered a tiny kernel of discontent. Perhaps that was what set up the dichotomy between his hands and his mouth, because the two seemed to be receiving different messages. And while the former rubbed her back in soothing circles, the latter muttered, "There. Happy now? You won. I conceded control."

He wished the words back the minute they left his mouth. But it was too late, for she went from soft and malleable to stiff as a statue in his arms. Without a word she sat up, dislodging him from his snug berth inside of her, and climbed from the bed.

Her silence was a roar that beat against his eardrums as, without so much as a glance in his direction, she gathered up her clothes, strode into the bathroom and closed the door.

CHAPTER TWENTY-ONE

Headline, *Country Billboard*:
A Big Congratulations to Priscilla Jayne on The RIAA Platinum Certification of Her Sophomore Album *Watch Me Fly*

AFTER THE CONCERT the following night P.J. lay in her bed in the stateroom she shared with Nell. "Men are scum," she informed the ceiling she couldn't see in this small, dark hour of the morning. The bus tires hummed with a whoosh-thump, whoosh-thump rhythm as they crossed a bridge. "Well, okay, maybe not scum. But big ol' pains in the butt for sure."

Covers rustled from the other bed as Nell turned to face her. "You and Jared have a fight?"

"He holds something back, Nell. Every time we… you know…do it." *What are you, nine years old?* "When we make love. Or maybe screw is a better word, because that's the thing—he sort of controls me with killer orgasms while holding something of himself back until the last possible moment. And God forbid he should allow himself even that unless he's already taken care of me several times." Rolling over, she turned on the little lamp attached to the nightstand between them, blinking against the sudden light. She eyed her friend. "I know that doesn't sound like something to complain about. You probably think I'm a whiner."

"No, no, I get it. Killer orgasms are nothing to sneeze at, and a guy who can deal them out in multiples—well, you should maybe hang on to him. All the same, if he's using sex to control you—"

"Exactly." Then she frowned. "I don't want you to get the wrong idea about him, though. J's not one of those I'm-gonna-cut-you-off-from-all-your-friends-so-I-can-direct-your-every-move kinda control freaks. It's more like...his father was really awful. He treated Jared like shit and one night when the old man got in his face, J shoved him and his dad fell and hit his head. Jared thought he'd killed him for sure, and he panicked and ran. That's how he ended up on the Denver streets where we met. That same night his father was murdered and for quite a while J believed he was the one who'd done it."

"Holy shit, Peej."

"Yeah. Plus his being the prime suspect was apparently what people remembered even after someone else was convicted of the crime. So what do you wanna bet the night he pushed his father in anger was about the last time he allowed himself to really lose control?"

"So what are you going to do?"

"God, there's the million-dollar question." She scrubbed at her face with both hands. *Happy now? You won.*

You won.

You won.

His words kept repeating in her head. And they hurt just as much as they had the first time. She felt as if she'd never be happy again, because what she felt for him didn't have a damn thing to do with competition. Never had, never would. And dammit, even if J didn't have the same feelings for her that she had for him, he ought to at least know her well enough to understand that.

"I don't know. But I've gotta figure something out. And soon. We sure can't go on this way."

THEY COULDN'T GO ON this way, Jared thought the next day. P.J. was polite and friendly toward him, but distant.

God, so distant, and it was driving him nuts.

It shouldn't. Her stepping back should have come as a huge relief, since he'd always known their time together was finite anyway. Yet relieved was not the word that came to mind.

He shoved aside the one that did. It was too frigging emotional and besides, he didn't have time for it now. "Marvin, you got a minute?"

The driver looked up from the map he was studying at the galley table. "Sure thing, Mr. Hamilton."

"I sure wish you'd call me Jared." But he knew it was a losing proposition since both he and P.J. had tried more than once to get Marvin to call them by their first names.

"I know. I'm sorry. I thought I could but I'm just too old school, I guess. Early training taught me never to treat my employers informally."

"Which, technically speaking, I'm not. But never mind, that's not what I want to talk to you about." Glancing at Hank and Nell, who were seated on the bench seat a few feet away wrangling over the finer points of her new song, he tipped his head toward the bus door. "Would you mind stepping outside with me for a minute?"

The driver followed him off the bus, but the minute they cleared the stairs Marvin cleared his throat nervously. "Am I in trouble, Mr. H? Over the other night?"

"No—hell, no. You did an exceptional job in a lousy situation." Opening the luggage hatch, he pulled out a couple of lawn chairs and carried them over to the shady side of the bus where he snapped them open and set them up. It was breathlessly hot, with humidity to match, but it was the best he could do. "Have a seat."

Marvin perched on the edge of his chair, his hands gripping his knees.

Jared shook his head. "Relax. Look, I heard from the sheriff from the other night's episode and I just want to give you a heads-up. Lay out your options."

"What do you mean?"

"I think you and I both realized right away that Luther Menks was behind running you off the road."

"Yes, sir, that's what I assumed."

"Me, too. And while the sheriff needed more proof than our word, he just confirmed it. Menks is a real loose cannon, which means something similar could happen again. And that puts you at risk. So I want to give you the option of going or staying. I want you to know that, whatever you decide, I'll give you the best reference I can put to paper. You've gone above and beyond the call of duty for us already."

Marvin straightened in his seat. "Oh, I'm sticking, sir. And if he tries it again, then he'll be the one who's run off the road."

"I'm glad you're staying. You've been professional and reliable and I'd have hated to see you go."

The driver's shoulders had a proud set. "It's my job, sir."

"And you're a pro, no doubt about it." He hesitated, then gave the other man a crooked smile. "Now if I could only get you to call me by my first name."

NELL SAT AT THE GALLEY table, her feet up on the chair across from her and a cold beer and a bowl of pretzels shoved aside on the tabletop as she worked at putting the final touches on her new song. Muttering to herself, she squinted to decipher her handwriting on the notes she'd scribbled during a brainstorming session with Hank yesterday.

"Hey, there."

She looked up to see Eddie standing hip-shot at the end of the table. For a brief moment, her heart did the pitty-pat thing it'd been trained to do at the sight of him.

Then it remembered it had been there, done that and settled down. She shot him a smile made wry by her own Pavlovian conditioning. "Hey, yourself."

Scooping a couple of pretzels from the bowl, he tossed them in his mouth and tipped his chin to indicate the music score spread out in front of her. "You still working on your song?"

"Yep. It's almost done."

"What's it about?"

She hesitated to tell him, because the day he'd pitched in to help them go through P.J.'s fan letters she'd seen a different side of him. And since then he'd actually been around more and didn't seem quite as shallow as usual. Then she shrugged and told the truth. "It's about a faithless womanizer."

"Huh. A jerk, I suppose."

"No, just clueless and not real deep."

Grabbing the chair nearest him, he swung it around, propped his boot on its seat and leaned to brace his elbow on his raised knee. Then he caught her in the crosshairs of the Eddie Special, a look she'd watched him bestow on countless women over the years, a killer combination of a crooked aw-shucks grin, a knowingly raised eyebrow and laser-beam eye contact designed to make a woman feel as though she was the only female he saw. "So," he murmured. "I couldn't help but notice the other night that you're way more built than I ever imagined."

Mouth dropping open, she simply stared at him for a second before touching a fingertip to her jaw to make sure it wasn't sagging like a halfwit's. Finding it where it belonged, she said, "Well, hmm, thanks." *I guess.* "And I noticed you wear your hat real well." She managed not to laugh out loud, but really. What an inane conversation.

"So, you wanna go out with me sometime?"

For a single suspended moment temptation sang a siren song in her veins. Okay, it was shallow—she knew it was shallow. But hell's bells, she'd spent what seemed like half a lifetime nursing a crush on this guy. So you'd just have to excuse her if for a few satisfying seconds triumph bloomed at the opportunity to fulfill those foolish dreams—should she so desire.

Then as fast as it had appeared, the sense of validation dissolved. Because she realized she didn't desire. Not when she had Hank. A date with George Clooney in his Lake Como villa couldn't tempt her to blow that relationship. Eddie didn't even run a distant third.

Hank made her feel smart and beautiful and special, and she intended to hang on to him with both hands. She didn't question that for a minute. Her certainty was like a primal imprinting that her mind recognized well before some sixth sense made her look over to see the man himself standing in the narrow hallway leading to the back of the bus. She shot him a grin.

He didn't grin back and she didn't need a knack for clairvoyance to understand he wasn't half as certain of her intentions. Staring at her and Eddie, Hank's expression was shuttered. His knuckles, however, stood bone-white against the weathered skin of his hand where he gripped the edge of one of the sleeping compartments.

Tearing her gaze away, she turned her attention back to the guitar player. "I'm flattered by the offer, Eddie, but no. Thanks. You're a sweetheart, but Hank's my guy."

He shrugged. "Okay. I just thought I'd put the offer out there." Straightening, he dropped his foot from the chair seat and shoved his hands in his pockets. "Well, gotta go. I'll see you later, hey?"

"Yeah. See you at sound check." She watched him walk away, then turned to watch Hank approaching.

He dropped onto the seat next to her and for a moment simply looked at her. Then he blew out a soft breath. "He seemed to take the rejection pretty well."

"You think?" She laughed. "What do you bet that even as we speak he's slapping the moves to another woman?"

"I wouldn't have let you shut me down so easily."

The look in his eyes made her heart kick like a confined stallion at the wall of her chest. "I know."

"So…I'm your guy?"

"Oh, yeah."

"Good. Because I thought for a minute there I was history. What with your longtime dreamboat offering to tie up at your dock and all."

"Well, I'll tell you what—it was flattering after all that time spent yearning over him. But it's you I love, Hank."

His eyes went still. "God." Slipping an arm around her shoulders, he bent his forehead to hers. "You sure?"

"I've never been surer of anything in my life."

"Good. Because I love you more than I knew a man could love." He lowered his head to kiss her.

They were straining together and breathing heavily by the time he tore his mouth away. He slid his hand from her breast. "Damn! Who thought this bus was a good way to travel, anyway?" He shot his narrow sleeping compartment a considering glance but shook his head. "No room, no privacy." Then resolve filled his expression. "But you can take this to the bank, sweetheart. The very next town where we have a two-day gig you better do everything you need to do the first day. Because you and me are getting us a room at a hotel.

"And we aren't coming out until it's time for me to have my butt onstage for the concert."

P.J. STUDIED JARED'S profile as they strode toward the arena, where he planned to double-check the security. His gaze was alert to their surroundings, to the people in the parking lot, to everything but her. Her stomach churned because, dammit, every time she looked at him she wanted to both burrow into his arms for the sheer safety of it and smack him silly for being such a bonehead. And she was sick to death of feeling torn in two.

She couldn't do this anymore. She couldn't be practically joined at the hip to a man who refused to even acknowledge the elephant in the room, let alone talk about it. "I need a break from you," she heard herself say. It came out of nowhere, unplanned and unrehearsed, but it was the truth. It felt, in fact, like the reality of the century.

"Don't be ridiculous," he said, glancing down at her, then back toward the flurry of activity going on over by the venue's service entrance.

His dismissiveness shattered what little composure

she had left and she stopped dead. "Who the hell are you to call me ridiculous?" she demanded, grabbing him by the arm and jerking him to a halt, as well. Part of her was appalled by the hysteria starting to bleed into her voice but she felt helpless to stem it. Besides, a larger part of her frankly didn't give a rip. Tough patooties if she lost control. Unlike some she could name, she didn't think the world would come to a flaming end if she failed to hold it all together. "*I'm* not the one who thinks being a freaking *robot* beats expressing a few real feelings. You're the one who's ridiculous, J, and I can't stand another minute of your company." Standing on tiptoe, she got as close to being in his face as she could manage. "I need a break, Ineedabreak, I NEED A *BREAK!*"

She all but roared the last and he gaped down at her as if volatile vapors were steaming from her pores to envelop her in a dangerous cloud. "Okay, okay," he said in a careful, create-no-sparks tone of voice, and, wrapping his long fingers around her upper arms, he backed her up a step. "But it's not safe for you to be on your own. So I'll take you to Nell. You can hang out with her while I conduct the security check."

"*Now!*" She wanted away yesterday and feared if she didn't get some space between them soon she'd do something that could never be undone.

By the time they tracked Nell down, however, she was beginning to feel a little foolish. Anxious to be shed of him all the same, she gave Jared a terse nod.

"I'll see you in a bit," he said and looked down at her, dissatisfaction evident in his gaze. "Stay put."

"Uh, that might not be possible," Nell said, and when he bent a hard stare on her, she shrugged apologetically. "I've got a lot of ground to cover before the sound check, so we're going to be all over the place. But all within the building."

"Okay." He looked back at P.J. "Just take care." He started to turn away, then executed a militarily precise right turn, bringing them back face-to-face. "Jesus, Peej," he muttered and, reaching out, wrapped his hand around her nape. Bending his head, he kissed her.

It was brief, hard and full of frustration. When he lifted his mouth from hers, he stared down at her for a moment, swore under his breath, then set her loose and strode away.

P.J. watched him go until Nell's heartfelt "Whew!" redirected her attention. She turned to find her friend fanning herself with her fingers.

"I bet make-up sex with that man is almost worth the crap that comes before it."

"Everything's so screwed up, Nell."

"I know. I can see how unhappy you are." Wrapping an arm around her shoulders, Nell gave her a warm hug. "I'm sorry, Peej. Men are idiots sometimes—a sad fact but true. Still, let Mother Nell take you in hand. Maybe I can help soothe your bruised soul."

She let her friend do exactly that. Accompanying her on her tour-manager rounds helped to settle P.J.'s jangled nerves. Nell's warmth kept the unhappiness if not at bay, then at least at a manageable level. Little by little the knots in P.J.'s stomach unwound and by the time they were strolling down the wide, echoing corridor that contained her dressing room, she'd even laughed once or twice.

As they started to walk past the dressing room, however, she suddenly recalled something she'd meant to do. "Oh, crap! The top!" Bouncing the heel of her hand off her forehead, she came to a halt in front of the room's door. "I need to stop here."

"What? Why?" Nell glanced around as if looking for what had sidetracked her. But they were the only ones around aside from a workman in a toolbelt squatting in front of an outlet fifty feet down the corridor. And he wasn't paying the least bit of attention to them.

"I need to change my top before sound check. An underarm seam pulled apart in my silver blouse the other night and between one thing and the other I forgot all about having it fixed. I've got that red bustier I bought in L.A. in my wardrobe trunk. It turned out to be a little over the top for every day but should pop well enough to work as stage duds. I'd like to give it a whirl during sound check though, before I commit to it. If it's not gonna work I'd as soon find out before I'm standing in front of thousands of people." Afraid she was rambling, she shook her head. "Look, I'll just be five minutes. Ten tops, if it's not where I think it is."

Nell looked at her watch. "I'm sorry, Peej, but I've got an appointment in about four minutes with the will-call people about that block of tickets the local radio station is giving away and it's gonna take me five to get there as it is. We'll come back here soon as I'm done, okay?"

"No. That is, yes, you go ahead. I'll just stay in the dressing room until you get back. That will actually give me time to organize some stuff."

"I don't think leaving you alone is a good idea. Jared told you to stay with me."

"Yeah, but I don't think he meant for me to go outside to the will-call booth." She reached for Nell's hand and gave it a squeeze. "I could use a little time to get my head together. I've let so many things slide lately. And if the bustier doesn't work I need to figure out which of my other stage outfits I can reuse in a pinch. You know how I sweat during performances. It may not always be possible to get my costumes cleaned between shows, but I at least like to give them a couple of days to fully dry before I have to use them again."

"Okay. But I'm not leaving you in the dressing room without at least checking it out first."

"Good idea."

It only took them a moment to make sure the room was empty, and reluctantly Nell headed for the door. "I'll be back as soon as I can. And I'm warning you right now, if I run into Jared between here and the will-call office I'm sending him back to stand guard."

Swell, she thought but merely nodded. "Fair enough." She waved her friend off. "Go take care of business. I promise I won't step foot outside this door until you return."

"See that you don't." With a final concerned look, Nell left the room, closing the door firmly behind her.

P.J. had barely turned away to start going through the pile of stage stuff she'd hauled over from the bus earlier when there was a thump against the door. Laughing, she crossed the room. "Nell, come on, I'm fine," she said, opening the door. "You really are going to be late if you don't—"

A man burst into the room, one hand clamping over her mouth. His momentum sent them both stumbling deeper into the room and he kicked back with one foot, slamming the door shut behind him.

For a minute her eyes went blurry with fear and all she could hear was the roar of her own heartbeat in her ears. Her only thought was a befuddled, *Why does an electrician want to hurt me?*

But the man with his hand over her mouth and a fierce grip on her arm wasn't one of the arena workers, of course. And once she got past the fear of expiring on the spot of a heart attack or—nearly as horrifying—wetting her pants, P.J. recognized his face. It was the police artist's rendering come to life, except that Luther Menks's eyes were more fanatical than any artist could ever capture. They burned with a zealot's fervor.

Looking into them now made her heart thunder in her chest and sent her pulse racing off the charts.

"I gave you every opportunity," he said, removing his hand from her mouth and rubbing it furiously against his pant leg as if to remove some invisible substance. He loosened his grip on her arm, as well. "If you'd just paid attention, if you had bothered to read even one of my letters, this would not have been necessary. All I asked was that you honor your mother—even though it's since become apparent that you have committed other equally unforgivable sins." His hand kept rubbing, rubbing, rubbing against his navy-blue cotton pants while spittle gathered in the corners of his lips.

P.J.'s blood ran cold, an expression until now she had always assumed was invented by someone with a propensity for melodrama. Now she understood if anything it was an understatement, for she felt frozen to the marrow.

With no time to worry about it. "I didn't get your letters."

"What?" It broke his rant and seemed to throw him off-stride.

Menks was old enough to be her father but he was fit, bigger and stronger than she was and standing between her and the door. She took a stealthy step to one side anyhow.

"I'm so sorry," she blurted, "but I never received them. I get hundreds of letters a week and they're all sent on to the Priscilla Jayne fan club. I'm afraid it's often months before I see them and even then I only see a select few." She took another careful step away.

"They should have come to you," he grumbled. "I thought you were a good, moral—"

"Yes, they should have." She knew she was taking a chance interrupting him, but it seemed an acceptable risk if it kept him from getting all wound up again.

"And I apologize again for the error that prevented them from doing so. This fame thing is pretty new yet and we're still adjusting, trying to find better ways to be organized." Watching his continuous rubbing of his hand against his pant leg, she blurted, "Would you like to wash your hands, sir?"

He stared at her, the repetitive motion halting mid-action. "What?"

"You seem to have something on your hand and I've got a sink over there if you'd like to use it." She pointed toward the bathroom in the far corner.

When he turned from her to look in the direction she indicated, P.J. broke for the door. This was her best chance, her only chance, and she ran as if the hounds of hell were nipping at her heels, which was pretty much the case. She heard Menks bellow behind her but didn't look back. Panting, she snatched open the door and was two steps into the corridor when he grabbed her ponytail, stopping her in her tracks.

It felt as though her roots were being ripped from her scalp and, reaching back, she covered his hand with her own, first prying at his fingers, then clawing at them in an attempt to ease the pressure.

"Don't touch me with your whore's flesh!" His arm crossing her chest, he released her hair at the same time that he spun her around with the hand he'd clamped to her far shoulder. She twirled dizzily and his elbow, which was still raised from his hold on her hair, connected solidly with her cheekbone.

Black stars exploded in her vision and she staggered several steps back until the wall brought her up short.

"It's your fault," he snapped, half pulling, half carrying her back into the room. "You're so little you came around faster than I expected."

Yeah, great, blame the victim, she thought groggily but was smart enough to keep her mouth shut. Those black spots threatened again when he shoved her into a high-backed wooden chair with enough force to snap her head back. For a moment she was really, really afraid she was going to be sick.

By the time her head quit spinning she realized he'd tied her ankles together with her own belt.

"Ungrateful child, wanton woman," he muttered, jerking her hands together in front of her and whipping her narrow Indian gauze scarf around them several times. Adding insult to injury, the beads that made up its fringe clinked cheerfully as he jerked the ends together and knotted them over her wrist bones.

"Wicked Jezebel. I thought you were pure, but you've been fornicating with that man." His eyes burning with the conviction of his own righteousness, he scowled into her face. "Well, I know how to deal with you, missy." And reaching into the toolbelt slung around his hips, he pulled out a long-bladed pair of shears.

Her heart stopped dead. Oh God, he was crazy. And she wanted Jared, wanted him with every fiber of her being.

Menks yanked the rubber band from her hair. "You

won't use your woman's wiles to entice men after I rid you of your crowning glory."

"My hair? You're going to *cut off my hair?*" Rage battled with horror as she watched him go from air-snipping the scissors open and shut to rubbing the side of his hand down his pants. Rage won. "Who do you think you are? I'm not a whore, and you don't know the first damn thing about my relationship with my mother." And what was the deal with all that hand rubbing, anyway? The man was too freaking scary for words.

"I know you. I know your kind." Additional saliva joined the bubbles in the corner of his lips. "I thought you were a good, moral daughter, an icon for our youth to look up to. You needed guidance, but I excused the lack because you're surrounded by immoral people. But you're like a rotten apple, juicy on the outside, corrupt at the core." He leaned down until his weird-ass eyes were only an inch away from hers. "You think I don't see you? You think you're so smart and above the rules? I know what you do, and the wages of sin must be paid. You failed to set a good example in life. Now, I'll see to it that you set one in death."

He was going to *kill* her? Oh God, she more than wanted Jared—she *needed* him. How had she let that awful distance between them grow to this point? Suddenly her pride didn't seem all that important. *It doesn't matter if he's an idiot about some things. I'm going to die and I never even told him I love him.*

But she couldn't think about that now. "You won't

get away with this," she whispered, her voice raspier than usual.

He didn't seem particularly worried, merely staring at her with those judgmental eyes. "Right is on my side," he said solemnly. "Behold. You're Delilah, a snake-kissed Eve, the whore of Babylon. Women like you were turned into pillars of salt in Sodom and Gomorrah, stoned at the walls of Jericho." For a second rationality returned to his gaze. "And what can you do to stop me, anyhow? Yell?" His tone mimicked her speaking voice. "Go ahead. No one will hear you." Lifting the shears, he yanked up a hank of her hair and lopped it off.

Shock reverberated down her spine and her lip quivered. But she was damned if he'd see her cry. And if he truly believed she'd simply sit here and take this quietly he was even crazier than she'd already realized.

She met his zealous gaze squarely. "I'm guessing you've never heard me sing." Since anyone who had would know she could project her voice to the back row of a thirty-thousand-seat arena.

He paused with another handful of hair draped over the bottom blade to look down his nose at her. "Your pride doesn't interest me. That you can speak with conceit at a moment like this only proves that you deserve to die."

Not if I have anything to say about it, Bub. And figuring she had nothing left to lose, she screamed the house down.

CHAPTER TWENTY-TWO

Publishers Monthly magazine online
Publisher's Brunch:
Priscilla Jayne Biography Pulled. Jodeen Morgan
Dropped from Agent's Roster.

Earlier

IT WAS WAY PAST TIME somebody yanked him off this case.

Jared scowled as he realized he'd just missed the start of the venue's gate security procedures report. It wasn't the first time in the past half hour he'd found his thoughts straying. Hell, it wasn't even the second or third. He hadn't been able to concentrate worth spit since the moment he'd left P.J. with Nell. What the screaming eff had possessed him to let a little bit of five-foot-nothing titanium-laced femininity dictate the terms of how he did his job?

The fierceness of his dissatisfaction must have shown on his face because the young man giving him the overview began to stutter. Jared forced himself to concentrate on the report. It was vital information and considering he'd been the one to request it in the first place, the least he could do was give it the courtesy of his full attention. The very fact that he had to work this hard to focus, however, merely deepened his self-disgust.

As he walked away a few minutes later he blew out a breath. Inhaling another, he drew it deep and held it in the bottom of his lungs as long as he could before exhaling again. Breathing was supposed to be soothing—or so he'd always heard. According to his sister it even helped minimize the pain of childbirth. So was it asking so goddamn much to hope it might elevate his mood to a calmer plane?

Apparently so, since he didn't feel a freaking bit more tranquil. *Shit.* Another deep breath and he finally faced the bottom line he'd been tiptoeing around.

There wasn't a rationale on God's green earth that excused him for putting P.J.'s safety into someone else's hands. Particularly when the someone in question was a mild-mannered songwriter without an iota of training in personal security. And the fact that he'd let Priscilla Jayne's minimeltdown make him forget the bedrock basics of said personal security—many of which he'd frigging perfected—was unforgivable. Rocket was going to have his balls in a basket when he told him about this.

The cold, hard truth was he'd gotten much too close to P.J. It might have been acceptable if he'd managed to keep some separation between his personal and professional personas. But today's screw-up was just another reminder that there were good, solid reasons for his cardinal rule to never, but never, get involved with a client. His emotional entanglement in P.J.'s life had made him careless and if anything went wrong she'd be the one to pay the price.

"Entanglement," he muttered and a harsh, humorless laugh escaped him. There was a prissy-ass word if he'd ever heard one. This went so far beyond that it wasn't even funny. He'd allowed his feelings to cloud his judgment right down the line.

In the course of his career he'd worked with some of the most difficult clients a man could ever care to meet and not once had he let his feelings interfere with the job at hand. He'd stuck to them like flies to a glue trap no matter what their mood, their attitude or the amount of lip they'd given him. Yet had he done the same with P.J.? Oh, no. She had one little hysterical moment, said she needed a break from him and he'd backed off like a goddamn rookie.

Well, break time was over. As of now, he was back on the job.

But that was easier said than done, he discovered after searching in fifteen different places without seeing so much as a glimpse of her and Nell. And while several people reported sighting them, every time he chased down a new lead it was to find himself once again having just missed the duo.

With every minute that passed he grew more uneasy. He wanted to believe it was merely a continuation of that mistake-to-let-her-out-of-my-sight edginess scratching low and deep in his gut. But it was more than that. Something else was nagging him.

The security in this place had more holes than a slab of Swiss cheese. Take for example the nervousness of the young man who'd given him the report. The thought of it had him picking up his pace. Because no one involved in gate security should be rendered jumpy by one unhappy expression. You had to be ready to push back when someone gave you grief. Anything else rendered you worthless at manning the entrances of a venue of this magnitude.

Then there was the fact that the arena's head of security had sent a kid to do the job in the first place. A kid who hadn't even been familiar with the sketch of Menks that Jared had sent over the minute they'd hit town.

Jesus. If Menks had decided to come after Peej again…

His gut churning and, finally running out of people who'd seen P.J., he headed for the dressing room. It was the only place he could think of that he hadn't already checked. He'd left a trail of his business cards, handing them out like kisses from a politician to everyone he'd come across, along with strict instructions to tell P.J. or Nell to call his cell number the instant they were spotted.

Meanwhile, the churning in his belly was growing worse. If anything happened to Peej it was on him. He had one area of expertise in his life and he'd blown it big-time today.

A woman's scream suddenly rent the air as he was approaching the intersecting hallways where he'd turn off for her dressing room.

Son of a bitch! Heart slamming, adrenaline spraying through his system like fire laid down by a semiautomatic, he sprinted toward the sound echoing down the tunnel-like corridors. He'd know that voice anywhere.

He moved faster than he ever had in his life, yet still felt as if quicksand sucked at his feet, as though hours passed before he spotted the tinfoil-covered cardboard star that P.J. always nailed to her dressing-room door. Blood pumping hot and furious through his veins, he burst into the room. "P.J.!"

For one awful second, as he tried to make sense of the scene before his eyes, he felt as though his entire system had stopped in its tracks.

Muttering incoherently, a hunched man jerked awkwardly toward him then lurched a few steps in his direction with a Quasimodolike gait. It only took one look to know it was Menks and Jared tore across the room, his gaze on the long-bladed shears in the man's hand.

Shit, shit, shit! Where the hell was P.J.? It took a moment for his cognitive processes to clear, then he saw her feet and lower legs, which were partially blocked by the man between them. They stuck up in the air at a forty-five degree angle, and he realized that not only were her ankles bound together but she was tied to a chair that was tipped over on its back. Sucking in a deep breath to stave off the rage trying to shanghai his reason, he gritted his teeth over his inability to go to her aid until he had Menks secure. He could only demand, "Peej. You okay?"

For a heart-stopping moment, she didn't reply. Then her voice, low and raspy, said, "Yes. That is, I think so—only…I don't know. He said—" Her voiced trembled. "Oh, God, J, he said I set a hor—a horri—an awful example in life but he'd see to it that I set a good one in death." She swallowed audibly, clearly fighting back rising hysteria. "I think I kicked him in the nuts."

That would explain the bastard's posture.

"Be not deceived," Menks croaked, waving the shears as he backed away from Jared. "Neither fornicators, nor idolaters, nor adulterers, nor—"

Not about to let him close to P.J. again, Jared lunged, grabbing Menks and twisting the shears from his hand. For one enticing moment the thought of plunging them into the asshole's neck beckoned like a Belgian beer on a blistering summer day. Then, grabbing hold of his professionalism, he tossed the implement aside. Yanking the older man's hands together behind his back, he looked around for something to bind them.

When Menks twisted to stare at him over his shoulder, however, Jared left off searching to study him in return. A cold shiver worked its way down his spine, leaving a wash of goose bumps in its wake. The guy had seriously crazy eyes.

"Let the marriage bed be undefiled—for fornicators and adulterers God will judge." In a sudden, unexpected movement, Menks jerked half-free of Jared's hold to lunge toward P.J.

She screamed and Jared caught his first entire-Peej glimpse since entering the room. Stuck like a turtle on her back, her eyes showed too much white and tendons stood like overburdened cables in her neck. A chunk of hair had been hacked off about chin length on the side nearest him, but it was the knot on her cheekbone, which was beginning to bruise, and the blackening eye swelling shut above it that really made Jared see red.

His professionalism went up in flames.

He swung Menks around by the arm still in his grip, then sent him crashing to the floor with a powerhouse right hook to his jaw.

The guy screamed like a girl and stared in horror at the blood that spattered the hand he'd raised to his mouth. "You can't strike me! God has charged me with a mission."

"Yeah, me, too. And I'm glad you're at peace with Jesus, buddy," he growled through clenched teeth, "because I'm gonna send you home to Him." He hauled Menks to his feet only to flatten him once again. "Oops. Look at that. It appears I missed the damn chair entirely when I tried to seat you. Tell you what, Luther. Why don't you go ahead and take a swing at me just to even things out."

Menks didn't move an inch from where he was sprawled on the floor. "The law of Jesus Christ has made me free from the law of sin and death." He pinned Jared with his fanatic's eyes. "I have no argument with you. May God grant you repentance so that you may know the truth, that you may come to your senses and escape the snare of the devil. My mission is with *her,* the devil's whore."

Jared's temper spiked another degree hotter. "Get up, tough guy," he said. "You're real free and easy with your fists and your scissors when your opponent is a woman who weighs maybe a hundred pounds soaking wet. Let's see how you deal with someone your own size." Oh, man, he wanted the SOB to take a swing. Just one lousy swing. It was all the excuse he'd need to lose that last thin thread of control preventing him from annihilating the bastard. Without taking his eyes off his downed quarry, he leaned down and righted P.J.'s chair.

"You sure you don't want to take a shot?" he demanded of Menks when she tried to stifle a gasp of discomfort. "No? Okay then, don't say I didn't offer." And filled with a cold, killing rage, he put the power of his shoulder behind the punch he threw. Pain sang up his arm when his knuckles connected with Menks's face, and cartilage popped audibly in Menks's neck as the man's jaw followed the trajectory of Jared's fist. "I'll make you a deal, Luther. If you're still alive when the cops arrive we'll call it even. That's better odds than you gave Priscilla."

"She is Jezebel." Menks's eyes burned with conviction even as he cowered away from Jared. "I thought she was pure but—"

"She *is* pure, you son of a bitch!" And damn it to hell, although her bruises were Menks's responsibility, the situation was *his* fault. His father had always said he was a fuck-up and he'd just proved the old man right. His pride and goddamn need to allow P.J. her distance for his own emotional safety had almost cost him the woman he needed more than—

No. He gave himself a mental shake. This was not the time to get into this. His lack of professionalism had already nearly cost P.J. her life.

Stowing his guilt in a dark corner of his mind already teeming with like-minded emotions, he shoved Menks into a chair, then bent down and whipped P.J.'s belt from her ankles. "Change of plans. I'm not going to jail for stomping the life out of a twisted bastard like you," he snarled as he secured Menks's legs. When he untied the bandana from around P.J.'s wrists and saw her swollen fingers, however, he didn't hesitate to wrench Menks's arms behind his back with unnecessary force. And if he tied the bonds a little too tightly…?

Tough shit.

He lifted P.J. from her chair, supporting her when her legs buckled. Fighting the rage that threatened to consume him all over again when he assessed her bruises and contusions, he touched them with gentle fingertips. He could feel the tremors that racked her body as she leaned against him. "Easy, baby, just hang on," he murmured as gently as he could manage with all this unspent adrenaline thundering through his veins.

Just then Nell burst into the room. "Oh, God, oh shit," she moaned when she took in the situation.

"Here." Pulling his cell phone from his belt loop, he

tossed it to her. "Call 911. We need the cops and an EMT. Then get hold of Security." Looking down at P.J. again, he assured her quietly, "The paramedics will be here to check you out real soon."

It only took minutes for word of P.J.'s encounter to spread. Hank arrived and a mere moment later so did Eddie. In short order the room started filling up with roadies, extra musicians, the sound guy and two women from the front office. Last to appear was a man Jared recognized as the arena security head.

"I don't need the paramedics," P.J. said, and to his horror her eyes filled up with tears that silently spilled over.

"Aw, man, don't cry," he pleaded, wrapping his hand around the back of her head and pressing her face into his chest. God, she was killing him here. His control had all but disappeared this afternoon. For the first time in fifteen years he'd failed to stop and count the consequences before he'd acted, and only some failsafe embedded deeply within had prevented him from beating Menks into a coma for what he'd done to P.J. He needed to get back command of his emotions. "Please, baby, don't cry." Over the top of her head he watched the security guy approach and narrowed his eyes. He had more than a few choice words to say to the man.

"I'm not crying," she denied gruffly, rubbing her uninjured eye against the swell of his pec. "But I don't want a paramedic. I just need you. I was so scared, J." She pressed herself against him as if trying to climb inside. "God, I thought I was dead for sure and I hadn't even told you I love you."

He froze. Joy warred with terror and he couldn't say which was winning. A dozen thoughts and twice as many emotions jumbled his mind. But only one emerged.

"You don't really mean that, Peej," he assured her coolly. "You've been through hell and had the crap scared out of you. You're not thinking straight."

A couple of uniformed cops entered the room barking questions. He felt a shameful sense of relief as he turned Peej over to Nell and left to go answer them. Then he'd have to see about canceling tonight's concert and imparting a few home truths to the head of security.

P.J. was finally safe and his job was done. It was hard to believe, but the two facts were bound to sink in any minute now.

And as soon as they did, he was sure this two-ton rock crushing his chest would lift.

CHAPTER TWENTY-THREE

Hyperlink, www.NightTrainToNashville.net: Three Priscilla Jayne Concerts Canceled in Wake of Stalker Attack

FOR THREE LONG DAYS NOW, in the wake of Luther Menks's assault, P.J. had held it together. She was still holding it together when Jared came barging into her dressing room in Cleveland's Gund Arena and blew her hard-earned calm all to hell and gone.

"You don't have to do this, you know," he said, banging through the door without so much as a hello. "You *shouldn't* do it. It's too damn soon."

She shrugged, hanging on to her composure by refusing to look directly at him.

But he just couldn't let sleeping dogs lie. "Are you nuts, Peej?"

Everything inside of her coalesced into a hot ball of anger and slowly, breathing carefully, she redirected her attention, bringing her gaze from just beyond his left shoulder to meet his stormy eyes. "Excuse me?" Her voice was quiet, but if he was half as smart as she'd always thought he was he'd be very, very careful about what came out of his mouth next.

Apparently she'd overestimated his intelligence.

"Look at you!" He took a step closer, scowling down at her. "The swelling might have gone down, but your cheekbone still looks tender and your eye's still black." He squinted at the orb under discussion. "Well, more green and purple, but the point is, you've got a way to go yet in your recovery. You sure as hell don't need to put yourself through a big-ass press conference. What was McGrath thinking to set it up so soon? What are *you* thinking to agree to it?" He took another step nearer. "I repeat, are you *nuts?*"

Tossing aside the stage makeup she'd been contemplating using to minimize her black eye, she marched up to him. "I guess I must be or I would have wised up by now and stopped putting up with your lame game of emotional dodge-'em."

"Huh?" He stilled, looking down at her with eyes gone wary. "What did I do?"

I will not lose it, I will not lose it. "Aside from insulting my intelligence and treating me like a five-year-old, you mean?"

"What the hell are you talking about?" he demanded indignantly, bending his head until their faces were nose-to-nose. "I've never treated you like a five-year-old in my life."

"The hell you haven't!" Her last fragile grasp on the react-first-think-second temper she'd worked so hard to rise above simply came undone. She thumped her finger into his sternum. "Don't you pretend to be concerned about me," she snarled, jabbing his chest in cadence with every word.

He had the nerve to look thunderstruck. "I *am* concerned—"

"You've been avoiding me like an Ebola outbreak!"

"That's bullshit." Wrapping his fist around her drilling finger, he prevented her from poking at him any further but tightened his grip when she tried to snatch it away. Dark brows gathering over his nose, he looked down at her. "Jesus, Peej, I've just been busy. Between dealing with the cops, the press and the arenas for the concerts we had to cancel, there were a hundred things to do."

"My God, you are so full of it it's amazing your eyes aren't brown," she marveled. "Well, you just keep telling yourself that, pal. Never mind that two thirds of your busywork is Nell's job—you and I both know the real reason you haven't been around."

"Maybe you do, baby. I don't have a clue what this 'real' reason might be."

"You've been running scared because I brought up the dreaded L-word."

"What?" He dropped her hand like a hot brick. "No." Stepping back, he thrust his fingers through his hair, his eyes growing shuttered. "I told you then that I understood you didn't really mean it."

"Yes. And how special that you seem to know my feelings better than I do." She didn't bother disguising her disgust. "But hey, good thing you're not treating me like a five-year-old or anything." Clenching and unclenching the hand he'd turned loose, she looked him in the eye. "No, wait. That's exactly what you're doing."

Then she took a giant step back, suddenly worn to the bone. "I'm so tired of chasing after a love that no one wants to give me I could spit. I did it for way too many years with Mama—damned if I plan to start begging for yours, too. What are you still doing here, anyway, J? Menks is in jail, the danger to me is past." She laughed a little wildly, because what a load of horse manure that was, considering that the very definition of danger stood right in front of her. She'd rather be back in that room with Menks than standing here feeling her heart shatter to pieces in her chest.

But she'd be planted six feet under, pushing up daisies and feeding the nightcrawlers, before she'd let it show. She thrust up her chin. "I think it's time for you to go home."

Face blank with—what? shock? relief, maybe?—he stepped forward, one long-fingered hand reaching out to her. "Peej."

There was a sudden rap on the door, then the portal swung open and her manager, Ben McGrath, strode into the room. "There's quite a crowd out there," he said in his crisp New England voice, pocketing a cell phone on which P.J. knew he'd have just that moment concluded a call. "You ready?"

"Yes." Taking a quick peek at her reflection in the makeup mirror, she rearranged a few strands of her new haircut, which curled just about chin length now, then shrugged at the bruising she'd thought to disguise. What the hell. Let the whole damn world see—what did she care? It wasn't like she'd done anything to warrant the beating Menks had dealt her.

It was simply one more case of attracting the emotionally bankrupt. She seemed to have a real flair for it.

"Dammit, P.J." Jared's voice was urgent, commanding her to look at him, and once again he reached out for her.

Ignoring the demand, she dodged away from his touch and his fingertips merely grazed her forearm. Ignoring as well the heat that seared her skin where they had brushed, she looked at Ben. "Let's go."

She left the room without a backward glance.

She thinks I should go home? Gut feeling as if a host of maniac grasshoppers danced hip-hop inside it, Jared stalked down the hallway behind P.J. and Ben.

Hell, she was probably right. That's exactly what he ought to do. In fact, that's what he'd sort of assumed his plan was, anyway. He'd thought to see her recuperate, to see her settled, then blow this popstand and never look back.

Now that she'd told him to go, however—

Before he had time to follow that snippet of thought to a conclusion that didn't involve him being one of those stubborn don't-tell-*me*-what-to-do kind of idiots, they'd reached the stage.

It was like walking into a room you believed empty only to have someone flip on strobe lights and crank up the sound to ear-bleed level. Flashbulbs exploded like the blitz over London, blinding in their proliferation and blue-white intensity. A cacophony of voices shouted questions on top of overlapping questions, all of which seemed to begin with "Ms. Morgan! Ms. Morgan! Is it true that...?"

Blinking against the spots floating across his retinas, he put himself between Peej and the press until they reached a catering table set up at center-front stage. He had originally planned to observe the proceedings from the arena floor until Ben had insisted that he join them at the mics, stating that the press would likely have questions Jared could answer more easily than P.J. Recognizing the truth of it, he'd reluctantly agreed and now he was glad he had. Because the mosh pit swarmed with far more print reporters and TV crews than any of them had anticipated.

They settled themselves at the table and the grasshoppers hip-hopped with increased frenzy when Peej shifted unobtrusively away from him as he seated her. Ben opened the press conference by reading a brief statement.

It didn't begin to satisfy the fourth estate. "Ms. Morgan! Ms. Morgan!" A dissonance of questions peppered them.

Ben, smoother than a White House press officer, fielded as many of them as he could. Most were directed at P.J., of course, and were worded in such a way that only she could respond. She did so with polite composure.

But from the corner of his eye, Jared saw her hands clench in her lap and knew it was costing her.

As Ben had predicted, Jared, too, came in for his share of attention. "So who are you?" demanded one bubble-haired blonde. "Mr. McGrath is Ms. Morgan's manager, but why are you on the dais with her?"

"My name is Jared Hamilton, Ms. Grabowski," he said, reading her press tag. Not about to share that P.J.'s label had hired him to protect their investment in the wake of the bad press generated by her mother, he fell back on the liar's friend and offered up a partial truth. "I'm a security specialist from the Semper Fi agency in Denver. Ms. Morgan began receiving threatening correspondence and Wild Wind Records hired me to keep an eye on her." Not necessarily in that order, but they didn't need to know that.

The woman scrutinized P.J.'s discolored eye and still-bruised cheekbone, then glanced back at him with raised eyebrows. "You didn't do a very efficient job of it, did you?"

"That's very unfair," P.J. said, giving the reporter a look of cool censure. "My label hired one man. How efficient can any one person be trying to be everywhere during every minute of every hour of every day? Mr. Hamilton did an outstanding job with the tools he was given. He's the one who figured out that Luther Menks was my stalker. He's the one who had fliers made up of Menks's likeness and saw that they got passed out to every security team in every venue I played. And if he hadn't arrived when he did I'd most likely be dead."

He turned to stare at her for a second before remembering where they were and jerking his attention back front and center. But Christ on a crutch. She was *defending* him?

Never mind that she still angled herself subtly away from him—that big heart of hers just flattened him like a rockslide. P. J. Morgan was a bigger man than he'd ever be and he didn't deserve her generosity. Because Ms. Grabowski had it right. He'd done a piss-poor job of protecting her.

Despite the fact that his old man had never hesitated to tell him he wasn't worth the space he took up, he couldn't complain about his life up until now. From his seventeenth summer he'd had a family to tell him he had value, people to comfort him when the idiots of the world believed he really had killed his own father. He'd had a strong male influence in John, had plenty to eat, money in his pocket, an elegant roof over his head and access to a first-class education.

P.J., on the other hand, had been dragged from trailer park to trailer park by a mother who'd disdained everything that made her special until Jodeen discovered she could make a buck off Peej's musical gift. But had she turned bitter or self-pitying? No. She was sweet and talented and kind to everyone she met. And she was generous to a fault to give him credit for saving her life when it was his—what had she called it?—his lame game of emotional dodge-'em that had driven her to escape his company in the first place. That had left her vulnerable to a madman's attack.

She'd had every excuse to turn into a stone-cold bitch like her mother, but she'd refused to cling to the past. Instead, putting the ugliness behind her, she had made the best of her present and was heading into one hell of a future.

Which begged the question: If she could put her past behind her, what the hell kind of excuse did he have to hang on to his?

Wonder beginning to suffuse his chest, he turned to look at her.

"Ohmigawd! My baby!" a voice suddenly bawled from the back of the arena. Then, only a shade more quietly, "Let go of me, you ham-fisted moron. My baby needs me!"

P.J. swore softly beneath her breath and Jared didn't need to see the woman slapping at the security guard preventing her from getting near the stage to know that the infamous Jodeen Morgan had come to cash in on her daughter's misfortune.

He surged to his feet, but before he could push back from the conference table to hustle her mother the hell out of there, P.J. leaned into the microphone. "It's okay," she said softly. "Please. Let her go."

He sat back down as the guard promptly stepped back from Jodeen, the man's hands going wide of his body in a you're-the-boss posture.

Jodeen gave him one last slap.

"Mama, stop it. What are you doing here?"

"Oh, my poor daughter," Jodeen crooned, rushing the stage. "I just hadda come see how my darling baby is doing after such a horrible ordeal—even if you did turn your back on your own flesh and blood."

P.J. winced and Jared's ire spiked. So this was P.J.'s mother. She was smaller than he'd expected, which, considering her daughter's petite stature, shouldn't be a surprise. But where P.J. had a softness to her, her mother looked exactly what she was—a hard, self-serving bitch. And he wasn't about to let her just show up and start putting her daughter down.

He leaned into the mic. "I wonder why she would do that, Mrs. Morgan?" he asked in an interested, non-confrontational tone. "Could it have anything to do with the fact that you stol—"

"And you are?" The older woman interrupted with saccharine sweetness even as her eyes narrowed in sour assessment. Then, without taking her gaze off him, she gave her brittle ash-blond hair a little pat and strode through the parting press until she stood in the pit directly below their table. "No, don't tell me. You must be the new manager Priscilla replaced me with when she tossed her own mama aside."

"No, ma'am," Ben said, leaning forward. "That would be me."

"Oh." Hands on her hips, she turned her attention to the New Yorker, taking in his faultlessly tailored suit and patina of sophistication until the flashbulbs going off around her like paparazzi covering the red carpet seemed to recall her to her mission. The hard-edged calculation melting from her expression, she turned a tragic face toward the press. "Then who is this other man?" she asked piteously. "Is he some hanger-on, hoping to get his hands on my baby's money?"

"Interesting question, coming from you," Jared said. "Sorry to disappoint you, but I neither want nor need Priscilla Jayne's money. And frankly I'm not sure why you would assume I'm after it in the first place." She was drunk, he suddenly realized. Not falling down, sloppy drunk, but he recognized the exaggeratedly careful mannerisms for what they were. "However, please allow me to put your mind to rest. My name is Jared Hamilton. Your daughter's record label hired me."

"You!" For an instant unbridled hatred twisted her features. Almost immediately, she wrestled her expression back into her oh-so-sad poor-abused-mama look. "You're that young man she mooned over—the boy who killed his own father!"

"Mama!"

Like Romans uncaring whether the gladiator or the lion won as long as it was a good, bloody fight, the press turned on him, shooting off questions right and left. They quieted, however, when Jared looked at Jodeen with a cool, shuttered gaze and said, "Careful, Mrs. Morgan. I doubt you can afford to be sued for slander."

"I apologize," she said hastily. "I meant to say the young man wanted in *questioning* for killing his own father."

He had to hand it to her, that was pretty slick. She'd managed to cover her ass and still get that killing-your-own-father bit in twice in thirty seconds.

"Someone else was convicted of Jared's father's murder, Mama," P.J. snapped. "As you very well know, since I told you all about it when you finally let me come home."

"Don't you take that tone with me, missy!"

P.J.'s jaw went up, but her pointed little chin wobbled for a second before firming up.

Jared's heart clenched so hard that for a second he thought it was going to seize. Ah, man, she was killing him, sitting there taking it on the chin and refusing to let the world see how much it hurt. He was mad as hell at Jodeen for wounding her this way.

He was even madder at himself for having done the same. That didn't stop him, however, from taking his wrath out on Jodeen.

"Don't *you* take that tone with her," he snapped. "Your daughter's still recovering from a fundamentalist right-wing whacko who tied her up, struck her, cut her hair and threatened to kill her, which he would have done in a New York minute if he hadn't been stopped. She's been traumatized and she's been hurt, and so far the only thing I've heard you ask, Mrs. Morgan, is if I'm after her money."

"Well, of course I'm worried about her! Haven't I said so a hundred times?"

"No. You haven't. You've wailed about your 'baby' and you've claimed that you just had to see her after her ordeal. Yet not once did you ask her how she's faring." Taking off the gloves, he demanded in clipped tones, "Isn't it true that your main concern here is to regain your meal ticket?"

Still playing the room, she fluttered a hand to her breast as she weakly gasped, "That's a *horrible* thing to say!" But if eyes could morph into knives, hers would have eviscerated him.

"Yep, it's pretty lousy," he agreed. "Still, you kind of set yourself up for a few sticks and stones when you embezzled from your own daughter."

"I never! You better watch yourself, sonny—that suing for slander can go both ways!"

"Except it's not slander if you've got the books to back up the claim. And isn't it true that you're jealous of your daughter? That you've always *been* jealous because she's sweet and has talent and is everything you never were?"

"I made her career! If not for me, she'd still be playing bars and honky-tonks. But when she started to get somewhere, what did she do? Dumped me like yesterday's dirty dishwater for Mister Fancypants there."

"So your contention is that it had nothing to do with your helping yourself to her earnings."

"I deserved that money! Anyway, she was starting to make pots, so I don't see what a dollar or two here and there matt—" She cut herself off, but more flashbulbs flashed and voices erupted and it was too late to take the words back.

P.J. pushed back from the table with a screech of her

chair. Ignoring the pandemonium breaking out all around her, she strode from the stage.

Shit. *Shit!* What the hell had he done? He, too, pushed back. "Take over," he said to Ben, who was all but rubbing his hands together in satisfaction over Jodeen finally having been outed for the crook she was.

Then Jared hotfooted it into the wings after P.J., covering ground as fast as he could without pulling attention to himself by actually running.

CHAPTER TWENTY-FOUR

"Rumor Has It" column,
Country Connection magazine:
What Mama's Girl's Mama's Been Stealing Her Baby Girl Blind?

"PEEJ."

P.J.'s footsteps faltered at the sound of Jared's voice. Then she caught herself and picked up her pace once again. Just a few more yards and she'd be at her dressing room where she could close out the world, if only for a little while. "Go away, J."

"I can't. I can't just leave you to deal with this all on your own. I think you've had to do way too much of that already."

She moved even faster, but he closed the gap between them just as she reached the dressing-room door. Before she could open it he was behind her—crowding her backside, caging her between his arms, his hands spread on the wood entry on either side of her head. He bent to bring his lips close to her ear.

"I'm sorry, baby," he said in a low voice that sent

goose bumps shivering down her spine. "I didn't mean to embarrass you in front of the press. I was just so pissed at Jodeen for all the crap she's dealt you over the years. I hate that she doesn't value you, but I should have left it alone instead of pushing her the way I did."

"That would have been nice," she whispered to the door. "I could have lived very nicely without the entire world knowing how little my own mother likes me."

Still, honesty compelled her to admit, "But you know what? Humiliating as it's going to be reading about it in the papers, I've moved beyond my need for Mama's affection. It hurts and it sucks that she's such a bitch, but I can survive perfectly well on my own."

"P.J.—"

She turned to face him, pressing her back against the door to avoid brushing up against his hard body. Looking him in the eye, she said, "I deserve better than to beg for the crumbs of anyone's affection."

He stepped back, giving her breathing room. "I was an idiot."

"Which time, exactly?"

Amusement lit his eyes and tugged up the corner of his mouth. "Yeah, that's the question, isn't it?" Stroking his fingers along her cheek with heartbreaking tenderness, he gazed down at her. Then he stuffed his hands in his pockets. "I was an idiot when you told me you loved me and I blew it off. A fool when I decided I knew better than you what you felt. But I was the biggest dumbshit of all when I ran scared from the one thing I want more than anything else in the world."

Her heart began to pound with...well, not hope. No, sir, she wasn't doing hope anymore; she'd finally learned her lesson on that score.

All the same, she mentally held her breath even as she scoffed at the notion he could ever be scared. "You're not afraid of anything."

"You always did give me way too much credit," he said softly, easing near again. But his hands remained deep in his pockets. Then his gaze locked with hers and what she saw there sent a jolt clear down to her toes. "But everyone's afraid of something. And my fear is that I'll disappoint you. That you'll see what a flawed man I am and think as little of me as my old man did." His Adam's apple took a slow ride up and down his throat. "That you'll take off—like you did fifteen years ago—and I'll never hear from you again."

"That's not how it was!" she denied instinctively. Then she shook her head. "That is, I guess it was, but not because I wanted it to be!"

This time it was Jared who made a skeptical noise.

"I didn't! Look, I tried to explain this before, but I only made you angry by bringing up your wealth. But give me a break here, J—I was thirteen years old! When Mama finally let me come back home, I knew darn well it was only because Gert had somehow forced her to. You had come to mean more to me than anyone I'd ever known, but I'd seen the way you lived. So I was already intimidated by your big, fancy mansion and your cook and your maid and...and...the way you'd corrected my grammar! I mean, I know you did that sometimes when we were on the streets but when you did it in your big ol' hotel of a house, I just felt...I felt so—"

She cleared her throat. "Well, I was primed to believe Mama, is all, when she insisted a rich boy like you wouldn't want anything to do with trailer trash like me. But I *missed* you, Jared. God, I missed you so much and—"

He hauled her in, wrapping her up in his arms and pressing her head to his chest. "I love you, Peej. Don't send me away. I don't think I could stand it."

"I... You... What?" Like a tender frond of a fern, the hope she'd refused to believe she harbored began unfurling in her heart. Yet she did nothing to break the light grasp of his fingers in her hair, because what if she was somehow hallucinating? He'd been her high mark, the standard she'd judged all men against, for nearly half her life. And if she was merely hearing things, she'd just as soon not know.

"I love you. I think maybe a part of me always has." Jared pressed his lips against her warm hair at the crown of her head and gathered encouragement from the fact that she didn't pull away from him. She was actually leaning into him, her arms sliding around his waist to hold him tightly in return. He couldn't remember another time when he'd felt this right. When he'd felt this...whole.

Because he knew her. And Priscilla Jayne Morgan had a generous heart. She wouldn't turn him away, even if it was what he deserved for being such a self-protective ass.

He stroked his hand down her newly shortened hair. "When you disappeared from my life, you took an important part of me with you," he admitted hoarsely. Using his thumb on the point of her chin to tip her face up, he bent his head and kissed her brow. "I lost the part that knew how to give myself to a relationship—and I feel like I'm just now getting it back."

A sudden thought occurred to him and he grinned down at her. "I don't have to be a goddamn glacier peak any more." Like it had worked worth a damn around her anyhow.

"Huh?"

"Never mind, it's not important. Tell me that you love me."

"I love you, J."

"I love you more. That's what I should have said the last time you told me. I love you more." He kissed her lips softly, sweetly, and opened the door at her back. Easing them into the room, he kicked the door shut behind them, then turned until her back was pressed against the wood portal.

Worshipping her with his lips, he took the kiss deeper and deeper as he slid her clothes from her body. Then, lifting her against the door, he bent his head to string kisses from her throat to her collarbone to her breast. He'd barely gotten started, however, when she caught a fistful of his hair and tugged.

"I want to feel you inside me," she said. "Now."

He was so lost in her that it didn't even occur to him to fall back on his old habits. Setting her back on her feet, he handed her his wallet with a murmured, "condom," then pulled off his shirt, toed off his shoes and kicked free of his pants while she fished it out. This wasn't about getting her off a number of times before he allowed himself to cut loose. It wasn't about control.

This was about making love to Peej.

Clad only in socks, he picked her up, crossed the room in a few huge strides and bounced her onto the mattress of the daybed in the corner. After dancing on one foot while yanking the sock from his other then repeating the process, he dropped down over her, catching himself on his palms.

For a second he simply stared at her flushed skin. She was still a little beat up, but the look in her eyes made his knees go weak.

"God, I love you," he said. Then, fitting himself between her thighs, he eased on home.

He meant to love her slow and tender. And he started out doing exactly that. But she was so hot and slick, and she clung to him like a treed cat and whispered hot promises of a future he wanted so bad he could taste it. And he began to thrust more emphatically, to twist against her at the apex of each lunge like a tomcat stropping against the first person to ever offer a friendly hand.

Then before he knew it, he was starting to plead.

"Please, Peej. Come on, baby, you gotta—oh, God, *I've* gotta—" His hips began to pick up speed, to slap into her faster and harder, and there didn't seem to be a damn thing he could do to stop it. "Sweetheart, you gotta come now. I'm begging you, I don't know how much longer I can hold on. Please, baby, please, baby, I love you soooo—!" Slamming his hips forward one last time, he held himself deep inside of her as the world went up in flames. Red-hot sensation and screaming pleasure colored his universe as he blasted over its edge.

Then miracle of miracles, despite the fact he had the attention span of a gnat while his brains pumped into the reservoir tip of his condom, that slim fraction of his awareness not focused firmly on himself heard P.J. cry out, and he felt her hips rise and her body start clamping down around him. He had just enough resources left to see her through her orgasm and to say, "Thank you, thank you, thank you, Jesus." Then he collapsed on her like a horse that'd had its legs shot out from under it.

A while later he raised his head out of the curve of her neck and shoulder, lifted his chest enough to allow her to breathe and gazed down at her. "Sorry," he muttered. "It was touch and go there for a minute whether I was going to leave you high and dry."

"I know." She gave him a big, dazzling smile. "That was our best lovin' ever."

"'Scuse me? I forgot damn near everything I ever knew about taking care of a woman's needs, and you're telling me you *liked* it? Say you're kidding."

"I've told you before that I don't require multiple orgasms before you finally let go of the reins."

"And I get that, I honestly do. But *one* would probably be nice."

Reaching up, she gently brushed back a strand of hair that had fallen over his eye. "For the first time I really felt you were here with me one hundred percent."

"Yeah." And it had been better than anything he'd ever known. "Yeah, I suppose that's true." He grinned at her. "And damn, it was good, too. So I hope you're ready to take responsibility for your own orgasms, honey, because from here on out it's all about me."

She laughed. Then she gave him a poke. "You are so full of it. Not to mention threatening the wrong girl. I could play you smoother than Hank plays the fiddle if I had a mind to."

He made a rude noise.

"I could. I could make you spend your every waking minute concentrating on nothing but my pleasure."

"You wish."

"I'm telling you, piece o' cake. I'd just say, 'My *last* lover made sure I had five, six orgasms before he got his—and you can't even give me one?' The next thing you know, you'd be working like a Trojan to make me happy."

He laughed in her face. "I'd get myself off, roll over and go to sleep."

"You forget, I know you. You'd morph into Mr. Competitive just…like…that!" She snapped her fingers.

"Not anymore. Now I'd just say, 'That loser? I know guys like that. They're all style and no substance. And I want to be substance for you.'" His playfulness disappeared. "Did you mean it when you said you want to be with me for the rest of your life? Or was that only heat-of-the-moment, he's-not-getting-the-job-done-but-maybe-if-I-tell-him-something-he-really-wants-to-hear-he'll-be-motivated type sex talk?"

"Oh, I meant every word. Although I don't know how we're going to work out the logistics exactly. I mean, I can always sell the house in Aspen since your work's in Denver. But I'm going to be on the road a lot and you do have a job and—"

He kissed her into silence. When he lifted his head a few moments later, he said, "You're not planning on touring three hundred and sixty-five days a year, are you?"

"No, of course not. But some tours can last two, three, even four months."

"Well, my assignments rarely last longer than a week or two and I can always take time out between jobs to join you on the road. We'll work it out, Peej.

The important thing is that I love you and you love me and we want to be together, to be a family." He kissed her longer this time and smiled at the dazed pleasure on her face when he finally came up for air.

"And when two people love the hell out of each other the way you and I do?" he said. "Baby, the rest is just details."

EPILOGUE

Headline, *Modern Twang Weekly*:
Priscilla Jayne Sighted at Denver's Clerk and
Recorder's Office With Security Specialist Honey.
Do We Hear Wedding Bells in the Future?

Six months later

P.J. WAS LATE TO HER OWN bridal shower. John and Victoria's early-nineteenth-century brick home was ablaze with warm, golden light by the time she and Jared pulled into the driveway. Her plane had been delayed nearly forty minutes, her baggage had taken its own sweet time getting to the carousel and just when she'd finally been reunited with Jared and thought nothing more could go wrong, they'd gotten caught in a big backup on I-70.

While Jared hung her coat in the foyer closet moments later, she straightened her gold wool dress, smoothed her hair and practiced some basic breathing exercises to calm her nerves. It was silly to feel anxious, but all the same…

"You're going to knock them dead," Jared murmured as he rejoined her. He bent to give her a reassuring kiss. Then, tucking her hand in the crook of his arm, he steered her toward his sister's living room. "Sounds like they started without us."

The noise of a successful party—clinking glassware, hearty laughter, rapidly-escalating-in-volume conversation—rolled out of the archway like a friendly greeting, and her tension eased. Jared's family had made it clear she was family now, too, so she had no real reason for feeling so nervy. It was likely just the accumulated stress of running late all day.

Or it might be from trying to deal with her mother this past week, attempting to include Jodeen in the wedding festivities. She should have known better. The public had rallied behind P.J. after the press conference last summer following Luther Menks's attack and Mama wasn't happy that the tide had turned against her. She didn't seem to care that Menks was now confined to a mental institution and was no longer a threat to her daughter. Instead she blamed Jared for exposing her own bad behavior. Still, P.J. had done her best to make her mother feel involved. It was largely a wasted effort, but Mama was the wall she couldn't seem to stop banging her head against.

Reaching the doorway, she stopped in her tracks,

staring at the crowd in the elegant room. This was like no bridal shower she had ever attended.

There were men here. Hank, for starters, who hadn't said a word about coming. He and Nell were over near the open pocket doors that led to the dining room. There was a man she didn't know talking to John and Tori's son, Grayson, and oh my God, was that *Eddie* talking to a redhead about Esme's age over by the laden sideboard? This wasn't even close to what she'd expected. Spotting Gert, she wiggled her fingers in greeting. The old woman saluted her with a champagne flute and, tugging on Jared's arm, P.J. started across the room to her.

"You made it!" Esme rushed up and gave them both a hug. "Come in, come in. Welcome to your couple's shower."

"I never knew there was such a thing," P.J. admitted as she shrugged at Gert and allowed Esme to drag her into the room. "I've only been to maybe three showers in my life, but I didn't think men were usually invited to these shindigs."

"They aren't," Esme said. "But Daddy's best buddies insisted they couldn't allow Jared to marry a woman they haven't blessed with the Marines' seal of approval."

"You're kidding me," she said faintly. Jared had told her stories of the three former Marines, of course. But she hadn't realized she'd have to audition for them.

"Queen's honor. Coop, Dad and Zach are tight."

Jared snorted. "They believe Dumas wrote *The Three Musketeers* just for them, Es. That goes a smidge beyond tight."

"You saying he didn't?" a deep voice demanded, and P.J. looked up to see a dark-haired man approaching them, his arm hugging a plump, pretty blonde in killer red heels to his side.

"It was written about a hundred years before you were born, old man," Jared informed him dryly, exchanging a hug that involved a lot of hearty back-thumping with the man before leaning down to gently kiss the woman. "Lily, you look beautiful as always."

"Aw, you're such a lovely-mannered boy," she said, patting his cheek. "I've always adored that about you."

Grinning, he pulled P.J. to his side, his long fingers splayed possessively over her hip. "Peej, this is Zach and Lily Taylor. Zach, Lily, this is my fiancée, Priscilla Jayne Morgan."

"And I'm Coop," another voice said, drawing P.J.'s gaze from the kind-eyed Lily, whose hand she'd been shaking, to a very large, dark-browed, blond-haired man. Whoa. *Very* large. Both former Marines were older, around her future brother-in-law's age. But like John, neither possessed an iota of the softness that one usually associated with middle age. "Hello," she said politely, offering her hand.

Coop enveloped it in both of his and gave her a leisurely once-over. "You're a little bit of a thing, aren't you? You sure you're up to the challenge of taking on Jared?"

She'd worked with men for too many years not to recognize a tease hoping to provoke a reaction when she saw one, and she had to squelch a grin at his good-natured cockiness. Instead she narrowed her eyes at him. "Oh, I'm up to it. Don't let my size fool you. I make up for it in pure mean."

He cocked his head, his mouth twitching. "That a fact?"

"Don't go scaring the bride, Cooper," Tori ordered, joining them. She leaned to give P.J. a hug, then said to her husband's longtime friend, "Where's your better half? Shouldn't she be here hauling on your leash?"

He laughed and leaned down from his impressive height to give P.J. a kiss on the cheek. "I like a mean woman," he told her, then turned his attention back to Tori. "Ronnie's calling home to check on the kids. They're staying with friends of ours this weekend."

"And she let you run loose on your own?"

He shrugged one large shoulder. "She did say something about behaving myself."

"A feat he's constitutionally incapable of," a brunette with pale skin, red lipstick and a striking white streak in her black hair said as she joined their group. "You must be P.J." she said warmly, eschewing a handshake to give her a hug. "I love your music."

"I love the way Jared's been all smiles since she agreed to marry him," Tori said.

P.J. dove right into getting to know this group. They were important to Jared. He'd told her stories of how the men in particular had included him in pranks and projects—how they'd made him feel a part of something. Since the Miglionnis and Gert were doing the same for her she knew firsthand how that must have made him feel. And she wanted to know everything about the people who'd given him that.

She was leaning back against Jared, talking to Zach about his boot camp for troubled boys, when Gert came up.

"There you are!" Slipping from Jared's arms, she stepped forward to greet her. "Esme whipped me in here so fast I didn't get to say hello." She gave the old lady a hug.

"Now, don't you be fussing," Gert said gruffly even as she hugged her fiercely in return. She kept an arm around P.J.'s waist when she turned to Jared. "You are one lucky man. Slow, but lucky. I was beginning to think I was going to have to knock some sense into you last summer."

"I was a little backward on the uptake," Jared agreed with a smile. "But once things clicked for me, they stayed clicked." He curled his fingers in a gimme gesture at the old woman. "My arms are starting to feel empty here. You gonna give me my girl back?"

"If I must." She turned P.J. loose but fixed a stern

look on Jared. "I've said it before but I'll say it again. You be good to her or you'll have me to answer to."

Jared snorted. "Do I look stupid to you?"

Gert merely elevated her eyebrows above the rims of her cat's-eye glasses, and he laughed. "Okay, Mama Bear."

A faint flush stained the cheeks of a woman who probably hadn't blushed since the Eisenhower Administration, but Jared didn't tease her about it. He simply said, "I know exactly what I've got with Peej." He pulled her in front of him again and wrapped her in his arms. "I'm the luckiest man on the planet."

P.J. laughed and snuggled in, beaming over her shoulder at him. She felt as if she could burst, she was so happy. She'd thought she'd hit the pinnacle of contentment when her career had finally taken off, never dreaming that such happiness could exist for her on a personal level. Yet suddenly she had it all: the man she loved beyond anything in the world, her music, good friends and now a close-knit family and *their* good friends. She purely couldn't imagine life getting any better than this.

"This is just the beginning," Jared murmured, as if he somehow had a direct line to her innermost thoughts. "You and me, Peej? We're just getting started."

She smiled up at him and didn't care that her heart was probably right there for the entire party to see. What the heck, this was her wedding shower—she was supposed to wear her heart in her eyes.

"Yeah, just getting started," she whispered, going up on her toes and twisting to give him a peck on the chin. "How great is that?"